Praise for the novels of T.J. MacGregor

The Hanged Man

"Taut, tricky, and terrifying . . . a dark and suspenseful page-turner."

—Nora Roberts

"A tense and provocative suspense novel."
—*Publishers Weekly*

"A gripping tale of revenge and obsession that's filled with pulse-pounding suspense, bizarre twists, and non-stop action

—*Booklist* (starred review)

The Seventh Sense

"MacGregor combines a riveting story, memorable characters, and heart-pounding suspense in this outstanding supernatural thriller."

—*Booklist*

"MacGregor keeps the suspense rising . . . in her creepy exploration of the power of human perception."
—*Publishers Weekly*

"*The Seventh Sense* grabbed me, pinned me to my chair, and kept me there until the last page. I loved it."
—Nancy Pickard, author of *The Whole Truth*

"*The Seventh Sense* is superb. MacGregor's writing blazes through the twisting catacombs of the heart and mind, leading you deep into new terrain so fascinating you almost forget to breathe. Don't wait for Thomas Harris. Read this book."

—Steven Spruill, author of *Rulers of Darkness* and *Daughters of Darkness*

BOOK YOUR PLACE ON OUR WEBSITE AND MAKE THE READING CONNECTION!

We've created a customized website just for our very special readers, where you can get the inside scoop on everything that's going on with Zebra, Pinnacle and Kensington books.

When you come online, you'll have the exciting opportunity to:

- View covers of upcoming books
- Read sample chapters
- Learn about our future publishing schedule (listed by publication month *and author*)
- Find out when your favorite authors will be visiting a city near you
- Search for and order backlist books from our online catalog
- Check out author bios and background information
- Send e-mail to your favorite authors
- Meet the Kensington staff online
- Join us in weekly chats with authors, readers and other guests
- Get writing guidelines
- AND MUCH MORE!

**Visit our website at
http://www.pinnaclebooks.com**

VANISHED

T.J. MacGregor

PINNACLE BOOKS
Kensington Publishing Corp.

http://www.pinnaclebooks.com

This one is for the Megger, who started it all when we swam with the dolphins; and for my mother, Rose Marie Janeshutz, 1916–2000.

Special thanks as always to Rob, my first reader; to Vivian Ortiz for all the stuff on dolphins; to Al Zuckerman and Kate Duffy, every writer's ideal for an agent and editor; and to Sam Gelfman for his discerning eye.

Part One

Vanishing Point
June 9–25, 1999

"No energy is ever lost. It may seem to disappear from one system, but if so, it will emerge in another."

—Jane Roberts
The Unknown Reality

One

The birds had been gathering since Max Thorn had gotten up an hour ago. A hundred or more of them now fluttered and twittered in the branches of a pair of maples that stood just outside his kitchen window. Crows and doves, bluejays and finches, grackles and cardinals.

Every few minutes, another flock arrived and jockeyed for space in the trees. Those birds that couldn't find a spot hovered around the branches, squawking and fussing to be let in. None of them seemed to even notice the bird feeders that hung from the lowest branches, three feeders filled to the brim with choice seeds. That in itself struck Thorn as odd. In the seven years he and Ellen had lived here, he'd been feeding birds and had never seen one yet that wasn't interested in food.

He filled a mug with coffee, splashed in milk, and stepped out the back door, onto the porch. To either side of him stood waist-high wooden planters billowing with ivy and wildflowers that Ellen had been tending since spring. He peered through the leaves and fragrant buds, watching as another large flock of birds fluttered around the upper branches of the maple tree closest to him. How many now? Two hundred? Four hundred? They made one hell of a racket. Even though he didn't want to frighten them away, he needed a better look, so he stepped out from under the wooden awning.

So many birds filled the maples now that he could barely see any green. The noise level rose steadily with warbles, whistles, sudden bursts of trilling that traveled through the still, pleasantly cool air with the clarity of sound through water. In his twelve years as a veterinarian, his experience with birds had been minimal—a parrot suffering from an embedded egg and a depressed canary who had responded to Saint-John's-wort. The little he knew about birds had come from observing them in the wild. But he'd never seen anything like this. Even to Thorn's untrained ears, the noises sounded alarmed, disturbed, a call to arms or a warning issued to other birds. It made him distinctly uneasy.

The trees now looked as dark as india ink. Just above them, where more birds fluttered, the blue of the sky was no longer visible. A flock of geese approached from the south, probably coming from the lake itself. They flew just above the tallest trees in the woods, their honks echoing.

"Max?" Ellen called.

"Outside, hon."

Ellen appeared, dressed for her morning run in tight white Spandex pants that outlined every curve, every muscle and bone. The matching top left her arms and midriff bare. She'd gathered her black hair into a ponytail that bounced against the back of her neck. "I could hear the ruckus at the other end of the house. What's going on, anyway?"

"I don't know. There must be seven or eight hundred birds up there now, with more on the way." He pointed at the geese.

"Scenes from *The Birds* in our backyard." Ellen shaded her eyes with a hand. "Bacall wouldn't even come out here," she remarked, referring to their golden retriever. "So what's it mean, anyway? Is bad weather on the way? Are we about to have an earthquake or something?"

"Beats me. I'm a vet, not a biologist."

The geese circled the fields behind the house, honking loudly. Another huge flock of grackles appeared, several hundred strong, Thorn guessed. Flocks of pigeons joined them. How many now? he wondered. A thousand? They chattered from the trees and circled above the house as he and Ellen stood there, watching.

Thorn ran inside for the videocamera and returned just in time to see the geese sweeping in low toward the house, more geese than he'd ever seen in one place before. They circled the house at about two hundred feet and his camera whirred, getting it all.

Then the birds in the maples fell utterly and completely silent.

It spooked him, that abrupt silence punctuated with the geese's honking and an occasional whisper of wind from the woods. It spooked him so deeply that he thrust the videocamera at Ellen and ran out into the yard, shouting and waving his arms. The birds lifted like smoke from the trees, their wings beating the air and frightening off the geese. He stood with his arms spread open until the sky swallowed the last of the dark smudge. A memory stumbled around inside him, something that begged to be recognized, but he couldn't seize it.

"Got it all on tape." Ellen came over to him and fit the strap of the videocamera over his shoulder. "Maybe the local Audubon chapter will know what to make of it. Maybe they've gotten other reports." She bit at the inside of her cheek, pensive. "We should check the Web and CNN, Max."

"Under what? Weird shit?"

She began to jog in place, her ponytail bouncing. "We've got two horses reserved over at the stable for nine." She paused long enough to buss him on the cheek. "I'm off. Set your timer."

He pressed the timer on his wristwatch and before he could say anything, the woman he'd lived with for the last seven years jogged away from him, the clean, sweet scent of her skin lingering in the air. She kept her arms tucked just so against her sides and her long legs swept her forward.

They'd met eight years ago, when she'd brought her ailing Persian cat to the office he used to have in town. Ellen had moved recently to Blue Mountain Lake from Manhattan, moved there with her menagerie of pets and her childhood furniture, to teach at the local high school. The chemistry between them had been immediate, but they were both gun-shy from recently failed relationships, so for the first three months they were simply riding buddies.

Every Saturday, they met at the local stable, tacked up their horses, and spent the day following trails through the Adirondacks. During those long rides, they never stopped talking and exchanging personal histories and stories. They'd been friends first and regardless of how hokey it sounded, friendship had allowed them to get to know each other in a way that was impossible once sex had entered the equation. Then one day in

early October, when the air had been scented with the
sweet crispness of autumn, all that had changed. They'd
stopped to look for stones in a creek and had become
lovers. The physical act had confirmed everything he'd
felt about her since he'd first laid eyes on her. It had
smacked of destiny.

Unfortunately, her father had detested Thorn right
from the start and that hadn't changed one iota. If anything, the old man hated him more now than he had
in the beginning and it wasn't just because Thorn had
stolen the heart of the old man's youngest daughter.
The real problem, the absolute bottom line, was that in
terms of professional hierarchies, the old man considered veterinary medicine to be on a par with cleaning
toilets. Why hadn't his daughter fallen in love with another attorney? Better yet, why hadn't she fallen for
one of Manhattan's young, hotshot attorneys who also
came from the same blue-bloodlines that had spawned
the old man himself?

And Ellen, despite her rebellion against her Manhattan upbringing and all that it represented, had refused
to marry him because she would become the family
outcast, the prodigal daughter. There was just enough
of that upper class bullshit left in her for that, a lifestyle that had smacked of the rich and famous: summers on the Vineyard, supper with the celebrities next
door, foxhunting on two continents, college at Vassar,
Daddy's favorite little girl.

Ellen, of course, had never admitted any of this to
him—or to herself. Her argument came straight out of
the sixties: why did they have to validate their relationship according to the mores of mainstream society? The
irony didn't escape Thorn. He'd finally met a woman
he wanted to marry and she wouldn't marry him. So

for seven years, they'd lived together here in their little Walden, fifteen acres of land that Ellen had bought with part of her trust fund, another strike against Thorn in Daddy's eyes. Their lives were as intimate and intertwined as any married couple's and the only time it made a difference was on those rare occasions when they saw her old man.

He glanced down at his watch, checking the time, then watched her in the distance. As she picked up speed, she became a vision in white against the green fields, the perfect blue sky, a breathtaking figure of lightness and grace. Every morning, six days a week, for as long as the snow didn't fly, Ellen jogged the same four-mile route. It would take her past the kennel, empty now, past the fenced area and the stable that had once housed three mares and a pony, and into the woods that surrounded their fifteen acres on three sides. The footpath would take her a mile into the woods, then back out and around the small lake.

Thorn knew the path by heart because he'd walked it with her a couple of times and had ridden it when they'd still had horses. It had been a while since he'd done either. They'd sold the horses three years ago, when it had become apparent that neither of them had the kind of time the horses required. Although Thorn practiced out of an office here on the property, he traveled every other week to treat larger animals in the area, horses and cows and hogs, pigs and sheep and even several llamas. Several times a week, Ellen commuted into Saratoga, where she taught English lit at one of SUNY's satellite campuses. Since her job had ended until the fall, she and Bacall would go with him when he left tomorrow on his rounds.

Ellen reached the paddock, where the fence seemed

to lean permanently to the right and the grass looked so vivid and green it made Thorn's heart ache. He could almost smell the grass from where he stood, that peculiar sweetness of upstate grass that mingled with the scent of early summer. For the years they'd lived here, summers had meant some of their best times together, and this scent seemed permanently etched within those memories.

From just this aroma, for instance, Thorn could conjure a morning six years ago when they'd ridden their horses out into the woods and had discovered a spot that reminded him of Tolkien's Middle Earth. He and Ellen had made love in the grass and afterward had talked honestly about their difficulty in starting a family. Did they want to go the route of other couples they knew, in vitro or surrogates or adoption? They'd lain there in the sunlight of this place, talking quietly, holding hands, and had decided that if she got pregnant, great. If not, that was okay, too, but they weren't going to subject themselves to any of the rest of it. In short, they'd agreed to let nature take its course.

Nature's course hadn't produced any Thorn or Bradshaw rug rats. He knew she regretted it as much as he did, but they'd simply accepted it and had gone on with the rest of their lives. And those lives, he thought, had been good to them.

He started to go back inside to replenish his mug when he suddenly heard the birds again—a cacophony of screeches, caws, whistles—and he spun around. The dark cloud approached from the east this time, twice as large, an undulating wave in which no single bird was visible. Once, years ago out West, Thorn had watched a cloud of locusts sweep down over a field of corn and it had looked no different than this.

The wave circled a hundred and fifty feet above Ellen, who had stopped dead near the paddock, her head back, hands cupped like visors around her eyes. Then her head dropped forward, as if she'd noticed something on the ground more interesting than the birds, and her entire body snapped around and she screamed, *"Max, get out here fast!"*

Her voice echoed shrilly across the field, a staccato sound, like gunfire. But she didn't move. She seemed paralyzed. Thorn lurched forward, his bare feet slapping the soft summer grass. The noise of the birds grew louder and so did her screams. A stitch exploded in his side, his breath burst from his mouth, everything took too long. And when he was about forty yards from her and closing as fast as his unfit body would take him, she started to fade.

Fade, for Christ's sake.

Her shoulders and arms went first, fading the way an object does when struck by the full glare of summer light, as if the light were swallowing it. He could suddenly *see through* her shoulders, see the velvet green of the woods behind her and a curve of the corral fence. For a wild, crazy moment, he knew that if he touched her now, his hands would go straight through her.

The top of her head began to lighten, the hair first, all that black paling. Then her forehead started to fade. Then her nose, her cheeks, her mouth and neck. Thorn could see through her thighs now, the tall, rustling summer grass visible through her skin. Her shrieks sounded shrill enough to shatter crystal.

The mass of birds seemed to spiral steadily downward, a wide, dark ribbon loose in the wind. He ran faster, harder, arms pumping at his sides. Thirty yards. Twenty. When he reached her, the only parts of her that remained visible were her strong, muscular thighs and the pale blue points of her eyes. She looked like a toddler's drawing, hastily scribbled lines that merely suggested something human.

Terror swam through those points of blue that were her eyes. Her thigh muscles bulged. He threw his arms around her legs, seizing them. Solid, they were solid. They were real. Even when her thighs faded completely, he still felt them. Still clutched them. He screamed, but had no idea what he screamed.

He felt her nails scrape across the backs of his arms. Heard her labored breath, her gasps. And he heard the birds, screeching as they spiraled downward. Then her legs felt less solid. It was as if they were turning to sand or water. He lost his hold on her and clutched air, empty air, and the birds slammed into his back, his head and shoulders, one after another, again and again, pummeling him, driving him to his knees.

Thorn threw himself to the ground and rolled up into a ball, arms covering his face and head as the birds struck him, rained down over him.

At some point, he tried to crawl away, but the birds kept falling, hitting him until they covered him completely. Buried in feathers, in flesh and blood, his mind too shocked to grasp what had happened, he surrendered to a thick, suffocating blackness.

Thorn came to on his side, arms tucked under his head, soft *stuff* stuck to his face. A terrible stink hung in the air, a smell like an open sewer or rotting eggs or decaying flesh. He coughed and some of the soft stuff drifted into the breeze. Feathers, the stuff looked like feathers.

"What the hell." He rubbed his hand over his mouth and sat up slowly, his body bright with aches and pains, as if he'd slept the entire night on the ground.

Long shadows fell across the field. A sweet summer wind blew against his face. He didn't have any idea what he was doing out here. His head felt twice its normal size, his neck had gone stiff, his eyeballs had been scrubbed with sandpaper. Mostly, he wanted to lie back down in the soft grass and shut his eyes again. Instead, he called, "Ellen? Bacall?"

His voice drifted out over the field, a hollow, empty sound without substance. Thorn rocked back onto his heels and looked around. The field, the paddock, the woods, and way over there, the house. Where were the horses? Three mares and a pony that Ellen . . .

And suddenly it all rushed back, crashing over him. *Ellen, fading.*

And the goddamn birds filling the skies, falling . . . hitting me . . .

Thorn shot to his feet and stumbled away from the spot where he'd lain. He shouted Ellen's name, stopped, shouted again and turned in a circle where he stood. The shadows that fell against the grass told him it was midafternoon. Maybe later.

Impossible.

He looked at his watch, frowned, tapped it, held it to his ear, looked at it again. The watch had stopped at 7:42.

Deep inside his chest, a beast went on a rampage, throwing its body around, slamming against his ribs. His throat flashed dry, his head spun, and he squeezed his eyes shut, holding on to whatever vestige of ordinary life he could dredge up. The weight of the watch on his wrist. The stink in the air, the silence. Yes, most of all that. A silence that rippled beneath the softness of the wind.

People do not fade and vanish.

Of course not. And when he opened his eyes, the world would be as it had been when he rolled out of bed this morning. Ellen would be up already, the perennial early riser who started the coffee, and she would be standing in front of the fridge when he came up behind her. He would slide his arms around her waist and nuzzle her neck and she would laugh in that way she had and turn in his arms.

When he opened his eyes, he would be in that world.

So he opened his eyes.

Nothing had changed. The hands of his watch still stood at 7:42. The wind still blew. The shadows against the grass still screamed that it was early afternoon and he had lost five or six hours, maybe more.

And I know what I saw.

He had seen Ellen fade and vanish.

And he had seen birds.

Hundreds of birds, maybe a thousand birds.

If he could find the birds, he would find Ellen.

He lurched forward, slapping the tall grass with his hands, shouting for her, his panic so extreme he could taste it. He stumbled over something and fell to his knees, clawing through the grass. A bird. A dead crow. He tore off the denim shirt that he wore over his T-shirt, snapped it in the air, and laid it on the grass. He lifted the crow by the legs and dropped it onto his shirt. He stared at it, studying it, waiting for its body to yield some small clue. Then habit kicked in.

Rigor mortis.

No broken neck.

Blood had dried in and on its slightly open beak and leaked from its open eyes.

Did birds die with their eyes open or shut?

He didn't know. His lack of knowledge about birds now mocked him. Besides the animals, horses, and domestic pets that he treated, he got an occasional oddball, a raccoon, a fox, a coyote. A couple of times, zoo animals had ended up in his office for intricate surgeries or alternative therapies like acupuncture. But birds were a specialty all their own. He'd never even owned a bird.

Using a stick, he turned the bird over on its back. "Jesus," he whispered and jerked back.

Its chest had exploded open, the gaping hole wide enough for his index finger, maybe his thumb. He quickly pulled together the corners of the shirt, covering the bird, and tied the sleeves, making a hobo sack. He started to weep. He screamed her name. He grabbed the hobo pack with the bird in it, and lurched forward again, eyes on the grass.

He didn't know how long he searched. At one point, he became utterly certain that Ellen had shrunk to the size of a pea and when he found her she would be tiny enough to stand in the palm of his hand, a real Thumbelina. Her little mouth would open and he wouldn't be able to hear her unless he got down very close.

But he didn't find Ellen in any version at all. He found sixteen more birds of various types, all with the same hole in their chests. He picked out the largest birds and tossed them into his shirt and slung it over his shoulder again. Now and then he called her name, but his throat felt dry and his voice got so hoarse he fell silent. His stomach growled, he had to piss, his body hurt, his head pounded.

Thorn made a beeline into the woods, certain now

that she'd gone into the trees. Whatever he'd seen had been an optical illusion of some sort, a short circuit in his brain.

Ellen had fallen and hurt herself. Of course. It made sense. She'd panicked as the birds had descended and had fled into the trees. She'd stumbled, fallen, maybe broken her foot.

Thorn shouted for her again and hurried along the footpath where she usually jogged. Nothing moved in these trees—no birds, no insects, not even the wind. Light slanted through the branches and fell in erratic patterns across the ground. The bag over his shoulder got progressively heavier.

A quarter of a mile into the trees, a movie began to unroll in his head, slow-motion frames of what had happened. The birds, Ellen fading, vanishing, and himself curled up on the ground as the birds slammed into him. He tore up the path as if a part of him believed he might outrun the truth. But the mental movie replayed again and again, driving him off the path and into the trees.

He crashed through undergrowth, into and out of shadows. His breath came hard and heavy. The bag knocked against his shoulder blades. He stumbled over something and went down on his hands and knees, shaking his head as if to rid himself of what he kept seeing.

A terrible keening started somewhere in the woods, somewhere close, and when he slapped his hands over his ears to block the sound, he realized it was coming from him. But he couldn't stop it. Everything inside him had begun to unravel, to come undone. He began to weep, to sob, and rocked back and forth, arms clutched against his waist as if to hold something in. And that was how they found him, his dog and a neighbor and a battalion of cops.

Piper Key Gazette
Wildlife Column
June 11, 1999

   As I'm writing this, it's early spring. I hike into
that part of the island which we locals call the
horse's ears. All of you know this place. It's our
woodland hills, our nature preserve. It's where the
last of the island's cedar trees grow and where the
air smells as it did a century ago.
   This isn't my first hike. Periodically, I unplug
from my creature comforts and go into the woods
to challenge myself, to discover who I am stripped
of my phone, my computer, my fax. I go alone and
I travel light. In my pack, I carry: a camera, two
canteens, a fishing line and hook, a six-inch knife
in a leather sheath, a hammock and a change of
clothes and shoes, a metal frying pan and pot, a
magnifying glass, slivers of dry wood, a length of
rope, a basic first-aid kit.
   Sometimes, I also carry a plastic tarp, two lightweight cotton blankets, a solar-powered light, a bar
of soap, a razor, packets of oatmeal, and a box of
kitchen matches. None of these things existed a century ago, at least not in their present form. But I've
found that despite my yearning for a simpler life,
I'm very much a product of the twentieth century.
I enjoy having light to write by at night. I like feeling clean. And yes, I like the security of knowing
that if it rains and my fire won't light, I can spread
my tarp over my head and light a match to some
dry wood. So sue me.
   On my first day, I hike from shortly after sunrise
to midmorning before I stop to make camp. The heat

and humidity are savage things that leech my body's moisture. My muscles aren't accustomed to all the hiking and beg for a respite. Besides, why not stop? I don't have any appointments. I'm not even wearing a watch.

I string up my hammock at the edge of one of the little plantations and leave most of my supplies bundled inside of it. Then I head off in search of water. Thanks to the spring rains, fresh water isn't that difficult to find here in the hills. I follow the tracks of raccoons and deer and come upon water that has pooled in a rocky depression. As I'm filling my canteen, a wolf appears on the other side of the pool. As far as I know wolves don't inhabit Florida. Coyotes have been infiltrating the state since the late eighties, but this is definitely not a coyote. It's a gray wolf, a female with ocean-blue eyes that watch me warily.

I freeze. I barely breathe. In these moments when we simply stare at each other, I frantically search my mental database for what I know about wolves. The only wolves I've ever seen have been in zoos, joyless creatures who pace and try to hide from the endless parade of spectators. I know wolves are pack animals and on occasion, a wolf is ousted from its position in the pack and can be attacked or even killed by other members of the pack. That's about it for my databank on wolves.

I slowly sit on the ground next to the pool, in what I hope is a nonthreatening position, and remain very still.

After a few minutes, the wolf apparently decides I'm not a threat and proceeds to drink from the pool. She lifts her head again and looks over at me,

*then raises her beautiful head to the sky and howls.
There is something plaintive and lovely in the
sound, something primal and timeless. I wonder if
she's alerting her pack to the presence of fresh meat
and an easy prey or if she's simply warning me to
keep my distance. Maybe the howl means neither of
these things.*

*Suddenly, a wolf pup trots out of the brush near
the pool. The she wolf yelps, three yelps in quick
succession, and the pup limps over. One of its rear
legs is injured and it stops frequently to lick at the
leg and whine. The mother goes over to it, picks it
up by the scruff of the neck, and carries it over to
the pool, urging it to drink.*

*The pup laps at the water a couple of times, then
lies down in the sunlight, whining softly, obviously
in pain. The mother drinks from the pool again and
moves to her pup's side. She opens her mouth, releasing the water she has just taken in, and the
water runs over the pup's leg. She repeats this several times, washing, then licking the injury, and I
snap several photos of them. She finally stretches
out beside her pup, in the warm light.*

*When I finally slip away, the shadows are longer.
I'm astonished at what I have been permitted to
witness.*

*It's dark now. I'm sitting by my fire, cooking din-
ner—fish that I have caught, papaya that I have
picked. Despite my satisfaction at how today has un-
folded, I feel lonely and out of sorts. It would be nice
to have company, to talk with another human being,
to share what I witnessed today with the wolves.*

The only way they could get to the island is the

way most of us do who come by land—by following
the road from the mainland. At night, when there's
no traffic, the wolves could make the trip easily.
Perhaps the mother was pregnant when she found
her way here and the pup was born in the hills. Or
maybe there's a pack of them. This seems unlikely,
though, because wouldn't some of us on the island
have heard their howls? Would someone have
sighted them?

As I'm writing this, I hear noises in the woods.
The firelight doesn't extend too far into the thick
darkness that surrounds me and I'm seized by an
atavistic urge to leap into my hammock for safety.
But my fear of such darkness is just one of the many
reasons I make these hikes, so I stay where I am
and turn the fish. I add a bit of coconut juice in
the frying pan and toss in some sliced bananas.

Then I see her, the she wolf carrying her pup by
the scruff of the neck. She approaches me warily,
coming fully into the glow of the firelight, her eyes
bright with intelligence. My heart pounds as she
moves toward me and sets the pup on the ground
beside me.

It whimpers and whines, this skinny little thing,
and tries to rise, but its leg is a suppurating mess.
The mother whines and extends her paw toward me,
as if asking me to help her pup, then she sinks to
the ground, licking the pup's head and leg.

I speak softly to her, to both of them, and reach
into the pot that holds a filleted, uncooked slice of
fish. I remove it from the pot and set it on the
ground, close to her. Then I rise slowly and back
toward the hammock to get my first-aid kid and the
solar-powered light.

Most pet owners know a little something about how to treat their animals when they're hurt. A wolf, of course, isn't a pet, but I can tell the pup's leg is badly infected and the least I can do is try to treat it.

With the light attached to a low-hanging branch and the first-aid kit resting on the plastic tarp, I begin to clean the wound with hydrogen peroxide. The pup whimpers and the mother growls. It scares me and I pause, speaking to her in the same quiet voice, trying to communicate that the pup will feel some discomfort while I treat the injury.

The pup stops whimpering and the mother stops growling. I realize the growl was intended for the pup, not for me.

When the wound is clean, though still oozing pus and a little blood, I can see it more clearly. It looks as if something sharp poked deeply into the leg, then tore a gash about three inches long. I treat it topically with an antibiotic ointment and give the pup a penicillin tablet hidden in a chunk of raw fish. Finally, I wrap the wound in gauze and put everything away.

I get one of the lightweight blankets from the hammock, spread it on the tarp. I reach into the pot of uncooked fish, cut it in half, and put it on a plate. I mash it with a fork, then set the plate at the end of the tarp and move back to the fire to finish cooking my own meal. While I'm eating, the mother gets up and goes over to the fish. She sniffs it, samples it, then returns to her pup's side and picks it up by the scruff of the neck again. She carries it over to the tarp and proceeds to share the rest of the fish with her pup.

Before I retire to the hammock, I fill the pot with water from my canteen and set it on the tarp.

The next morning, mother and pup are still there, the two of them playing on the tarp, rolling around on it like a couple of rambunctious kids. The penicillin obviously kicked in, but I want to check the pup's leg. I don't dare do it, though, without an invitation. So I go about my business, washing up, boiling water for oatmeal and coffee. I make enough oatmeal for the three of us, crush another penicillin tablet in one portion, and set the bowls on the ground. To my surprise, they gobble it up.

As I wash the pot, the she wolf approaches me, whining, submissive, and rubs up against my arm. Then she sinks to the ground and allows me to pet her. Her fur is shockingly soft, yet coarse. She likes to be scratched on the head.

Pretty soon, the pup comes over and mimics her and I have a chance to unwrap the gauze. Already the swelling has vanished and the wound is closing. The mother licks my hand, a quick lick, and sniffs her way up my arm, as if committing my scent to memory. There, in the half-light, in the strange morning stillness of the woods, we understand each other, she and I. She yelps twice for her pup and they trot off into the trees. I have been touched by the miraculous.

Witness
Visit our website at:
www.piperkeygazette.com

Two

Pensacola Naval Air Base
Florida

Gail Campbell sat at the edge of the catwalk that surrounded the holding tank. The weather was summer perfect, with winds at a gentle five knots out of the west, air temp at eighty-three, water temp about seventy-nine.

She slipped on her flippers, cleaned her mask, drew it over her head, and fitted it across her eyes. The strap was too loose and she adjusted it. When she got it exactly right, she pushed it back onto her head and picked up the buoyancy vest beside her. She ran her fingers over it, searching for nicks, tiny holes, anything that might compromise her when she was underwater. She slid her fingers into the side pocket, removed her whistle, put it around her neck. Then she drew the vest on over her wet-suit jacket. It fit well. Everything she wore when she dived fit well. It had to. Her life might depend on it.

Steve Dylan came over, carrying a pair of oxygen tanks. He set them both on the walkway and sat down on the other side of them. "I'll have the cell phone in the dinghy. You think we need a radio, too?"

"No. Let's keep this as simple as possible."

She proceeded to connect the pressure-gauge hose and the regulator hose to the tank's valve. Dylan began to suit up. "You're quiet, Campbell. You sure you're up to this?"

"If I weren't up to it, I wouldn't be here." She blew into the regulator's mouthpiece, testing to make sure it was clear. "Is everything else ready?"

"Green lights all the way."

She slipped the tank onto her back and strapped it around her waist. She flipped open the lid of the Igloo cooler to her left. It held a small explosive mounted on a device that she would attach to Alpha's snout. The dolphin would secure it to a target and the explosive would be detonated from the control room.

This particular technique had grown out of the navy's early "biological weapons system" in Vietnam, when dolphins outfitted with carbon cartridges and hypodermics were trained to protect U.S. Navy bases. These techniques had been further honed during the Gulf War and were now being taken to another, higher level in submarine defense. The Department of Naval Intelligence funded the program covertly, of course, otherwise every animal rights group in the country would be up in arms. She suspected that Dylan, as head of the program, also had a personal agenda that he hadn't shared with her. He denied it, naturally, but she knew better.

She put the device into a lead-lined pack that she snapped onto her weight belt. She secured the weight belt around her waist, then reached into a second, smaller cooler. This held twenty pounds of herring, Alpha's favorite food. She took several handfuls and stuffed them in another pocket of her vest and sealed the Velcro shut again.

She glanced over at Dylan, forty-four years old last

week, his blond hair shaved down to a fine stubble so that the gray didn't show. His neatly trimmed beard and mustache hadn't gone gray yet, but here and there she saw fine threads of white. All the hours of diving and swimming kept his physique trim, almost sinewy. He'd spent so much time outside the past few months that his skin looked like a Coppertone ad.

She was Dylan's age, but didn't feel as though she was in shape at all. She worked here on weekends and elsewhere during the week and the strain of balancing her two lives was beginning to show. No, she hadn't gone gray yet. Her hair was the same glossy mahogany it had always been and she wore it short and sassy, as Dylan put it. Her body wasn't bad, either. She worked out at a gym several times a week, using machines as well as free weights. This discipline kept her weight at 118, her clothing size at a perfect eight, the same it had been in college, and her stomach as a flat as a dollar bill. She looked good, but inside she felt ragged and she blamed it on the dichotomy of her two very different lives.

She watched him getting ready for the dive. He did it in much the same way she did, with a focused intent that blocked out everything else. They both wore short-sleeved wet-suit jackets and booties, but no pants. The gulf was warm enough so they could get by without suits at all. They both felt more comfortable with the jackets, probably a vestige of their childhood diving experiences.

They'd grown up together, she and Dylan, navy brats who had been born at Guantanamo's naval hospital, on the same day and year, two minutes apart. Six months before Castro had won the 1959 revolution, their families had been transferred to a naval base in Key West, where they lived two blocks from each other. After that, there were a succession of moves—Virginia and Maryland, California and Oregon, Europe and Asia and South America. By the time they'd hit their teens, they'd moved a combined total of thirty-eight times and had lived many of their childhood years in the same neighborhoods. Not surprisingly, they'd been lovers off and on since they were fifteen.

Dylan, like his father, had gone to the naval academy, a course of study that she equated with being assimilated into the Borg of the military collective. She'd gone to Berkeley and rebelled. Perhaps that was the result of the two minutes of difference in their birth times. At Berkeley, she'd gotten married during her junior year, a drug-induced deception that had lasted about ten months.

On the day her divorce had become final, Dylan had called her at 11:01 that night to tell her he was getting married. It was the only time in her life she'd contemplated suicide. She even had written a suicide note and a letter to Dylan, then she'd ridden her bike out to the Golden Gate Bridge and had stood at the railing for hours, sobbing, raving at Dylan. She had imagined her body plunging over the side and had thought about Dylan's reaction when he heard the news. She knew that he would mourn, that he might feel guilty, but that his life would go on. And that was when she'd pedaled home.

A year or so before his marriage had fallen apart, they'd started seeing each other again. He'd been living in Hawaii at the time and she'd landed a job at a dolphin research center in Honolulu, a bit of strategic planning on her part that had paid off when his marriage had collapsed completely.

They had a couple of great years together until Dylan had been transferred to Norfolk in 1980 and promoted into the naval intelligence division. It had taken her a year to find a job close by, at a federally funded research center, training dolphins for the mammal defense program. She'd started out as an assistant director and within a year, landed the directorship. Much of her good fortune during this time had been due to Dylan, of course, pulling strings to get her the job and the funds that she'd needed. His career had benefitted as well because the dolphins she'd trained had been trained specifically to Dylan's specifications and had been used in the Gulf War.

That job had lasted until 1988, when she was offered a teaching position in marine biology at a university in Australia. Dylan had balked. Professional suicide, he'd said. She was a researcher, not a teacher, he'd said. Besides, it was too far away; how would they see each other? The real reason he didn't want her to take the job was that she would no longer be under *his* control, doing *his* bidding, which was precisely why she'd accepted the job.

In retrospect, those three years now seemed like paradise to her. She'd loved everything about Australia and for the first time since college had flourished despite the fact that Dylan hadn't been in her life. She'd had a passionate affair with an Aussie and probably would have married the guy except that Dylan showed up two nights before the wedding.

His timing had been impeccable and he'd known exactly what treats he should dangle: a job in Pensacola, where he was now stationed, in a research program that she would direct, at a salary she couldn't refuse. That had been eight years ago.

In the end, her forays into rebellion hadn't amounted to much. She and Dylan, after all, had ended up in the same place, on the same research project, fighting for the same side. A year into the deal, he'd asked her to do a bit of spy work at a private dolphin center on Piper Key and her life had split in two, as tidy as a sliced apple. Except that it wasn't tidy. Every weekend that she spent here in Pensacola made her job on Piper Key that much more difficult.

Gail glanced at the large round clock outside the control room. The hands stood at 2:58. She wanted to be submerged by 3:15 at the latest. A front was supposed to move in later this afternoon, the usual summer shit of thunderstorms and rough seas, and she didn't want to be diving when it hit. "You almost ready?" she asked.

"Just a final check with the camera." He fiddled with it, loading film, testing the light.

"How long?"

"Three minutes."

And he meant exactly that. Not three minutes and forty seconds, not two minutes and twenty seconds. Three minutes. Dylan was the only man she'd ever known who was as precise as she was. His ex-wife hadn't understood that side of him.

She picked up Dylan's cell phone and called the tower. "Control, we're on a countdown to three minutes in phase one. Is the target ready?"

"Hey, Dr. Campbell. It's Jackson. The target is being deployed now. Stay in touch."

Gail tossed the phone in the dinghy Dylan would use and slid into the water with the ease of someone born to that element. In fact, according to family myth, her mother had given birth to her in a warm pool in the naval hospital, an outrageous thing to do in 1955, but the birth had gone without a hitch. Five hours of labor and she'd come out into a watery world that hadn't been too different from the embryonic world where she'd spent the previous nine months.

Dylan's mother had opted for a hospital room and after thirty-two hours of excruciating labor, he'd been born by C-section, lifted out of the womb with his lungs filled with phlegm and his body a daffodil yellow. Or so his family mythology claimed. In her mind, it was one more vital difference between them. And yet, his name meant "man from the sea," as if he were some throwback to Atlantean times.

Fully submerged now, she and Dylan swam side by side. Periodically, he aimed his underwater videocam at her. Later, he would do the voice-over, adding details about water temperature and other minutiae that the military brass rarely paid attention to but which pleased them because the details gave it all such authenticity.

The water seemed shockingly clear, with visibility more than thirty feet. Alpha appeared, a twenty-five-year-old female bottlenose dolphin who weighed in at just over six hundred pounds. In the years before Gail had begun working with her, she had given birth to five of the dolphins here at the base. She was now ailing, could no longer give birth, and had been deemed "expendable."

Gail felt bad about it because Alpha was bright, often playful, and Gail had enjoyed working with her. But she held no ethical qualms about her work. The knowledge she'd gleaned from Alpha was already being applied to her research and, ultimately, would help to make the world a safer place.

Alpha veered in front of her, less than a half foot

away, an invitation for Gail to grab on to her dorsal
fin. She pressed the first of four buttons on her weight
belt, a signal to the control room to raise the gate on
the holding tank. Then she flashed a thumbs-up at Dylan, seized Alpha's dorsal, and they took off.

The dolphin swam fast but not so fast that Gail's
regulator hose would be knocked out of her mouth. Alpha knew the routine. As the gate went up, she dived
deeper and swam out into the canal and headed for the
open gulf. The other dolphins had already been removed from this tank, so there was no danger of escape.

About four minutes later, she surfaced for air, and
Gail pressed the second button on her weight belt, a
signal to the control room that it would be another four
to six minutes before they reached the floating dock
offshore.

Through trial and error, she'd found this routine
worked best when Alpha was hungry and when Gail
swam with her as far as the dock. There, she would
attach the device to the dolphin's snout, toss her a
handful of herring, and direct her to the target site half
a mile away and two hundred feet down. In the past,
Alpha had attached the explosive to the target and had
swum away before the explosive was detonated. That
would not be the case today.

By now, Dylan would be in the dinghy with the outboard motor, putting toward the floating dock. He
would videotape the sequence of events on the dock
and get a shot of Alpha as she sped away from the
dock; then they would both wait for the first signs that
the experiment had been successful.

As they neared the dock and the next surfacing, Alpha emitted a series of clicks. Gail felt a burst of sonar

as the dolphin scanned whatever lay in front of them. Seconds later, a school of yellow-tailed fish swam past them. If Alpha had been living in the wild, she would have gone after the fish. But due to years of captivity, she was addicted to herring and knew that if she deviated from the course at this point, the herring in Gail's buoyancy vest would be denied her.

This kind of human conditioning often had dire effects on the very abilities in dolphins that the navy valued so highly. Like their sonar. Early on in her work with dolphins, Gail had discovered that dolphins in captivity were unable to use their sonar because the sound bounced off the sides of the tank. Eventually, the ability began to atrophy. So before she'd agreed to join Dylan on this project, she'd insisted that any dolphins she worked with would be allowed daily access to the gulf. They'd lost quite a few dolphins over the years, but the ones that remained had sonar abilities that almost matched those of dolphins in the wild.

Alpha, despite her health problems, could locate, when blindfolded, a vitamin capsule at the bottom of a tank. She could distinguish between identical sheets of aluminum and copper and could detect a stainless steel sphere only three inches in diameter. But in the opinion of the committee that held the power of life and death, her sonar ability alone wasn't enough to keep her around. They wanted younger dolphins that could reproduce and that were still "malleable"—i.e., trainable.

They reached the floating dock and Gail grabbed on to the ladder, removed her mask and flippers and tossed them onto the dock, then climbed onto it. As she removed her tank, she glanced out across the flat gulf water. Half a mile out, she saw the boat that had deployed the target, a humanlike figure decked out in full diving gear and filled with oxygen, and lowered to two hundred feet. Alpha would hear the signal the figure emitted and as she was attaching the explosive to it, the control room would detonate it, taking Alpha with it.

Gail knelt at the edge of the platform, rocked back on her heels, and greeted Alpha as she surfaced, clicking for a treat. Gail tossed her a couple of herring to whet her appetite. Dylan's dinghy drew alongside the dock and he hopped out, tied it to a post, then reached inside for a waterproof bag. Out came the videocamera and the cell phone, which he clipped to the pocket of his wet-suit jacket.

He lifted the camera to his eye, scanning the water and the sky in the distance, where dark thunderheads climbed thirty thousand feet. "That storm's moving in pretty fast," he remarked. "Let's wrap this up."

Gail blew her whistle and Alpha swam toward the dock, eager for more herring. She came right up to the edge, opened her mouth, and Gail tossed in a handful. Alpha clicked and whistled, her way of saying thanks, and sped around the dock for a few moments, as if playing to Dylan's camera. She swam backward, half her torso out of the water, a trick she'd learned at the marina where she'd lived before her life in the navy.

Gail blew her whistle again, a signal that Alpha should return. But she'd gone under again. "Shit, she dived, Dylan."

"So blow the whistle again. She can hear it."

She blew the whistle a third time. A hundred feet away, a pair of dolphins surfaced. She couldn't tell from here whether they were males or females, but there were definitely wild. She suspected that Alpha's presence had drawn them and worried that Alpha would swim off with them.

Instead, Alpha surfaced close to the dock and Gail went over to the edge and knelt down again. "You want more herring, Alf?"

She clicked and Gail reached into her pack and brought out the device with the explosive mounted on it. She signaled for Alpha to rest her snout at the edge of the dock and quickly attached the device. Gail rewarded her with a big handful of herring and pushed the last button on her belt, alerting the control room to activate the signal on the target.

"You know what to do now, girl." She gestured for Alpha to dive, seek the signal, and attach the explosive to it.

The dolphin swam away from the dock, air rushing from her blowhole, Dylan's videocam whirring, recording it all for military posterity. Then she dived and Gail reached into Dylan's pocket for the cell phone. She punched out the number for the control room and Lieutenant Jackson picked up. "Got her on radar, Dr. Campbell. She's moving fast."

"How fast?"

"Bursts."

That meant her speed ranged from eighteen to twenty-two miles an hour. "Is she headed toward the target?"

"Yeah, but she's not deep yet, only about thirty feet."

She should be much deeper than that, Gail thought, pacing from one end of the floating dock to the other, her eyes on the water. "Anything else unusual, Jackson?"

"No . . . wait. . . . There're two blimps on the screen, joining her. Are there more dolphins out there?"

"Yeah, two. Crank up the signal on the target."

"Right."

"Keep the line open."

"What's going on?" Dylan asked.

"I don't know." She stared out across the water, an alarm shrieking at the back of her mind. She could still see the boat that had deployed the target. No dolphins broke the surface of the water. "Jackson? You in contact with the guys on the boat?"

"Yeah, their radar's jammed. They're moving away from the target now, Campbell. And I've got Alpha on radar, two hundred feet down, barely moving. . . ."

The cell phone went dead.

"Shit, your cell phone's dead, Dylan."

"Impossible. I charged it up last night."

She tossed the dead phone to him and ran over to the edge of the dock. She had a very bad feeling about this. "Something's wrong," she said and hurried over to her diving gear to gather it up. "Let's get back to the tank. Fast."

Dylan tossed his bag in the dinghy and ran to untie the rope. Just as Gail scooped up her gear, a tremendous explosion tore through the air. She whirled around and saw plumes of greasy smoke billowing up from where the boat had been anchored. And then, off to the right, three dolphins broke the surface, fleeing for the open waters.

The last of the evening light leaked from the seam of the horizon and spilled across the water behind Dylan's place. Big Lagoon, they called it, a misnomer, for sure. It was just an open body of water that separated the mainland from Perdido Key.

She pressed her bare feet against the wooden deck. The wicker rocker where she sat creaked and moaned as it moved. Out in the yard, fireflies darted about. A cacophony of noises drifted up from the lagoon. *What went wrong?*

The three men on the boat had died. One of them, the youngest, had lived long enough to make it to the hospital, but had died within an hour of third-degree burns that covered ninety percent of his body. A cover story had been issued to the press to explain the explosion. The men who had died would now become heroes and no one outside their circle would ever know the full truth.

But she knew and what good did it do her? She couldn't explain it. Alpha had spent most of her life in captivity, with humans, dependent on humans for virtually everything. During her years in the military, she had been trained and programmed to perform certain tasks in a certain way. And yet, in the space of a few minutes, the unexpected appearance of a pair of wild dolphins had overturned all that training, all that deep and fundamental need for humans.

She hadn't just ignored a directive; she had displayed forethought, strategy, intent. She and her buddies from the wild had jammed radar signals, Alpha had removed the explosive and attached it to the boat, and then she'd fled.

She turned on us.

Of all the things that might have happened, this was so low on her list she had never even considered it. Not from Alpha. Not from any dolphin she'd ever worked with.

She knew she was going to be killed.

Impossible.

Gail rubbed her eyes and sat forward in the rocker, sipping from the bottle of beer that Dylan had handed her a while ago. She heard his voice through the screen door, a low, urgent voice, his military voice, the voice he probably had been taught to use at the naval academy. She entertained that idea for a few minutes, of Dylan in a course taught by the navy's equivalent of Lon Chaney.

She heard him slam down the receiver. Heard the fridge door open and shut as he helped himself to another beer. Then the screen door creaked and he came outside on the deck and dropped into the hammock to her right. The light had bled completely away. Stars popped out against the black skin of the sky. The hammock squeaked as it swung. He said nothing, a brooding silence that could quickly turn ugly. "I've got to get some food," she said finally. "I haven't eaten since breakfast."

"Today is Saturday, June thirteenth," Dylan said, as if she hadn't spoken. "We have exactly forty days to train two dozen dolphins to locate and destroy targets on demand, Gail."

Gail exploded with laughter. "In your dreams, Dylan."

"Otherwise this project is scrapped."

Her laughter died. Her feet no longer pressed against the wooden deck. She had gone utterly and completely still inside. *Scrapped?* Just like that? A snap of the fingers and an entire program was wiped out? "When did all this come about?"

"I'm not at liberty to say."

"They can't afford to get rid of us."

"Right now, Gail, we're a liability."

"That'll pass. It always does. The funeral's tomorrow,

there'll be press for another couple days, then some other scandal will come up. And if there's no legit scandal, they'll create one."

"I need dolphins, Gail."

She squeezed the bridge of her nose, shook her head. "And I need food." She pushed up from the rocker. "I can't think on an empty stomach."

"What's there to think about? You've mentioned at least six dolphins at the research center that sound like prime candidates for our program."

"Most of the center's dolphins are either injured and recuperating or they're being untrained for release into the wild. You know that. You know they wouldn't work. Besides, there are eight dolphins here at the base that are qualified and probably another four or five that need a little more intensive training. That's twelve or thirteen."

"I need more than that."

"The cold war's been over for years, Dylan. What's the rush?"

"I told you, I'm not at liberty . . ."

"Yeah, yeah," she snapped. "So go pillage some other dolphin centers in the keys where you have spies, Dylan. I like my job and I'm not putting it in jeopardy for the navy."

"I pulled the strings that got you that goddamn job."

True. Seven years ago, he'd gotten a small grant for the dolphin center where Gail worked and Gail had been part of the package. But so what.

"I'm outta here." She trotted down the steps and around the side of the house to where her car was parked.

"Gail, you can't just run away from this."

"Who's running?" she called back, and kept on walking.

They'd played this game many times over the years and she knew how it would go. She wouldn't hear anything from him for the next few days or even the next few weeks, depending on how angry he was that she hadn't gone along with *his* agenda. Then he would call or send her flowers or show up unexpectedly and would try to convert her without telling her what was really going on.

Usually, she gave in at this point because she was lonely and missed him. But this was precisely why he'd married someone else all those years ago and fathered two children with the woman. He simply figured that good ole Gail would always be there.

Not this time, Dylan.

Three

Natalie Thomas pedaled fast and furiously through the sunrise, her blond hair flying out behind her as she headed for the forbidden place.

She crossed the runway, a strip of asphalt too short for jets and just long enough for the single-engine planes that connected the island to the rest of the world. The bridge also connected Piper Key to the mainland, the bridge and a two-lane strip of asphalt that unrolled for fifty or sixty miles to Gainesville, the nearest major hub. But the road often flooded during storms and the rich weekenders who had homes here hated to drive. So they hopped into their expensive little planes and their hired help picked them up in electric cars or golf carts. Most of them had left before Easter and they wouldn't be back until the weather turned cooler in the fall.

Personally, she didn't mind the snowbirds. But her mother did. She griped about the traffic they created, their lack of consideration, their rudeness. She claimed they tied down their planes in the area where her employees at Dolphins on the Gulf parked their bikes, golf carts, and cars. Last winter, she got so mad about it she brought it up at a town meeting. It didn't change things. According to Natalie's mother, the island commission wasn't about to pass any laws that would make life difficult for the folks whose property taxes paid for new roads, computers in the schools, and basic services like electricity and water.

The dolphin research center, on the other hand, was nonprofit and didn't pay a penny of tax on its five-acre spread. But the center did bring in tourists, Natalie thought. In the last year, the dolphin swim program had lured more than fifteen hundred tourists, which was more than half the year-round population on Piper Key. The island commissioners, though, had ignored that part of it and Natalie didn't understand why. There were many things in her mother's world that she didn't understand.

Why, for instance, had her parents gotten divorced when Natalie was five? *We weren't compatible,* her mother had said. But what did that really mean? Was incompatibility the reason her father had never bothered to contact her? And why had her mother split up with Ian Cameron last year? *I didn't love him,* her mother had said. But why hadn't she loved him? Of the several boyfriends her mother had had over the years, Ian was the best, an animal abuse cop in a nearby town. If she couldn't love him, then she probably couldn't love anyone.

There hadn't been any other special men in her mother's life since Ian Cameron. No one would put up with the hours her mother worked, Natalie thought, and what man would choose to play second fiddle to dolphins? And that was what it amounted to, even for Natalie.

Ever since Natalie had been in second or third grade,

her mother had worked twelve hours a day, seven days a week. Occasionally she took time off to attend a school function with Natalie, but they rarely did things together just for *the fun of it*. If she wanted to see a movie, she went with a friend. Picnics, outings, shopping: her mother didn't have time for any of that. Natalie had learned early on that if she wanted to do any of these activities, then she went with a friend's family.

Ian had taken her a lot of places during the six months he and her mother had dated. Baseball games, bookstores in Gainesville, horseback riding in Ocala, to the sinkholes on the mainland for snorkeling and swimming. The best part about Ian was that he loved animals as much as she did.

Not that her life was all bad or anything. She loved Piper Key and the freedom she had here, and at least twice a year she and her mother went on her mother's version of a vacation. Alaska, Hawaii, Australia. But once they got to these cool places, Natalie usually discovered that her mother had gone for work purposes and had hired a sitter to do things with Natalie.

She sped past the dolphin center, a wooden building that stood on concrete pilings ten feet high. It didn't look like much from here, but on the other side, which faced the cove and gulf, it resembled a crazy web of layered wooden catwalks that surrounded the dolphin holding tanks.

The center was deserted at this hour. Her mother wouldn't arrive until eight and, with any luck, wouldn't check on Natalie's whereabouts until ten or eleven. She would make her usual calls to Natalie's friends, tracking her the way a bloodhound tracked criminals, unless Natalie called her first on the cell phone.

Then she would start with the questions and demands. Was there an adult in the house? How long would she be there? Please call if they left the house. Stay away from the water. No boats, no strangers, no junk food. In some ways, her mother treated her like a preschooler, not like a teenager who would be sixteen in October. But in other ways, she considered Natalie a grownup and in terms of dolphins, treated her like a peer.

Trade-offs. Life was a series of trade-offs.

She passed the downtown area, several blocks of shops and real estate offices. On a map, Piper Key looked like a horse's head, with the downtown located in the horse's mouth. Her destination lay just north, in the horse's nostrils. In Corinne's neighborhood, none of the houses stood on pilings or stilts because the area was five feet above sea level. The only place where the altitude was higher was the wilderness preserve in the horse's ears, where the land rose steeply several hundred feet into the hills.

Natalie turned into the driveway of the square yellow house where Corinne lived. Both of her parents worked in Gainesville, so they were hardly ever home. But her grandmother lived with them and Corie was always eager to get away from her.

The old lady answered the door in her bathrobe, her mouth turned down at the corners like usual. Instantly, a wave of loathing crashed over Natalie. She stepped back quickly, trying to put enough distance between herself and old lady Laker so she couldn't feel what she felt. "You again," the old woman muttered, the flap of skin at her chin trembling as she spoke. "I suppose the two of you are up to no good again today."

"Morning to you, too, Mrs. Laker."

Little snit.

The words resounded in Natalie's head and she stepped back a little farther. "We're going bird-watching."

"It's barely dawn yet."

"It's the perfect time for bird-watching."

She rolled her eyes and planted one hand on her fat hip, so that she resembled a chubby little teapot. "How stupid. Birds just crap and chirp. Who needs them?" Then she shuffled away from the doors, her slippers slapping her heels, and shouted, "Corinne, your friend's here."

Your friend. As if she didn't have a name, Natalie thought.

Natalie remained outside, where the waves of loathing and bitterness couldn't reach her. Mrs. Laker turned around. "You coming in or staying outside? The cool air is escaping."

"I'll stay here, ma'am."

"Suit yourself."

She slammed the door and Natalie sat down on the step to wait for Corie. Moments later, she heard shouting inside, then the garage door went up and Corie hurried out, pushing her bike, her pack slung over her shoulder. "The shit bitch is on the warpath big time," she muttered.

The shit bitch threw open the front door just then and shouted, "No swimming, Corinne, you hear me?" Then, almost like an afterthought, she shouted, "And what about food and water?"

"In my backpack, Mrs. Laker," Natalie called, and sped on, catching up with Corie.

"She doesn't really care about the food and water,"

Corie said. "She just asks because she figures it's her duty to ask."

"Forget her. We'll stay out all day and tonight you can stay at my house and tomorrow we'll putter around the center. It's our first day of summer vacation."

Corie let out a whoop and they both raised their fists into the air and shrieked, "Girl power!" They laughed and swung out into the middle of the road. They raced out of the city limits and north through the string of smaller islands, onward to Boogie Key.

Corie was a year older than Natalie, but in the same grade, and at least a head taller, dark hair to her blond, a knockout who couldn't care less about all the guys that clamored constantly for her attention. Her passion, like Natalie's, was animals, and animals had been their strongest link ever since they'd met in kindergarten. The only secret that Natalie had ever kept from Corie was about to end today, at the forbidden place.

"So is my dad going to let me get a dog?" Corie asked. "You get any feelings about that?"

Corie was one of two of Natalie's friends who knew about the feelings she got, about the *routes* she could see in her head. She usually had a couple of questions for her when they were together. The problem, though, was that she knew Corie and her home situation so well that it interfered with these feelings. The bottom line was that old lady Laker hated animals as much as she hated people and since she paid the mortgage on the house, Natalie's parents weren't about to cross her. "No, I don't get any feelings about it. Ask me something else."

"Are we ever going to move into our own place and get away from shit bitch?"

A *route* appeared in her mind, several lines shooting

out from a central point, Corie's present home. One line seemed particularly thick and bright, indicating that it was the most probable *route* to the future of Corie's question. Natalie followed it in her head and saw a house on stilts somewhere here on Piper. The walls looked nearly solid, so she knew it wasn't that far in the future. "It's a house on stilts somewhere on the island. I think your parents have already looked at it."

Along this *route* she saw a bank. "They've already talked to the bank."

Corie's face lit up. "So it's soon, then."

"I think so."

Corie looked over at her. "Spooky, how you do that, Nat."

No, she thought. The spooky part was how it had started, a story she'd never told Corie because it was part of The Secret.

"You leave your mom a note?" Corie asked, changing the subject.

"I'll call her. I've got the cell phone in my pack."

"I asked my mother if I could have a cell phone and she laughed."

"It's different for you. Someone is always at your house."

"Well, you'd better call your mom before she calls my place. The shit bitch really gets off on telling parents what absolute horrors their kids are."

She didn't need to get grounded for the next two months and reminded herself to call her mother by 9:30. Last summer had started off with her mother grounding her for a week because she'd gone swimming with wild dolphins. Ridiculous, but there you had it. Her mother definitely fell into the obsessive category and when it came to the dolphins—which she always referred to as *her* dolphins—she could be a real control freak.

When they reached Boogie Key, they slid off their bikes and walked them into a thicket of bushes at the edge of the salt marsh. "This is it?" Corie asked, wrinkling her nose as she glanced around. "This is the forbidden place?"

"No. We have to get into the boat."

"What boat?"

"My boat." Natalie ducked under an arch in the bushes and led her friend through a tunnel of green, where she kept the small aluminum canoe she'd bought two weeks ago from a kid who was in the senior class.

"Cool," Corie said. "I guess your mom doesn't know, huh."

"She'd have a fit." She turned it over, exposing the paddles and the outboard engine wrapped in a plastic tarp. "Grab the paddles, will you?"

Natalie attached the engine to the back of the canoe, then she and Corie pulled and pushed it through the brush. They emerged on a narrow beach that ran parallel to the salt marsh for several hundred feet.

"You think there're any wolves around here?" Corie asked, glancing around uneasily.

"On the beach?" Natalie laughed. "No way."

"In the *Gazette*'s wildlife column this week, the whole thing was about a gray wolf and her cub up in the horse's ear. Did you read it?"

"Sure. I always read it. That wolf is in the woods, Corie."

"Yeah, but there've never been wolves in Florida. So what's it doing here?"

"I don't know." She'd wondered the same thing when she'd read the column and then, as now, the wolf's presence on the island disturbed her in a way she couldn't explain. "Who do you think the witness is?"

Corie shrugged. "Probably someone we all know. I got the feeling it's a woman."

"I think it's a man."

Corie giggled. "Maybe it's a kid."

"Yeah, sure."

"A really smart kid. Like Tom Maynard."

Natalie rolled her eyes. "He's not exactly a kid. Besides, he's too busy with computers to be writing that column. And he would've told me if he was doing the column."

"Maybe." Corie snickered again. "Unless college has changed him a lot."

Natalie knew that her crush on Tom amused Corie and merely shrugged, refusing to be goaded.

"So where's this forbidden place, anyhow?" Corie dropped her pack in the canoe. "How far do we have to go?"

"Out past the salt marsh to a cove."

"Digger's Cove?"

"Yeah. You been there?"

"Nope. I've heard stories, though. Everyone has."

Stories told over campfires, Natalie thought. Island legend said that pirates used to hide out in Digger's Cove after they'd raided other towns up and down the Florida coast. "You scared to go?" Natalie asked.

"Me?" Corie ran her fingers back through her short hair. "No way."

They drifted out into the salt marsh, Corie paddling up front and Natalie steering from the back. She kept the engine out of the water until they had cleared the hyacinth. Then she set it back into the water and cranked it up, opening it as wide as it would go. The summer wind bit her eyes and all the smells she loved best filled her lungs. Salt, the marsh, the sky, and, most of all, the open spaces.

Ten minutes later, they plunged into a thick hammock and followed a briny river through an overhang of branches. Birds twittered in the shadows, fish swam through pools of sunlight. The county or the state had posted various signs along the channel. NO TRESPASSING. NO SWIMMING. NO FISHING. PROPERTY OF THE STATE OF FLORIDA.

"Hey," Corie said. "How long does the gas in the engine last?"

Corie, the worrier, Natalie thought. "Long enough."

"I sure don't want to get stuck out here."

"We're nearly there."

When the river forked, Natalie steered to the right, where the water deepened and flowed back into the gulf. Pretty soon, the trees on their left ended and the world opened into Digger's Cove, a paradise of turquoise water surrounded by mangroves, a narrow curve of white beach, and the vast blue sky above them.

"Incredible," Corie breathed.

"I told you."

"No condos, no boats, no people." She tore her T-shirt off over her head. "Is it safe to swim here?"

"It's really deep. One of us needs to stay with the boat unless we pull it up onto the beach."

"Let's take turns," Corie suggested. "Me first." She leaped over the side.

Natalie tipped the engine out of the water, stripped down to her bathing suit, then sat back in the canoe and pulled her flute from her backpack. She briefly shut her eyes, waiting. When the music drifted into her head, she raised the flute to her mouth and began to play what she heard.

Always, it had been like this with her and the flute. First she would hear the music in her mind, then she would play it. She'd been playing for more than eleven years, since she was four, but back then, her fingers and her mouth always seemed to be out of synch. She could never quite match the beauty that she heard in her head. She still couldn't. But she was much closer now to the ideal.

The music drifted out into the warm light, mingling with the noise of Corie's splashing. The canoe rocked as Corie tugged on the rope, pulling the canoe toward shore. Natalie's eyes scanned the mangroves as she played. She could feel the music deep in her bones now, in her very blood, and knew the moment was close.

Suddenly, Corie scrambled back into the canoe, almost tipping it over, her face flushed with excitement. "Dolphins, do you see them?" she whispered.

Natalie rolled onto her knees, the flute silent. Three dolphins. She started playing again, watching them. One of the dolphins separated from the other two and came toward them. Corie looked worried. "They going to tip over the canoe?"

Natalie shook her head.

"Do they want us to swim with them?"

She shrugged.

"Should we be worried?" Corie asked.

Natalie lowered her flute and grinned. "Not with Kit. That's the one coming toward us."

"She's from the center?"

"A long time ago."

Corie frowned. *"The music?* You called her with the flute?"

Natalie smiled and raised the flute to her mouth again. More than thirteen years ago, she'd waddled out of her mother's sight at the center and had fallen into one of the holding tanks. She'd sunk to the bottom, down through the strange and trembling light, down through the hiss of bubbles, down to the bottom. And she hadn't come up.

Natalie couldn't remember much of what happened while she'd been down there, trying to breathe like a fish. But she did remember the moment when the dolphin had bumped into her. She recalled looking into its eyes and hearing the music, sounds so beautiful, so different, so completely alien to her experience, that she didn't panic. The music had swept through her like a wave of electricity, then it had swallowed her.

Suddenly, she'd sped toward the surface and exploded into the bright light, a little thing that arced through the air like a beach ball. She remembered that moment, then nothing else. Nothing until she'd come to on the dock, her sobbing mother hovering over her.

Until then, Natalie's vocabulary had been limited to *Mama, Dadda, kitty, poop,* and a few other basics. But after that, she hadn't even uttered those words. After all, what was the point? Her voice would never sound like the music she'd heard underwater, the song of the dolphin. Besides, she didn't need to speak. She could hear what other people were really saying.

All of that had changed when she'd turned four and her mother had sent her to preschool. If she wanted friends, she would have to speak. She would have to join the tribe. So she eventually began to talk and a few months later, her mother had bought her a flute. When she played, her need for language went away.

"Oh, my God," Corie whispered, eyes wide, staring at Kit as she circled the canoe, air whooshing from her blowhole. "What's she doing?"

Natalie stuck her flute back into her pack and leaned over the side of the canoe, clicking her tongue against her teeth. "Kit," she called, and set her palms flat against the surface of the water. She didn't pat or slap the water, just kept her hands still. The dolphin swam up closer to the canoe, clicking and whistling, a dolphin Morse code, then came up under Natalie's hands.

In the moments that it took for her hands to pass completely over the dolphin's back, *routes* exploded across her inner vision. She couldn't decipher what she saw, couldn't follow any single path to the next moment or the next. In this moment, all things seemed possible because time had collapsed into an eternal *now* riddled with excruciating urgency.

She gestured for Kit to return. Instead, the dolphin sped away from the canoe and Natalie suddenly understood. She leaped up, shouted for Corie to stay in the canoe, and jumped over the side. Kit reversed directions and swam toward her. Natalie grabbed on to her dorsal fin and they sped toward the other two dolphins that had accompanied Kit into the cove.

As they neared, Kit slowed and Natalie got a good look at the pair. She recognized the male, Rainbow, from the fold in his dorsal fin. He'd been released from the center about a year ago, after treatment for a bacterial infection, and had been sighted maybe half a dozen times since then. Natalie had never seen the other dolphin, but Rainbow seemed to be supporting it, holding it up.

All three dolphins clicked and whistled at each other.
Kit came up close to them, so that Natalie was now
trapped in the middle. She held on to Kit's dorsal fin
with her right hand and held the palm of her other
hand against the surface of the water, not knowing exactly what she should do or what Kit expected of her.

They swam slowly in a circle, Kit towing Natalie,
until Rainbow nudged the other dolphin toward her.
Even as it changed directions, Rainbow continued to
offer his body as support. Natalie placed her left palm
on the surface of the water, something she never did
with dolphins in the wild because they might interpret
it as aggression. The dolphin seemed to understand,
though, and clicked as it approached, scanning her.

Then it came up under her hands. Instead of seeing
routes, exquisite sensations coursed through her. Her
entire body felt like a tuning fork that hummed at the
same pitch as the dolphin's whistle. Colors and geo-
metric shapes danced through her mind. Fragmented
images, as if viewed through a prism of glass, floated
through her awareness. She sensed these fragments
were pieces of some giant puzzle that pertained to the
unknown dolphin, but didn't have any idea how to put
the pieces together.

She suddenly knew that it was a female and sick,
very sick. "I'll get help. Or I can take you to a place
where you'll get help."

The female swam past her, Kit came alongside her,
and Natalie grabbed on to her dorsal again. As they
swam toward the canoe, Rainbow and the female
clicked and whistled and started to follow. Kit picked
up speed and just short of the canoe, veered sharply to
the left and Natalie let go of her fin. Then she scrambled into the canoe.

"What's going on?" Corie asked.

"The female's sick. I'm hoping they'll follow us to the center. Call my mom on the cell phone. I need to put the engine in the water."

Natalie put the engine back into the water and started it up. Corie tossed her the cell phone. "It's ringing."

"Dolphins on the Gulf. Dr. Thomas speaking."

"Mom, it's me. I'm bringing in a sick dolphin. A female. She's with Rainbow and Kit and . . ."

"Slow down, Nat. Just slow down. Where are you?"

"Digger's Cove."

"Digger's Cove? You need a boat to get there."

"Yeah, Mom." She steered the boat to the right, where the deepest part of the channel lay. "Can you get a holding area ready? Just in case Rainbow and Kit come in with her, maybe you should clear holding areas one and two. We'll be there in thirty minutes."

In an icy voice that promised Natalie would be grounded for the rest of her teenage life, her mother said, "The tanks will be ready. But you don't have any guarantee the dolphin will last until then. Or that it'll follow you."

"It will. Hey, Mom?"

"What?"

"Eu coosi dao, Mikana."

Despite her anger, her mother laughed. "I love you, too, kiddo. But we're still going to talk about this later."

She disconnected before her mother could say anything else.

As they emerged from the mangroves, the dolphins' clicking turned to high-pitched whistles, a complex series of them. The rapid pitch changes brought goose bumps to Natalie's arms.

"What're they doing?" Corie asked.

"Calling for help."

She knew that bottlenose dolphins could pick up each other's signals from a distance of six miles and that Kit's pod was probably much closer than that. So it didn't surprise her when several dozen dolphins appeared. The air exploded with whistles, clicks, squeals. Natalie stopped the engine and titled it toward her chest, out of the water, so none of the dolphins would be injured if they swam close to the canoe.

Corie clutched the edge of her seat. "They're surrounding us."

"Sit down. Fast."

Natalie removed the engine from the back of the boat and set it under her bench. She propped her pack against it and leaned against the pack so the engine wouldn't slide. Corie now sat on the floor at the other end, gripping the sides of the canoe, eyes wide with fear.

Within minutes, dolphins seemed to be everywhere, appearing as if by magic. Hundreds, Natalie thought. There were hundreds of dolphins now. They converged on the area, a dark, quivering wave of dorsal fins, beaks, and arching bodies. Four swam alongside the canoe, their clicks and squeals almost deafening, their flukes splashing water over the sides. "Oh God, oh God," Corie muttered over and over again, her face utterly white.

The four dolphins pressed up against the canoe and it pitched violently to the left. Natalie grabbed on to the sides, Corie moaned and squeezed her eyes shut, then suddenly the canoe flew across the surface of the water like some kind of hydrofoil. The wind stung Natalie's eyes, making them tear. The canoe rocked and rolled and she leaned back as far as she could against her pack. The clicks and squeals deafened her.

Once, just once, she managed to turn her head enough to glimpse the endless wave of dolphins behind the canoe. She could no longer distinguish one from the other. Their bodies formed a dark mass as far as she could see.

She groped inside her pack until her fingers found the flute. She gripped it tightly and sank down lower in the canoe so the wind wouldn't whip it out of her hands. Then she brought it to her mouth and started to play, her fingers flying over the holes, the music bursting forth. It wasn't clear to her whether she played to talk to the dolphins or to calm herself.

Four

Mom, it's me. I'm bringing in a sick dolphin. Lydia Thomas kept hearing her daughter's voice in her mind, a reminder of her ex-husband's complaint that their daughter wasn't normal. Actually, what he'd said was, *She's a freak.*

She'd thought a lot about that in the years since he'd run off with an eighteen-year-old bimbo, shortly before Natalie's fifth birthday. Lydia had heard he was out West somewhere, living with his third wife, her three kids, and two of their own. She and Natalie had heard from him only once, when he'd called and asked Lydia to ship his bike to him. She'd told him to fuck off and had hung up.

In all fairness to him, though, he'd never understood what had happened to Natalie that day that she'd stumbled into the holding tank. She wasn't so sure she understood it, either, but she had a better grasp of the ramifications than he did. Somehow, her daughter had emerged from that experience with an uncanny ability to understand animals. Natalie claimed she *communicated* with them, and although Lydia couldn't go that far, she had to admit her daughter was exceptionally intuitive.

And now little miss Natalie Dolittle was bringing in a sick dolphin. What next? Whales?

Eu coosi dao, Mikana. She knew these particular words of her daughter's secret language had been intended to soften the sting of her anger. The phrase literally meant "I love you, Lydia," the sweetest words any mother could hear from a teenage daughter. But at the same time, the language itself underscored Natalie's intrinsic eccentricity, her marked difference from other kids.

The language, in fact, had evolved over a period of several years, but Lydia was convinced its source lay in whatever had happened the day she'd fallen into the holding tank. At times, a part of her even believed this secret language was the human equivalent of the dolphin's clicks and whistles.

Lydia stood on the uppermost deck and scanned the waters with a pair of binoculars. Her height was a definite advantage; at five-eleven, she didn't have to stand on a chair to get a better view. But even so, there was no sign of them yet. The gates to the two largest holding tanks stood open, though, ready to receive the sick dolphin. If Rainbow and Kit accompanied the dolphin into the tanks, there would be enough room, since these two tanks alone covered about two acres.

"You see them yet?" Armando "Arnie" Pintea ran up behind her, breathing hard, and stopped at the railing.

"Nope. Is everything ready down there?"

"As ready as we'll ever be." He moved around as he spoke, quick, nervous movements, as if stillness were anathema to his personality. He was her only Latino biologist, a short, wiry man with dark hair as curly as the matted hairs on his chest. "The doc is on his way, Gail is contacting everyone scheduled for swims and asking them to reschedule, and all the dolphins have been moved to other tanks. I'll be at the control panel, ready to shut the gates on your signal. Anything I've forgotten?"

Lydia smiled and shook her head. "Yeah. Tell me how we can get our grant approved so we can afford to take in one more dolphin."

Pintea's bushy brows lifted, forming little peaks over his dark eyes. "We can say no to one more dolphin?"

Lydia made a face and combed her fingers back through her curly hair. "C'mon, Arnie."

"Okay, we can't say no. We should maybe develop a media program? Get more exposure so our donations increase?"

"In other words, you don't think the grant will be approved."

He shrugged. "Our fiscal year ends June thirtieth, Lydia. You tell me how it looks."

Bad, she thought. It looked very bad. They had about a month's reserve for salaries, operating expenses, and disasters and that was it. She'd bought the center sixteen years ago, on her twenty-fifth birthday, with an inheritance from her mother's sister. Nothing remained of that money. She'd poured her profits into the center and it had been a constant struggle to keep the place solvent. Nearly always, help had come through at the eleventh hour. Even though she was grateful for that, the eleventh-hour shit was getting old. Just once in her professional life, it would be nice to know she had the next six months covered.

"You're depressing me," she replied.

"Shit, I'm depressing myself."

Already, the center had twenty dolphins in various stages of rehab. Most of them were bottlenoses, but they also had spotted and common dolphins. Another dozen or so checked in at least once a week to play and, yes, they usually stuck around for chow, too. At twenty to twenty-five pounds a day per dolphin, this added up to more than five hundred pounds of fish a day, most of it squid, mackerel, and fish native to the gulf. Some of it was donated. But the rest had to be purchased from local fishermen or from suppliers. Food remained the most expensive item at the center, with vet bills a close second, and salaries trailing behind the two.

Could she afford to feed and care for one more ailing dolphin? No. Twenty more pounds a day added up to another 7,300 pounds of fish a year. But, somehow, she would do it. Maybe she would give Ian Cameron a call. He had great local contacts and had come through for her several times in the past. But she hadn't spoken to him since she'd walked out of their relationship nearly nine months ago, and if she called him now, he might think she wanted to start things up again.

"Hey," Pintea said suddenly, pointing in the distance. "What's that?"

Lydia shaded her eyes against the sun and looked in the direction that he pointed. A dark mass as large as an island headed this way, moving quickly. It was perhaps a mile out and changed shape every few seconds. On the beach below them and off to the left, sunbathers had lined up, watching the spectacle. Swimmers scurried out of the water.

She raised her binoculars to her eyes again. "My God. Dolphins. Hundreds of them."

"Let me see."

She passed Pintea the binoculars. *"Caramba,"* he breathed. "Six or seven hundred easy." He thrust the binoculars back at Lydia. "I want this on videotape."

He ran off and Lydia looked through the binoculars again. The pod seemed to be growing even as she watched. She didn't think they would descend en masse on the holding areas, but dolphins in the wild were rarely predictable and she simply couldn't risk it. She slipped her radio out of her pocket. "Gail, this is Lydia. Open the gates on the other side of the canal. There's a pod of hundreds out there and if they enter the cove and try to get into the tanks, we're in deep shit. Over."

"Hundreds? How many hundreds? Over."

"I don't know. Hundreds. Open the gates just in case. Over."

"Okay, I'm opening them. I've never heard of a pod this large in the gulf, have you? Over."

"No. Over and out."

She continued to watch the pod, roiling like some huge protoplasmic mass, shifting this way and that. The cove marked the beginning of the center's property. Shaped like a U, with a very narrow mouth, it could be sealed off with a polyurethane net. But she knew it wouldn't withstand an assault by a pod this large and the risk of injury to some of the dolphins would be too great. Better to open up the other end of the deep-water channel that connected the cove to the holding areas and led back into the gulf.

The pod lay about half a mile out now. Something just behind the leading edge of the mass glinted. Lydia adjusted the focus on the binoculars and everything around her screeched to a halt. The only thing that existed was the aluminum canoe that the undulating pod of dolphins seemed to be carrying through the water. The canoe with two kids inside it.

She grabbed her radio, spun around, ran for the stairs. She pressed a button for an open channel.

"Natalie and Corinne are in that pod, people. In a canoe. Just behind the leading edge. Stand by."

Voices crackled over the open channel. Lydia raced down two flights of stairs to the lowest level of catwalks, flew down another four steps, and hit the beach at a full run, heart pounding in her throat. She raced up the long curve of the cove, arms pumping at her sides.

Please don't hurt my little girl. Please.

A pair of helicopters chattered past overhead, one of them sweeping around, rotors chattering. *News choppers.* Christ almighty. All this would be on the news this evening, the greatest dolphin fiasco in the history of the gulf, the center's holding areas destroyed, hundreds of the mammals killed, two human fatalities. . . .

No. As she tore up the rocky slope on the left side of the cove, a sense of déjà vu swept over her. *I've lived this moment before.* What? Where the hell had *that* thought come from?

The radio in her hand crackled as Gail's voice came through. "Lydia, the gates at the other end of the channel are open and the doc is here and ready. Do you need a boat or anything? Over."

A boat? A goddamn boat? What the hell difference could a boat possibly make with a pod this immense? "I need wings, Gail. Wings." She disconnected and ran up the slope on the left side of the cove, a rocky jetty some twenty feet above the water. She could now see the pod clearly. The air literally rang with their clicks and whistles. The mass seemed to be shifting direction and the canoe pitched from side to side, her daughter's head bobbing up and down, visible one moment, gone the next.

Lydia scrambled down the jetty of rocks. She knew

she couldn't do anything, that her proximity to the water wouldn't make any difference in whatever happened. But she needed to be as close as possible to Natalie so that her daughter could see her, hear her. Her foot slipped, she nearly lost her balance. The choppers swept past again, low enough to startle the dolphins, and Lydia waved her arms frantically, motioning for them to get away. She moved more quickly, using her hands, her buttocks, descending the rocks like a crab.

At the bottom of the jetty, water broke over her sneakers. The clicks and whistles crested, ebbed, crested again, and kept on rising in pitch and intensity. The mass, less than a quarter of a mile from the mouth of the cove now, closed in fast.

She shouted her daughter's name and waved her arms. The choppers swept past again, much lower this time. She would never know whether the proximity of the choppers caused the mass to break abruptly away from the canoe or whether the signal had come from the lead dolphins. But suddenly the canoe pitched violently to one side and the pod veered away from the jetty as if governed by a single mind. Walls of water rose up, blocking Lydia's vision.

Her panic broke loose and she tore off her sneakers and threw herself into the water, swimming like someone possessed by unspeakable energies. When she came up for air, she saw her daughter madly paddling the canoe toward her, her soft moon face flushed from sunburn, excitement, fear. Corinne sat on the floor of the canoe, sobbing into her hands. Behind them swam Rainbow and Kit, with a third dolphin between them. Beyond them, the dark mass had stalled, clicking and whistling, waiting—*for what?*

Lydia swam over to the canoe and climbed inside. For a moment, she and Natalie just looked at each other. In her soft blue eyes, Lydia recognized Natalie's father. Her pale blond hair also belonged to him. But the rest of her, from that ski slope of a nose to the pouting mouth to the high cheekbones, was a pure blend of them both.

"I'm okay, Mom."

"I'm not okay. You took ten goddamn years off my life." She started the engine. "Corinne. Hey. Listen up."

Corinne sniffled and rubbed at her eyes.

"Once we're past the jetty, I'm going to pull up close to the seawall and I want you to get out."

"But . . ."

"No buts," she snapped. "You get out and go straight to the holding areas."

"What about me?" Natalie asked.

"I need you to stay in the canoe, so that trio back there follows us."

"We were never in any danger, Mom."

"We'll talk about it later. Is this your boat, Corinne?" She caught the look the two girls exchanged.

"It's mine," Natalie said softly.

"Uh-huh. Add that to what we'll discuss later." Lydia looked back at the dolphins, trailing them at about fifty yards. A quarter of a mile away, the pod still waited. "Was that entire pod in Digger's Cove?"

"No." Natalie shook her head. "They showed up once we'd left the mangrove."

Corinne spoke up for the first time. "Rainbow and Kit called them."

"Why would a pod this huge show up for one sick dolphin?"

"Because there's something special about Alpha,"
Natalie said.

"Alpha?"

"That's her name."

Lydia didn't ask how she knew. "Special how?"

"I don't know. I felt it when I touched her."

This was the I-talk-to-animals shit again, now carried
way too far. She would save that one for later, too.

Lydia steered the canoe through the mouth of the
cove, past the jetty, and pulled alongside the seawall.
Corinne climbed out and Lydia steered the canoe out
into the channel again, the dolphins trailing some thirty
feet behind them now.

As they neared the holding areas, Kit and Rainbow
emitted a series of whistles that the pod a quarter of
a mile out responded to. These whistles sounded different from the ones she'd heard earlier, and when she
looked around, she saw the pod splitting in half, then
into quarters, then into eighths. The choppers chattered
past again. One followed a pod out to sea and the other
followed the canoe.

Bastards, she thought. If they came down any lower,
if she lost this dolphin because of the goddamn
press . . .

They rounded the bend and chugged into the holding
tank. Lydia brought the canoe flush with the wall,
killed the engine, and leaped out, Natalie right behind
her. Pintea helped her haul the canoe out of the water
so it wouldn't pose a threat to the dolphins.

"The doc's standing by." Pintea stabbed a thumb toward the floating catwalk on the far side of the tank.
"Do we try to separate the sick one from the other
two?"

"No. I don't think she can stay afloat by herself for very long."

"Then I'll radio Gail to close the gates as soon as they're in."

"And call someone to get that chopper the hell out of here."

"I already did."

Lydia grabbed the packs out of the canoe and ran over to Natalie and Connie. They huddled together at the edge of the seawall, a pair of skinny little things with adolescent curves in all the right places. In another year, Natalie would be more interested in boys than in dolphins and Lydia knew she would be worrying about worse things than her daughter sneaking out to swim with dolphins at Digger's Cove. She reminded herself to take that into account later, when they discussed all this.

She dropped their packs on the ground. "One question, Natalie. Were you playing your flute when the dolphins came into the cove?"

"Yes."

"Then play it now. Fast. And be ready to get into the water if I signal you." She looked at Corinne. "You okay?"

"Yeah. Now I am."

"Good. Get vests for you and Nat. Put them on. If I give you the signal, I'd like both of you to get into the water with the dolphins. You don't have to do anything in particular, Corie. Just be there. They like kids."

"Okay, sure, Ms. Thomas."

She seemed grateful to have something to do and ran off to get the vests. Natalie, flute in hand, began to play. The haunting notes drifted out into the warm air, the chopper lifted away from the center, and the three dolphins entered the holding area. These three events happened seamlessly, as if one hinged on the others. The gates began to close.

Lydia tore off her T-shirt and shorts, stripping down to her bathing suit, and ran over to the rack of vests. She pulled one on and joined the doc, Bill Sinclair, on the floating catwalk. "Let's give them a few minutes to calm down before we get into the tank, Bill. Then we'll slide in nice and easy."

He looked at her, the sunlight burning his white hair even whiter. "It's your call, hon. I'll need to draw blood before I can determine anything."

"I know. If we can get them calmed down enough, taking blood won't be a problem. Just have the syringe ready."

The dolphins moved slowly through the holding area, the female still sandwiched between Rainbow and Kit. Natalie's music seemed to calm them. "I'll go first," Lydia said quietly.

She eased her body into the water, careful not to splash, and swam slowly toward the trio. They clicked, scanning her, and she felt it right down to her bones. In the thirty-five years since her first swim with a dolphin at the age of six, this sensation had never deviated. It always felt indescribably pleasant and utterly alien. The intimacy of a dolphin's sonar scan surpassed orgasm. It was like being embraced by some vast and incomprehensible intelligence offering unconditional love. But in another sense, it was an invasion, a violation, a serious breach in interspecies etiquette.

Rainbow and Kit swam close to the tires that lined the holding area. They whistled, obviously communicating something. Then Rainbow slipped away and Kit maneuvered the female up against the tires for support.

Rainbow swam toward Lydia, whistling as though Lydia understood his language. In a way, she did. She knew that he was asking for her help and offering his own help to facilitate the job. Treading water, she placed her palms flat on top of the water. He swam under them, so that her hands passed over his immense body. He felt rubbery, soft.

She closed her fingers over his dorsal and held on. His dorsal was comparable to the cartilage in the human ear. If she gripped too tightly, it would hurt him. If she didn't grip tightly enough, the speed at which he traveled would whip her off. He sped back across the holding area, whistling to the other two, and brought her right up to them.

The female, so weak that she could barely keep her head out of the water, looked at Lydia with eyes that screamed with pain. Instead of touching her, Lydia ran her hands over Kit's beak. *See? I'm okay. Kit isn't freaking.* Kit, in fact, opened her mouth and allowed Lydia to stroke her tongue.

Kit clicked and the other female whistled weakly. And only then did Lydia touch her, speaking softly to her, assuring her they wouldn't hurt her. Her hands found evidence of abuse—a jaw that had been broken somewhere in the past, old scars, a dorsal with a chunk missing. The air that rushed from her blowhole didn't sound right.

Aquarium, she thought. This dolphin had been at a sea aquarium somewhere, living on a diet of herring, in a tank that was much too small. No telling what other horrors it had known. Lydia raised her right hand slowly from the water. She signaled the kids first and once they were in the water, she signaled the doc.

Rainbow swam in short, nervous circles some distance away as the girls approached him. Natalie had a ball that she tossed to Corinne. It distracted Rainbow, who joined in the play, tossing the ball back to the girls.

Sinclair approached Lydia and the female. The female clicked several times, scanning them, and suddenly jerked her snout away from Lydia's hands, and whistled, a weak, pathetic sound punctuated by the wild thrashing of her flukes. Rainbow instantly broke away from the girls and raced across the holding area.

Lydia glanced around, trying to determine what had spooked the female, and saw Gail Campbell standing at the edge of the tank, near Natalie and Corinne. Gail's appearance was the only obvious thing that had changed in the moments since Lydia had slid into the water.

Lydia motioned for Gail to get out of sight. Dolphins had good vision both above and below the water and maybe if the female couldn't see Gail, she would calm down. Gail quickly darted behind the wooden panel that shielded the outdoor shower.

The female kept thrashing and now Rainbow reached her, whistling rapidly, urgently, and placed himself between her and the others. Natalie continued to play the flute. The doc stayed where he was, close to the catwalk, floating, waiting for Lydia's signal.

Within minutes, the dolphins had calmed considerably and Lydia swam toward them first. They scanned her, but remained calm. She motioned for Sinclair to join her. The dolphins clicked, scanning him once more. They seemed to accept him, so he went to work, with Lydia assisting him.

During the twenty minutes that he worked on the female, she never drew away from him, never thrashed, and neither Rainbow nor Kit acted aggressively. If anything, they seemed to understand that his intent was to help. They even allowed him to listen to the female's heart and lungs. He ran his hands over her body, checking it for wounds and scars.

He talked the entire time that he worked on her, his soft, southern voice drifting into the hot summer air. Before he finished, he injected her twice.

Afterward, as they headed up the catwalk, Sinclair said, "I won't know for sure until I get a look at these blood samples, Lydia. But her lungs sound like she's got pneumonia and there may be a secondary infection, too. She was definitely living in captivity and was subjected to some insidious forms of abuse. Her jaw has been broken, she has scars on her back and sides that suggest physical beatings, and she's malnourished. In addition to a broad-spectrum antibiotic, I gave her a vitamin booster to bolster her immune system. But I have to be honest with you, Lydia. It may be too late."

"Will we know within twenty-four hours?"

"Give her forty-eight. I'm going to leave some antibiotics with you. She'll need a shot twice a day."

"What do you suggest we feed her?"

"Whatever she'll eat."

"How the hell am I going to keep her afloat, Doc?"

"I suspect Kit and Rainbow will do what they can. But in a pinch, you can rig up a net."

She'd done that only once before and the net had terrified the dolphin so deeply that it had died. "I'll think of something. Maybe tonight we'll keep an eye on her in shifts."

"If she survives the night, then she should begin to improve." Sinclair waved a hand toward the sky. "Those choppers . . ." He shook his head. "This will definitely be on the evening news. Maybe it'll help churn up business, huh?"

Commotion erupted in the tank again and Lydia glanced back. Gail Campbell had stepped down onto the catwalk with Natalie and Corinne to hand them a bucket of mackerel to feed the dolphins. The female saw her and now thrashed more furiously than before. She whistled shrilly and threw herself against Kit, trying to get away. Rainbow's flukes slammed against the edge of the platform, rocking it so violently that Gail slipped and went down hard on her knees.

The female broke away from Kit and struggled out into the holding area alone, her burst of strength ebbing so rapidly that Lydia knew that within ten or fifteen seconds she would sink. And if she sank, she wouldn't come up. If she didn't come up, she would drown.

"Get the hell off the catwalk!" Lydia shouted.

But Gail seemed oblivious, her eyes fixed on the dolphins, her blond hair wild around her head. Lydia shot toward her, leaped onto the catwalk, and grabbed the back of Gail's T-shirt, jerking her away from the platform and the dolphins.

Gail wrenched around and slammed the heel of her hand against Lydia's throat. Lydia gasped. She felt like a diver at five hundred feet whose source of air has been completely cut off. Her brain went ballistic. She had a vague sensation of falling forward. Then air rushed back into her lungs and she coughed and leaped up, rubbing her throat.

Gail seemed as stunned as she was.

"Get . . . the fuck . . . off . . . the platform . . ." Lydia sputtered.

The hardness in Gail's features seemed to soften all at once and she rushed toward Lydia, murmuring,

"Christ, I'm sorry. I didn't mean to . . . My God, are you okay, Lydia?"

Okay okay okay: The words echoed in her skull as Gail took her gently by the arm and helped her to her feet. Lydia, still rubbing her throat, pulled her arm away. "I'm fine. Get out of here, Gail, just get the hell out of their sight."

Gail hurried away and Lydia rolled onto her knees, rubbing her throat and watching as the dolphins came together again, whistling and clicking in agitation, but no longer terrified.

Gail Campbell, her most qualified marine biologist, terrified the ailing female dolphin.

Why?

Five

As soon as Joe Nelson's truck hit the main road out of Saratoga Springs, Max Thorn rested his head against the back of the passenger seat and shut his eyes. He didn't want to talk. But it was a long ride from Saratoga, where he'd been in a hospital for almost a week, to Blue Mountain Lake, and he knew Nelson had a lot of questions.

Nelson, after all, wasn't just his closest neighbor and one of the people who had found him. He was also a county cop who wanted to know where Ellen was and why he'd spent at least forty-eight hours in the fields behind his house, carting around a bundle with dead birds in it.

But Thorn had no answers, at least none that made any sense. A single lucid memory haunted him, of Ellen fading, then vanishing. Beyond that, he knew nothing. But he suspected he had lost it big time out in the fields, that his mind had cracked like a nut. His doctor said that when he'd been brought in, he was out of his head and had a temp of nearly 105 from an infection that was resistant to most antibiotics. His fever had finally broken two days ago and, with the breaking, came the memories.

Of birds, hundreds of birds. And of Ellen fading, then vanishing out there in the fields, near the corral.

Who would believe it? Not Joe Nelson. Not Ellen's old man, who had more connections than God. Right now, he wasn't even sure that *he* believed it. Other things were easier to believe: an alien abduction, memories implanted by the government for motives yet unknown, some weird breach in the space-time continuum. Hell, almost anything was easier to believe than what he'd seen.

Other memories stirred. He couldn't put it into words, the memories weren't specific, but he began to feel short of breath, choked, and knew that a tidal wave of raw emotion lay on the other side of this feeling. He inhaled deeply, trying to calm himself, and just then Nelson popped in a country-music tape.

No wonder Nelson's two Labradors had hearing problems, listening to this shit all the time.

"Joe?"

"Sorry." He turned the music down. "I didn't mean to wake you."

"How'd you find me?"

He didn't hesitate at all. It was obvious that he'd been waiting for Thorn to ask. "Bacall showed up at my place the night of the eleventh. She was starved and refused to come in the house, so I fed her outside. I knew something must've happened for her to trek three miles to my place. I called your house and when I didn't get an answer, I got worried. Bacall and I drove over there. Soon as I pulled into the driveway, she leaped out the window and ran for the house. The back door was open, the lights were off. The coffeepot was on, but everything inside it had burned away. The table was set, but there was garbage all over the floor. . . . Looked like a coon had come right in and made itself at home.

"Anyway, no one was around, so I checked the garage to make sure the cars were there. Then Bacall took off into the field and I grabbed a flashlight and went after her."

"That was Friday night?"

"Right."

"And today's Friday, a week later."

Nelson nodded. It didn't seem possible that so much time had elapsed. When he'd been out there, in the fields and in the woods, everything had been compressed. "And you found me that night?"

"Nope, found you Saturday, around noon. Bacall and the other dogs had problems picking up your scent. You were so far back in those woods we might not have found you as soon as we did if we hadn't heard you. You remember what you had with you?"

"Birds. Dead birds."

"Why?"

Jesus God, Joe, there were hundreds of them. . . .

He suddenly saw himself leaning into the floor freezer in the garage, the cold air drying the sweat on his face. This memory connected to nothing else, though, so he didn't have any idea what it meant.

"Max?"

"I don't know why I had dead birds with me."

"They'd started to rot," Nelson said. "I think that was part of the reason the dogs had trouble following your scent." He paused, ran his fingers through his reddish hair. "You have any idea where Ellen is, Max? She hasn't been seen since she walked out of a pharmacy downtown on June eighth. You two were supposed to ride horses on the ninth over at Mountain Stables, but you never showed."

Birds, a thousand or more birds . . . And then she just vanished, Joe.

Thorn blinked, rubbed his eyes, and looked at Nelson, waiting for him to say something. *Make it good.* "She left," he said hoarsely, his voice cracking.

"Left? Left for where?"

The twilight zone. "I don't know. She . . ." *Faded.* ". . . said she needed time to think. Then she . . . left." *Vanished.*

"You mean, there's another guy?" He sounded incredulous.

"I don't know."

"But that was your impression, right?"

The birds, Joe. All those goddamn birds. And then she went for her run and screamed and started to fade and winked out like a star and I must've lost it bad.

"Yeah, that was my impression."

"But both cars are still in the garage, Max. How'd she get to wherever she was going?"

"I don't know. I . . . I went into my den and shut the door and when I came out, she was gone."

"Did you argue?"

"No. We rarely argued."

He glanced over at Nelson again, his compact body leaning forward, as if to see the road more clearly, elbows resting against the steering wheel. His reddish hair shone in the light.

"The whole thing was very . . ." Thorn groped for the right word. The *convincing* word. ". . . I don't know. Very civil. Very calm. She said what she had to say. . . ." *Kissed me on the cheek before she jogged off into the field, Joe.* "I think I asked her some questions, I think she responded. That part's foggy. I was in a kind of shock, I guess. I mean, it was so goddamn sudden."

"Did she have a suitcase packed?"

"I don't know."

"How was she dressed?"

"Jesus, Joe. I don't know. I wasn't interested in how she was dressed. The only thing that mattered right then was what she was saying. I don't know what she was wearing, I don't know if she'd packed a bag, I don't even know how the hell she left the house. Christ, maybe she walked down the street and her lover picked her up." He nearly choked on the lie and looked quickly down at his hands again. "I just don't know," he finished, softly.

"Christ," Nelson spat. "What the hell should I tell her old man?"

Thorn tried to keep his voice controlled. "You talked to him?"

"He must've left a dozen messages on your answering machine. Then he called the station yesterday and again this morning before I left to pick you up. He's concerned because he hasn't heard from Ellen in a week."

Ellen's old man would never buy the truth about what had happened to his daughter. "What'd you tell him?"

"That you were in the hospital and I'd get back to him. Unless you want to do it."

"What the hell am I going to say to him, Joe? That Ellen left me? He'll celebrate. The prick can't stand me."

"Look, we'll deal with him later. Right now, let's just get you home and pick up Bacall from my place."

A good plan, Thorn thought. Not too complicated, not too far in the future.

"Have you, uh, looked in the mirror in the last week, Max?"

Thorn rubbed his stubbled jaw, shook his head. "I guess I'm growing a beard."

"That's not what I mean." Nelson reached over and snapped down the visor over the passenger seat. "Take a look."

Something inside him resisted doing this. Just from the way his clothes fit him, he knew that he'd lost ten or fifteen pounds and probably resembled some haunted survivor of war. But he would have to look at himself sooner or later, so what the hell. He adjusted the mirror—and drew back in shock. His hair, once a chestnut-brown, had gone completely white.

Thorn headed out the back door, the videocamera slung over his shoulder and Bacall hugging his heels. The dog hadn't left his side since they'd picked her up at Nelson's several hours ago. Her soft whimpers let him know, however, that she wasn't too crazy about this and might not go the distance with him. He knew exactly how she felt.

A pleasant breeze blew through the maples where the birds had congregated that morning. Only a few grackles twittered in the branches now. The leaves rustled and across the field, the high grass swayed in the breeze. He glanced right and left across the slice of sky that curved over the field and the woods, a part of him expecting to see a dark swarm. Other than isolated scarves of clouds, the sky was clear.

"Let's go, girl."

Bacall licked his hand and they headed out into the field, alive with butterflies and bees, dragonflies and birds, all the summer critters. Hundreds of birds had fallen on him. He remembered that clearly, remembered curling up into a ball on the ground, in the grass, as they'd struck him. Where were all their corpses?

Even without the paddock as a landmark for the vanishing point, he would have found it anyway because all the grass within two or three feet around it had died.

He and Bacall stopped just outside the perimeter of dead grass, an erratic ring. The dog growled and crept back, away from the ring of dead grass, and Thorn suddenly understood why she hadn't gone on her usual run with Ellen that morning. She'd sensed a *wrongness* in the air, the same wrongness that had brought the birds, killed the grass, and caused Ellen to fade away to nothing. It was as if Bacall had tuned into a frequency that Thorn couldn't perceive, into the collective mind of nature, into its primal soup. It didn't explain what had happened—that would be his job—but it made him feel utterly sane and less alone.

Just the same, when he moved closer to the ring to videotape the barren area, beads of sweat popped out on his forehead and the terror sprang to life again, nibbling at the walls of his chest. He fought the urge to flee and raised the camera to his eye, getting the place on tape. Then he crouched down, eyes scanning the ground for a clue, a hint, anything. He found a long stick and poked at the dirt, dug at it, turned over clumps of it.

He didn't know what he hoped to find, perhaps some vestige of Ellen. Instead, he uncovered dead things—dead bees, dead dragonflies, dead butterflies, even a dead snake.

In fact, nothing living came within three yards of the dead grass.

What's that prove?

Maybe nothing, maybe everything.

Thorn set the stick down and passed his hand through the air about a foot above the ring. The air felt ten or fifteen degrees colder. He was even able to define the shape, which felt like a tube of cold air roughly the same size as the ring of dead grass. It ended about four feet above the ground, a very definite line of demarcation where the colder air abruptly turned warmer.

He stood and stepped into the ring, into the cool tube of air. *Beam me up, Scotty.* He shut his eyes and conjured an image of Ellen as she had faded. *Take me, too.* Nothing happened. The anomaly or the primal force or whatever the hell had taken her was gone and only this barren, cold vestige remained.

Bacall barked and started running around the ring, snapping at the air. Alarmed, Thorn quickly backed up, out of the tube of cold air, and Bacall ran over to him, licking his face. "Hey, calm down, it's okay. Nothing's going to zap me into the twilight zone."

He decided he should document this change in temperature. It would be his proof that something weird had happened right here, even if he didn't have any idea what was entailed in that weirdness. He whistled for Bacall and they loped back through the field to the garage, where the old floor freezer was. He would remove the old thermometer inside the freezer and would videotape the thermometer's temperature outside the ring and then inside it.

He raised the garage door and he and Bacall hurried inside, between the Cherokee and the Explorer. He

lifted the freezer's lid, frowned. The contents looked as
if they'd been rearranged by some kid stoned out of
his mind. Packages of frozen goods stood on end, soy
burgers spilled from their boxes, containers of juice had
popped open and the liquid had frozen in colorful layers on the floor of the freezer.

Thorn pawed through everything until he found the
thermometer, frozen to the side of a box of Popsicles.
As he pulled the box out, a pyramid of other boxes
toppled to the side, exposing what lay buried in a corner. A crow. One of the dead crows from the field.

In that time of madness, he must have returned to
the house and put one of the crows in the freezer, so
that he could autopsy it later. He may have been out
of his goddamn mind, he thought, but old habits died
very hard: he had even sealed it in a plastic freezer
bag. He brought out the Baggie, rubbed the frost off
of it, and turned the bird over. The gaping chest wound
was there, all right. He hadn't imagined it. And if he
hadn't imagined that, then he hadn't imagined what had
happened to Ellen.

Certain that the crow held genuine clues about what
had happened out there in the field on the morning of
June 9, Thorn set the crow in the utility sink to defrost.
Then he went back outside with the thermometer.

Thorn, so absorbed in conducting his experiment before the light ebbed completely, didn't hear anyone behind him until Bacall barked. He glanced around and
there stood Joe Nelson, a muscular silhouette against
the plum-colored sky.

"You want to tell me what the fuck is *really* going
on, Max?" His eyes darted from the dead ring of grass

to the videocamera to the thermometer, and back to Thorn's face. "You want to tell me why the shovel in your garage is covered with dirt? Maybe it's related to that dead grass there, huh, Max? And I can't believe that you don't remember why you collected a bunch of dead birds with holes in their chests. And most of all, I can't believe that Ellen left you for another guy. I don't buy that one at all, Max. I mean, man, it's so fucking obvious that she's nuts about you, that she would've married you in a second if you'd asked."

This last remark rendered Thorn speechless. Where the hell had Nelson been living for the last twenty years? On Mars? Had it ever occurred to him that women were no longer like his own mother? That the world had evolved beyond such black and white roles?

Then he realized that Nelson's opinion probably represented that of most of the people in Blue Mountain Lake who knew him and Ellen. In the consensus mind of the town, *he* was the schmuck who had never popped the question and had been taking advantage of Ellen for the last seven years. Yeah, suddenly the picture snapped into clarity. He would have to be very careful from this instant onward.

"Well, Joe, it happened. I don't know what else to tell you."

Nelson crouched and plucked a blade of grass. He slipped the tip between his lips, savoring it like a cowboy with a strip of fresh meat cooked over an open fire. "That isn't how it looks."

Those few words, uttered so softly, confirmed the menace that Thorn felt in his very bones. He knew that Joe Nelson, neighbor, client, and a friend for more than eight years, was about to cross a boundary that would take them both into a darkness where he really didn't want to go.

"I can't help how it looks. I don't know what the hell you want to hear."

Nelson gazed at him for a long moment, his red hair tipped with the last of the light, then flicked the blade of grass away. "The truth, Max. I want to hear the truth."

Thorn said nothing.

After a moment, Nelson muttered, "Shit," and got up and walked away.

Thorn sat back on his hands, watching Nelson until he vanished around the side of the house. *So this is how it starts,* he thought, and stretched out in the grass again with his dog and watched the sky go black.

Piper Key Gazette
Wildlife Column
June 18, 1999

Last Monday morning, I was having breakfast at one of the cafés on the pier. I looked up from my menu and saw a dark continent where only blue water had existed moments before. Then I realized this continent was moving and that it wasn't a land mass, but a tremendous pod of dolphins. Like everyone else on the pier, I ran down to the water's edge to watch this phenomenon unfold.

The pod was perhaps a thousand strong and seemed to move as if governed by a single mind. Just behind the leading edge of the pod was a canoe with two kids inside. At times, the canoe was raised entirely out of the water, borne along by the immense pod.

As the pod neared the cove, which is the entrance to the dolphin research center, it began to disperse, exposing the three dolphins that followed the canoe. The two flanking the middle dolphin appeared to be holding it up, so that it wouldn't drown. The pod regrouped some distance away and seemed to be waiting for the three to get to safety. Once the trio entered the cove, the air exploded with whistles and clicks and the pod dispersed.

Altruistic acts aren't uncommon among dolphins. Wild dolphins have been observed holding up dolphins who are having trouble breathing, just as the two dolphins apparently did for their ailing companion. They've been seen rescuing other dolphins from human attackers by biting the lines of harpoons and nets that have captured one of their own.

Dolphin midwives routinely help newborns to the surface so they can breathe. There are also many documented cases in which dolphins have saved humans who otherwise would have drowned.

But yesterday's incident goes well beyond any of these examples. Why did such a large pod accompany the trio of dolphins? Were they merely spectators or does this hint at some deeper meaning that deserves our scrutiny? Perhaps the truth lies with the ailing dolphin that was brought into the center. Maybe we should be asking ourselves if this dolphin has a special role or place within the larger community of dolphins in the gulf, and if so, what is that role?

Perhaps the answers to these questions will usher us into a century and a millennium that isn't merely new, but profoundly different from anything we've known. My sense is that something unusual and transformative is happening on Piper Key. And if it's happening here, then maybe it's happening elsewhere, too. If you or anyone you know has observed erratic or unusual behavior among wildlife, please let us know at: pipergazette@island.net.

Witness
Visit our website at
www.piperkeygazette.com

Six

Lydia and Natalie sat at the edge of the catwalk between holding tanks one and two, their legs dangling in the water. Just beyond them, Rainbow and Kit swam along on either side of Alpha. They no longer had to hold her up, but they rarely left her side for very long.

"Why don't you play the flute and let's see if she'll come over to us without the other two," Lydia suggested. "Then I'll feed her the mackerel with the antibiotic inside of it."

Natalie plucked her flute from the back pocket of her shorts. "We trying to save money on vet bills or something?"

"You got it."

Her frown jutted deeply between her eyes. "I was kidding, Mom."

"I'm not."

"It's gotten that bad?"

"Yeah, it's gotten that bad."

She'd been so busy trying to keep the center solvent that she never had bothered to explain the full financial realities to her daughter. Oh, over the years Natalie had known when they were having *problems,* but in her world, problems were solved and life went on. But every day, financial disaster crept more closely and her answer had been to work longer hours, write more grant proposals, and cut every corner she could without having to lay off any employees.

She still couldn't bring herself to lay off anyone or to feed the dolphins less food. But two days ago, when she'd received Doc Sinclair's latest bill, she'd decided she could do just about everything he could do, as long as he or another vet supplied her with the antibiotics the dolphin needed. So she'd contacted the university vet school and they'd worked out an arrangement.

In return for periodic visits by someone at the vet school and the antibiotics she needed for Alpha and her other charges, the school would send students to the center for "on-hands training" with dolphins. If there were no more sudden and unexpected expenses, the arrangement would buy her a little time.

"Then let me help out more around here, Mom."

"You do enough already."

"I can do more. I can do exactly what Gail does. If you fired her, you'd saved a ton of money."

She said this with a certain vehemence that surprised Lydia. "I thought you liked Gail."

Natalie shrugged. "She's okay. I just don't think she does as much as she should around here. You do three times the work she does."

"I should. It's my center."

"You know what I mean."

"No, I don't. Give me an example."

Natalie raised the flute to her mouth and played a string of quick, high notes that caught the dolphins' attention. The trio made a wide turn at the far end of the tank and started toward them. Natalie stopped playing and glanced at Lydia. "She doesn't work weekends. You and Arnie do."

"She works one weekend a month, exactly what her

contract stipulates, and puts in about fifty hours a week, without overtime pay."

"I could do that and you wouldn't have to pay me anything."

Lydia smiled and ran her fingers through Natalie's hair. She wondered how much longer she would be able to do that without her teenager daughter flinching. She'd seen other teens do exactly that, saw it one night when she and Ian had gone to a movie in Gainesville and stood in line behind a mother and her teenage daughter. The mother had smoothed her hand over her daughter's hair and the daughter had wrenched back as if she'd been burned and hissed, *Please, Mom, not here.*

"I appreciate everything you do around here, Nat. But even if I wanted to fire Gail, I can't. We renewed her contract last year and it would cost me a small fortune to break it. One thing you could do, though, is not bring in any more dolphins."

"She was sick. What would you have done?"

"The same thing."

Natalie grinned and poked Lydia playfully in the ribs. "There's something about her. I can't explain it, but she's . . . I don't know . . . unique, I guess. Special somehow. And I . . ."

An eruption of clicks and splashing interrupted her and they simultaneously glanced out at the tank. The three dolphins approached the catwalk, Alpha in the lead. She came right up to the edge, rested her beak on the edge, and clicked softly. Those soulful eyes met Lydia's, then flickered to Natalie, who immediately tossed her a handful of mackerel with the antibiotic hidden inside one of the fish. Alpha clicked in gratitude, then extended her tongue and Natalie slowly reached out and stroked it.

"I'd say she trusts you completely," Lydia said quietly.

Natalie just smiled, leaned forward, and bussed Alpha on the tip of her snout. The dolphin clicked again and, as she swam off with her buddies flanking her, slapped her flukes against the water, splashing them both.

Lydia and Natalie laughed and kicked their feet, trying to splash her back, but she was already out of range.

"That was pretty cool," a man called from the other end of the catwalk.

The sun burned against Lydia's eyes as she glanced toward him. She saw only his silhouette, but she didn't have to see him to recognize Ian Cameron's voice.

"Ian!" Natalie's squeal echoed through the morning light. The catwalk rocked and rolled as she scrambled to her feet and raced toward him.

Shit, Lydia thought as she got to her feet. *The great reunion.* But how could she blame Natalie? Ian was the closest thing she'd had to a father since her own flesh and blood had departed with the bimbo. But she felt odd watching their embrace, Natalie's arms clenched around Ian's waist, his arms holding her as though she were, indeed, his daughter, both of them talking fast at the same time, laughing, then both of them saying, "You first," and laughing again.

When Ian's eyes finally met hers, memories rushed back, condensed and vivid. Ian Cameron, fellow vegetarian, animal abuse investigator, ex-lover whom she hadn't seen in nine months, looked pretty much the same, his thick, pale hair still rather long, tucked back behind his ears. His face still held a perpetual burn from wind and sun and his eyes still smoldered. He wore faded jeans and a T-shirt with a tree frog on the front. Under the frog were the words: *I'm an endangered species.*

"Hey, Lydia."

"Hey, yourself."

"You look great."

"Thanks, so do you. What brings you over here?"

He walked toward her then, his arm and Natalie's linked together, as if to say it was two against one. "I had business out here this morning. One of those calls you get about the neighbor who's abusing the family pet."

"And?"

"False alarm. Don't get many of those anymore." He paused and gave Natalie's hand a quick squeeze. "There's something out in my car for you, kiddo. Why don't you go get it?"

Natalie gave them both a *look* that made it clear the ploy didn't fool her for a minute. But she grinned like the teenager she was and in a breathy voice said, "Be back in a jiffy."

Suddenly alone on the roiling catwalk, Ian stabbed a thumb toward the holding tank. "I heard about the sick dolphin that two kids brought in."

"You and the rest of the island. She's doing a hell of a lot better now than she was a week ago."

"What was wrong with her?"

As Lydia recited the litany of injuries for which Doc Sinclair had treated Alpha, she kept noticing Ian's strong, beautiful hands and thought of those hands on her body. Yeah, the sex between them had been good. And they had plenty of interests in common, with animals foremost among them.

Cameron had been raised in Ocala, Florida's horse country, the only son of the town's most eminent horse breeder. The lifestyle had instilled in him a passion for horses and, later, for animals in general. When he joined the navy, the military failed to brainwash him of that passion, but it had stolen just about everything else from him. Now forty-three, he'd never been married. Back before she'd known him, there had been an engagement and two live-in, long-term relationships that had ended bitterly.

He left the military six years ago and had become the town of Roberta's only cop on the animal abuse beat. She'd introduced him to the world of dolphins, so it was no surprise when he asked, "What's your take on the size of that pod?"

"Bizarre." It was the only adjective that described it.

"The two kids were Nat and Corie, right?"

"Of course."

He chuckled and shook his head like a proud father who has long since accepted his daughter's quirks and now feels proud that she isn't like every other kid on the block. "Since the dolphin has been abused and is in my jurisdiction, it's technically entitled to veterinary care at the county's expense, Lydia. If you send me Doc Sinclair's bills, the office will reimburse you."

From anyone else, Lydia thought, the generous, unexpected offer would trigger an immediate suspicion that she must give something in return. But this was Ian, after all, a man she might have loved if things had been different, a man whose kindness toward animals had also encompassed kindness toward her, in whom he had seen a kindred soul. He had no private agenda. He knew the center was always cash short, that vet bills were one of her major expenses, and he was offering to help within the parameters that his job permitted. End of story, she thought.

But she knew herself well enough to realize that if she accepted his offer, all the old softness would rush into her again. They would walk over to the office, they would chat, they would laugh, they would trade animal stories. They would slide so easily into the past that they would walk down to the pier for an iced cappuccino and if they got that far, they eventually would end up at his little house in Roberta. And there they would screw their brains out and she would regret it later because her feelings for Ian would never match her daughter's expectations or her Beaver Cleaver view of family life.

So she thanked him and replied it had been taken care of already and told him about her deal with the vet school in Gainesville. They headed up the catwalk as they talked and, once, his arm brushed hers and a sort of electricity sped through her. By the time they reached the shaded deck, she felt herself weakening, felt all these months of celibacy rushing up behind her.

Then her cell phone rang, saving her from doing something stupid. It was Pintea, babbling away in Spanish, then English, then in Spanglish, a meld of the two, and most of what he said was incomprehensible. "Hold on just a second, Arnie." She covered the mouthpiece with her palm. "I've got to take care of this, Ian. It was great seeing you and thanks for the offer." She backed away from him, her abrupt dismissal like a gaping wound in his eyes. She turned quickly and walked on toward the office with Pintea babbling about their fish order, and didn't look back.

Seven

She's hiding in the deep chasm where the shallows slope steeply into the deep end of the ocean. Her breath lies still and hot in her lungs. She hears the boats circling above her, the men shouting. She wants desperately to swim deeper, down where the light can't touch her, but her lungs ache. She needs air.

Now one of the boats stops directly above her. The engine goes silent, the men's shouts echo through the water. Have they seen her? She clicks, defining the shape and length of the boat, and swims fast toward the other end of it. Suddenly, she's tangled in a net and thrashes wildly to free herself. Her shrieks and whistles erupt through the water, but no other dolphins come to her aid. The net is lifted, air rushes from her blowhole, but already the sun beats down, stealing moisture from her body.

One of the men jumps into the water. For seconds, their eyes lock and she recognizes him. The man is Dylan. He frowns, as if recognizing her as well, then jabs a needle into her back, just to the side of her blowhole, and she shrieks and thrashes, but he just laughs. Dylan laughs.

Gail snapped upright in bed, gasping for breath, her eyes bulging in their sockets. She swung her legs over the side of the bed and doubled over at the waist. Blood rushed into her head, clearing it. She drew air into her lungs. *Just a goddamn dream.* But her years in Australia had taught her that dolphin dreams were never to be dismissed so lightly.

On the island of Groote in northern Australia, where she'd spent time observing dolphins in the wild, the aborigines believed themselves to be direct descendants of dolphins. At the ceremonies where they celebrated their rich mythology, they chanted and danced themselves into trance states so they could enter into "dolphin dreamtime." These sacred rituals supposedly allowed them to fish cooperatively with the dolphins, a phenomenon that Gail had witnessed. As the women of the tribe sang, the dolphins herded fish toward shore, where the men speared them. Each family took only one fish and the rest were returned to the dolphins.

But she wasn't an aborigine and the dream sure as hell wasn't going to allow her to fish cooperatively with dolphins. This dream, she thought, concerned her relationship with Dylan, specifically that he would use her for his own agenda—*or is already using me*—and not think twice about it.

She raised her head and the utter silence in the house struck her. An unnatural silence. Gail remained completely still, listening hard, trying to figure out what made her so uneasy about this silence. She heard the air conditioner as it clicked on, but that was all.

Gun, she thought.

She reached under a pile of T-shirts folded on a shelf on her nightstand, and brought out a thirteen-shot automatic, fully loaded. She flicked off the safety and, hunkered over, moved around the foot of the bed, senses jammed into a kind of hyperalertness. She darted to the side of the door, stopped.

Like most of the homes that bordered the salt marshes, hers stood on stilts. It had only two entrances—the front door, reached by an exterior staircase at the east side of the house, and a door in the kitchen, reached by stairs under the house, where she parked her car, bike, and golf cart. She'd locked both before she'd gone to bed.

Back to the wall, Gail moved out into the hall, alert for any movement, any sound. Several places on her block had been robbed in the last few months, but those houses were boarded up for the summer, obviously empty. She suspected that teenagers had been behind those robberies and doubted they would be foolish enough to break into a house that was occupied.

She reached the kitchen; the dead bolt hadn't been touched. She made her way back into the hallway, her heart hammering, her hands damp with sweat. She paused at the end, where the hallway opened into the living room.

Moonlight streamed through the windows that faced the salt marsh, illuminating the furniture and throw rugs—and the front door, standing open to the night air. On the coffee table sat a tremendous bouquet of flowers that hadn't been there when she'd gone to bed.

"Very funny, Dylan," she said, and marched into the living room and turned on the floor lamps.

The room was empty.

Gail walked through the open door, noting that the chain had been cut, and found him on the side of the porch that faced the salt marsh. He lay in the hammock, arms tucked under his head. He looked like some executive on a Caribbean vacation: denim shorts, T-shirt, sandals, a two-day growth of beard. "Nice place, Campbell. No wonder you don't want to jeopardize your job at the center."

"You're lucky I didn't shoot you. And it's a really bad idea for you to come here, Dylan."

"You didn't leave me much choice. I left eighteen messages on your machine."

Yeah, and each one was more threatening than the last. Dylan had seen the dolphin spectacle on the national evening news, had recognized Alpha, and called her within the hour, demanding that she "take care of the fiasco." His last message, three days ago, had made it abundantly clear about his position. *You handle it or I will.*

"And just how the hell do you expect me to *handle* it without incriminating myself?"

He sat up, swung his legs over the side of the hammock, and laughed. "C'mon, use your imagination."

"You don't get it." She sat back in the wooden rocker and rested her feet on the edge of the coffee table. "You don't understand what the situation is. Alpha is in a tank with two other dolphins. I can't get anywhere near her because she recognizes me and freaks. My boss has already noticed it."

"So what. Anyone who works with dolphins knows they don't like every person they come into contact with. It doesn't prove anything."

"If something happened to her, I'd be the first person to come under suspicion."

"Not if it looks like a natural death. I mean, Christ, she's got pneumonia, a secondary infection, and . . ."

"How the hell can you possibly know that?"

Dylan realized he'd said too much. "Her immune

system is compromised. No one would be surprised if she died. And she has to die, Gail, no question about it."

"You didn't answer my question."

"Give a hacker a computer with a modem and nothing is private, Campbell. Nothing. That's basic."

"Terrific."

He rose from the hammock now and rubbed at the stubble on his jaw. He walked over to the railing and gazed out at the salt marsh for a few moments, then turned, leaning against the railing. "The grant that Ms. Thomas has applied for doesn't have a prayer. Once the center closes, we step in—through a third party, of course—and offer to provide for the dolphins. Our price will be generous. That takes care of the dolphins we need. The problem, though, is that it has to happen soon. That means we have to apply pressure."

"What's this *we* shit, Dylan?"

"Okay, *you* have to turn on the pressure."

"First you tell me you have forty days to find and train a group of dolphins for some sort of top secret project. Now you're telling me the plan is to force the center into bankruptcy, to kill Alpha, and take all the dolphins. You still haven't told me what's behind this and until you do, count me out."

At some point during her little speech, he had come over to the rocker and crouched in front of her. Now he slipped his hands up under her long nightshirt. He had given it to her a few years ago when they'd gone to the islands for a long weekend. A huge queen of hearts graced the front of it. He ran his fingertips down the sides of her thighs and legs. She knew this routine, too.

"Why is it, Dylan, that whenever you don't want to

tell me something, you think sex is going to make me forget what I want to know?"

"That's unfair," he said.

She laughed. "It's true."

He rolled the end of her nightshirt up over her knees and thighs and brushed his mouth over her kneecaps. "I just happen to like your body." He leaned forward and tongued her nipple through the nightshirt. "And your body likes me."

Also true. "That doesn't change anything, Dylan. If you don't tell me what's going on, I won't help you."

"Then I'll help you."

He kissed her deeply, the sort of kiss that ignited memories of their teenage hormones running amok, the two of them groping at each other in the backseats of cars, on beaches, wherever they could steal space and time. She thought briefly of the dream and started to break their embrace, but Dylan slipped his arms under her, lifting her from the rocker, and set her down in the hammock. As he stood over her, pulling off his T-shirt, he seemed to be sculpted from moonlight and shadows, an ephemeral figure, a phantom. But his hands against her skin weren't those of a phantom. They felt warm and eager and as familiar to her as her own bones.

"This is how it should always be with us," he whispered, his mouth hot against her ear, his fingers slipping deep inside her.

"It could be if you were honest with me, Dylan."

"I'm as honest as I can be."

She didn't like the way that sounded, but didn't have a chance to comment on it because his mouth now roamed across her belly, slipping lower. The hammock rocked. Night sounds drifted upward from the salt marsh. Now and then, one of them moaned softly. From the very first time they'd made love, they'd known each other's bodies so intimately that sex remained their strongest language and the one area about which they never disagreed. She attributed it to the mere two minutes that separated their births.

In fact, years ago in Berkeley, during that dark period after Dylan had announced he was getting married, Gail had gone to an astrologer to have their birth charts drawn up. The astrologer had assumed from the charts that she and Dylan were identical twins. Upon discovering that they weren't, he'd informed her their relationship was about power, its use and abuse and how they wielded it against each other. *It can only go one of two ways—complete transcendence or total annihilation. There's nothing in between for you two.*

They hadn't annihilated each other yet and the transcendental part of the equation happened only during sex. But for right now, that was good enough for her.

Afterward, they lay side by side in the hammock, the breeze rocking it, her head resting on Dylan's shoulder. She felt peaceful and even though she knew it wouldn't last, she shut her eyes and drifted in the sensation. "Have you ever wondered why Alpha has that name?" Dylan asked her.

"I figured it was just a military thing. I never thought of it as having any special significance."

"When Vietnam ended, we had a lot of data on training and using dolphins as weapons. We knew they could plant explosives and find targets at depths of a thousand feet. We knew we could make them aggressive by the way we trained them. We knew they could attain bursts of speed as high as twenty-five miles an hour under their own steam and much faster than that by riding the bow wave of a fast-moving vessel. We knew that some of them could be trained to use their sonar to stun a target. But the problem with all this was that even the best-trained dolphins proved to be unpredictable."

After twenty years of working with dolphins, she knew all this. "They're erratic because even the best-trained dolphins are essentially wild. You can feed them all the herring they can eat, treat them with compassion, make them so totally dependent on humans that they'll die in the wild. But the fundamental wildness never vanishes. Alpha wasn't the first to prove that and she won't be the last."

"Exactly. So in 1972, the military decided to try an experimental strategy. They caught half a dozen dolphins in the gulf—Alpha was the first and the only one of the six that survived. She was about a year old then, still malleable, that was how the military looked at her. Instead of receiving her schooling from her mother, aunts, and grandmother, the military schooled her. They taught her that she was one of them.

"They used a lot of John Lilly's theories back then, studying the sounds she made, duplicating them, using them to communicate with her. She was treated as a spiritual being, capable of abstract thought."

Gail laughed. "The military has a concept of spirituality? Shit, it's news to me."

"That's my word for it, not theirs. Alpha was also treated as if she had the capacity to analyze situations rather than just react to them. They found that she was able to make decisions on the basis of information she had, just as we do. She demonstrated the ability to invent, to plan ahead, to be creative, abilities we also have. For all practical purposes, she was treated as a human being who just happened to live in an aquatic environment."

Gail had a sudden image of the dolphin seated at an underwater table set with porcelain plates and silverware, sampling escargot as Mozart was piped in through underwater speakers. "All the data says that she lived at an aquarium, in a theme park, for four or five years."

"That's the official story."

"Christ, Dylan." She sat up in the hammock and swung her legs to the floor. "How many other goddamn lies have I been fed over the years? Just tell me that, okay? I need to know."

"Just this lie."

"So you're really divorced?"

He laughed then, a quick, tired laugh. "Yeah, Gail. I'm really divorced. The only lies I've told you have centered on Alpha and the mammal defense program."

He touched her back, urging her to lie down next to him again. But her nudity no longer felt comfortable. It made her too vulnerable to his lies. She pulled her T-shirt back on and remained sitting up. "So go on," she said. "Tell me what else I don't know."

"In 1982, Alpha had her first calf. A female. In 1984, she had her second calf, a male. It was immediately apparent that these two dolphins were very different. It was like . . ." He paused, seeking the right word, the right phrase. ". . . like these two calves had inherited everything that Alpha had learned in her interactions with humans. Like they had inherited her entire memory bank."

Anthropomorphism. As far back as elementary school, one fact had been drilled into her: The greatest travesty a biologist could commit was to ascribe human characteristics to an animal. Yes, the kitten was cute and cuddly. But that didn't mean that it could think or feel anything when its skull was opened and electrodes were attached to its brain. Yes, the white rabbit made a neat pet. But to a scientist, it was a testing ground for perfumes, hair dyes, and Wite-Out.

Always, there had been a professional horror when some biologist even suggested that animals might have feelings, that they might feel pain, grief, joy. The consensus made it clear they were too far down the food chain to feel or think.

This attitude actually began in the seventeenth century with Descartes. He believed that only human beings were spiritual; their rational minds made them so. Everything else in nature, including the universe itself, was simply a machine. In his scheme of things, only man had a soul and that soul was confined to only one area of the brain, the pineal gland.

This belief in a mechanistic universe had prevailed until the present day with only one small change, that the seat of the soul was now believed to be centered in the cerebral cortex—or in the computer's mother-board. It prevailed in the sciences, from biology to medicine, and allowed man to feel intellectually and spiritually superior to all other forms of life.

Personally, Gail felt divided on this issue. She had never felt like a machine and didn't know of anyone else who did, either. And yet, on the rare occasions when she saw a doctor, her body was treated like a machine. In her work, she generally treated dolphins like machines—intelligent machines, for sure, but machines nonetheless. She did this even though she knew they didn't act like machines. They had highly organized societies, were capable of communicating with each other and with other species, and exhibited so many of the traits humans ascribed to intelligence that it was foolish, as a biologist, to believe they were less intelligent than man.

It was, however, equally foolish to believe that one dolphin's experience could be genetically transferred to its offspring. This went beyond anthropomorphism; it collapsed into the domain of British biologist Rupert Sheldrake.

"Say something," Dylan said.

She shrugged. "What's there to say, Dylan? You're talking about Sheldrake's morphic resonance, about a cumulative memory in nature. It's the hundredth monkey bullshit and I don't buy it."

"You don't have to buy it." He sat up, reached over the side of the hammock and scooped up his shorts, which he put on. "We have endless supportive data on this. By the time Alpha's daughter was a year old, she was doing things it had taken us five years to teach Alpha. When the son was born two years later, he was even quicker. We're talking about the inheritance of *acquired characteristics.*"

This, she thought, was another manifestation of the two minutes that separated their births. Despite Dylan's indoctrination by military life, a part of him always had been looking for deeper explanations, deeper mysteries, cosmic bullshit. Drugs at Berkeley had purged her of that. "You're talking bullshit, Dylan. This is all speculation that . . ."

"Let me finish," he snapped. "In Sheldrake's theory, acquired characteristics can be inherited without *any transfer of genes* because of the morphic field."

Now she got really irritated. "You've gone off the deep end, Dylan."

"Just listen," he said. "That's all I'm asking, Gail."

"Okay, okay, I'm listening." *Listening and trying not to hear a nutcase.*

"We found that other dolphins in our program, dolphins unrelated to Alpha, exhibited some of the same traits that she and her offspring did."

"Which they supposedly learned through the morphic field, right?"

He nodded.

Gail rolled her eyes. "Oh, *please.*"

"Let me finish. How long did it take you to learn how to use a computer?"

"Years."

"It took my oldest nephew ten months. It took my youngest nephew about five weeks. It took my niece, who's nine, five or six days. She was surfing the Web at the age of four, Gail. And it's not because she's brighter than everyone else. It's because she inherited the knowledge and experience of all those kids who preceded her in the computer age. So it wasn't just Alpha's offspring who knew what she knew. Dolphins as a species benefitted."

"That's a stretch, Dylan, even for you. You haven't met every dolphin on the goddamn planet. Give me a specific example."

He rubbed his hands over his face and didn't say anything. She fully expected him to pull his usual bullshit, citing security issues and all that. Instead, he said, "After Alpha's female calf was born and the people in charge began to suspect that the calf had inherited certain traits, they decided to teach Alpha a specific set of behaviors to see if her next offspring would know how to do it without being taught. At that time, they suspected the traits were inherited genetically.

"So the first thing they taught her was how to toss a Frisbee. The second thing they taught her was that it should always spin away on her left side. It took her about six days to master the whole thing.

"When her female calf was eight months old, one of the trainers tossed her a Frisbee, which she'd never seen before. The calf did it right within an hour, spinning the Frisbee away to her left."

"Oh, c'mon, Dylan. That doesn't prove squat. The person throwing the Frisbee may have inadvertently given her clues."

"No. These were trained biologists, Gail. Like you. You don't make those kinds of mistakes."

Yeah, her mistakes centered on Dylan.

"When the male calf was born two years later, he did the same thing, too. There were dozens of simple experiments like this, Gail, and in each instance, the task was mastered more quickly. If you don't believe me, take a Frisbee out to your center tomorrow."

"It still doesn't *prove* your theory, Dylan."

"This will. The people in charge of the Frisbee experiment decided to be really adventurous. They took their Frisbees out into other oceans, the Pacific, the Indian Ocean, the waters off the coast of Africa. They even took their Frisbees to the Amazon and to the Ganges River, to see if the river dolphins got the trick."

"All at taxpayers' expense, no doubt," she said dryly.

He ignored the remark. "In every instance, the dolphins knew the trick."

Ludicrous. Impossible. Laughable. While her mind threw up a word bank of similar synonyms, she blurted, "Even the river dolphins?"

"Yes."

"And this is documented?"

"Absolutely."

"I want to see the documentation."

"Fine. I'll fax it to you as soon as I can."

Even if she conceded that dolphins could communicate ideas and experience, the sheer distance made it unlikely that an Amazon *boto,* that pink beauty that inhabited the freshwater rivers of South America, or the nearly blind Ganges *susu,* would have any contact with ocean dolphins. And without contact, how could an experience or an idea be communicated?

If she conceded that Sheldrake's morphic field was the means, then what the hell *was* this field?

"What happened to Alpha's offspring?" she asked.

"The female escaped and the male died." He paused, then went on in the same quiet, haunted voice. "I have a tape from the news station in Gainesville that got the original footage on that massive pod. The dolphins on either side of Alpha are her daughter and her grandson."

She had played the odds many times in her life and knew that the odds of this happening were beyond comprehension. And yet, according to Dylan, it had happened.

"We believe that every dolphin in that massive sighting—and there were more than a thousand, Gail, that was the computer tally—are *informed,* okay? They know what Alpha knows. Her experiences are theirs. It goes back to the Frisbees and then collapses into the really weird. In some way we don't really understand, Alpha is revered. The closest analogy we have is the Christ figure, the Buddha, the guru, the spiritual master. That's why those dolphins showed up, Gail. Their spiritual leader was in jeopardy. Kill Alpha, and the masses mourn and eventually disperse. *The movement dies with her.*"

Prickles of alarm raced up and down her spine. This went well beyond Sheldrake or anthropomorphism. This smacked of breakdown, the nuthouse, delusion. She rose quickly from the hammock, as if his insanity might be contagious, and went over to the railing. She turned, facing him, and kept her voice neutral.

"Let me get this straight. You're saying that Alpha is the head of a spiritual movement that somehow is a threat to us, right?"

"Exactly." The word came out as an anguished sound.

"In what way is that a threat to us, Dylan? You think she's going to hold a press conference? Is that it?"

"Spare me the sarcasm, Campbell."

"Then spell it out for me, for Christ's sake."

"Three nights ago, a pod of five or six thousand dolphins and orcas descended on Sea World in San Diego. They crashed through the holding tanks and freed three-quarters of the mammals at the park. That same night, another pod that was just as large descended on the navy harbor in Norfolk. It destroyed docks, piers, fifty small vessels, and damaged three subs. There were six fatalities. At Pensacola, another pod freed every dolphin we have. At the naval base in Pearl Harbor, eight subs were damaged. These attacks all took place at four A.M. eastern daylight time." He paused, letting this sink in. "In other words, Gail, these were *planned* attacks, coordinated to take place when the targets were most vulnerable. It's exactly the kind of strategy *we* taught *them.*"

She just stared at him, trying to absorb everything

he'd said. "How . . . I mean, I haven't heard anything about this, so the navy must have covered it up."

"Yeah, except in Hawaii, where it happened during the daylight. And that's all over the Web. Fortunately, the only videos that exist were taken by navy personnel."

"What about attacks in other countries?"

"None at our bases. If any attacks happened at foreign bases, they aren't talking. But the whole point is that we believe Alpha coordinated these attacks. That she's the strategist."

Gail refused to comment on that. She needed to think things through first. "So where does the navy go from here?"

"I can't speak for the navy. But I know what I have to do." He reached down and picked up the small cooler from the floor next to the hammock. "I know you'll find this totally repugnant. But it's no more repugnant than anything else we've done to dolphins over the years." He stood and came over to the railing where she stood. He set the cooler between them and unzipped it. He brought out a syringe and set it on the railing. "It's ready to go. Just attach a needle and inject it."

He hasn't heard a damn thing I've said. "Hello, Dylan. I just finished telling you I can't get anywhere near Alpha."

"Then I'll take care of it."

"Right." She laughed. "Imagine how she'll freak when she sees you."

"I meant that I've got divers who will do it."

"No." The word echoed between them. "I won't have some schmuck navy diver coming in and fucking things up. I just won't allow it."

She caught his quick, furtive smile and realized he'd set her up for exactly this. By showing her the options—which he would act upon, she knew that much—he hoped to bring her around. "You prick."

He shrugged. "It'll be easier and faster if you do it, Gail."

"It's the same ole tune, isn't it, Dylan."

"What the hell's that supposed to mean?"

"Forget it. What's in the syringe?"

"Antifreeze. Death isn't fast, but it's certain. Every naval base has been placed on alert. Any dolphins sighted within half a mile of our bases will be killed. That's phase one."

"And what's phase two?"

"Poisoning the surrounding waters at each base."

Overkill, for sure, she thought. But that was the way the military had always done things. "That will also kill a sizable portion of the area's ecology, Dylan. We can't even guess what the larger repercussions would be."

"Yeah, the butterfly effect." He pushed the syringe toward her. "This is the best way. If you can't do it, I'll have it done by someone else. In the meantime, the dolphin center will be pushed into bankruptcy and . . ."

"I know," she said coldly. "You already told me that part."

"Look, there're four syringes in here. I'll leave them with you."

The sky over the salt marsh now turned a soft, pigeon gray. It was nearly daybreak. "I don't want anyone seeing you leave here, Dylan. You'd better go before the sun comes up."

He looked wounded. "I was going to work here today and figured we could do something this evening."

"No. Bad idea." She didn't want him around just now. She needed to think, to be alone. "Does that syringe have to be refrigerated?"

"Yeah, keep it in the cooler, in the fridge. If you need to get in touch with me, call my office. They'll forward my calls. Or there's e-mail." He leaned toward her and brushed his mouth against her cheek. It felt like a burn.

She rubbed her cheek, picked up the cooler, and turned away from him, never giving him the chance to whisper more sweet nothings in her ear.

Eight

Shortly after midnight on June 25, after five hours of dreamless sleep, Max Thorn walked out of his house with his dog and crossed the bank of grass and maple trees that separated his house from his office. He breathed in the sweet night air and the deep silence and hoped he could finish what he needed to do before the sun rose.

He unlocked the office, marveling that the place where he'd spent most of his waking life now felt as though it belonged to someone else. His things were still inside—the wicker furniture in the waiting room, the receptionist's desk, the humorous posters of animals—but he no longer felt connected to any of them.

He hit the *Play* button on the answering machine and listened to sixteen messages from patients, all of them canceling appointments. No surprise. The scuttlebutt around town was that the cops smelled something awry in Ellen Bradshaw's disappearance, an opinion her old man probably had a lot to do with. Bradshaw, in fact, had been up here twice—not to see Thorn, but to talk to the cops. He'd left Thorn a single chilling message on the answering machine: *Have Ellen's clothes and personal belongings packed up and ready to go. My driver will be up in the next few days to collect everything.*

He felt certain this also meant that in the next few days, he could expect Joe Nelson to arrive with a search warrant for the house and his office. Or maybe even an arrest warrant. They didn't need a body or a weapon to arrest him, only sufficient motive. And her old man undoubtedly had supplied that.

The cops had spent the last three days scouring the acres behind the house with a portable sonar machine, presumably looking for the buried body. He expected them back as soon as it got light, which gave him about six hours to finish cleaning out the crawl space and packing up whatever he wanted to take with him.

He wasn't sure when he'd decided to leave and didn't know yet where he would go. But the urge had grown steadily in the last three days.

He went into his lab, Bacall tagging his heels, and glanced around at the neat piles of *stuff* that he'd cleaned out of the crawl space above the storage closet during the last two nights. Boxes of old files. Old suitcases. Camping equipment. A leather briefcase with about nine grand in cash, some of Ellen's family jewelry.

He'd stashed the money away over the last year, intending to surprise Ellen with a cruise to some exotic port. The jewelry had belonged to her grandmother and great-grandmother and she hadn't wanted to stick it in a safety deposit box, so she'd kept it in the crawl space. Now the cash and the jewels would finance his getaway.

He loaded the camping gear and briefcase into the pop-up camper in the garage. He'd already packed some of his personal belongings and clothes, a supply of Bacall's food, and a shitload of pharmaceuticals and herbs suitable for animals and humans alike. He had a cooler in the car that he would have to fill on the way, but had several bags of freeze-dried stuff and water that would see him through to wherever he was going.

Last night, it had seemed like a good plan. Tonight he wasn't so sure. He simply knew that he couldn't remain here.

He ran back to the lab, Bacall racing alongside him, and entered through the back door. He turned on his computer. He'd finished making backups of every program and file on his PC last night and now had to transfer everything to the laptop. Then he planned to remove the hard drive and dump it somewhere en route. Extreme, perhaps, but he lived in extreme times.

Only in extreme times, after all, would a common black crow die from what appeared to be a coronary implosion, apparently caused by an aneurysm on the vertical wall of its heart. Terror might do it, but what had caused the crow such fear? Had it felt whatever had taken Ellen and turned the ground barren at the vanishing point? He clearly remembered being struck by falling birds and if those birds had died in the same way the crow had, then they, too, had been terrorized by something. Even more to the point, what had happened to the rest of the dead birds?

Hey, that's easy. They went to the same place as Ellen. The goddamn twilight zone.

A part of him believed that if he could solve the puzzle about the crow, he would have a vital clue about the larger puzzle, about what had caused Ellen's disappearance. If he knew what had caused it, then he would find a way to undo it and get her back.

He finished loading the backup programs onto the laptop, then started with the backups of files. The laptop had actually belonged to Ellen, but he sure as hell wasn't about to let her old man haul it away with her clothes and whatever else he seemed to think he was entitled to. The legal bottom line, after all, was that Ellen had bought the place with *her* money and in the event of her death, her will stipulated that he would inherit it.

She's not dead, Thorn. Don't even think like that.

Right. Gone but not dead.

Gone where?

"I don't know," he whispered to himself. But one way or another, he would find her.

When he completed loading the files, he went through various directories, spot-checking to make sure everything worked. He ran across a directory of files that Ellen had downloaded from the Web. She'd been a far more accomplished and dedicated Web surfer than he ever hoped to be, but he hadn't realized how odd some of her interests were until he glanced through the contents of the directory. Earthquake predictions. Earthquakes on a given day, worldwide. The predictions of Nostradamus. Millennial predictions. Volcanic eruptions in the Caribbean. The Y2K bug. The anomalous world of Charles Fort.

He recalled that Ellen had mentioned Fort a number of times in the last few months. The man had lived in the early part of the twentieth century and had collected anomalies—factual events for which science had no explanation. That sure seemed to fit his life since June 9, so he opened the file.

He uncovered a gold mine of articles about every weird and inexplicable phenomena on the planet, from red rains to rains of frogs and rocks to mysterious appearances and disappearances. For obvious reasons, he clicked on the articles about mysterious appearances and disappearances. One article discussed the top twenty-five most puzzling disappearances of the twentieth century: Amelia Earhart, Jimmy Hoffa, Colonel Percy Harrison Fawcett, the crew of the Mary Celeste, West Point cadet Richard Cox, Michael Rockefeller, the skyjacker D. B. Cooper. Fascinating stuff but none of it was what he needed.

The second article, downloaded only two weeks before Ellen disappeared, was so relevant to his life that it spooked him.

Anomaly As Proof?

On November 25, 1809, Benjamin Bathurst, a special envoy of the British government, stopped at the village of Perleberg, Germany, to change horses. In full view of his two traveling companions, he walked around the horses and was never seen again. Some versions of this story say that flocks of birds were sighted just before the disappearance.

A similar eerie disappearance supposedly happened in Tennessee in 1880. Farmer David Lang stepped off his porch one September afternoon, strolled across his field, and vanished. This happened in full sight of his wife, children, and two other witnesses.

Charles Fort and others have suggested that such disappearances may be tied up somehow with alternate Earths or universes. In Fort's era, this sort of theory constituted heresy of the highest form. But as we head into the millennium, it sounds a lot like the Many Worlds Theory of quantum physics.

To understand this theory, think of it like this. As you're reading these words, other YOUs are reading this in an indefinite number of parallel universes.

All possible universes exist. Perhaps junctures are created between these universes, through forces we don't yet understand, that allow movement from one universe to another. At the juncture point, these two universes don't simply merge. Reality itself is changed in the most fundamental ways. Call it a reality quake, for lack of a better term. It's not very scientific, but it captures the essence.

> Karl Stevenson
> Chairman, Global Watch
> KSte@globalwatch.com

"It's happened before," he whispered. "And there were birds."

Bacall, curled up on the floor next to his chair, raised her head and whimpered.

"If it's happened before, girl, then maybe I can get information from this Stevenson guy. I mean, is there a follow-up to this story? Where'd Stevenson get it from?"

Excited, Thorn jotted down the man's e-mail address, connected the laptop's modem to the phone, and went online. But when it came right down to composing the e-mail, he didn't know what the hell to say. *Send me more info on disappearances?* He would probably get some brochure in the mail on Global Watch. What he wanted to know was whether any similar disappearances had happened recently. If so, he wanted details, all the details. Were there any witnesses? What were the weather conditions? Were large numbers of animals or birds involved? Did the person fade slowly or quickly? Was the person's voice audible afterward?

He needed a *pattern.*

He finally fired off a note to Stevenson, passing himself off as a novelist doing research for a novel. The plot, he wrote, concerned a young woman who faded and vanished as her brother witnessed the event. He explained the details—the birds, the barren ground at the vanishing point, the explosion of the crow's heart.

He sent the e-mail, then explored the Web, clicking on Ellen's bookmarks for various sites. The most informative proved to be a site called *Weird News,* where he ran across a wildlife column published by a paper called the *Piper Key Gazette.* The piece that had been picked up by *Weird News* concerned a hiker's experience with a female wolf and her cub. Intrigued, Thorn clicked on the newspaper's website and clicked around until he found the most recent column, entitled, *A Thousand Dolphins.* He read it twice, his excitement mounting, then read it a third time and knew he'd found the lead he so desperately needed.

Thorn downloaded the piece, with two photos, and printed everything out. The pictures, though grainy, astonished him. The pod resembled a very large island, a dark mass so thick that hardly any water was visible within it. And there, toward the front of the mass, glinted a canoe, two kids huddled inside.

A thousand dolphins and a thousand birds, separated by more than a thousand miles, had acted atypically. Did it mean something? Did it qualify as a *pattern?* Or was it just one more anomaly to add to Fort's puzzling files?

Bacall suddenly started barking, leaped up, and ran to the door. Thorn rose quickly, whispering, "Sshh, girl, it's okay," and hurried through the lab, past the empty examining rooms, to the waiting room. He doubted that the glow of the laptop's screen would be visible through the lab's only window and didn't turn on any lights in the hallway or waiting room.

He peered out the side of the venetian blinds. Joe Nelson's truck had pulled into his driveway and now the driver's door swung open and Nelson got out. In the dim wash of light from the inside of the vehicle, Thorn could see that he wore street clothes. That meant his visit was unofficial. But if Nelson walked in here and saw the boxes, he would become a cop again. Thorn couldn't risk it.

He unlocked the front door and rushed back to the lab, Bacall's claws clicking against the wooden floor as she followed him. The Glock, he thought, and ran into the storage closet. He quickly retrieved the gun from beneath a stack of cushions that had once graced the chairs on the back porch of the house. The clip was in, ready to go. He stuck it under his shirt, against the small of his back, then walked over to Bacall and crouched down.

"You've got to do exactly what I tell you," he said softly.

She cocked her head, listening, those amber eyes locked on his. Thorn placed a hand at either side of her jaw and kept looking at her. Most dogs that he'd known couldn't maintain eye contact with humans for very long. They glanced to the side or down, feigning interest in something else or outright indifference to the human doing the looking. Bacall had never done that. When she locked eyes, it became a commitment.

"You have to remain very quiet. . . ." He brought a finger to his lips. "And you have to stay in there." He pointed at the storage closet without taking his eyes from hers. "Otherwise we're up shit's creek. Do you understand what I'm saying, Bacall?"

Bark once for yes, two for no.

She cocked her head and kept looking at him. Thorn stood and pointed at the closet. "Go," he whispered. "Now."

She got up, walked into the closet, turned so her head faced the door, and lay down, head resting on her paws. "Good girl," he said, and stooped to stroke her. "Now." Finger to the mouth again. "Sshh. Very quiet. I'll leave the door open."

With that, he slipped off his shoes and put them inside the closet, next to Bacall, a promise that he would definitely be back for her. He slid across the wooden floor in his socks, shut the door partway, and slipped behind it. His breath seemed to stall in his chest. His heart did a drumroll.

It didn't take Nelson long to get to the office. He rapped twice at the door, then opened it and called, "Max? Hey, it's Joe."

Thorn noted the usage of first names. Definitely an unofficial visit.

Footsteps, headed this way. "Max?" he called again.

From the closet, Bacall whimpered.

No, Christ no. Shut up. Please. Beads of sweat rolled down the sides of his face.

"Bacall?" Nelson whistled. "Max?"

The golden retriever let out a weak, pathetic sound, a sound of anguish, and Thorn heard her claws scratching at the floor. *I'm fucked.*

She came across the floor on her belly. He knew it even though he couldn't see her, and he suddenly understood she had a strategy. His dog had a *plan.*

Another whimper, another pathetic bark, and Nelson practically ran across the waiting room. Thorn watched him through the crack in the door, Nelson as a shadow with substance and shape. An instant before he reached the door, Thorn slammed the heels of his hand against the wood. The door struck Nelson so hard the impact reverberated through Thorn's hands with the power of a living thing. Nelson grunted like a pig and fell back, crashing to the floor. Thorn sprang out from behind the door, the Glock clutched in both hands, aimed at Nelson. But he was out cold, blood oozing from a nostril, his lower lip split open.

Heart hammering, Thorn moved toward him, reached down and checked under his windbreaker for a weapon. He found it, tucked neatly into a shoulder holster, and removed it. Bacall darted out through the door, tail wagging. Thorn grinned at her. "Clever, kiddo. Very clever. I'm impressed. So just guard him until I find something to tie his hands with."

She plopped right down as if she understood every word he uttered. Thorn ran over to the receptionist's desk, jerked open the bottom drawer, the nightmare drawer where homeless things went. He pawed through the mess until he found a pair of scissors and two lengths of rope that had been wound around a cat carrier a couple of months ago. He remembered because the ropes were pink.

He flew back to Nelson, crouched beside him, set the Glock on the floor. Thorn cut up the ropes, turned Nelson onto his side, then rolled him onto his stomach, and pulled his arms behind his back. He tied Nelson's hands, then his ankles. He grabbed his bound ankles, and pulled him across the floor to the couch. He took another length of rope and tied one end to the rope that bound his wrists and the other end to the rope that secured his ankles. Joe Nelson, human rocking chair. He threaded the last piece of rope around the ankle ropes and tied it to the foot of the couch. Unless Nelson was a closet Houdini, he wouldn't be able to get out of this one.

Redundancy, he thought, was the battle cry of extreme times.

He checked Nelson's injuries to make sure he wouldn't bleed to death before someone found him. Blood had dried around his nose, but the stuff appeared to be congealing. His lip would look like a curb, but he wouldn't bleed to death from it. His breathing sounded weird, though, a nasal wheeze that worried him. Suppose Nelson's nose were broken? Could a man die from a broken nose?

Thorn leaned close, listening to Nelson breathe. It would be okay, he decided, and wondered if he should gag him.

If he screamed, who the hell would hear him?

No one.

He would call 911 from elsewhere sometime tomorrow morning.

He told Bacall to stay, to guard Nelson, and ran back into his lab to get the rest of his stuff and stow it in the camper or the Explorer, wherever it would fit. Anxiety nibbled away at his insides like some sort of insidious cancer. Once, he had to stop because his head spun, his stomach heaved, he thought he would puke. But it passed and that surprised him. Already, he had decided that in the time of extremes, nothing ever went on to become something else, but was fixed in a pattern incapable of improving, a pattern that only got weirder and stranger. Now he realized that couldn't be true. His nausea and dizziness had passed; therefore his confusion eventually would pass as well.

He continued on to the lab, mentally ticking off the

tasks that remained before he could blow out of Blue Mountain Lake. Then he reached the reception area, where Joe Nelson was now conscious and talking to the dog.

"C'mon, Bacall, honey. Bite these ropes. Chew my way out of here. C'mon, sweet pea, you can do it."

Bacall, naturally, would have none of it. She growled and snapped at Nelson's feet, and barked once, loudly, when Thorn walked in.

"Sorry about this, Joe."

"You're making a big mistake."

"I'd be making a bigger mistake if I stayed." He patted his thigh and whistled for Bacall, who came running, pleased to be let off the hook. "The sonar guys will find you tomorrow morning."

Nelson struggled frantically against the ropes and shrieked, *"Help! Someone, help me!"*

"No one's going to hear you, Joe."

He fell silent, opened his eyes, rocked. "Listen to me, Max. I came here tonight to tell you Ellen's old man pulled strings and got a search warrant for your place. I . . . I wanted to warn you. I . . . Jesus, Max, if you're innocent . . ."

"Once Bradshaw got into the act, you and everyone else assumed I'm guilty. But you know what, Joe? No one will believe the truth and I don't intend to rot in jail for something I didn't do."

Nelson stopped rocking and glared at him. "She didn't leave you for any guy. She's buried out back somewhere."

"Birds, Joe. A thousand birds. That's what came first. Then she went out for a run. . . ." He hesitated, momentarily puzzled because this moment seemed familiar. It was as if he and Nelson had already had this conversation. Impossible. ". . . When she got down near the paddock, she started screaming and then she began to fade." Thorn let out a clipped, ugly laugh. *"Fade,* okay? And by the time I reached her, she had vanished. I could still hear her for several minutes afterward. And I'll tell you something else, Joe. The vanishing point is fifteen to twenty degrees colder than the rest of the air. You can feel it. Nothing living goes near it, not even insects."

"You're right. No one will believe that, Max." His face got bright red and he screamed, *"Because it's a goddamn lie!"*

Thorn shrugged. "Go to sleep, Joe. It'll make the time pass faster." He whistled for Bacall and headed for the door.

Minutes later when he pulled out onto the road, he felt a sharp stab of regret that his life had been reduced to this. He didn't have any idea what he would do once he reached Piper Key, but it was his only lead and, Christ, it felt *right.*

He would drive at night, hole up during the day, and his route would be erratic, a jagged line that cut south and west and east and south again. He would make sure that Ellen's father and Joe Nelson lost his trail. He would disappear just as completely as Ellen had.

Part Two

Flows
July 1–August 4

"Modern researchers in 'earth mysteries'—the hidden powers and qualities of places—have found that the location of major sacred sites is often associated with particular patterns of underground 'energy flows' revealed by the techniques of dowsing, akin to water divining. . . . There is no doubt that some places are agreeable to live in, while other places create a sense of unease, and it would be foolish to rule out the possibility that underground patterns of activity could affect the quality of places."

—Rupert Sheldrake
The Rebirth of Nature

Nine

Natalie pedaled across the runway, a beach bag over one shoulder and her pack hugging her spine. A pencil-thin line of milky light seeped above the horizon. Already the air felt warm and humid to her, but she didn't mind. It meant the water in the holding tanks would be just perfect.

She'd left her mother sleeping and had set her alarm clock an hour later than usual because she needed the sleep. Natalie had heard her typing away on her computer at two o'clock this morning, probably trying to juggle the center's finances so they wouldn't run out of money before her grant was approved.

As she came up over the slope in front of the center, into the area where wood chips and indigenous plants covered the ground, she struck something. Her bike careened into a skid and gathered speed as it headed down the hill. Her leg shot out to keep her upright, but the handlebars twisted around, spilling her to the ground. Natalie landed hard on her side and knocked the air from her lungs.

Stunned, she lay there until she caught her breath, then slowly raised up and brushed the dust off her legs. A nasty scrape ran from her calf to her thigh, blood seeped from a cut in her knee. "Shit," she murmured, and glanced back for her beach bag.

In the predawn light, with shadows shifting across the slope behind her, it was difficult to distinguish one shape from another. But she thought she saw her bag near the top of the slope, where the bike had gone into the skid. She got up, limping on her injured leg, and started back up the hill. Before she reached the top, she heard noises that stopped her dead.

Let me be wrong. But her body knew that she wasn't wrong. Sweat erupted from her pores, her heartbeat went ballistic. She turned her head slowly to the right. Three or four feet away from her, the ground seethed with rattlers, dozens of them all piled on top of each other, wiggling and hissing and vibrating their rattles. Natalie could see the diamond shapes on their backs. Their diamond-shaped heads came into view.

And just beyond this group lay another mound of rattlers, which she must have hit with her bike. Her muscles and tendons twitched, shrieking at her to run, now, fast, but terror pinned her to the spot where she stood.

One of the snakes in the mound she'd hit began to free itself from the pile of snakes. This, in turn, freed the snakes beneath it and so on, down through the pile, until the rattlers seemed to explode outward from a central point, all of them slithering across the wood chips. Some headed into the brush, others dug into the wood chips, but one came straight toward her. A Diamondback could strike accurately at up to half its body length and it could do it faster than the human eye could follow, in a quarter of a second. But it wouldn't jump at or chase an intruder and wouldn't go out of its way to bite. Her best bet was to step back very slowly.

She lifted her right foot ever so slowly, just a bit higher than the ground, then glanced quickly at the mound that was closest to her. Here, too, a snake began to pull free from the pile, and suddenly she knew these two snakes were in communication, that the clicks of their rattlers weren't just sounds.

It's a strategy. They're going to close in on me. A planned attack. Diamondbacks don't act like this.

She wanted to glance behind her, to see if there were more snakes in her path, but she was afraid that if she looked away one or both of the snakes would coil and strike at her. She eased her right foot back, regretting that she wore sandals, and kept her eyes on the snake closest to her. It was coiled now; in her peripheral vision, she saw that the other snake had also coiled. *Spin around and run like hell.*

She couldn't. There might be more behind her and . . .

. . . and a *route* suddenly appeared across her inner vision, as if she had eyes in the back of her head, and she saw her way clear of danger.

Natalie brought her left foot down directly behind her, then stepped sideways and back about six inches with her right foot. She no longer saw the rattlers; she saw only the *route,* a bright web of pulsating lines juxtaposed over the slope behind her. Left foot again, right, left, and with each step, she turned her body another twenty degrees until she was facing what had previously lain behind her. Then she ran, arms tight against her ribs, her breath slapping the humid dawn air.

She didn't stop until she reached the picnic table just outside the gate. She leaped onto the bench, then the table, and sank to her knees, her hands pressed hard against her thighs. The keys to the center were in her bag. So were her sneakers and her cell phone.

And who're you going to call, jerko? Mom?

She knuckled her fists against her eyes and rocked back on her heels. She would make a run for it to the side of the building, where one of the center's golf carts was parked. The key was taped to the inside of the back bumper. Then she would drive the cart up the slope to her bag. A fine plan. A safe plan.

Natalie glanced back.

She saw nothing but wood chips, small sea grape trees, wilted impatiens, clusters of other plants that Gail and Arnie had put out here. No snakes.

Impossible.

Natalie peered over the side of the picnic table, checking beneath it for snakes. Clear. The whole area was clear. She stepped down from the table, alert for the slightest noise, the smallest irregularity. She moved swiftly up to the slope, eyes darting here, there, but didn't see anything. She scooped up a long stick and when she reached her towel, she poked the stick at it, flipped the towel over, then lifted it from the ground. No snakes. She did the same thing with her bathing suit, her sneakers and socks, her cell phone, everything that had been in her bag. There wasn't a snake anywhere.

She glanced down at her leg, making sure that she hadn't imagined falling off her bike. The scrape looked even uglier now that the sun was rising. The blood from the cut on her knee had begun to dry up. *So I fell off my bike and must've hit my head and imagined the whole thing, right?*

Wrong.

Natalie grabbed her bag, stuffed her belongings back into it, and tore down the hill.

She felt considerably better when she slipped over the side of the platform into the holding tank. She knew she hadn't imagined the snakes, she knew what she'd seen. What she didn't understand was where the snakes had gone during the short time she'd been on the picnic table. She supposed it was possible that in those few minutes, the snakes had burrowed under the wood chips or scattered into the brush.

She would have to alert her mother and the others and signs would have to be posted in the area. The whole thing still spooked her, though, because she sensed there was more to it than that. In some ways, it was just as mysterious as the appearance of hundreds of dolphins that had accompanied Alpha, Kit, and Rainbow into the center.

She figured she had another hour or so before anyone arrived at the center, enough time to swim with Kit and Rainbow and Alpha, too, if the dolphin would allow it. Alpha and Rainbow, however, seemed oblivious. They played at the far end of the tanks, close to the gates that opened into the cove.

Natalie and her mother were the only people who could get close to Alpha. Sometimes she tolerated Arnie's presence, but whenever Gail was anywhere within sight, Alpha freaked.

Kit swam up under Natalie's hands and she felt a strange tingling in her fingers and across the surface of her palms. Images flitted through her, disconnected mind pictures of dolphins and orcas. A *route* accompanied it, but it wasn't clear or bright.

The dolphin turned and came back. Just before she reached Natalie, she went under and came up under her legs, so that she straddled the dolphin's back. Exhilaration swept through her. She hadn't done this since she was a kid, but her body remembered what to do. Her legs tightened at Kit's side and she leaned forward and gripped her dorsal.

The dolphin took off, racing across the two acres of the holding tanks. The warm wind bit at Natalie's eyes and whipped her hair around her head. She tasted salt on her tongue. Then the images started again, brilliant mind pictures of thousands of dolphins and orca whales, racing toward a harbor somewhere, descending on it, crashing into piers and docks, overturning boats. She saw marine animals of all types racing for open waters. Before she even had a chance to grasp what any of this meant, Kit turned sharply and Natalie tumbled into the water.

The vest kept her afloat, but she realized she'd fallen off near the gates. Kit raced away from her, clicking madly. She heard cries from the other two dolphins, but couldn't see what had disturbed them. The dock and finger of land that jutted out from shore blocked her view.

She swam toward the closest shore and suddenly saw Gail hurrying along the catwalk between tanks two and three. She held a red Frisbee in one hand and her head was turned away from Natalie, watching the dolphins in tank three. "Okay, guys," Gail shouted. "We're going to test Dylan's little theory."

Who's Dylan? What theory? She quickly deflated her vest, slipped it off over her head, and sank underwater. She swam hard and fast toward the dock. If she positioned herself just right, she might be able to see Gail without Gail seeing her. She opened her eyes to narrow slits and the salt water bit at them. The water was too murky to see much of anything so she shut her eyes again. Underwater, the dolphins' clicks and cries traveled clearly, high-pitched, terrified sounds.

She surfaced just under the end of the dock and swam to the middle. She couldn't see much from here, so she swam to the other side of the dock, gripped the edge, and pulled herself up so she could see Gail. She shouted at the dolphins again. "Ready, guys? Here it comes." And she flung the red Frisbee out into the holding tank.

Her mother had forbidden the use of Frisbees with the dolphins because most of them were made of plastic and might injure the dolphins' mouths if they bit through them. So none of these dolphins' had ever seen a Frisbee, at least not at this center.

The Frisbee sailed out over the tank, about eight feet above the water. One of the spotted dolphins, a young female named Iris, leaped up, sped back on her flukes, caught the Frisbee, and flung it to the left. A male bottlenose, Jake, caught it, and hurled it left to another dolphin. This round-robin game was repeated three more times, always with the Frisbee thrown to the left side of the dolphin's body, before it was tossed back to Gail.

She stood there with the dripping Frisbee in her hand, then whipped her cell phone out of her pocket. Natalie ducked down and swam to a post in the middle of the dock. She waited, treading water, listening. She heard Gail coming this way, pacing along the dock, her voice irritable.

"C'mon, Dylan, answer your goddamn phone. . . ." Then: "Colonel Steve Dylan, please. . . ." Moments passed. "Hey, it's me. . . . Uh-huh. I just did it, Dylan, the thing with the Frisbee. . . . There are five dolphins in the tank and every single one of them knew what to do with the Frisbee and always tossed it to their left. . . . Okay, okay, so I'm a hardhead. But I'm convinced, all right? I also went onto the Web after you left. The San Diego Sea World has announced that they're closed temporarily, but don't say why. There are supposedly still photos of the Pearl Harbor fiasco that are going to be posted on a site called, *Weird Happenings* . . . No, I don't know the URL."

Gail stopped almost directly over where Natalie clung to the post. She tried not to move, not to breathe too loudly.

"You hear all that racket?" she was saying. "That's Alpha. That's what I was talking about, Dylan. . . . No, I can do it. Just give me some time. . . . Okay, talk to you later."

Natalie peered up through the slats between the planks; Gail was moving away, up the dock. Gail Campbell, PhD, had secrets, Natalie thought. And from this second forward, she would always be Campbell to Natalie, not Gail, not Dr. Gail, and definitely not Aunt Gail, as Natalie had called her when she was much younger.

She had a very bad feeling about this, about Campbell. She'd never liked the woman very much, but could never figure out why. Even though she still didn't know why, she at least knew her feeling was right.

"Hey, Alf," Campbell shouted.

The cries and whistles grew louder again and the three dolphins now appeared at the far end of the tank, near the gates, Kit and Rainbow flanking Alpha. Natalie moved to the other side of the post, where she would be less visible if Campbell came this way again.

"Alf, I hear you're responsible for all the shittin' chaos. That time, girl? You the spiritual guru of every dolphin on the planet?" Campbell laughed, a quick, cruel laugh. "Well, it doesn't wash with me, you hear, Alf? You outsmarted us once. There won't be a second chance."

The boards creaked as Campbell made her way up the dock. Moments later, her legs and feet passed through Natalie's field of vision. *Yeah, keep going, Gail, into the building so I can get outta here.* Still under the dock, she swam to the rocks at the shoreline, waited until Campbell entered the building, then scrambled up the rocks and onto solid ground. She ducked out from under the dock, checked to make sure Campbell hadn't returned outdoors, then ran like hell for the side door.

It would take Campbell at least this long to get up a flight of stairs to her office, where there was a window. Natalie slammed her hand over the latch and slipped out the door, into the garden where she'd left her bike and backpack. Her beach bag was in the locker room, but she could get it later.

Her head raced with everything she'd heard. *Dylan. The thing with the Frisbee. San Diego Sea World. The Pearl Harbor fiasco. Spiritual guru.* What did any of that mean? Gail had definitely met Alpha before, too, which explained why the dolphin was so afraid of her. But where had she met her?

Natalie didn't want to go home to use her computer because her mother would be waking up about now and would have five million questions about why she'd gone to the center at the crack of dawn. She couldn't go to

Corie's either. She'd been grounded after the canoe incident. Forget the computer at the center as long as Gail was around. That left one spot: The Loft.

Natalie pedaled through town, still slumbering in the early morning light. Piper Key, that very large horse's head, stretched twenty-two miles wide at its widest point and about twice as long if you went all the way to the end of the horse's muzzle. A bridge connected the muzzle to the two-lane road that tourists detested, which twisted through high hills to Gainesville.

The upper third of the island, from the horse's eyes up to the tips of its ears, was a state preserve that consisted mostly of salt marsh. Everything from the eyes right down to the lower part of the horse's jaw and the beginning of its neck was developed or under development.

She and her mother lived near the horse's neck, on the west side of the airstrip; the center stood on the other side of the airstrip. Just above the neck, Piper Key linked with other, smaller keys where the rich snowbirds lived. The Loft stood at the edge of a salt marsh in the horse's lower jaw, the largest marsh on the island, in the most exclusive niche on the island.

She turned down the main street in the neighborhood and found the bike path that took her through pines and oaks. All the homes, raised on stilts, began at about half a million bucks. Most were snowbird places, abandoned by the owners for the summer and rented out to families in the northeast who had time and money to burn.

The Loft appeared at the end of a cul-de-sac, a rambling two-story building, vaguely L-shaped, that dated back to the mid 1880s, when the railroad between here and Gainesville was a whisper in Henry Flagler's ear. It had been the hub of a red-light district in those days, with women brought in from all over the state. They only serviced the very rich, the movers and shakers of Florida history. In terms of customers, The Loft hadn't changed. It still serviced only the rich, but as a bed-and-breakfast rather than a whorehouse.

At the mouth of the driveway, Natalie hopped off her bike and glanced at the mailbox. The angel on the top stood upright, a signal that Tom's parents had left for the day so it was safe for his friends to come on in. She walked her bike to the side of the building, leaned it against the cedar wall, and headed up the wide cedar steps. The door, also cedar, had been inlaid with stained glass from Paris or Rome or someplace over there. As usual, it didn't have a single fingerprint, smudge, or streak on it. The three housekeepers made sure of it.

She pressed down on the heavy metal handle, found the door unlocked, and stepped into the strange, waiting silence of another time. The original gas lamps graced the walls. Antique lace curtains hung over the windows. The original floors remained, now covered with a hundred coats of stuff that made those old boards shine. She passed the curved reception desk, moved silently through the lobby, past the ballroom, the bar, the coat room, to the foot of the tall, winding staircase.

"Tom?" His name came out like a croak. Natalie cleared her throat and called again.

"Up here, Nat," Tom shouted. "The place is empty. The housekeepers have the day off."

She didn't feel comforted by that bit of news. This place scared her, it always had. She gripped the railing and started up the stairs, her eyes fixed on a spot at the very top. Maybe it was the dim light, maybe it was just that she always felt as though she wanted to be someplace else when she was here, but suddenly her vision went fuzzy. And in that fuzz, something weird happened to her peripheral vision. She glimpsed movement, colors, shapes. And she also heard music, drifting up the staircase from the first floor.

Still gripping the railing, she glanced back. Women in tight, sequined dresses went up and down the stairs, laughing, their heads thrown back, some of them carrying tall wineglasses. Several women stumbled up the stairs with men who wore stiff, dark clothing. None of them seemed to see her. It was as if she weren't there, as if she were a ghost in their world.

Natalie felt so dizzy she sank to a step and rubbed her hands over her face. Her palms still smelled faintly of salt from the holding tanks. She thought she was going to throw up. Then she heard Tom's voice again and the dizziness and nausea vanished as rapidly as they'd appeared. When she lifted her head from her hands, the women and men were gone. Silence clamped down over the rooms again.

Really spooked now, she tore up the rest of the steps and burst into Tom's room at the end of the hall. She slammed the door behind her and said, "This place scares me, Tom."

"You oughta be here at night."

"No, I mean, I think it's . . ."

"Haunted?" He chuckled. "Yeah, probably." He motioned her over to where he sat. "Pull up a chair, Nat."

Both she and Corie were only children and had turned that intrinsic solitude toward animals. Tom, the only child of indifferent parents, had spent his solitude learning about computers—how they worked, how to build them, what made them tick, and how he could make them tick faster and more efficiently. He had more than a dozen computers now, all of them up and operating at the moment. He owned so much software that it filled two of the walls in his room. The third wall consisted of a bookcase that held videos and books. The fourth wall was all glass, a gigantic window that overlooked the marsh.

"This is the coolest game," he said. "The biggest and most complex maze I've ever been in."

Natalie peered over his shoulder, knew immediately that it went beyond her abilities, and sat down. "I've got enough mazes in my life, Tom. Listen, I need a favor."

He turned his pale blue eyes away from the screen. He had a great face, handsome without vanity, with a pronounced jaw that made him look stubborn even when he wasn't. He wore his dark hair very short, except for a long slender tail in the back. He was three years older than she, already a sophomore at MIT and studying—what else?—computer science. She fully expected that one of these days he would be the next Bill Gates, an "aw, shucks" sort of guy who talked to the masses in a red pullover sweater and jeans.

"What kind of favor?"

"I need to know why Sea World in San Diego is closed and what happened recently at Pearl Harbor."

"Any specifics?"

"Yeah, a site called *Weird Happenings*."

He thought a moment, nodded, then his long, graceful fingers flew over the keyboard. He got up suddenly and moved to another computer, and then another, until five of his twelve computers churned through endless sites in cyberspace.

He finally sat down again in his rocking leather chair and reached for a pack of thin cigars. He tapped one from the box, ran his fingers down it, lit it. "You smoke yet, Nat?"

She wrinkled her nose. "Nope."

"Cigars are okay. All natural stuff. All sorts of indigenous people smoke cigars. So does Arnold Schwartzenegger."

"He's an indigenous person?"

Tom got a big kick out of this and laughed. "In some circles that's what they'd call him. How're the dolphins?"

"Weird shit going on, Tom."

"Yeah, I heard about you and Corie and the canoe. Weird shit going on all over, Nat. Down on some remote beach in Venezuela, eleven dolphins beached themselves. Why? Because their sonar went haywire? Because magnetic north ain't quite where it used to be? And in Norfolk? At the naval base? A bunch of marine mammals wrecked docks and piers and boats, even some subs. Nature's in rebellion, Natalie. That's what's happening."

One of his computers beeped and he got up again and went over to it. "Yes," he said softly, and struck the air with his fist. "Okay, we've got a board here, a message board. Sea World, what really happened at Sea World." Tom scrolled down the screen, scanning the messages. "How about this one, from a guy who claims he's an employee. No name, that's fine, right? He says that a pod of dolphins and orcas about the size of Maine assaulted the holding tanks three days ago. Assaulted, Nat. A strong, active verb, isn't it. And hey, he even mentions the huge pod sighted here on Piper as 'one more anomaly.' "

Anomaly or miracle, Natalie thought, the incident had gotten her grounded. Despite all this, she'd managed to convince her mother that she should be allowed to keep the boat.

"Anomaly of what? Dolphin behavior?"

"Of nature."

She leaned over his shoulder, reading the message, then another computer beeped. Tom hurried over to it, sat down. "Okay, chat room shit from a San Diego contact. Blue."

"Blue? What kinda name is that?"

"It's complicated. His wife left him a couple months ago. He works at the naval base there."

Natalie pulled up a chair and read the e-mail.

Friends and foes: here's the scoop. At approximately 1:01 A.M. PDT, a pod of dolphins and orca whales descended on Sea World at San Diego. The pod destroyed every holding tank with an ocean access. About eighty percent of Sea World's mammals were freed. The theme park is trying to keep the truth under wraps.

At the same time on the east coast, a pod of dolphins and orcas at least as large as the pod in California destroyed docks, piers, at least fifty small vessels, and damaged three subs.

Another computer beeped and Tom moved again, with Natalie right behind him. He glanced at the screen and nodded. "Good, here's the link I was hoping for." A weird image came up on the screen of a hooded figure holding a book in one hand and a lit candle in the other. At the hooded figure's feet were the words *Welcome to Diogenes. Enter password.* "The guy at the other end is wired to a string of underground information centers," Tom explained.

"Who is he?"

"A classmate."

Tom's hands played the keyboard. The screen blanked, then a maze appeared and a message flashed:

Lo, Joe. What's cooking?

Hey, Brain. What's the real scoop on Sea World San Diego and Norfolk?

Just like it says on the Web. But it wasn't confined to those two areas. At Pearl Harbor, eight subs were damaged and at Pensacola, captive dolphins were freed and four subs were damaged. It all happened at 4:01 EDT. In other words, it appears to have been planned.

Anywhere else?

Yeah, the naval base in King's Bay, Georgia got hit, too.

Any takes on what it means, Brain?

No scientific takes yet. But hey, check out Sheldrake. I'll be in touch when there's more. Signing off.

The screen blanked again. "Who's Sheldrake?" Natalie asked.

"A visionary biologist," Tom said, and explained Sheldrake's theory of morphic resonance.

Most of it went over Natalie's head, except for the part about the blue tit birds in England. In 1921, the birds began opening bottles of milk that were delivered to homes early in the morning. Blue tits rarely venture more than fifteen miles from where they live, but the habit somehow spread to Sweden, Denmark, and Holland. "During the war, milk bottles just about disappeared in Holland," Tom said. "But by 1947, the blue tits were at those bottles again. It's unlikely that any of the birds that learned how to do this before the war were still alive after the war, but somehow, the habit survived. Habits acquired by some of the birds facilitated the acquisition of the same habits in other birds, even without any known means of connection or communication."

. . . the thing with the Frisbee . . . every single one of them knew what to do with the Frisbee and always tossed it to their left. . . .

"Let's say I taught a dolphin a new trick, Tom. If this morphic stuff is right, then in weeks or months or years or whatever, other dolphins would know how to do that trick even if they'd never seen it before, right?"

"Exactly. That's an acquired characteristic, something that mainstream science says is impossible."

"It sounds like telepathy."

"It may someday explain telepathy. Let's say that your mother played a really mean game of Ping-Pong, right? But she never had taught you the game, you'd never seen her play, and you'd never even seen a Ping-Pong table. Yet, as soon as you were old enough to hold a paddle, you played the game better than she did. That would be an acquired characteristic. But I don't know if it completely explains a systematic, planned assault by marine mammals on naval bases and theme parks." He frowned and it brought his bushy brows so close together they seemed to form a straight line over his eyes. "Now you want to tell me what's going on, Nat?"

"As soon as *I* know, I'll tell you." She gave him a

quick hug and hurried back down the stairs, through the strange, waiting silence.

This time, she didn't see any women in red sequined dresses; instead, her mind filled with little birds opening milk bottles all over Europe.

Ten

Dear Ms. Thomas,

Thank you for allowing us to see your grant proposal. Your research program concerning dolphins is most intriguing. However, due to budgetary cutbacks, we are unable to approve your grant. We wish you the best of luck in finding funding. . . .

The rest of the letter blurred. Lydia crumpled the piece of paper and hurled it across her office. It hit the far wall, bounced off, and she marched over to it, swept it up, tossed it into the trash. "Fuckers." She pressed the heels of her hands into her eyes, hating the bureaucrats who didn't get it, hating herself for not having stuck money away over the years. Then her arms swung to her sides and she dug the letter out of the trash and smoothed it out on her desk. She stared at it.

No grant.

Okay. This had been her worst-case scenario all along and now it had happened. It meant that in about four weeks, maybe five if she was really tight with money, the center would close. Shut down. It meant foreclosure, the auction block. *Kiss fifteen years good-bye, Lydia.*

She pressed her fist to the tightness just below her

breastbone and told herself she'd been through worse. *Yeah? Like what?* Her divorce? No. The marriage had been worse than the divorce, but even the marriage wasn't as bad as this. Closing the center meant professional failure.

She supposed she could take out cash advances on her credit cards, but they were already strained to the max. She could beg the city council, beg for donations, beg on the goddamn streets, but that wasn't likely to yield much at all. Although the press from the dolphin incident had brought in far more summer tourists than any other summer, the increase in business barely covered fish for a week.

She shoved the letter down into her purse, then buzzed Gail and told her she was sick and was going home for the day: Gail clucked about long hours and too much stress and told her not to worry. *Sure. Don't worry, be happy, have a nice fucking day.*

She drove her golf cart into town and, on the way, called the house and asked Natalie if she would take her out in her boat today. The request, of course, stunned her daughter. "My boat? Uh, yeah. Sure. Okay."

"I mean, if you don't have any other plans."

"No plans, Mom. I'd love to take you out in the boat."

"Great. I'm on my way to the market to pick up stuff for a picnic. I'll be home in about an hour. Should we take bikes or the car?"

There were no chain supermarkets on Piper Key. Despite the influx of snowbirds every winter, the year-round population of twenty-five hundred wouldn't support a major chain. The only market, Vega Foods, was family-owned, but didn't suffer because of it. In here, Lydia always found the most delectable of treasures—soy cheeses laced with hot peppers, mangoes still warm from the trees, papaya from South Florida and the Dominican Republic, and a vast array of vegetarian delights.

Even though Natalie still enjoyed an occasional junk meal from McDonald's, she seemed to be leaning more and more toward a vegetarian diet. Lydia had never pushed it on her, never insisted that she eat every green pea on her plate. She'd trusted that her daughter's passion for animals would bring her around, just as it had brought Lydia herself around when she was in college. If you worked with animals long enough, you invariably reached the point where you had to think about what you ate. That chicken on your plate, roasted to a fine golden brown, had suffered excruciating pain in its short and frantic life: debeaking, living in a cage jammed with dozens of other chickens, no place to scratch or to nest, fattened up with hormones. It was the same sordid story for the cow and the lamb that had provided that six-inch steak, that slice of veal.

In the earlier days of her vegetarianism, she still had eaten seafood, but then she'd become a marine biologist and that had ended. Now her diet consisted mainly of fresh fruits and vegetables, pasta and soy, cereals and breads. Fortunately, vegetarian foods had proliferated in the last ten years and she no longer had to figure out how to put together an interesting dinner.

At Vega Foods, in fact, the vegetarian products filled an entire wall. As she pushed her cart slowly down the aisles, studying new products, reading labels, she managed to forget about the grant rejection. She was so involved in the array of foods, she failed to pay attention to where she was going and suddenly crashed into another cart.

When she looked up, there stood Ian Cameron. "Lydia." He looked as surprised to see her as she was to see him.

"Ian." She didn't see the guy for nine months, then suddenly sees him twice in as many weeks. If she didn't know better, she would think he was following her. "Since when do you shop here?"

"Whenever I get called out to the island, I stop by. This time I got a call about a sighting of a wolf and cub."

"You think it's the same pair Witness wrote about?"

"Christ, I hope so. Otherwise we've got at least four wolves on Piper."

"You saw them?"

"Saw their tracks, up in the preserve."

As they chatted, he turned his cart around so that he was moving in the same direction that she was. She kept glancing at his hands, she had always loved his hands. She stopped that thought before it could progress any farther and, in the first pause, said, "Were you serious about the animal abuse department picking up the bills for Alpha?"

"Absolutely. Why? You change your mind?"

"Yeah. My grant was rejected."

His expression captured everything that she felt just then and he reached out and gave her arm a quick squeeze. "Christ, Lydia. I'm really sorry. Those bozos just don't get it. They never have."

Emotion swelled in her throat; she swallowed it back and shrugged. "One more day of remedial measures."

"Look, send me the vet bills and a bill for whatever

you think her food and other requirements cost you. The department will pay for it. I'll make sure of it."

"Thanks, Ian. I appreciate it. The next time your sister and her kids are in town, they get to swim with the dolphins for free, for as long as they want." They had reached the end of the aisle, both of them had stopped, and she suddenly leaned forward and hugged him. "You bought me a little time."

Lydia stepped back quickly, not wanting him to get the wrong idea. But she knew from the soulful look in his eyes that he already had the wrong idea, that he had missed her these past months. "Fax the stuff to me in the next few days. I'll get a check out to you by the end of the week," Ian said.

"I will." Then she tapped the face of her watch. "I've got to scoot. Nat and I . . ." She started to tell him that Natalie was taking her out in her boat, to the beach, but sensed that he would want to come and would be hurt if she didn't extend an invitation. So she said, ". . . We've got to go to the dentist."

"Fax me the stuff," he called after her, and Lydia waved her hand in the air, acknowledging that she'd heard him.

She felt, just then, like the lowest shit in the universe. *Use him and push him away.* She moved more quickly through the last aisle, as if speed could erase their past.

Digger's Cove reminded Lydia of her own childhood in the Florida Keys, where her mother had taught hormonal seventh graders and her father had taught high school science. Thirty years ago, keys existed in the Florida straits that were like the cove, undiscovered, pristine, utterly devoid of people. Fortunately, the state had become more aware of its resources in those thirty years and, with any luck, Digger's Cove would remain undeveloped, while Key West would march on into Guinness records for T-shirt sales.

She and Natalie swam and snorkeled and played a game of Scrabble while consuming the lunch that Lydia had packed. "How come you took the day off from work?" Natalie asked her as they put away the Scrabble game.

"I felt like it." Lydia rolled onto her stomach, brought her hands up to her face, and rested her cheek against them. "I deserve a day off now and then, you know."

"Yeah, I know." Then, after a brief hesitation, she said, "But what's the *real* reason? I can't even remember the last time you took a day off during the week."

Lydia sat up, knees together, and looked at her daughter. Natalie wore a two-piece bikini that showed her deepening curves. A baseball cap, pulled low over her eyes, shaded her face. Her hair, burned almost white by the sun, grazed her shoulders. She was drawing designs in the sand with her fingertip. And suddenly, Lydia panicked. Her throat closed up, she couldn't speak. *She's a teen. Where the hell have the years gone?*

No mystery to that one, she thought. The years had gone past by while she worked twelve-hour days, seven days a week. And for what? Endless aggravation? Imminent bankruptcy? Lydia said, "I didn't get the grant."

"Oh, Mom." Natalie's face softened and she leaned forward and hugged Lydia. "I'm really sorry."

Emotion swelled in Lydia's throat. She squeezed her eyes shut, tried not to cry, and failed.

"Are you going to close the center?" Natalie asked.

"We've got enough money to see us through this month, as long as we don't have any large unexpected expenses."

"I thought the summer tourists were helping the money situation."

"They help, but it's not enough. I may be able to go through Greenpeace or one of those other organizations, but right now I'm just not sure which way to turn."

"Ian has a lot of connections."

Here it was, Lydia thought. Natalie's reverence for Ian Cameron.

"His department's going to foot some of the bills for Alpha. But I need more than that." A lot more.

"Talk to Gracie."

"Great idea."

"Let's go do it now," Natalie said.

"This second?"

"Yes." Natalie started gathering up her things. "C'mon, let's get going."

What the hell, Lydia thought. They loaded up the canoe and paddled off through the cove again. "Hey, Mom," Natalie said. "You ever heard of a biologist named Sheldrake?"

"Sure. But where'd you hear about him?"

"From Tom Maynard."

The MIT whiz kid. "What'd Tom say about him?"

"That his theory of morphic resonance is brilliant. What do you think?"

"That he's right. The theory explains a lot of things about dolphins that have puzzled me for years."

"Let's say we teach a dolphin to play with a Frisbee," Natalie said. "Would other dolphins know what to do with a Frisbee even if they'd never seen one?"

"Probably. They're naturally playful. That doesn't seem to fit Sheldrake."

"Suppose we taught the dolphin to do something specific with the Frisbee and other dolphins did that behavior when they played with the Frisbee?"

"It would depend on the behavior."

"What if the behavior was tossing the Frisbee in a certain direction?"

"And dolphins you'd never met before tossed the Frisbee in that direction?"

"Yeah."

"I think that would qualify."

Natalie nodded but didn't say anything more.

"Why do you ask, Nat?"

"Just curious."

Ha, she thought. Natalie never asked out of mere curiosity. "C'mon," Lydia said. "Come clean."

"Really. I'm just curious. I was thinking about it the other night, after I saw Tom."

It sounded convincing, but Lydia sensed there was more to it. She didn't press, though. Her daughter never succumbed to pressure or threats and, if she explained at all, would do so in her own time, at her own pace.

As they entered the tunnel of green formed by the braided mangrove branches, a pair of dolphins suddenly appeared, one on either side of the canoe. Their abrupt appearance, without any warning ripples, startled Lydia. "See, Mom? It's a sign that Gracie will have answers for us."

"I don't . . ."

She stopped in midsentence and turned, frowning, to watch the dolphins. The shadows darkened their bodies, that had to be it, she thought. They dived again and she slid to the floor of the canoe, where she could turn more easily without rocking the canoe so much.

"What's wrong, Mom?"

"What kind of dolphins were those?"

"Bottlenoses, probably. I didn't get that good a look."

"No, they weren't bottlenoses."

Then the pair surfaced again and she saw them clearly. Black backs, flukes, snout, flippers, and the undersides of the tail stocks. The flanks were white, except for a black band that ran back from the eyes, widened to meet the black on the backs, then sloped downward again. "Hourglass dolphins," she breathed.

"That's impossible," Natalie said. "They live off the coast of Argentina, right?"

"And in very deep ocean."

Natalie slid to the floor of the canoe with Lydia, pulled her pack toward her, and brought out her flute. "Maybe they'll come closer if they hear music."

She started to play, her paddle forgotten. The music, breathtaking in its beauty and innocence, drifted through the green tunnel. The dolphins answered with their own songs, their own music, a mysterious, joyful resonance. As Lydia listened, she became aware of patterns in the music, as if it were some sort of dolphin code. If she could decipher it, break it down, perhaps she could understand how the hourglass dolphins got here.

Pretty soon, two more hourglass dolphins surfaced and now the four surrounded the canoe, bumped up against it, clicking and whistling almost continuously.

No one will believe this. Four hourglass dolphins here in the gulf, thousands of miles from their native waters around Tierra del Fuego and the South Shetland

Islands. Lydia intended to take advantage of the moment.

While her daughter played her bewitching music, Lydia reached over the side of the canoe and touched her palms to the water. One of the dolphins swam up under her hands, a touch that seemed electric, alien, and yet totally visceral. It scanned her repeatedly, bursts of sonar that she actually felt in her tissues and her bones.

Lydia suddenly felt strange, sort of light-headed, her body rubbery and loose. A wave of nausea clamped down over her and she rocked back on her heels and gripped the edge of the bench to steady herself. The light that spilled through the mangrove branches seemed different, too, hazy, with bits of luminous dust floating in it.

She started to say something to Natalie, but the dolphin in her line of sight suddenly arched gracefully upward, air *whooshing* from its blowhole, then began to fade like an old photograph. For seconds, no more than that, its pale shape seemed to linger in the shadowed air, ghostly and strange. Then it disappeared.

Lydia shot to her feet; the canoe rocked violently. Natalie shouted, "Mom, you're about to tip us over!"

Lydia dropped to her knees, her head whipping this way and that. All four of the hourglass dolphins were gone. She didn't see any dorsals or telltale ripples, nothing to indicate they'd ever been here.

"No way." She leaned over the left side of the canoe, then the right. "That's impossible. Her head snapped up. "Did you see that, Nat? Did you see what happened?"

"My eyes . . . were closed."

Lydia peered behind them, in front of them. Nothing. Not a goddamn thing. "What'd you see, Natalie? Tell

me what you saw before and after you started playing
your flute."

"Before I started playing, I saw two dolphins. They
startled me because they were suddenly just *there*. No
warning at all. That only happens when we're out at
sea, where the water's really deep."

"Exactly." Lydia grabbed her paddle and thrust it
down into the water. "Look, Nat. The water here is
about five feet deep. That's dangerously shallow for
hourglass dolphins. It's so shallow they would swim
very close to the surface. And that means we should
have heard them before we saw them. *But we didn't.*
And then there's the fact that hourglass dolphins inhabit
waters eight or nine thousand miles from here."

Natalie frowned. "So what're you saying, Mom?"

"I'm saying . . ." What the hell *was* she saying? "I
don't know what I'm saying."

Lydia tried to reconstruct what had happened, but
now the whole thing seemed vague and unreal, like a
dream fragment that didn't fit with anything else.

"Something like this happened to me twice. Remember the snakes I'd told you about?"

"It's not likely that I'd forget, honey." Natalie had
told her about the snakes the same day the incident had
happened. She'd alerted the staff to watch out for them.
"What about them?"

"There weren't just two, like I told you. There were
dozens," and she quickly told Lydia what had happened
to her. "That same day, at Tom's house, I was going
up the stairs to his room and suddenly I felt really
dizzy and I had to sit down. When I . . . I opened my
eyes, I saw all these women in red gowns, with sequins
on them, tight gowns, prostitutes. They were laughing
and drinking. . . . Men were with them. I . . . and

then . . . then they all faded away. That's how it was with the dolphins just now, right?"

Yes. No. Maybe. "I'm not sure."

"Did you feel dizzy?" Natalie asked.

"Yes. And nauseated."

"Me, too." Natalie bit at her lower lip. "What's it mean? What's going on?"

"I don't know, sweetheart. But let's get outta here." *And fast.*

Eleven

Ten or fifteen miles outside of Piper Key, deep in the high hills that separated the island from Gainesville, Gail Campbell turned left onto a dirt road. Barbed-wire fences sprang up on either side of her, with NO TRESPASSING signs posted every few hundred feet. Beyond the fences sprawled rural Florida at its worst. Broken-down trailers and wooden hootches were partially visible behind copses of Florida pines and isolated live oaks draped in Spanish moss.

For the hicks and rednecks who inhabited these hills, the ten or twelve miles of countryside along this part of the road, the Civil War had never ended. They hated Yankees, blacks, and everyone else who was different than they were. She felt vulnerable and uneasy just driving through here.

Half a mile in, she hung a right onto another dirt road, lined by more barbed-wire fences. A quarter of a mile later she spotted the listing she'd found in the yellow pages: *Livingston Farm Animals.* The rusted gates stood open, but looked as though they might collapse in the next high wind. Her unease hitched up another notch as she drove through.

Garbage cans spilled over with *stuff,* a rusted Pontiac without wheels or windshield stood next to a metal shed that leaned to the right. Scattered around in no apparent order were numerous cages and small, crowded fenced areas that held chickens, rabbits, cats, goats, geese, ducks, and assorted other wildlife.

She pulled up in front of the trailer, another disaster of neglect, and suddenly a pack of dogs raced out at her, all of them barking and snarling and leaping up around the Cherokee. One of the monsters, which looked as if it probably weighed a hundred and fifty pounds, leaped at her window and snapped at the glass, its huge fangs dripping saliva.

Gail pounded her fist against the horn until the trailer door swung open and a man sauntered out. He looked old, but didn't move as if he were. His beer belly strained at the fabric of his denim coveralls, his bushy, gray beard touched his chest, and gray hair the texture of a Brillo pad sprang out from every side of his head. An aging hippie, she thought, who hadn't moved on when the sixties had died. In the crook of his elbow, he cradled a riding whip.

"Hey, dogs!" he shouted in a thick southern drawl. "You mutts back off now, y'heah?"

The dogs ignored him until he cracked the whip. It caught one of the Dobermans on the back and the animal yelped in pain and ran off, whimpering. Another crack of the whip and the animals parted like the Red Sea. The guy strolled over, cracking the whip near the ground. Gail lowered the window.

"Is it safe now?" she asked.

"Sho' thing, ma'am."

She opened the door, stepped out. "I'd like to purchase a rabbit."

"Ayuh." His eyes slipped over her body, openly lascivious, a look that made her skin crawl. "What kinda rabbits you be lookin' for, ma'am?"

"Whatever you've got, but preferably one on the large side. My niece just loves fat rabbits."

"Uh-huh. No problem." He stabbed a thumb over his shoulder. "Back this a-way."

Gail followed him and a couple of the dogs followed her. They continued to growl, but kept a respectful distance. They passed cage after cage of chickens, twenty or more of them crammed into a space about the size of a carrier for a large dog. The branches overhead got thicker, the stink got worse, a stink she couldn't quite identify, death and decay and something else.

The rabbit cages stood in the shade at the border of the woods behind his trailer, two rows of six cages each. The old man snapped his whip over the top row and the rabbits scurried to other parts of their cages. "Not the brightest critters to ever walk the face of the earth, y'understand, but they make nice pets."

"How much for one?"

"D'pends on the rabbit, ma'am. Just have a look."

"You look and pick out one that's at least ten pounds and no more than twenty bucks."

"They start at forty."

She burst out laughing. "C'mon, I can go to the local pet store in Gainesville and get a rabbit for about fifteen bucks."

"Then reckon that's where you're gonna have to go."

"Fine." Except that she couldn't. She might be remembered at a pet store. "Thanks for your time."

As she started to turn away, the guy said, "Okay, thirty. Ah cain't go no lower than thirty."

She smiled. "You've got a deal. I also need a goat that weighs at least seventy-five pounds."

"Got just the critter. He ain't cheap."

"How much?"

"One-twenty-five."

"Just for the *goat?*"

"Goats give milk."

"I'll give you a hundred for the two of them."

He grinned, exposing teeth that screamed for a dentist, and picked at the space between his front teeth with the long, dirty nail on his pinky finger. "You tryin' to drive me outta business? On the open market, ah can git sixty for the rabbit and two hundred for the goat. Ah cain't go no lower than one-forty for them both."

"One-twenty-five is my best offer. With the rabbit cage tossed in."

He ran his long fingers through his beard, pensive. "Cash?"

"Yes."

"Ah reckon that'll make up the difference. You be wantin' feed?"

"If it's included."

"I'll toss in a one-pound bag."

Ten minutes later, the old man loaded a cage into the back of her Cherokee, then went over to the tree where he'd tied up the goat. "Bubba heah is one fine goat, ma'am. He likes folks, y'know what ah'm sayin'? He'll be sittin' up front with you if you let him."

"I don't think so. Could you put him in the back?"

But when the old man brought the goat around to the back of the Cherokee, tugging on the rope around its neck, it bleated shrilly and dug in its back hooves, refusing to go a step farther. The old man looked around. "Goddamn animals been actin' strange for weeks now. Cain't figure what's got into 'em."

She thought of Alpha, and asked: "Strange how?"

He whipped a checkered bandanna from a pocket in

his coveralls and wiped his face with it. "Ah come out heah one mornin' and sees a fox and one of my rabbits touchin' noses out there near the cages. *Touchin' noses,* huh? Ah mean, the rabbit shoulda been freakin' in that cage and the fox shoulda been tryin' to get into the cage. Nope. They's touchin' noses.

"Then, couple two, three weeks back, ah git home one afternoon and find, Jesus, ah don't know, maybe six or eight hundred birds in the middle of mah clearin' here. They cover my trailer. They cover the ground. They're sittin' in the trees, on the power lines. It was like somethin' outta that Hitchcock flick, know what ah mean?"

She'd never seen the movie. She avoided animal movies. Too much anthropomorphism, too much bullshit. "So what'd you do?"

"Stopped mah truck at the gate, got out nice and slow like, and suddenly ran into the clearing screamin' and wavin' mah arms. They flew away, all them beatin' feet at once. Never done seen nothin' like it." He tugged on the goat's rope again and this time succeeded in getting the animal right up next to the back of the Cherokee. "Reckon ah'll jus' lift you in now, baby."

But when he reached out to slide his arms under the goat's belly, the goat reached back, grabbed hold of his beard, and began to eat it. The man screamed and tried to pull away; the goat kept munching. Gail didn't know whether to laugh or take off, and before she really had any time to think about it, the old guy fell back, hit the truck, and sat there, groaning and touching his ragged, torn beard.

"Forget the goat," she said.

"The goat's goin'," he snapped, and sprang to his feet. The goat had taken off, dragging the long rope that encircled its neck. The man, really pissed now, sprinted after it, his long, skinny arms pumping at his sides, and stomped on the end of the rope, nearly decapitating the goat. It bleated and struggled to escape, but the man hurried toward it, wrapping the rope around his hand, and then he kicked it hard in the side. The goat went down, bleating softly, and Gail, disgusted by the whole thing, headed back to her car.

"Hey," he called, and loped after her, with the goat now in his arms. "Y'bought Bubba, he's yours, lady."

Christ. "Put it in the back."

He hoisted the animal into the Cherokee, slammed the lid, held out his sweaty palm. "One and a quarter, cash."

Gail, anxious to get away from him and his little spread of horrors, dropped a wad of bills in his hand and got out of there. All the way up the dirt road, the goat bleated and tried to climb over the backseat, the rabbit scratched madly at its cage, and the car slammed into every pothole. Her head ached, she thought she might scream.

Fuck Dylan and his schemes.

She'd put this off for nearly two weeks now and would be smart to put it off forever. But she knew that she wouldn't. She had to know.

She hit the main road and drove another two or three miles along it until she turned right, onto another dirt road, into another pine and live oak thicket, into the sticks again. Isolated, she thought. Exactly what she wanted. She stopped and the goat instantly stopped bleating. Even the rabbit paused in its relentless clawing at the wire cage.

Gail reached over to the floor in front of the passenger seat and picked up the small cooler that Dylan

had left her. One syringe, she thought. She had to know
if Dylan had told her the truth. She slung the cooler
over her shoulder, got out, and went around to the back
of the Cherokee.

"Okay, Bubba." She raised the lid. "We're going for
a walk."

The goat peered at her intensely for a moment,
bleated once, and tried to scramble over the backseat.
Gail picked Bubba up. "I liked the way you tried to
eat the SOB's beard, but don't even think about trying
it with me, got that?"

She set the animal down about thirty yards from the
car and tied the rope to a branch. Bubba immediately
starting munching on the leaves of the nearest tree and
ignored her completely. Gail crouched, set the cooler
on the ground, and unzipped it. She brought out one
of the syringes, attached a needle, and touched the
plunger enough to send out a little stream of antifreeze,
just like they did in those grade-B horror films she
used to watch as a kid. She walked over to Bubba.

She lacked experience with goats. Hell, she was a
marine biologist. But even a goat undoubtedly had a
carotid artery or something similar. So she stroked
Bubba's head and talked softly to him, just as she always had done with Alpha. Dylan had commented once
about how much he liked her voice when she talked to
animals. Low and seductive, that was how he'd put it.
Frankly, she'd never heard it and she sure as hell didn't
hear it now. Bubba didn't seem to hear anything at all.
He just kept munching those leaves, chowing down like
some sucker on death row consuming his last meal.

She slipped her arm around his neck, tight but not
tightly enough so that he would wrench away from her,
and slid the needle into his neck. It must've stung be-

cause he jerked back hard, kicking and bucking. The needle snapped off in his neck and she lost her hold on him and fell back on her ass, clutching the syringe. He bleated and kept bucking and she scrambled back to avoid his hooves.

Within seconds, the goat went into convulsions. Blood poured from its mouth and eyes. *Stuff* foamed from its nostrils and ears. The air that she breathed turned foul with the stink of death and she started to gag. Gail stumbled to her feet and lurched back, back, back, one hand clamped to her mouth, the other still clutching the spent syringe.

She backed into the front fender of the Cherokee and felt her feet take root in the soil. She squeezed her eyes shut, but it didn't help. In her head, she saw the goat convulsing, bleeding, dying. She smelled its death, heard its death, tasted it in the air that she breathed.

And when she couldn't stand hearing it anymore, she pressed her hands over her ears and breathed into the sleeve of her blouse. She stumbled away from the fender, groping blindly for the door handle. She threw herself into the car and pressed her forehead to the steering wheel, damning Dylan and his bullshit and his lies. That wasn't antifreeze. It was something much worse, something concocted in a navy lab somewhere by a bureaucratic researcher who had documented the end result on rats or white mice, not on a goat and definitely not on a dolphin.

And why does all of this seem like a replay? A memory?

An hour and a half later, the goat's convulsions stopped.

Gail peered at the corpse through the windshield. The heat had climbed into the nineties, the inside of the Cherokee steamed like the air in the Amazon jungle. She lowered the window and the influx of fresh air left her slightly dizzy. She threw open the door, swung her legs out, and filled her lungs with the scent of salt and sunlight and deep summer.

Now march your ass over there. You need to get rid of the carcass.

Gloves, she needed gloves. She couldn't touch the goddamn thing with her bare hands. But she hadn't brought gloves. She rifled through the drawer under the driver's seat, looking for something—anything—she could use. The only things she found were small plastic bags, grocery store bags. She could use the bags to fashion gloves, but then what? If she tossed the goat in the woods, whatever had killed it might contaminate the water and kill off everything within a mile. She couldn't leave it here because eventually it would draw vultures and someone would investigate. It wouldn't be difficult to trace the goat to the weirdo with the beard and he would lead to her.

The tarp, she thought. She had an old plastic tarp under the backseat. She would wrap the goat in the tarp and deposit it in a Dumpster in one of the rural outposts between here and Gainesville. People out here in the sticks rarely questioned the weird shit found in Dumpsters.

She opened the back door and saw the rabbit cage. She'd forgotten all about the rabbit. It huddled in a corner of its cage, watching her warily, its little pink nose working frantically at the air. As she reached past its cage to pull the tarp out from under the backseat, it made a strange, oddly human sound, a sound she knew meant fear, and scampered to the far end of its cage.

It knows. It knows just like Alpha knows.

Ridiculous. It didn't *know* squat. It had been terrified since the second she'd laid eyes on it and who could blame it, living with that nutcase back at Livingston Farms? "Look, if it's any consolation, you've won a reprieve, okay?" she said to it.

The rabbit just stared at her.

"I'll take you back to the farm."

It began to gnaw wildly at its cage.

"Shit, I can't take you back there."

It stopped gnawing and looked at her again.

It understands.

"Fuck that," she muttered, and reached past the cage and pulled the tarp out from under the seat.

She sat in the doorway, on the floor, and tied double plastic bags around her hands. She flexed her fingers, then picked up the tarp and carried it over to where the goat lay. She shook the tarp loose and spread it open on the ground about a foot away. She would roll the goat onto the tarp, she thought, bring the four corners together, and drag the bundle over to the car. Simple. Any idiot could do it.

The goat lay on its side, its back to her. As she neared it, she saw the blood that had seeped into the ground around it. Copious amounts of blood. She walked around to the front of it and a violent surge of bile flooded her throat. *It bled out. Pools of blood where the eyes were, blood covering its nostrils, its mouth.* She gagged and spun around, but her knees buckled and she went down on all fours, her stomach heaving.

Jesus God, Dylan, what the hell was this stuff?

Gail didn't know how long she remained on her hands and knees, puking, the humidity eating away at

her. Hours, it felt like hours. When she finally rocked
onto her heels, she knew that if she didn't act quickly,
she would flee. She would just run for her car and get
the fuck out of here. So she stood and hurried past the
goat without looking at it, and grabbed the edge of the
tarp. She tossed it over the animal's body, then tucked
the edges in and rolled the goat into the tarp.

Blood poured from a crease in the tarp and it looked
menstrual dark, almost black. *A soup of blood in its
belly.* Gail dragged the goat over to her car, trying not
to see the trail of blood in the dirt, trying not to breathe
too deeply, to imagine too much.

Before she hoisted the body into her car, she tilted
the tarp to the side, hoping the excess blood would run
off, then tied the ends securely. She lifted it, seventy-
five pounds of dead goat, and pushed it back toward
the rabbit cage. The rabbit made that sound again, that
noise of terror, that terrible, human sound that sundered
the most intimate part of her. That sound which said,
I know what you've done, killer.

Gail slammed the door, wiped her arm across her
forehead, and scrambled into the Cherokee. She sped
north on the miserable two-lane road, the cold air from
the AC vent blasting into her face. Her mouth tasted
sour, her head ached. Her rage at Dylan increased in
direct proportion to these physical factors. It was like
a mathematical equation, this rage, or like a scientific
axiom, an immutable truth.

All her life, she'd been there for Dylan. Even when
she was at Berkeley, married to the perennial rebellious
asshole, her relationship with Dylan had taken prece-
dence. But it had been unilateral. Dylan gave only
when he needed something in return. He always had
an ulterior motive, some higher, hidden scheme.

Never again, Dylan. You do your shit work yourself from here on in.

No more charm, no more heavy confessional stories, no more no more no more. She didn't give a shit if the navy sank, if Dylan got fired, if the military collapsed over her inability to do what Dylan believed was required. Let him do it.

Thirteen miles outside of Gainesville, in a park where the rivers teemed with water moccasins and gators, she dropped the tarp in a Dumpster. The metal clattered as the animal struck the bottom. Gail tore the plastic bags off her wrists and dropped them into the Dumpster as well. Then she fled, fled with the rabbit scrambling madly in its cage, and the stink of the dead goat—*it bled out*—clinging to her.

Twelve

(1)

Thorn hosed off the concrete slab outside his camper and wondered what he would do today. Another bike ride around the island? Another visit to the dolphin center? Stock up on more food? He'd become quite adept at killing time.

In the ten days since he'd pulled into the Finch Campground on Piper Key, he'd kept such a low profile that sometimes he felt he didn't exist at all. He was the only camper here, with a choice spot that backed up to the island's wooded preserve. His human contact had been minimal—gas station attendants, clerks, and the woman who owned the campground.

Fortunately, she didn't ask questions. He'd paid for his site in cash, a month in advance. She'd given him a map of the island and some tips on local restaurants, shops, and tourist hot spots. She'd commented that Washington state was one of her favorite places in the world and it had taken Thorn a few moments to remember that he had Washington plates on his car and camper now. He'd stolen them to replace Kansas plates, which he'd stolen to replace California plates, which he'd stolen . . . Hell, he couldn't even remember now.

In all, since the night he'd fled Blue Mountain Lake, he'd had ten or eleven sets of license plates.

And because he didn't want to seem so mysterious that he aroused the Finch woman's suspicion, he told her that his wife had died and he'd taken a sabbatical. The wife part had just spilled out, a blatant attempt on his part for sympathy. It had worked, she hadn't asked him any questions since, but he felt lousy about it. Lousy and superstitious.

Ellen wasn't dead. She was merely *absent*. That was how he'd come to think of it, how he *had* to think of it. Otherwise, he would lose his mind. He would become a permanent version of the man who often haunted him in the middle of the night, the guy who woke short of breath and panicked from dreams of his lover fading, then vanishing.

Even more to the point, Ellen wasn't his *wife*. For seven years, he had felt as though they were married and had convinced himself that the legal tie was superfluous. But in the end, the reason they weren't married—Ellen's old man—had made the critical difference for Thorn, forcing him to flee.

What the hell had she been thinking all these years? That she would wait until her old man died and then get married? Despite his best efforts, his anger toward her had rooted so deeply that when he lay awake at night, it was all he could think about.

Sometimes he would follow a trail of *what-ifs* to their probable conclusions. What if, for instance, they'd gotten married seven years ago? Would her old man and the whole meddling family have dropped out of their lives? Or what if they'd had kids? Would they have married then? And if they married, would her father have come around, hungry to see his grandchildren? Would he still be trying to run their lives?

All possible universes exist, wrote the chairman of Global Watch on that website Thorn had found. If the Many World theory of quantum physics was true, then there was a universe where Ellen *hadn't vanished,* right? A universe where their lives had gone on as before. And there was also a universe where they had gotten married and another universe where they'd had children and a universe where they hadn't met at all.

Perhaps junctures are created between these universes, through forces we don't yet understand, that allow movement from one universe to another. At the juncture point, these two universes don't simply merge. Reality itself is changed in the most fundamental ways. Thorn had committed these words from the website to memory and during the dark, sleepless nights here in this new world, he murmured them aloud, like a prayer, hoping to find an answer or at least a hint about how to find Ellen. By the time the first soft light appeared in the camper's window, his anger at her usually had returned full force and driven him out of bed and into some type of physical exercise. A brisk walk through the woods. A run down the dirt road.

Last night had been that kind of night and at five this morning, he and Bacall had run into town for a newspaper.

Thorn finished hosing off the slab, stuck his index and pinky fingers in his mouth, and whistled shrilly for Bacall. She usually wandered off into the woods to explore, but this time she trotted around the front of the camper and flopped down at his feet, begging for a belly scratch. He accommodated her, then rewound the hose and brought his laptop and cell phone outside to work for a while.

He'd rented the cell phone in town, without a credit card, by paying for everything in cash. When he'd given his address as the Finch campground, the cell phone guy hadn't even asked for a deposit on the phone. Apparently the Finch name carried weight on the island.

Thorn connected the cell phone to the laptop and went online to check his e-mail and his usual websites. He knew that maintaining his old e-mail address and server was a risk. But Joe Nelson wasn't cyberspace literate and Ellen had never communicated with her father by e-mail, so the chances were quite good that neither of them even knew he was online. If they ran a check on his credit card usage, they wouldn't find a charge for an online service because the charge went on Ellen's Visa. Eventually, of course, when the credit card bill wasn't paid, the service would be disconnected. Until then, however, he was online.

His mailbox was empty. The guy from Global Watch had never responded to his e-mail and Thorn couldn't risk writing him again. So he surfed his usual spots, seeking a clue to whatever course he should pursue next. He had no idea what this clue might be—another report about erratic wildlife behavior or just a hunch that he should move in a particular direction. He was open to anything.

Bacall, lying next to him on the slab, suddenly started barking and ran out into the road. Thorn whistled and called her back, but she plopped down in the middle of the road and refused to get up. The last thing he needed right now was to get kicked out of the campground because his dog was a pest. He disconnected the laptop from the cell phone, left everything on the chair he used as a table, and walked out to the road to get her.

Just then, a golf cart came up the road with a woman and girl inside. Bacall remained just where she was, sprawled in the middle of the road, blocking the cart's passage. The cart stopped and the attractive blonde behind the wheel said, "Is the dog okay?"

"She's just being stubborn. Sorry about this. I'll have her out of the way in a second."

"No problem," the woman replied, tipping her sunglasses back onto the top of her head. She had beautiful eyes, Thorn noticed, a liquid blue fringed in thick lashes.

"She's a golden," the girl exclaimed, and hopped out of the cart. "Can I pet her?"

"Sure."

As soon as the girl approached Bacall, the dog scrambled to her feet and greeted her like a long-lost friend, licking her face and hands, tail whipping from side to side. The woman laughed and shook her head. "That's my daughter, Natalie. I'm Lydia Thomas."

The woman who owns the dolphin center. The timing, the odds that she would happen along just now, when he'd been hoping for a lead, went beyond coincidence, Thorn thought. He grasped her outstretched hand, immediately noting the softness of her palm. "Max Howard," he said. "And that's Bacall." He held her hand a fraction too long and knew that she noticed it.

"As in Bogie and Bacall?" Lydia asked.

He nodded. "Ever since she was a pup, she's had a distinct preference for old movies."

Natalie ran over to the cart, with Bacall trotting alongside her. "Can I play with her while you're talking to Gracie, Mom?"

"If it's okay with Mr. Howard."

Natalie looked at him with those wide blue eyes just like her mother's and he laughed and nodded. "Sure, it's fine with me. I'll get you her Frisbee." With that, Bacall jumped into the backseat of the golf cart and made herself right at home. "She's adopted you. Be right back."

In extreme times, he thought, everything held special significance. Bacall's odd behavior hinted that she'd known what he had not, that the golf cart coming up the road held the very people who might shed light on the enigma of Ellen's disappearance. And the girl, he guessed, was one of the two who had been in the canoe that the thousand dolphins had surrounded. Now it was up to him to take advantage of it.

He returned to the cart and handed the Frisbee to Natalie. "Could you try to stay in Gracie's front yard? I'd like to keep Bacall out of the woods."

"Natalie isn't allowed into the woods by herself," Lydia said.

"She forgets that I'm fifteen," Natalie replied with a roll of her eyes. Then she flung the Frisbee up the road and Bacall leaped out of the cart and took off after it. Natalie raced along behind her.

"She's been bugging me for months about getting a dog," Lydia confided.

"She's welcome to play with Bacall any time. Goldens are great with kids."

"How do you think Bacall would be with dolphins?"

She inadvertently had given him the opening he needed. "Probably great. I've seen her take care of wounded raccoons, birds, cats, ferrets, horses . . ."

Lydia laughed. "You work for a zoo or something?"

Here comes the lie. "Nothing that exotic. I teach veterinary medicine in Washington state. I'm on sabbatical."

Her eyes lit up. "You're a vet? Fantastic. Then what I'm about to say might not sound as strange to you as it would to someone else. I've got one dolphin in rehab who might benefit from pet therapy, particularly with a dog like Bacall. Would you be willing to give it a try?"

"Love to. Dolphins are part of why I'm here."

"Great. We could do an exchange. You lend us Bacall in return for a swim with dolphins."

"Just say when."

"How about in the next few days, sometime after five?"

"Great."

"It's been a pleasure, Dr. Howard."

"Max."

She smiled. "See you then." She started the cart and it whispered on up the road.

(2)

"Hey," Gracie called, stepping out onto the porch. "Don't I even get a hug hello? And where's your mom?"

"She's talking to Mr. Howard." Natalie sprinted over to Gracie, Bacall at her heels, and hugged her hello. As she did so, she saw a grid of pulsating lines in her head, a different sort of *route,* one she'd never encountered before. She didn't know what it meant or how to interpret it. She stepped back from Gracie. "Is this a cool dog or what?"

"Very cool," Gracie agreed.

Magoo, the skunk, poked his little face out the door and sniffed the air. Then he waddled out and Bacall whined softly and flattened out against the porch floor, allowing Magoo to sniff his way around her. "She's like that with the cat, too," Gracie said. "Pretty amazing."

Gracie, now in her late forties, was older than her mother by seven or eight years, but she looked like some slender teenager growing up in cutoff jeans, cotton shirts, and bare feet. Even her thick, short hair, the color of cedar, looked *young*. "How'd you get your mom to take a day off from work?" Gracie asked.

"I think that's what she wants to talk to you about." Gracie nodded knowingly. "Here she comes."

Natalie left them to themselves and she and Bacall took off across the yard. Gracie had fifteen acres here, all that remained of the two hundred her family had bought in the 1800s. The property sprawled across the edge of the preserve in the horse's ears, a mysterious paradise of wildlife wonders.

She'd converted part of it into a campground with twenty gorgeous sites shrouded in trees. During the tourist season, every site was booked a year in advance by her repeat customers, snowbirds from Cincinnati and Pittsburgh, Syracuse and Flint, who pitched their tents and parked their campers and RVs for the winter. Howard was lucky he came during the summer, when the sites usually lay empty.

Natalie loved these woods, the quiet shadowed mystery of the place, the abundant wildlife, the sweet smell of the air. During second grade, when things at the center had hit a rut and her mother was working fourteen-hour days, Gracie used to pick her up some afternoons from school and bring her back here. They always had done fun things—hiked into the woods to collect herbs for Gracie's greenhouse, looked for new bird's nests, photographed wildlife.

When they'd hiked, Gracie had told her stories about when she'd been an emergency room doctor in Gainesville. She'd left that life eight years ago to open the campground. She now worked part time at the clinic in town just to keep her license active and sold her herbs on the side. She rarely spoke about her children, a boy and a girl, now grown and living on the other side of the country. She remained on good terms with her ex-husband, though, which was more than Natalie could say about her own parents. It depressed her to think about her father, silent all these years. But, as Gracie had said to her many times, if he couldn't even call once a year to say happy birthday, then why waste time thinking about the bastard?

When she was grown, she would have lots of land and animals would fill it. Wild animals, domestic animals, injured animals, she would welcome everything. Her land would be an ark. It would be *famous*. And if she couldn't have land, if in her future land simply wasn't an option, then she would have a slice of beach on the ocean and marine mammals would be her life. But unlike her mother, she would make sure that her home life was equally good. She would marry someone like Tom Maynard, some really smart and sexy guy who valued her as much as she valued him.

Natalie hurled the Frisbee and it sailed into the trees. Bacall raced after it, barking, and plunged into the woods. "Hey, not in there," she shouted, and ran after the dog, crashing into the woods.

Shadows shifted across the ground, the woods grew thicker, the trees more tightly packed together. She whistled and called the dog. Her voice echoed and the echo seemed to just go on and on, farther and farther out into the woods. She finally stopped, turned slowly, and glanced around. Which way was the house? What direction had she come from? She didn't know. She kept turning until she'd made a full circle, then turned halfway around and started walking.

It has to be this way.

But she couldn't be absolutely sure. She shouted for the dog again and this time she heard the *wrongness* in the echo, the unnatural way that it stretched, like a piece of fabric that might tear in the middle at any second. It scared her. The air now seemed to shimmer, too, which reminded her of the night at Tom's, there on the stairs, when she'd seen the prostitutes. Had the air shimmered when she'd seen the snakes? She couldn't remember. She stopped, shut her eyes, and willed a *route* to come to mind. But nothing happened.

Scared now, Natalie broke into a run. The shimmering air moved as she moved, as though it were breathing. A light mist swirled across the ground. The trees, ground, plants, even the glimmer of blue sky through the branches looked different, the colors richer, deeper. The shape of things stretched like elastic, trees and leaves, stones and stumps, until everything she saw resembled something else. Faster and faster she went, arms hugging her sides, hands hardened into fists.

And suddenly she tripped and stumbled forward, arms thrust out to break her fall, and her hands came up against the breathing air, the *wall* of weirdness. She *felt* it against her skin, a substance with the texture of Jell-O and the spring of a trampoline. Her hands and then her head went through it, into a space between words, between thoughts, between heartbeats, into a twilight place with smooth, dark walls. Terrible, high-pitched sounds echoed through the twilight, animal sounds, animals in excruciating pain. And suddenly she saw them, the animals, several of them, their heads protruding from rock or tar or some other dark substance that held the rest of their bodies trapped.

Natalie screamed, wrenched back, and ran. Everything blurred, the wind bit her eyes, her screams crashed along behind her. Then she slammed into something and everything went black.

She's sinking, sinking down through the turquoise waters, her eyes wide open. Little bubbles rise around her, hissing, whispering, rising upward toward the light. The water stings her eyes, but she's afraid to close them, afraid that she won't ever open them again.

Her lungs are beginning to hurt. She understands that she's supposed to do something, but doesn't know what to do. She keeps sinking. And suddenly, a dolphin appears. It swims alongside Natalie and pokes its beak into Natalie's side and starts pushing her upward, up through the sunstruck water, up toward the light, air, her mother.

Before they break the surface, Natalie hears the dolphin's music, the orchestra of its long, rich history, a dizzying spiral toward the last point in time. The notes become consonants and vowels. The letters become words and the message is simple. It is her curse and her gift to see what others cannot. Now she must use it to make a difference.

(3)

They sat in Gracie's spacious, sunlit kitchen, snacking on homemade cookies as Lydia recounted the center's financial woes. Over the years, this scene had been repeated many times, the two of them commiserating like sisters over men, money, and the general mayhem of life.

They'd known each other since the day Natalie had fallen into the holding tank. Even though Natalie had been conscious when the dolphin brought her to the surface, Lydia had rushed her to the emergency room in Gainesville, where Gracie had been the attending physician. They'd seen each other through their respective divorces, affairs, and the ups and downs in their professions. As usual, Gracie listened to her without interrupting, then reached for a pen and a napkin.

"What's the center worth, Lydia? With buildings and all."

"With the improvements we've done, the holding tanks . . . I don't know."

"How much did you pay for the center fifteen years ago?"

"Three hundred and fifty. Cash."

Gracie jotted that figure on the napkin. "Since then you've added the holding tanks, refurbished the building, and improved the property. If you were going to sell the place, what would you ask?"

"Eight hundred. But I'd take seven."

"Do you owe anything on the property?"

"Yeah, I owe about seventy-five grand on a loan I took out against the property four years ago."

"So it's essentially a first mortgage."

"Yes."

"Anything else?"

"I owe nearly as much on credit cards."

Gracie slapped down the pen and grinned. "We'll call it one-fifty. Christ, this will be a cinch. I'm going to call Jim Farris, who's head of Piper Key Union Bank. He'll give you a line of credit against the value of the property, Lydia."

about the approaching millennium. I'm no exception. But because I believe that wildlife senses change and transition before we humans do, I can't help wondering what the message is.

The wolf, the dolphins, the fire ants. In each instance, these creatures acted atypically. I recognize a pattern here, but I don't know how to decipher it, to break it down into its simplest components. I don't know what it means. Until I do, I'll be alert and wary and, yes, I don't mind saying it, I'll be afraid.

Last Witness
Visit our website at:
www.piperkeygazette.com

Thirteen

(1)

Blue Mountain Lake
Upstate New York

Joe Nelson walked restlessly through the same rooms that he'd walked dozens of times already, the video-camera panning from one wall to the next. He didn't notice anything new.

He made his way through the waiting room of Thorn's veterinary office, past the area where that bastard had tied his wrists and ankles together. As soon as he thought of that night, his nose began to ache. It was still twice its normal size and felt as if it were stuffed with cayenne peppers. His doctor had told him he was fortunate he had only hairline fractures in the bridge of his nose, but the bottom line was that it hurt like hell and wasn't likely to improve by tomorrow.

When he reached the lab, he turned off the camera and slung the strap over his shoulder. He turned slowly in place, his eyes sliding over everything in sight. The computer with no hard drive. The open door to the storage area. The answering machine with the old messages that he'd listened to a hundred times. The nearly empty crawl space above the storage closet.

Somewhere here lay a clue about where Thorn had fled.

"Find anything?" asked William Bradshaw, coming up behind him.

"Nope." Nelson turned and faced Ellen's old man. He didn't look old; at sixty-eight, he looked younger than Nelson felt. Tall, gray-haired, with a thick white mustache. An athletic body. Dressed casually but impeccably, he wore khaki chinos that probably had cost what Nelson made in a week, a crisp sports shirt and deck shoes. "I found a photo album with a recent picture." He flipped open the album and handed Nelson a five-by-seven-inch black-and-white photo.

"Perfect. I'll scan it onto our website and get it over to the feds today."

"I've already contacted my sources in the media," Bradshaw said. "By tomorrow morning, his photo will be in every major newspaper in the country and on every search engine on the Web."

Nelson frowned and glanced up from the photo. "The feds have a tough time pulling that off with the top ten most wanted. How'd you manage that?"

Bradshaw's smile seemed oddly chilling to Nelson, hinting at secret deals in darkened rooms. "I'm offering a reward of half a million dollars for information that leads to Thorn's apprehension." In a softer voice, he added, "And another half a million goes to the cop who makes the arrest, Lieutenant. That won't be public knowledge, of course, but I just wanted you to know."

Nelson's ears rang. Half a million would put his kids through college, buy his family a larger home, a new car, a real vacation . . . Hell, half a mil would buy them all a whole new life. "I . . . we . . . I mean, our department has a policy that . . ."

"This has nothing to do with the department, Lieutenant." Bradshaw made an impatient gesture with his hand. "This has to do with *justice*. That bastard *killed* her . . . buried her body somewhere . . . and then . . . then took off."

His voice broke then and he looked quickly down at the floor, his hands clutching the photo album so hard his knuckles turned white. For moments, everything in the room went still, silent, so silent that Nelson could hear Bradshaw's labored breathing, the ticking of the clock on the wall, and squirrels scampering across the roof. When Bradshaw finally raised his eyes again, Nelson couldn't read their expression—grief, fury, maybe some strange combination of the two, Nelson couldn't be sure.

"Find Thorn," Bradshaw said softly.

Nelson swallowed hard. "As I was walking through the rooms with the camera, it occurred to me that to find him, we have to think like he does." He knew he was on to something, but couldn't pull it closer so he could examine it. He started pacing the room, thinking out loud. "He mentioned birds. He was carrying dead birds when we found him. He said she faded right in front of his eyes. He said . . ."

"Lies," Bradshaw spat.

Lies, yes. But in his head, Nelson saw Thorn during those last few minutes that night, Thorn raving about what had happened to Ellen, about the cold spot down near the paddock—and it was cold, just as he'd said, Nelson had checked—and Nelson suddenly realized what had eluded him ever since. *Thorn believed the lies and acted according to that belief.*

"That's it!" he whispered.

"What?" Bradshaw asked impatiently.

Excitement coursed through Nelson. "I need to check a few things, Mr. Bradshaw. I don't have any jurisdiction outside the county—or the state, for that matter—but I can work with local law enforcement officials to bring him in. You need any more help around here?"

Bradshaw shook his head. "My driver's coming up this afternoon to pack up the rest of her things. You go on. You have my phone numbers if you need anything."

"I'll be in touch." Nelson hurried toward the door with the black-and-white photo, his mind buzzing along five minutes in front of him. The FBI would be his first stop. Then he would surf the Web and check out-of-state newspapers for any sort of animal weirdness. *Birds, Joe, a thousand birds* . . . Thorn would head where the weird shit was happening. For the first time since the night Thorn had split, his nose didn't hurt.

"Lieutenant?" Bradshaw called after him.

He stopped, turned. "Yeah?"

"It's about justice, son. Remember that."

Nelson grinned and rushed on to embrace the half million bucks that would be his.

(2)

On the morning of July 16, three weeks after Thorn had fled Blue Mountain Lake, he found his own photograph on page two of the *New York Times* online. Time screeched to a grinding halt and he simply stared at this old version of himself, Max Thorn, DVM, a regular Mr. Clean with his dark hair and Pepsodent smile.

Is that really me?

He felt only a vague connection with the man in the photo, as though he were someone Thorn had known long ago, an old high school classmate, or someone from vet school. And yet, he knew exactly where and when the photograph had been taken—last winter, outside his office. Ellen had been fiddling with the camera he'd bought for her birthday and had called his name just as he'd stepped out the door with a dirty kitty litter box.

Say sex, Max, she'd called.

This photograph had been in a photo album in the bedroom. He didn't have to be a rocket scientist to figure out how it had gotten into the *Times.* He quickly scanned the article, a short piece with few facts and only one statement that mattered: *A reward of $500,000 is offered to anyone with information that leads to the arrest of Maxwell Thorn. Contact . . .*

Half a million bucks. Sweet Christ. He shot to his feet and hurried over to the mirror that hung on the back of the door. He leaned close to the glass, scrutinizing himself. His hair was no longer dark—or gray, as it had been when Nelson had last seen him. He now had dark blond hair that he wore in a ponytail, a pierced ear, glasses, and a beard. He was also about twenty-five pounds thinner than he'd been when the photo was taken. He bore only a faint resemblance to the man in the photo.

But is it enough of a difference? Would anyone here on the island recognize him? Even more to the point, had the photo made it into a newspaper that people around here read? *What's the closest major newspaper?* Tampa, he thought. Tampa, Jacksonville, and then Miami. Those were the big three in the state and he felt certain that his picture would be in all of them and maybe even in some of the smaller dailies as well.

The dog. Was there any mention of a dog?

He flew over to the table again and read the article more slowly. Nothing about a dog. Good. Perfect. He at least had that in his favor. Nothing about a dog.

He searched the Web and came up with over a thousand references to Max Thorn. Of the first ten that he checked, only two involved him. The rest were simply people who had the same name he did. But still, twenty percent, for Christ's sake. Too high.

And what're you going to do about it, Max?

Lie low, watch his ass, and say as little as possible. That was all he could do.

He went off-line, shut the laptop's lid, and sat there staring at Bacall, sacked out on the floor several feet away. And then it began, that same shuddering dread that he'd experienced the night he'd split, that hollow, sick feeling in the pit of his stomach, that sense of the irrevocable, the irretrievable.

Thorn felt an overpowering urge to get out now, while he still could. He actually got up and went into his sleeping area to pack, then stopped and sat down hard on the edge of the bunk. No, he couldn't run. Not from here. Not now. Not yet. Not until he'd learned everything he could from the woman who owned the dolphin center and her daughter.

Even though he had no logical reason to believe they were key to what had happened to Ellen, he didn't care. He'd left logic down near the paddock behind the house upstate, the moment that the woman he loved had started to fade. If he ran now, he would never stop running.

Fuck the price on his head. He wouldn't leave here

until he understood the link between the dolphins and all those birds. He wouldn't leave until he'd vindicated himself.

Fourteen

(1)

Gail flipped open the lid of the rabbit's cage and reached inside to fill the bowl with fresh vegetables. The rabbit scurried to the back of the cage and cowered there, eyeing her warily and breathing hard. She'd had the damn thing in her carport for days and it was still scared shitless of her.

"Hey, the crisis has passed, okay? You got a reprieve."

At the sound of her voice, the rabbit tried to dig its way under the piece of fabric she'd put in the cage for it to sleep on. She thought about touching it, but figured it would die of cardiac arrest if she even tried. She brought out the bowl and dropped in chopped carrots, celery, apple, and bits of lettuce. She also put in some of the little pellets that passed for its usual food, the equivalent of army rations. She refilled the water bottle and changed the tray where the rabbit shit went.

Years ago when her family and Dylan's had lived in the Canary Islands, they'd caught a wild rabbit and kept it as a pet. She'd detested the thing, but Dylan had been so crazy about this silly rabbit that she pretended to love it, too. He'd cared for it most of the time and had actually tamed it. He'd walked it on a leash, trained it to use a cat litter box, and although he'd never admitted it, it also slept with him at night. She knew because once she'd sneaked into his room after their parents had gone to bed and she'd found rabbit hairs on his pillow.

It died about a year after they'd caught it and Dylan had called her to tell her about it. She'd rushed over to his house and found him weeping in the backyard as he buried it. Weeping, for Christ's sake. Over a silly rabbit. The whole thing had offended and angered her because she realized that Dylan had loved the rabbit more than he loved her.

Was there someone in his life now who was on an emotional par with that rabbit? It seemed unlikely, but then again, back at Berkeley she hadn't thought he would actually marry the bimbo he'd gotten pregnant. She presumed nothing with Dylan.

Gail shut the lid of the rabbit's cage, pulled out her cell phone, and called Dylan's private line at work. She reached a voice-forwarding service and quickly hung up and called his home number. No one answered, not even the machine. When she tried his cell phone number, an electronic voice informed her the phone wasn't turned on. So where were his messages being forwarded to?

She went into her house and booted up her computer to make the call to his office. Thanks to a nifty piece of software she'd gotten through the navy, she could trace call-forwarding numbers but her call couldn't be traced back to her. This time, she let the call forwarding at his end go through. The number rang once and she hung up and moments later, the number appeared on her screen.

The area code indicated he was in the vicinity of

Gainesville, which covered everything west of the city, including Piper Key. She ran a trace through the reverse directory and came up with exactly nothing. She fumed and mulled over her options and finally called an operator she knew at Alachua Bell, a woman for whom Gail had arranged several free dolphin swims.

"Hi, Carolyn, it's Gail. How's it going?"

"Oh, the usual stuff, you know. Overworked and underpaid. How're all those dolphins?"

They chatted for a few minutes; then Gail casually asked Carolyn to call her back on a line that wasn't bugged. Carolyn, understanding what this meant, hemmed and hawed, but finally agreed and called her back a few minutes later.

"I could lose my job doing this," Carolyn said.

"I could've lost my job getting you free swims, too, you know."

"What's the number?"

Gail ticked it off. Computer keys tapped in the background silence. "Penthouse suite at the Piper Lodge."

Here on the island and he doesn't even call me?

"Thanks, Carolyn. Come in any time for a free swim." *Bring your neighbors, your friends, your third cousins.* "I really appreciate this."

Five minutes later, she sped across the island, through the summer twilight, headed for the Piper Lodge. She was still wearing her jogging clothes, stank of sweat from her two-mile run, and was primed for blood. She didn't know what she would say to him, but knew that it wouldn't be pretty. And if he were with someone, Gail would make sure the bimbo never saw him again.

The Piper Lodge, like The Loft, its stiffest competition, catered to the well-heeled tourist and the businessman with a generous expense account. But unlike The Loft, it was snuggled in the hills near the preserve, on a freshwater, man-made lake stocked with fish. It boasted a helipad on the roof, its own cable system for faster Internet access, and underground parking. The Japanese businesspeople loved it and thought nothing of paying three hundred bucks a night in the middle of the hottest months in Florida.

Gail parked in a visitor's spot and marched through the ornate lobby to the house phones. She asked for Steve Dylan's room. The operator told her no guest by that name was registered at the hotel. She thought a moment. "It might be registered under his friend's name. Nicolas Clancy." The name came from two of Dylan's favorite celebrities—Nicholas Cage and Tom Clancy.

"Here it is," the operator said. "I'll connect you."

Gail quickly hung up the receiver. *Nicolas Clancy.* Christ.

She took the elevator to the housekeeping floor. Here, she found a Jamaican woman with a million keys hanging from her copious waist who believed Gail's story that she'd been locked out of her room. She unlocked the door to Dylan's room and Gail tipped her fifty bucks.

As she slipped inside, she heard the shower running. Dylan's wet swimming trunks lay on one of the king-size beds. His open suitcase lay on the other and it looked to be only partially unpacked. Gail didn't see any sign of a woman's presence, but that didn't mean anything. She went over to the suitcase and went through the clothes, looking for a packet of condoms. Dylan wouldn't screw anyone except Gail without a rubber and then it was only because she'd gone through menopause two years ago. He'd gotten trapped once and he'd made it abundantly clear over the years that he wouldn't get trapped again.

She found no condoms.

His briefcase rested on the floor beside the bed, the metal briefcase with the safety code that could probably withstand anything short of a nuclear blast. She noticed the cord that snaked away from it to a plug in the wall. It held his laptop, she thought.

She mulled over her own numerical preferences and spun in four eights, her favorite number. The briefcase clicked and she opened it. There were a few benefits, she mused, to being born only two minutes apart. The laptop, at least a size smaller than her own, was up and running. She pressed *Enter* and the dark screen lightened, displaying a schematic of some kind.

It looked familiar, although she couldn't say why. She studied it, noting the red blip that moved steadily across the screen, following one line in the schematic. She was so involved in what she was doing that she forgot where she was, what she should be listening for, forgot everything except the schematic. Suddenly, someone grabbed her from behind, grabbed her around the throat and jerked her back as though she weighed nothing at all.

"What the fuck are you doing here?" he hissed.

Gail slammed her elbow into Dylan's throat, the same move that had sent Lydia Thomas stumbling back that day at the center, gasping for air, and shot to her feet.

"What the fuck are *you* doing here?"

Dylan, wearing nothing but a towel draped at his waist, rubbed at his throat and grabbed on to the corner of the bed to pull himself up. "Jesus, Gail. You could've crushed my larynx." He sat heavily on the edge of the bed. "You can't just bust the fuck into people's hotel rooms."

She looked back at the computer, at the schematic, at the red blip that moved steadily across the screen. "That's the center," she said softly. "That red blip is just offshore from the center. You're going after Alpha, aren't you. That's what this is about."

He rubbed his throat and went over to the metal briefcase. "I think you'd better leave, Gail." He picked up the briefcase and set it on the table. "This doesn't concern you."

"Like hell it doesn't. You asked me to do a job and then lied about what was in that syringe, Dylan. That stuff blows open blood vessels so the animal bleeds out. If I'd injected Alpha while she was in a holding tank, the center would have shut down."

"That's the point."

"Not at *my* expense. I'm not going to get arrested for your dirty work, Dylan." She pointed at the red blip on the computer screen. "Call off your thugs or I'll alert the center to . . ."

"Don't threaten me," he snapped.

"Then don't keep lying to me." She went over to the phone, snatched up the receiver. "Call them off, Dylan. Now."

He moved at the speed of light, grabbed the receiver out of her hand, and slammed it down into the cradle. "Just calm down and listen to me."

"Listen to more lies? No, thanks."

"We're just going to release her from the holding tanks and get rid of her in open waters."

"The center is *my* domain, not yours."

"You're there because of the Department of Naval

Intelligence, Gail. The grant that Lydia Thomas got seven years ago came from us, through a third party, and you were part of the package deal. You seem to have forgotten that part."

"Contrary to what you've believed all these years, I'm not your fucking lackey. I'm not some puppet you can jerk around in any way that suits you. Either you do this my way or I blow the whistle on this whole thing."

She uttered this in a tight, seething voice and realized she meant every word of it. Dylan apparently realized she meant it, too. He looked stunned. "The heroine saves the day."

"Something like that. The other way, I'm just your fall guy, Dylan. And frankly, I'm tired of that role."

"I've never expected you to take the blame for my mistakes."

"Maybe you never expected it, but that's how it has worked out."

"Give me one example."

Christ, he didn't get it. It was as though he had one version of events and she had another. "In the eight years you and I have worked on this mammal defense program at Pensacola, you've never told me the whole truth. All that stuff about Sheldrake and Alpha . . ." She made a dismissive gesture with her hand. "That's just a small part of it. Why do you need the center's dolphins? Why is Alpha such a threat? And spare me the guru shit, okay? Just tell me what's really going on with the DNI's mammal defense program. Otherwise, I'll just go my way and you go yours."

His expression underwent subtle but definite changes, as if he were really seeing her for the first time. "That sounds like an ultimatum."

"Call it what you want." She walked over to the wall of glass on the far side of the room and gazed out into the darkness. In the distance, the last of the evening light faded away. "That's how I feel. We've known each other all our lives, but you've never trusted me enough to bring me fully into your real work for the DNI. That hurts. It's become a wall between us. It's created more problems than I'm willing to handle anymore."

"I see."

Did he? "Meaning what, Dylan?"

She turned. He stood with his back to her now, a show of modesty as he dressed. "That it's complicated." He pulled on khaki shorts and a T-shirt, then turned again. "I've ordered dinner. There's enough for two. Will you stay and have dinner with me?"

"If you call off your men."

He nodded, picked up his cell phone, and punched out a number. "It's Dylan. Bring the boat back in. . . . Yeah, I know. But it's scrapped for tonight. . . . Right. See you then."

Scrapped for tonight. What about tomorrow night and the night after that? Gail wondered.

As Dylan hung up, there was a rap at the door. "Dinner." He hurried over to the door and admitted a waiter pushing a serving tray.

(2)

Natalie stood on the platform with Bacall, watching her mother and Max swimming in the moonlight with Kit. She liked what she saw, her mother acting like a kid, her laughter ringing out across the holding tanks.

Maybe, she thought, her mother might be happy with a man like Max.

"Hey, Mom," she called. "I'm going to check on Alpha and Rainbow."

"See if you can head them back toward the tanks. We'll be finished here in a few minutes. Take your radio."

Natalie whistled for Bacall and they crossed the deck to the seawall and walked along it. The interaction between Alpha and Bacall had been successful in that they appeared to get along. Alpha had scanned Bacall from head to toe before she approached the dog, then had come right up and touched her beak to Bacall's snout. Alpha had done a lot of whistling, Bacall had whimpered and barked a lot, but Natalie had no idea what any of it meant. Afterward, Alpha and Rainbow had swum out of the tank and into the cove, where they were now.

As she and Bacall rounded the curve in the seawall, Natalie spotted the dolphins in the cove, swimming side by side. Alpha could now remain afloat by herself, but even so, either Rainbow or Kit were always somewhere nearby, her loyal bodyguards. She raised the binoculars to her eyes to get a better look and noticed the light of a boat about three hundred yards beyond the cove. A fishing vessel, she guessed.

Even though the polyurethane net blocked the entrance to the cove, the dolphins could jump it if they wanted to get out. But so far, none of the three had shown any interest in venturing out into the open gulf. Just the same, the presence of the fishing boat disturbed her and she picked up her pace. When they reached the beach, she heard whistles and cries, but these sounded agitated. Bacall started barking and ran up to the water's edge, then raced back and forth along the beach, alternately howling and barking.

Alpha and Rainbow sped away from the entrance to the cove, dangerously close to the shallow waters where Natalie now stood, the binoculars pressed to her eyes. Then Rainbow turned suddenly and sped back toward the entrance and Natalie suddenly knew he was going to leap over it.

She pulled her radio out of her pocket. "Mom, get out here fast. Something's going on. Rainbow's about to leap the net at the entrance to the cove. Over."

In the moments that it took her mother to respond, probably because she was still in the holding tank, Rainbow lifted majestically from the water, his body shimmering in the moonlight, and splashed down on the other side. Alpha whistled and shrieked and raced parallel to the shore. Bacall, barking ferociously now, ran along the beach, almost keeping pace with the dolphin.

"We're on our way, Nat," her mother said finally. "Do *not* go into the water under any conditions. Over and out."

Natalie peered through the binoculars again, trying to focus on the boat. And suddenly she saw more dolphins, surfacing near the boat, surrounding it. By the time her mother and Max appeared, the boat's running lights had come on, providing enough illumination to see that the water now teemed with dolphins. Dozens upon dozens of dolphins surfaced and dived, ramming the boat repeatedly.

Alpha, meanwhile, kept swimming back and forth, parallel to shore, whistling and crying out, and Bacall kept barking. Max ran after his dog, shouting at her, and Natalie and her mother stood side by side at the water's edge.

"Jesus," her mother said. "Whoever is on board is going to need help. I'm calling the Coast Guard." Her mother whipped out her cell phone, but Natalie touched her hand.

"The dolphins need help, Mom, not the people on that boat. They're protecting Alpha."

"You're assuming too much," Lydia snapped, and turned away to punch out the number for the Coast Guard.

(3)

"So explain why it's complicated," Gail said, unwilling to let Dylan off the hook.

They were eating out on the balcony, where the summer breeze felt warm and seductive against her skin. Candlelight softened the hard angles of Dylan's face, the fatigue that pinched the corners of his mouth. "It involves my old man's work with the navy in the late thirties and early forties."

Gail did some quick math in her head. Dylan's father had died in 1986 at the age of seventy-five. That meant that during the late thirties and early forties, he'd been in his late twenties and early thirties. "What kind of work was it?"

"Camouflage."

In the navy, camouflage spelled many things—the SEALS, dark ships that sped silently through even darker waters, subs that whispered through waters so deep that sunlight never penetrated. At these depths, fish were blind because they didn't need eyes. At these depths, the navy approached the abyss of the unknown, the unimagined. "What do you mean, camouflage? What kind of camouflage?"

"Of war vessels." Dylan swirled a piece of veal around in the sauce on his plate and popped it in his mouth. He washed it down with a sip of wine. "Tell me what you know about the USS *Eldridge*, Gail."

"Naval history was never my strong point. *You* tell *me* about the *Eldridge*."

Inside the room, his phone rang. He ignored it. "The *Eldridge* was a destroyer escort, a beauty of a ship, equipped to the hilt with the latest of everything that existed in 1943. In October of that year, while at the dock in the Philadelphia naval yard, the ship allegedly vanished and moments later appeared at its dock in Norfolk, Virginia. Half the crew supposedly went insane, some of them burst into flames. . . ."

"The Philadelphia experiment." Gail burst out laughing. "That whole thing is fiction, Dylan. The guy who first reported that it had happened was a hack writer of UFO books, for Christ's sake."

Dylan looked angry now. "His name was Morris Jessup and he wasn't a hack writer. He taught astronomy and math at the University of Michigan and his research led to the discovery of literally thousands of stars."

"Okay, okay. But the story is still bullshit. It's a myth of popular culture."

"My father worked on the project, Campbell."

"In what capacity?"

"The research end of it."

"Dylan, your father was a terrific person, but he wasn't a research scientist."

"He was the assistant to the man who did the bulk of the research with Einstein and John von Neumann."

Gail's parents had known Dylan's parents for all those years that their families had moved from base to base. Yet, she couldn't recall either of her parents ever mentioning that Dylan's father had been involved in any facet of research, especially with people like Einstein.

"When the experiment failed," Dylan went on, "my father was banished to Cuba, mostly as a way to keep him quiet. He met my mother, they got married, and life in Cuba was fine for almost sixteen years. Then I came along and so did the revolution and by the time my father left Cuba, his involvement in the *Eldridge* affair had been forgotten."

"I'm not real clear on how this relates to DNI's mammal defense program."

"The dolphin part came much later, around 1971, but it was an offshoot of the Philadelphia fiasco. For years, marine biologists have been puzzled about why dolphins and whales get beached. But we had the resources to research the question intensively. We tagged a group of dolphins so that we could keep track of them over a period of time. When one of them got beached, we went to the beaching site to try to determine what had gone wrong."

"And what'd you learn?"

"Well, there were some anomalies involved in all this. In many instances, it seemed the tagged mammals would head in one direction with their pods, then suddenly would be hundreds of miles away. We thought the tagging devices were faulty, so we tagged more dolphins with new electronic devices. The . . ."

His cell phone rang. He reached for it, but Gail covered his hand with her own. "Don't," she said quietly. "Just finish the story."

"This is just the confirmation call about Alpha, Gail. It won't take a minute."

She reluctantly withdrew her hand.

"Dylan here." Blood drained from his face, she could see it happening. It was like watching liquid drain from a hole in the bottom of a glass jar. Then he shot to his feet and hurried into the suite. "Where are they now? Right. I'll be there."

Gail hurried after him. "What's going on?"

"The boat we had out there is starting to sink. It's under attack by dolphins." He quickly packed up his laptop and made a beeline for the door.

"I'm coming with you."

"You can't, Campbell. Your security clearance isn't high enough."

"Fuck the security clearance. I . . ."

"No." He hurried past her and slammed the door.

Gail ran over to it, threw the door open, but the hall was empty. The elevators were too far for him to have gotten away so quickly, so she flew toward the closest EXIT sign. But inside the stairwell, she didn't hear any echoing footfalls. *The helipad.*

She ran up one flight, burst through the door at the top, and ran out to the flat part of the roof just in time to see the chopper lifting off.

Piper Key Gazette
Wildlife Column
July 25, 1999

I've received some intriguing e-mail and letters concerning the erratic behavior of wildlife here on Piper and in other parts of the country. I hope that by sharing some of these with you, we can piece together the meaning of what appears to be an emerging pattern.

From Port Orange, Florida (east coast, south of Daytona Beach): "In the last month, we've had some very strange incidents concerning birds. Only last week, the public beach was closed for two days because hundreds of pelicans filled the shore. City workers tried to scare them away and the pelicans attacked them. The week before that, thousands of sandpipers hovered over the downtown area for several hours. They formed such a dense cloud that cars and pedestrians were soiled by their droppings."

From New Orleans: "I'm a nature photographer and have spent a lot of the last twenty years out in the bayou. The gators here aren't aggressive unless you give them reason to be or if they're hungry. Neither of those things explains what happened to me a couple weeks back. I was out canoeing and taking pictures and a ten-foot gator bit off the end of my paddle, then went after my canoe. When he realized he couldn't bite through the canoe (it's aluminum) he swam under it and tried to tip it over. I managed to beat him off with a long metal pole I keep in the canoe.

"This wasn't just some isolated incident, either.

Three days after my experience, a man and his boy were out there and the boy was attacked and died twelve hours later."

From El Marmol (Baja California): "*My father is fisherman. Each morning, he go into Gulf of California and catch fish that he take to market. He sees many sharks on his trips. They not bother him, he not bother them. But on this day in June, I go with my father to fish and many sharks surround our boat, so many sharks we cannot count how many. They attack the boat, slam into it, but the boat it is bigger than them. My father he quickly turn on the engine. The engine it is powerful, noisy, fast. The propeller it cuts a shark, the water fills with blood, and suddenly the sharks attack the shark that is bleeding. Never do I see anything like this attack. Never. We escape. I do not go near the water now."*

From Cairo, Egypt: "*I'm an American archeologist working in Egypt. Whenever vehicles are hard to come by, we use camels to haul some of our supplies to a dig site. Camels can be quite cranky and aggressive at times and definitely aren't very lovable toward humans. At our most recent site, four of us were about to enter a chamber that appeared to be quite stable. The six camels we had with us suddenly lined up, blocking our entrance to the chamber. Nothing we did made them move—not threats or whips, not even a gun fired into the air.*

"We finally decided to back off and wait until they left on their own. Ten minutes later, they surged forward, away from the chamber door, and within seconds, the entire chamber collapsed. Did they save our lives? Absolutely. Did they act out of be-

nevolence? It sure looks that way to me, but my colleagues would call that anthropomorphism. Call it what you want. I know that I'm alive today because the camels sensed what was going to happen and prevented us from going into that chamber."

From Houston, Texas: "I live in a suburb south of Houston. I usually bike ride at night, when it's somewhat cooler, and take my two collies with me. The other night, as we turned down a street that parallels the park, I heard a horrendous screeching noise. It spooked my dogs, who took off into the park. I chased them and caught up with them in the playground. Just as I got their leashes on, I heard the screeching sound again. A huge flock of owls descended out of the dark, swooping toward us.

"We took refuge under a platform on the jungle gym, but the owls found us and tried to fly under the platform. We finally took refuge inside the jungle gym's large plastic tubes and I called 911 on my cell phone. Within minutes, a fire truck arrived and turned hoses on the owls, which chased them off. I have lived in this area all of my life and I've never seen owls act like this."

Two nights ago, just offshore our island, a boat was attacked by dolphins until it started to sink. No one seems to know who this boat belonged to or who was on it, but a chopper was spotted just above the boat, apparently rescuing the people on board. Who was on the chopper? No one seems to know that, either. The boat has now sunk to become part of the barrier reef just offshore.

That dolphin attack is just one more unknown in a string of unknowns.

I also have e-mails and letters from: the Midway

islands, a navy ship near the Canary Islands, Delhi, India, Saudi Arabia, and Marrakech. If you check a world map, you'll see that each of these places, as well as the locales of the e-mails I've included in the column, roughly fall along the same parallel as Piper Key, latitude 29N08. Even to a skeptic, this is too great a coincidence to ignore.

What do I, personally, make of this? I'm not sure. I've received reports from areas outside of this parallel, but nothing as consistent as the reports that fall around the twenty-ninth parallel. Something is certainly going on, but so far the mainstream media has pretty much ignored it. Why? There's plenty about these oddities on the Web, including a site similar to the Gazette's (but much larger), where people are invited to post their sightings and experiences and to talk about them during live chats.

True, this isn't "scientific"—i.e., no science organization has undertaken a study of what's going on. But this doesn't make the evidence any less valid. Anecdotal evidence, after all, is often the precursor to scientific breakthrough or understanding. The real issue, though, is whether we will be able to understand the pattern before it's too late.

Witness
Visit our website at
www.piperkeygazette.com

Fifteen

The alarm on Natalie's watch woke her at exactly 2 A.M. She bolted upright, listened to the silence, but heard nothing to indicate that her mother was still awake. For the last few nights, her mother always seemed to be at her computer, figuring and refiguring their finances, trying to determine how long they could keep the center functioning. But tonight, exhaustion must have gotten the best of her.

Natalie pulled on shorts and a T-shirt, stuck her sandals in her backpack, and shrugged it on. She stuffed pillows under her sheets, the oldest trick in a kid's arsenal of tricks, and one her mother had fallen for in the past. She felt guilty about sneaking out like this, especially after the other day, when she and her mother seemed to have arrived at some sort of understanding about each other. But it couldn't be helped.

She grabbed a couple of apples from the bowl on the counter, unlocked the kitchen door, and slipped out. She locked the door again with her key and stole silently down the stairs. Like many of the homes on the island, Natalie's was elevated on ten-foot pilings, with the carport under the house. They had sectioned off the carport so there was room for one car or the golf cart, with the rest of the area used as storage for bikes, camping equipment, and whatever else wouldn't fit in the house.

Natalie stashed the apples in her pack, put on her sandals, and pushed her bike out of the storage area. Before she pedaled off, she called Tom Maynard on her cell phone. It rang once.

"You on your way?" he whispered.

"Yeah. Just leaving."

"Meet you at Vine."

"Right."

Moments later, she pedaled out into the vast, moonlit silence that covered the island. No traffic, no people, just the way she liked it best. The air smelled sweet, of salt and jasmine and freshly mown grass. Now and then, she heard some distant sound, a dog barking, a shriek of brakes from outside of town.

Vine Street lay a mile east of her neighborhood and curved around the perimeter of one of the salt marshes. She spotted Tom's truck parked near the boardwalk. He leaned against the back of it, smoking a cigar. "Hey," she said, hopping off her bike.

"Hey, yourself."

"I hope the phone didn't wake your folks."

"No way. They're six sheets to the wind. Big party at one of the mansions in the neighborhood. They wouldn't give a shit about me leaving anyway."

He said this without bitterness or regret. But Natalie felt his hurt, an old hurt that he'd carried inside for all the years she'd known him. She gave his arm a quick squeeze. "Screw 'em if they can't take a joke."

Tom laughed, lowered the back of the truck, and lifted her bike onto the bed, next to his bike. He twisted the end of his cigar against the sole of his shoe, then stuck it behind his ear. "Let's get moving."

They drove north, toward Gracie's. Maybe tonight she would hear the monkeys that lived in the woods behind Gracie's place. Supposedly, there were several hundred of them now, descendants of twenty or so that had escaped from a traveling carnival about fifteen years ago. She'd glimpsed one on a walk with Gracie a long time ago. But she wouldn't be walking tonight. After what had happened that day at Gracie's, she didn't plan on ever going into that woods again.

The porch light came on before Tom had even stopped the truck and Gracie stepped out onto the porch to greet them. She had her reading glasses tucked back onto the top of her head. "Sorry to be so mysterious, kids, but what I've got to show you is most visible around four in the morning. I would've asked your mother to join us, Nat, but right now she needs her rest."

They went into one of two air-conditioned rooms in the entire house, Gracie's library. She had more than five thousand books, meticulously catalogued and arranged on the endless shelves that climbed three of the fifteen-foot walls. A movable ladder provided access to the highest shelves, where the oldest of the books had been boxed in special transparent containers to preserve them.

"Help yourselves." She gestured at the stone coffee table, where there were two platters of goodies and a pitcher of lemonade.

Natalie and Tom filled a plate apiece, then pulled up chairs on either side of Gracie, who sat at one of the computers. "Some of this is going to sound strange to you. And some of it won't." She looked pointedly at Natalie. "Does Tom know about what happened to you the day you followed Bacall into the woods?"

Natalie shook her head. "I don't even know what happened." Actually, that was only partially true. She knew what had happened; she just didn't have any idea what it meant.

"So is someone going to tell me?" Tom leaned forward, looking at Natalie.

The dog, the woods, getting lost, panicking: That was what she told him.

A quick, sly smile played across Gracie's mouth; her fingers danced across the keyboard. "I think there was a lot more to it, Natalie. I'll show you why I think so."

A revolving globe appeared on the screen. Borders firmed up. An interlocking grid of lines spun across the globe, linking areas. It looked a lot like the *routes* she saw in her head.

"Any idea what this is?" Gracie asked.

"Highways?" Natalie said, then shook her head. "No. Not across the oceans."

"An information grid," Tom said.

"Close," Gracie said. "But the grid doesn't exist in the conventional sense. We're not talking about Ma Bell cables. These are energy flows, invisible conduits of energy that connect the planet." She zoomed in on England. "See here?" She tapped the screen where a number of lines converged. "Stonehenge. And here." She zoomed in on Greece. "The Parthenon." Another zoom. "The Egyptian pyramids." Another. "Mayan pyramids." And another and another. Easter Island, Machu Picchu, the Alps.

"Where the lines converge, there are energy power centers. In other parts of the world, these centers usually have ancient structures on them—or the ruins of such structures. Some people believe that's part of the reason why these structures have lasted so long."

"What about the U.S.?" Tom asked. "Any energy flows here?"

"Sure." She zoomed in on the Southwest. "Anasazi ruins. The Hopi mesas. The Everglades. The waters between South Florida and the Bahamas. Areas in California, New England, Minnesota, the Adirondacks in upstate New York, Virginia Beach, areas in the Midwest." She swiveled around in her chair. "Even rooms have energy flow lines and points where the lines converge. She threw out her arms. "That potted plant by the window? It's an aralia, what Asians call a Ming tree. It usually doesn't do well indoors. But it flourishes over there—and not just because it gets a lot of light. It's sitting on a convergence of flow lines within this room. My greenhouse and the cellar are built on another flow line."

"How do you know?" Natalie asked.

"My ex is a dowser and he . . ."

"What's a dowser?" Tom asked.

"They find water," Natalie said. "Using a certain kind of stick."

Gracie nodded. "A good dowser can locate virtually anything in the earth—minerals, ore, oil, water. My ex dowsed the property and we mapped the flow lines. Then he taught me how to do it and I mapped the lines here in the house. He also created this program we're using." She hit another key and the horse's head of Piper Key appeared on the screen.

"And that brings us back here. Piper Key sits on a place where eleven major lines come together. Another eleven minor lines also go through here. That's *twenty-two,* guys." She glanced at Natalie. "It's part of the reason why your mother has had such incredible luck with dolphins here, Nat. It's why the wilderness preserve has withstood the assault of commercial development."

"Maybe it explains why my parents party so much," Tom remarked dryly.

Gracie laughed. "I doubt it. But it may explain why The Loft is so successful." She zoomed in on the area bordering the preserve. "That X marks my house." She moved the cursor again, highlighting a second X in the woods behind her house. "This is the exact point where four major flow lines intersect."

"So there's a lot of energy there," Natalie said.

"There's *so* much energy surging here that sometimes you can see it. The last few days, Nat, I've been exploring the area where you ran into Max. It was quite close to this intersection."

"Is that why I got so disoriented?" Natalie asked.

"Could be. I think you're sensitive to this type of energy. I think it's why dolphins and whales get beached. Surges of energy mess up their sonar. They think they're going after yellow fish for breakfast and end up on a beach in Bali. I think the surges on Piper Key are part of the reason why a thousand dolphins escorted a single, sick dolphin into a dolphin center. And why wolves have come here. And why a mother wolf sought human help for her wounded pup. Something's going on. Now let's take a closer look at the island."

She zoomed in on the horse's head. A map of Piper Key and part of the surrounding waters filled the screen: the salt marshes, the mangroves, the dolphin center, the airport and streets, all of it intersected by ley lines. "Three of the lines come together in Digger's Cove and remain together through the mangrove. Then they split apart again and are joined by three other lines in the gulf. These six shoot right past the dolphin center, Nat."

"That's the route the dolphins took Corie and me that day."

"Exactly. My theory is that animals are sensitive to the energy that hums through these lines. There's a growing body of evidence, for instance, that animals in quake areas act erratically a day or two before a quake hits. I think they pick up on the change in energy in the flow lines. Now apply this to what happened to you, Natalie, with the dolphins."

Natalie frowned. "There's going to be a quake here?"

"Not an earthquake, but I think something similar is happening. Dolphins and whales are particularly sensitive to fluctuations in the energy in the flow lines, probably because of their echo location abilities. Like I said earlier, that may be why they get beached."

"But what happened to Natalie and Corie didn't involve a beaching," Tom remarked.

"Exactly. It was something much stranger and very rare. Nearly a thousand dolphins came to the aid of a single, sick dolphin and the two kids who were trying to help it. It's virtually unheard of."

"And you think it happened because of something weird in these ley lines?" Natalie asked.

"I think the dolphins were responding to a fundamental change in the energy. And this isn't the only place it's happening." She clicked on another folder. "Over the past few weeks, I've collected over a hundred similar incidents."

She scrolled slowly down the screen. "At a naval base in Virginia, dolphins and whales descended en masse and destroyed a number of vessels. Sea World in . . ."

Natalie and Tom exchanged a glance and Gracie noticed. "You kids already know about this?"

Tom shrugged. "Some of it. Tell us more."

"Sea lions in San Francisco Bay, birds in upstate New York, condors in South America, fire ants in South Florida, coyotes in the Southwest, bees in Texas . . . Wildlife everywhere is exhibiting behavior that isn't normal or ordinary. But it gets stranger. There have been numerous reports of sightings of wildlife that aren't indigenous to the area where they're sighted."

Natalie immediately thought of her mother's experience the other day in the mangrove near Digger's Cove. "What kind of sightings?" she asked.

"Prairie dogs in Baltimore. Florida panthers in Colorado Springs. White wolves in Kansas. In each instance, the sighting is brief and usually described as 'shimmering.' "

Quietly, Tom said, "It happened to me. The other night I couldn't sleep, so I walked along the salt marsh and smoked a joint. I heard this really weird noise coming from the marsh and I saw a . . . a bear." He laughed, a quick, nervous sound. "A *bear,* for Christ's sake. A grizzly. There've never been grizzlies in Florida. Never. I . . . I figured I'd smoked too much dope and ran back to the house."

"It happened to Mom, too," Natalie said, and told them the story about the hourglass dolphins.

Gracie listened to all this, taking it in without interrupting. Then she picked up a pencil and on a piece of scratch paper printed an *A* on the left side and a *B* on the right side. "Say you're at A and you want to get to B on the other side of the ocean. It takes you five days by ship to get to B or eight hours in a plane. But suppose that by tapping into the flow lines you could get there in a matter of minutes? Or seconds? Or instantaneously? I think that's what's happening to the wildlife, except that they stumble into the energy and suddenly find themselves in a whole new place."

"Like 'beam me up, Scotty'? Is that what you're talking about?" Tom asked.

"I hadn't thought of it in those terms, but yeah, I guess that's as good a term as any. But this happens spontaneously. That's my theory, anyway."

"The quantum world." Tom's quiet voice held a reverence that Natalie had rarely heard from him.

Gracie nodded. "Yeah, it's the quantum world. But it's also the larger world, Tom. My theory is that something intrinsic to the nature of reality happens at the point where the energy converges."

"It's where the wave collapses into the particle," Tom said, excited now.

"Yes, I think so. And at the point where that happens, it's possible for psychics and other sensitive people to perceive it in some way."

"You guys just lost me," Natalie said. "What wave? What particle?"

Tom launched into a minilecture on quantum physics, but Natalie didn't understand a word of it. "What's causing it?"

Gracie shook her head. "I don't have a clue. Maybe it's the end result of what we've done to the planet in terms of pollution and everything else. Maybe nature is simply trying to balance things ecologically. For the last week, I've been going out into the woods at various times just to see what, if anything, I feel."

"And?" Tom asked.

"I want you to see for yourselves. Let's take the golf cart. I've got flashlights in the cart."

Natalie balked. "We're going out there *now?*"

"We won't get lost, Nat. I'm going to hang a bright electric light on the back porch."

"We can take a compass," Tom said.

Gracie shook her head. "No, the energy screws up a compass just like it messes up a dolphin's sonar. The porch light will be enough. And we'll have flashlights."

Natalie still wasn't crazy about this idea. But she didn't want to stay alone in the house, either. "How far do we have to walk into the woods?"

"We can drive in for about a mile, then walk about four hundred yards or so."

Gracie headed toward the door. Natalie glanced at Tom, who shrugged and mouthed, *Let's go.*

Outside, the moon had already set, but a million stars glinted against the black skin of the sky, providing enough illumination for them to see where they were going without using the flashlights. Gracie turned on the electric light that would serve as their beacon; then they got into the golf cart and headed for the dark, forbidding shape of the woods behind the house.

Sixteen

(1)

Lydia woke to the wind blowing in off the marsh and branches scratching at her bedroom window. Old fears clutched at her, silly fears that had followed her ever since the divorce: that someone had broken into the house, that Natalie had died in her sleep, that something had happened at the center. Ridiculous, she thought, but just the same she threw off the sheet and went to the bedroom doorway.

When you lived in a place long enough, its silences held meaning, nuance, coded messages. And this silence told her that Natalie wasn't in her room. Sure enough, the lumps under the covers of her bed were three pillows.

"Great. Just great." And where had her wayward daughter taken off for tonight? Tom's? Gracie's? The center? Digger's Cove? No, probably not there, not at night. And she wouldn't go to the center when the janitor was cleaning because he knew her and had instructions to call Lydia if she showed up there at night. That left Tom and Gracie.

Natalie probably wouldn't go to Tom's this late at night, unless they were sleeping together, which Lydia doubted. That left Gracie's place. Lydia ran back into her room to dress and brush her teeth, then raced downstairs to the carport. Natalie's bike was gone. She'd pulled this same stunt last summer and Lydia had grounded her. Now she intended to take away her bike.

As she backed her van out of the carport, the usual mother nightmares seized her imagination—that some cruising pervert had nabbed Natalie, that she'd been hit by a car, that she wouldn't be at Gracie's. She punched out Gracie's number on her cell phone and reached the answering machine. Gracie used the machine only when she wasn't home. So where was she at three-thirty in the morning? In Max's camper? No, he wasn't Gracie's type. He was more *her* type.

She called Natalie's cell phone number, but the phone wasn't turned on. Typical. When Natalie didn't want to be found, she turned the phone off. Angry now, she drove faster.

(2)

Bacall woke him with whimpers and scratches at the door. She needed to pee, for Christ's sake, in the middle of the night. Thorn kicked off the sheet and sat up. The portable fan next to the bed whirred softly and turned from side to side. Night sounds filled the air.

"Okay, okay, hold on."

He hauled himself out of bed, opened the door to the camper, and Bacall bounded down the steps. Thorn stood in the doorway, waiting for her. The night air felt good against his skin, even though it was a far shot from cool, nothing at all like summer nights where he came from. But he enjoyed the smell of the woods and the salt marsh and liked the endless orchestra of clicks and hums and croaks.

Here in the sweet richness of the dark, Thorn felt closer to wherever Ellen was. It was as if he could shut his eyes and reach out to touch her. Or he could cup his hands to the sides of his mouth and call her name and she would hear him. But in the next moment, the familiar despair and anger at her crowded in. *If we'd gotten married, I wouldn't be in this goddamn mess.*

Despite his despair and anger, the bottom line remained the same: No one returned from the twilight zone. Rod Serling had known it. Charles Fort had known it. Since he didn't have any idea what actually had happened to Ellen, other than her vanishing, he couldn't say with any certainty that she was still alive— *somewhere.* And yet, he'd always believed their connection was so strong, he would sense it if she died while they were apart. He would feel the *ripple in the Force.* Uh-huh, sure thing.

He may have believed their connection was strong, but it apparently wasn't strong enough for her to break away from her old man and marry him. Now Bradshaw had a price on Thorn's head and his photo had been blasted across the wire services.

He couldn't see Bacall now and whistled for her. She didn't appear. Since he wore only gym shorts, he stepped back into the camper and pulled on a T-shirt and sneakers. He grabbed a flashlight and Bacall's leash on the way out.

Headlights sped down the road from Gracie's place and he turned to see who it was. A blue van swerved to the shoulder of the road and Lydia Thomas hopped out and ran over to him. "Max, have you seen Gracie or my daughter?"

"Until five minutes ago, I was sound asleep. What's going on?"

"Natalie's friend, Tom, must've picked her up and they came over here. Tom's truck is in the driveway and Natalie's bike is in the back of it and no one's in the house . . ."

"Hey, slow down," he said gently, touching her shoulders. "Is Gracie's car at the house?"

"Yes."

He glanced toward the woods. "Bacall just woke me, asking to go out, then she vanished into the woods. I was just going to look for her. Maybe she sensed or heard them."

"Why would they go into the woods at night?"

"I don't know."

Just then, Bacall appeared at the edge of the trees, barked, and Thorn snapped, "Hey, get back here, Bacall."

She barked again, ran along the edge of the woods, stopped, barked, pawed the ground, and vanished into the woods. Thorn and Lydia glanced at each other, then he grabbed her hand and they ran after the dog. He felt certain that she'd awakened him because she heard or sensed people going into the woods. She would find them, too. Once she plugged into a particular scent, nothing stopped her.

The beam of his flashlight skimmed tree trunks, piles of fallen leaves, clusters of thick brush. He whistled and the sound echoed eerily. Lydia called her daughter's name and her voice echoed in the same way. Thorn wasn't sure how far they walked or how much time it took. Then they heard a noise off to their right and they both stopped and he whistled again. Bacall barked and moments later, the beam of Thorn's flashlight impaled her. She glanced back and the light caught her eyes, turning them red. Her tail wagged. Panting, she hurried on.

Lydia, several paces ahead of him now, suddenly stopped and hissed, "Max, you feel it?"

"What?"

Then he came up alongside her and felt it for himself. The air had turned noticeably cooler and it stunned him. *Like the vanishing point.* He stepped back three paces. Warm. Forward three paces. Cool. Another three paces forward brought him into air that was *cold.*

"What the hell," he murmured. "Right here it's downright cold."

"There's Bacall," Lydia said, pointing.

She stood about four yards from him, waiting, watching them. Thorn went over to her and reached for her collar. She growled and snapped at him and he jerked his hand back. "Jesus, what the hell's wrong with you?"

She barked and bounded forward, cutting through a clearing just ahead of them and into the trees on the other side. Thorn and Lydia hurried after her, into air that vacillated between cool and cold enough for their breaths to congeal. He heard Bacall's excited barks just ahead. Then: "Hey, Max. Lydia. Over here!"

Moments later, Thorn and Lydia emerged in an orchard of papaya trees. Gracie, Natalie, and Tom Maynard looked as surprised to see Thorn as he was to see them.

"I can explain, Mom," Natalie said quickly.

"Yeah? It'd better be good, young lady. The . . ."

"Hey, calm down." Gracie held up her hands. "I'm guilty. I asked her and Tom to come up here. Sit down, okay? And, Max, could you turn off your flashlight? I figure we've got just a few minutes till showtime."

Thorn turned off his flashlight and sat next to Gracie on the ground. Lydia remained standing. "Invited them up here for what, Gracie?" she asked.

"You'll see. C'mon, have a seat, Lydia. The show usually happens between ten and midnight and three and five A.M."

With considerable reluctance, she plunked down next to Thorn. "Exactly what're we waiting to see?" she asked.

"Just watch." Gracie pointed directly in front of her. "It should start right over there."

"The air's getting cooler," Natalie whispered loudly. "Feel it?"

"I went through cold spots on my way in here," Thorn said.

Natalie nodded. "So did we."

Thorn thought, again, of the vanishing point. "So what are these cold areas, Gracie?"

"I think they're points where energy converges."

"What kind of energy?" Lydia asked.

"Energy from the earth."

"I don't understand. . . ." And then she fell silent as the air two hundred yards away began to glow a pale blue.

"Jesus," Thorn whispered.

Bacall broke into a frenzied barking and lunged forward; Thorn grabbed her collar and snapped on her leash. "Stay."

The blue swallowed up the darkness in the immediate vicinity and climbed fifteen feet into the air. Its glow spilled across the ground and colored their hands and faces.

"Watch what happens to this rock," Gracie said, and hurled it into the blue.

The rock didn't go through the blue to the other side. It vanished inside of it, vanished just as completely and mysteriously as Ellen had. A soft humming filled the air, the sound of a thousand celestial voices tuning up for a choir. The blue shimmered and pulsed, like some tremendous lung inhaling and exhaling. The distinct chill in the air was like standing in front of an open freezer with the cold air drifting out of it. Bacall started howling and jerking on the leash, trying to escape.

Lydia shot to her feet. "I think we'd better get out of here."

"It won't come this far," Gracie assured her.

Suddenly, Bacall broke free and tore away from him, howling and barking, and headed for the spinning blue vortex. Thorn took off after her, shouting at her to stop, heel, return, every command he could think of. Her leash slapped the ground behind her and he lunged for it, missed, and nearly fell on his goddamn face. As she closed in on the whirling vortex, the humming reached a fever pitch that drove him to his knees. He slapped his hands over his ears, but the hum pierced his skull. It felt as though needles were being pounded into his eardrums, his sinuses, into his very eyes.

Then everything went black and silent.

He came to in a black silence. But this silence extended beyond his own consciousness and reminded him of the utter silence that had surrounded the vanishing point. No birds, no grasshoppers, no ants, nothing living. *Hey, this is it. The twilight zone. I'm where*

Ellen is. He actually called her name; then a giddiness seized him and he collapsed in a fit of laughter.

Losing it, lost it, gone. Christ oh Christ.

He pulled the flashlight out of his pocket, turned it on, shone it around. Okay, it would be okay. He located Bacall just ahead of him, lying on her side, and Lydia, Gracie, Natalie, and Tom, behind him, crumpled on the ground. Were they alive? *Please be alive.*

"Hey, rise and shine," he said loudly. "Hey, people, come on. Get up."

He started to stand, but his legs felt weird and rubbery, so he crawled over to where Bacall lay. She stirred, whimpering softly, then raised her head and licked his face. Thorn rubbed his cheek against her ribs, against all that soft and infinitely touchable fur, assuring himself that she was real. Alive. *Here.*

"Max?"

"Over here, Gracie." He shone the flashlight at her. "You okay?"

"I feel like a goddamn truck ran into me."

"Lydia?"

"Yeah. I . . . I'm okay. I think."

"Give me some light on the kids, Max."

He shone the flashlight on Natalie and Tom, who were now sitting up, rubbing their hands over their faces. "What happened?" they asked simultaneously.

"I don't know," Gracie replied, and glanced at her watch. "It's four-thirty. We weren't out very long."

Thorn had believed that, too, when he'd come to near the vanishing point, only to discover later that he'd been out in the field for two full days. "Let's get out of here." He still felt shaky when he stood. Even Bacall didn't seem to be herself. She stumbled once as they made their way to the others, then ran around, tugging on her leash, sniffing at everyone's feet.

It seemed to take them a long time to reach Gracie's golf cart and even longer to get situated, doubling up to make room for everyone. No one spoke as Gracie drove back toward her house. Thorn felt as if he'd swallowed a handful of hallucinogenic mushrooms and this was the crash at the other end.

As soon as they reached Gracie's, she handed out pillows and blankets and they stretched out wherever they happened to be sitting—Natalie on the couch, Tom in the recliner, Thorn on a beanbag chair with Bacall stretched out next to him. Lydia and Gracie fell onto opposite ends of the couch. Then he shut his eyes and fatigue crashed over him.

When he woke, he heard birds and smelled fresh coffee. The room was empty; even Bacall was gone. He heard no sounds from the kitchen, no sounds at all. His head ached, he had to piss, the inside of his mouth felt as if mold were growing inside it. He staggered down the hall to the bathroom.

When he emerged a while later, his first stop was the kitchen, where he filled a mug with coffee and helped himself to one of the Danishes on a platter on the counter. He headed back through the house to the porch. The screen door squeaked as he opened it. Lydia sat on the front steps, watching Bacall and the skunk checking each other out in the yard.

"Morning," he said. "Where'd everyone go?"

"Tom had to get home and Natalie and Gracie went into town for more coffee and eggs."

Thorn sat beside her on the lowest step. "How do you feel?"

"Me?" She laughed. "Considering how little sleep I got, I should feel like hell. But I actually feel pretty good. You?"

"The same."

He noticed how pretty she looked in the morning light, her blond hair like spun glass, her skin luminous, her shale-blue eyes quick to smile. She was wearing the same clothes, denim shorts and a halter top that showed every curve of her breasts, every step in her spine. He felt a sudden and inexplicable closeness to and attraction for this woman.

She sensed him staring at her and glanced at him. "What's your take on what happened out there?"

"I don't have a clue. I was still trying to figure out what happened with that fishing boat the other night, what that was all about."

"I called around, trying to find out who owned that chopper that showed up. But no one seems to know. The Coast Guard refuses to say who owned the boat. Or maybe they don't know."

It seemed easier to talk about this incident than what had happened last night, perhaps because the boat incident had occurred within a context that was more ordinary—except for the attack by the dolphins. He didn't understand that part. Last night, however, had no place in the ordinary world. It definitely belonged in the land of the weird and the strange.

"Gracie has theories that she wants to discuss over breakfast," Lydia said. "But I don't think any of her theories include getting zapped by weird blue light."

He laughed. In spite of everything, Thorn laughed and it felt good. It felt great. It felt as though he'd stepped back fully into the land of the living. And because he felt so good and wasn't thinking about what he was doing, he reached out and brushed her soft hair off her forehead.

She seemed startled by the gesture and gave a quick, nervous laugh. "That bad, huh? I left in such a hurry last night I didn't even bring my purse or a comb or anything."

"You look great," he blurted.

And suddenly Ellen's face loomed in his mind, a haunted image. Ellen, whom he had forgotten in these few moments. He stood quickly. "Want a refill on the coffee?"

"Yeah, thanks."

He hurried inside, wondering what the hell was wrong with him. He'd just come on to a woman he barely knew, had managed to embarrass her, and now he felt like a goddamn fool. Even worse, he'd betrayed Ellen's memory.

Breakfast suited Thorn, a vegetarian cuisine of pancakes and soy bacon, fresh-squeezed OJ and Colombian coffee. And while they ate, Gracie explained her theory. Thorn didn't have any trouble with the concept of flow lines. The Chinese used energy flow lines in the practice of Feng Shui, something Ellen had been interested in. And by now, he'd read enough of Charles Fort to get the general idea. His years as a vet had proven to him that animals sensed what people could not. But he had trouble connecting some of the dots.

"I think the glow we saw last night is produced by a convergence of these energy flow lines," Gracie said. "At these points, the surge of energy is like a surge of power on the electrical grid. You get too close and it zaps you. Shocks you. I think that's what happened to us last night."

Thorn appreciated the magnitude and force of electrical power, whether it came from a socket or from lightning. He could appreciate the power that had rendered them all unconscious last night. But the bridge between the two seemed to be missing. He couldn't quite reconcile what Gracie explained with whatever power had caused Ellen to vanish. And yet, the rock she'd thrown into the blue light had disappeared, hadn't it?

"That rock you threw into the blue light last night," he said. "Was it just me or did it vanish in the light?"

"I marked it before I left the house last night, so I would be able to find it," Gracie replied. "But when I checked the area this morning, there was no sign of it. I'm assuming it vanished."

Lydia spoke up. "Things don't just vanish, Gracie."

"Not according to scientific laws as we understand them now. But discoveries in quantum physics are changing those laws daily. Maybe the paradigm is shifting."

"The scientific paradigm?"

"The reality paradigm."

"Excuse me," Natalie interjected. "What's a paradigm?"

"A set of beliefs," Thorn replied. "We all believe that the sun is going to rise in the morning, that this table is solid, that the sky is blue."

"So you're talking about our beliefs about what's real?" Natalie asked.

Gracie nodded. "Yes, in a sense. Maybe at the most fundamental levels, the laws that govern what we believe is reality are in transition. Or maybe it's just that our awareness as a race has been raised to the point where we're able to perceive it. Maybe both. But suddenly, things are happening that simply aren't possible in reality as we know it. A rock disappears in a blue light. Dolphins native to the waters off the Argentinean coast are sighted around here. Florida panthers were sighted in Colorado Springs, white wolves were seen in Kansas . . ."

She listed one strange sighting after another. Thorn's ears rang, his head ached. He wanted desperately to tell her, to tell all of them, what had happened to Ellen, what he had witnessed. *Not a rock, Gracie, but a human being.*

Then it hit him. "A portal," he said softly. "What you're really talking about is some kind of doorway between places, between physical locations. Teleportation."

"That's how Tom phrased it. I think of it as moving space-time."

"Oh, c'mon," Lydia said. "That's science fiction."

"Call it what you want," Gracie said. "But it seems to be happening all over. How else do you explain the hourglass dolphins you saw, Lydia? How else do you explain panthers in Colorado Springs? Wolves here on Piper Key?"

"I don't know how to explain it. But assuming you're right—and I'm not saying you are, Gracie—then is it possible to go back through the portal? Did the wolves go back to where they'd come from? Or the panthers?"

"Suppose one of us walked into it?" Natalie asked. "Where would we end up? Would we be changed? Would we even remember where we'd been or what had happened?"

Gracie opened her hands. "We don't know."

"The hourglass dolphins just seemed to . . . to fade away," Lydia said.

"So we'd vanish," Natalie finished. "And maybe we'd come together again in another place. LA. Or New York."

"Or in the twilight zone," Lydia remarked dryly.

Thorn imagined himself walking into the swirling blue light, that spinning vortex in the papaya grove, and emerging into wherever Ellen had gone. Yes, it was nuts. The whole goddamn thing was nuts. But he couldn't deny what he had *seen or what he'd experienced*. Ellen had vanished in front of him. A blue light had appeared in the middle of the woods and when he'd gotten too close to it, he'd been knocked unconscious. Wildlife acted strangely, his life had collapsed into unimagined weirdness. In short, he had nothing to lose. One way or another, he would find the source of the light, that portal of blue.

Seventeen

Joe Nelson rented a car at the Gainesville, Florida, airport, a plain white Ford Escort that wouldn't attract anyone's attention. He bought a local map that he un- folded as soon as he scooted behind the steering wheel and used a red marker to draw his route through town to the two-lane road that would take him to Piper Key.

Fifty miles, he thought. Fifty miles might be all that remained between him and half a million bucks. In the bigger scheme of things, what was fifty miles when he'd already traveled fifteen hundred miles? *Spit in the wind.*

It had taken him eight days and endless hours of sifting through articles on the Web and in newspapers to narrow his choices to select cities along the twenty- ninth parallel: Port Orange, Florida; New Orleans; a town in Baja California; Houston, Texas; and Piper Key. All had reported strange animal or bird behavior, exactly the sort of thing that would suck Thorn right in.

Nelson had come to understand that after his ole buddy Thorn had killed Ellen and gotten rid of her body, his mind had snapped like a matchstick. Unable to accept the truth of what he'd done, he'd concocted the crazy-ass story about birds and Ellen disappearing and by the time he'd taken off, he'd believed the story completely. So, yes, it made perfect sense that he would head to a place where other, similar oddities had happened.

Nelson had wondered about all these oddities. He figured shit like this happened all the time but he just hadn't noticed because he'd had no reason to notice. He'd been too busy being a cop, a husband, and a father to his two kids. But the more he thought about it, the more it bothered him and he didn't know why. He shoved the weird stuff into a corner of his mind and congratulated himself on how cleverly he'd handled this whole situation.

His boss had sent Nelson off with the blessing of the department and the name of a contact at the FBI office in Gainesville. He hadn't contacted the guy yet; no point to it until he was sure Thorn was on the island. His wife had acted like he was made out of gold, fussing over him before he left, fixing a great meal that had been followed by the best sex they'd had in months. She knew about the half million bucks and he supposed—bottom line—that money really was an aphrodisiac.

He'd narrowed his first two selections by size: Houston as the largest city and Piper Key as the smallest. Thorn, a man on the run, might feel that he would be safer in a large city, where he would blend in with the populace. But because Thorn hailed from a small town, Nelson thought he would feel more comfortable in a town rather than a metropolis and had decided to check out Piper Key first.

He wasn't exactly sure what this "checking out" would entail, but how difficult could it be with a permanent population of about twenty-five hundred residents? His first destination would be the newspaper

office to track down the anonymous author of the wildlife series on the *Gazette*'s website. Even though he had
no official jurisdiction in Florida, he intended to convince the *Gazette*'s editor to run Thorn's photo.

If he turned up nothing on Piper Key, his next stop
would be Houston.

He got lost trying to get out of the city. Gainesville
wasn't that huge or anything, but, Christ, compared to
Blue Mountain Lake, it could've been Tokyo. His sense
of direction had never been very good to begin with
and here, he had no lake to orient him. Even when he
finally found the two-lane road that led out of Gainesville to the coast, it felt all wrong to him. The ocean
lay to the east, not the west, and the afternoon sun
burned through the windshield the entire way.

Twenty miles outside of Piper Key, his nose started
to ache—*the nose Thorn busted, let's not forget that*—
and his eyes felt dry and scratchy from the assault of
afternoon light. He looked for a place to stop—a bar,
a café, any place that sold cold water and sandwiches.
But the road had begun to twist upward into the tall
hills that separated the mainland from the island and
didn't even provide rest stops, much less a bar or a
café.

Signs promised that the town of Roberta lay only
twelve miles away. Then ten. He didn't know if he
could last another ten miles. He felt like hell and it
wasn't just his nose. His bladder ached and his vision
seemed fuzzy at times, as if he were peering through
a translucent fabric. He finally pulled off the main
route and onto a rutted dirt road with faded signs
posted along it that read NO TRESPASSING and LIVING-
STON FARM ANIMALS.

Backcountry hicks lived in here, he thought, and

pulled his gun and a clip out of his briefcase. A half mile in, he nosed the car into the thick pines, completely off the road, so it would be invisible to anyone who approached. He snapped in the clip and got out, gun in hand.

The air smelled sweet here, like home, except it was much hotter. And still, so goddamn still. Nothing stirred—not a leaf, not a twig. Beads of sweat rolled down the sides of his face, his shirt stuck to his spine like a Band-Aid. Nelson walked farther into the trees, glanced furtively around, and relieved his bladder. He felt light-headed, hungry, and very thirsty. All he wanted to do was get into Piper Key, his first—and, hopefully, only—stop en route to the half million.

As he zipped up his fly, something moved in his peripheral vision. Nelson glanced quickly to the right. Nothing. Then it happened again, on his left this time, but again he saw nothing. "Spooky place," he murmured. Spooky in a way he couldn't define.

He started back toward his car and stopped, listening to the silence. A car. Coming this way. *Shit.* Hoping to avoid a confrontation with the redneck who owned the land, Nelson dropped quickly into a crouch and moved behind one of the trees. Moments later, the vehicle came into view—a covered military jeep with four more jeeps behind it. The vehicles sped up the road, bouncing over the ruts, dust flying up behind them.

The last vehicle stopped and two men wearing jeans, T-shirts, and heavy-duty boots, got out. The driver stood at the side of the jeep, glancing around. Buzz cut, lean, dark shades. The other guy loped down the road in the direction they'd come. A few moments later, Nelson heard a clatter and the guy called, "Hey, Dylan, lock's rusted away."

"Shit," the man named Dylan muttered. "Just leave it."

The other guy trotted back into view. "Damn thing nearly dissolved in my hand."

"Old man Livingston assured me he'd fix it," Dylan said.

His companion laughed. "Hell, he probably sits in that trailer of his drinking rotgut all day."

"For what we're paying him for the use of his land, he'd better be inside that trailer welding a new lock."

The second guy swung his body back into the jeep, but Dylan walked around it, checking the tires, the fenders, the canvas covering. A cautious guy, this Dylan. "We've got a nail in the rear left tire," Dylan called out. "Talk to someone about leveling out this road."

"Tonight?" the other guy called back.

"By tomorrow morning." On his way back to the front of the jeep, he pulled out a cell phone and punched out a number. *". . . your fuckin' ass down here and fix the busted lock . . ."*

That was all that Nelson heard of the conversation, but it was enough to convince him to get out of here fast. As soon as the jeep sped out of sight, he got to his feet and hurried toward his car, anxious to beat feet before the hick who drank rotgut in his trailer showed up. The number one rule in his professional life had never changed in twenty-one years on the force: *Don't mess with the backcountry weirdos.*

Yards away from his car, he caught movement in his peripheral vision again. He spun to the right and froze. Dozens, maybe hundreds, of fine shimmering threads fell like a veil in front of him. And on each shimmering thread hung a spider. Little spiders. Medium-size spiders. Spiders nearly as large as his fucking hand. They came in every color imaginable, a living, shimmering canvas of exquisite colors.

He sucked in his breath, his mind racing and his body paralyzed by utter terror. Only his eyes moved, darting from the right to the left, where another shimmering veil dropped from the trees, each fine thread holding a spider. And now, directly in front of him, a third veil fell, and it began to swing slowly, in unison with the other two veils.

The inside of Nelson's mouth flashed dry. *Jesus God spiders no shit fuck . . . Move fast now . . .*

For a second, he thought he could hear their bodies scraping against the threads, a brittle, dry sound, like palm fronds scraping concrete. He'd heard that sound once, long ago, when he and his wife had honeymooned on Miami Beach before its Deco revival. The air conditioner in their room had broken, they'd been arguing, he couldn't get it up, and he'd gone out onto the porch to have a smoke.

The air had felt still and hot, like this air.

It had been about the same time of day, late afternoon, and he'd stood there smoking and wishing he hadn't gotten married. Suddenly, out of nowhere, a breeze had come up and the palm fronds had rubbed against the side of the building and made this sound. For some reason, it had scared him and it definitely scared him now—not just the noise, but the goddamn spiders, oh, Christ, hundreds of them rising and falling on those fine shimmering threads, the veil around him thickening . . .

He lurched forward like a madman, waving his arms wildly and screaming. He couldn't help it, the screams exploded out of him in some unintelligible language and he felt the first brush of the threads against his arm, his cheek . . . Then he hurled open the door of the rental car and threw himself inside, slamming the door behind him. He ran his hands over his head and face and arms, making sure no webs clung to him, to his clothes. Suppose one of the little fuckers had crawled down inside his shirt?

He ran his hand down into the collar of his shirt and glanced back, through the closed window, toward the trees. Nothing there now. He was too far away, he decided, and pulled his binoculars out of his briefcase and scanned the area under the trees. *Nothing.*

Completely spooked now, he cranked up the engine and jammed his foot against the gas pedal and the car screeched out of the woods in reverse. He jammed the gearshift into DRIVE and tore up the pitted dirt road.

At the end of the road, a metal gate blocked his way. Nelson slammed on the brakes, jerked the gearshift into PARK, and leaped out with the engine idling. He flung open the gates and raced back to the car and sped out onto the main road, rear end fishtailing.

He didn't stop until he reached downtown Piper Key.

Eighteen

(1)

Early morning and the air already steamed, the humidity as thick as butter.

Lydia sat on the catwalk, watching Bacall on the platform in front of her. The dog lay on her stomach, with her snout at the edge of the water, waiting for Alpha to make up her mind about whether she wanted to play. Max crouched next to Bacall, tossing a bright red ball from one hand to the other, an enticement for the dolphin.

But so far, Alpha hadn't approached the platform. She swam with Kit on the far side of the holding tank, the two of them whistling away at each other. The early morning light created a mirror of the water's surface, reflecting the perfect blue of the summer sky. As the dolphins cut a swath across the tank, the blue shattered into a million pieces.

She'd chosen the early hour—it was barely seven— because they wouldn't be disturbed. None of her employees would arrive until eight, Natalie was still home in bed, and the first dolphin swims of the day wouldn't begin until nine. Also, she'd noticed that Alpha was friskier early in the morning, less distracted, and more curious. Max had been good enough to accommodate the hour and had shown up fifteen minutes ago with two Cuban coffees and a couple of bagels.

Lydia finished the last of the coffee as the dolphins stopped whistling. Then Alpha broke away from Kit and sped toward the platform. "Okay, Max," Lydia said softly, leaning slightly forward. "Get ready."

Bacall raised her head, ears twitching, tail starting to wag. "You know the routine, girl," Max said. "I'll toss you the ball and you take it from there."

The dog cocked her head as he spoke. To Lydia, it seemed that the retriever understood every word that he said. When Gail had asked her what the hell she hoped to accomplish by an interaction between dog and dolphin, Lydia didn't have an answer. She couldn't explain it. It simply *felt* right. Perhaps, at the heart of it, lay her hope that Alpha would respond to the dog in a way that she hadn't responded to people, except for Natalie. Her daughter was the exception.

As she approached the platform, Alpha clicked and whistled. Max tossed the ball to Bacall and she leaped up and whacked it toward the tank with her nose. Alpha, in a burst of speed, caught the ball with her beak and bounced it back to Bacall. The dog barked and smacked the ball back to the dolphin.

This time, Alpha let the ball hit the water, then pushed it across the tank to the edge of the platform. She flipped it up onto the platform so that it landed at Max's feet. "Should I throw it to her?" he asked.

Lydia stepped down onto the platform. "Let's try something a little different. You toss the ball to me, I'll toss it to Bacall, and she'll toss it to Alpha." She positioned herself at the other side of the platform and Max threw her the ball. "Hey, Bacall, catch," Lydia

called, and volleyed the ball to the dog, who sent it
flying out over the water.

Alpha caught it in midair, but instead of knocking it
back toward the platform, she hit the ball toward Kit,
who sped across the tank to catch it before it struck
the water. Pretty soon, Rainbow joined them and Lydia
and Max donned flotation vests and got into the water
with the dolphins. Bacall didn't like being excluded and
ran back and forth across the platform, barking. Then
she leaped into the water and swam toward Max. But
Alpha, clicking loudly, swam in between them. She
came right up to Bacall, so that for moments they were
nose to nose, beak to snout, with Bacall treading water.
Then she gently nudged Bacall toward the nearest
shore, never pushing too fast.

Moments later, Bacall scrambled onto another platform and shook herself dry. Alpha whistled and sped
away, toward the ball. She batted it to Kit, who tossed
it to Rainbow, who sent it flying toward Bacall. The
dog batted the ball back to Alpha. Lydia and Max,
treading water, looked at each other and laughed.

"We've been excluded," she said.

"Knocked out of the loop."

"I want to get this on tape."

She quickly got out of the water and ran over to the
bench where she'd left her gear. The dolphins hadn't
just accepted Bacall as a playmate. They had made it
clear that she didn't have to be in their element for
them to accept her. In her fifteen years here, she'd
never seen dolphins interact in quite this way with another animal species. Perhaps this videotape, she
thought, would help her obtain a grant from Greenpeace or another similar organization in the event that
her loan from the bank didn't pan out.

Suddenly, the air exploded with whistles and shrieks and the dolphins scattered. Bacall erupted in frenzied barking, but it wasn't immediately clear to Lydia whether the dog was reacting to the dolphins or to the man who strolled through the side door.

He was slender, sinewy, with his hair cut to a fine stubble, and a neatly trimmed beard and mustache. He was also wearing a T-shirt and swim trunks. Lydia set the camera aside and walked over to him. "Morning," he said.

"Hi, can I help you?"

"I hope so. I'm scheduled for an eight o'clock swim."

"Our swims don't start until nine, Mr. . . ."

"Clancy. Nick Clancy."

"Nice to meet you, Mr. Clancy. I'm Lydia Thomas. I hate to make you wait an hour, so let me check to see who can do the swim with you."

"Thanks very much. I appreciate it. You mind if I walk around?"

Lydia glanced out over the tanks. The three dolphins had fled to the farthest corner of holding tank two, where Max and Bacall now were. "Actually, I'd rather that you wait in the tiki hut right over there."

"That's fine."

"Be right back."

It bothered her that the dolphins had reacted so strongly to a stranger. In all the weeks since Alpha's arrival, the center's usual swims had continued in tanks three and four, without any obvious reactions from Alpha, Kit, and Rainbow. In all fairness to the dolphins, though, recent events had prompted her to be constantly alert for significance and meaning in the smallest things. Portents in the wind, omens inscribed in wet sand: ridiculous. The dolphins probably just resented the interruption.

She hurried on toward the office to find Pintea and ask him to take the swim.

(2)

Thorn snapped the leash on Bacall. "What's gotten into you, anyway?" he scolded her. She got that hangdog look on her face, then plopped down at his feet, rolled over on her back, and refused to budge. Thorn tugged on her leash. "C'mon, please get up. I've got a treat for you, girl."

She wasn't buying it.

He finally picked her up, all seventy pounds of her, and carried her off the catwalk. He put her down when he reached the deck. She wagged her tail, trotting alongside him now, her nose to the deck. As they approached the tiki hut, her head snapped up. She glared at the bearded guy who waited there, then lunged at him, snarling and snapping at the air. Thorn jerked hard on her leash, wrenching her back.

The man looked startled. "Hope she's had her rabies shots," he joked.

"Sorry, I don't know what's gotten into her."

The sound of the other man's voice apparently enraged Bacall and she lunged again. This time, her collar slipped off over her head and she shot toward the man with her teeth bared. He scrambled onto the stone counter to his left, grabbed one of the flotation vests, and waved it in front of Bacall to keep her away from him. Thorn shouted at her, but some deep primal instinct had seized her. She snatched the flotation vest out of the man's hand and attacked it, tearing it to shreds. "Get that monster the fuck away from me!" the man screamed.

Thorn wasn't about to go near her. He ran over to the hose with her leash around his neck, and turned it on full blast. He aimed it at her and the sudden, powerful blast shocked her. She instantly backed off to escape the blast and started shaking herself free of water. Thorn dropped the hose, plucked a towel off the picnic table, and threw it over her back. Then he lifted her in his arms and hurried through the side door.

Outside, he slipped the collar back over her head and tightened it. He snapped the leash onto the bicycle rack, then rubbed her down with the towel, talking softly to her. She whimpered and licked his face, apparently aware that she'd pissed him off and anxious to make up for it. In the five years he'd owned her, he'd never seen her act even remotely like this. If anything, she went out of her way to avoid confrontations. That left two explanations: that she was sick or she sensed something threatening about the bearded guy.

Thorn ran his hands over her fur, checking for cuts, tenderness, abrasions. He touched his nose to hers, a quick way to take her temperature; it felt normal. He checked her ears for redness, which would indicate an infection, but her ears looked fine. "Shit, you just don't like that guy, do you," he said softly.

She licked his face again. He unsnapped the leash and put her in the car, where she had a bowl of fresh water and food. Then he went back inside the center to make sure the bearded guy wasn't hurt.

When Thorn came through the gate, the man was holding the flotation vest up by two fingers, examining the damage. "I hope you're all right," Thorn said.

The man whipped around, rage in his eyes. "That goddamn dog should be quarantined." He threw the flotation vest at Thorn and it struck him in the chest. "Look at that. It could've been me."

Two months ago, he would have gone to great lengths to appease a guy like this. Now the jerk only made him mad. He threw the vest back at him. "Hey, I apologized, you weren't injured, and it won't happen again."

"The dog's a menace."

"Is there a problem here?" asked Gail Campbell as she came up behind the man.

He turned and for a split second, Thorn thought he saw recognition on Gail's face. "Uh, no, no problem," the man said quickly. "Except that he's got a rabid dog that tried to attack me."

Gail laughed. "Bacall? No way. She wouldn't harm a fly. So, Mr. Clancy, I'm Gail Campbell. I'll be the facilitator for your swim today."

Grateful that Gail had intervened before he'd lost his temper, Thorn quickly left by the side gate. All the way back to the campground, he puzzled over the expression he thought he'd seen on Gail's face.

(3)

Neither of them spoke when the gate clattered shut behind Max. Gail marched over to the pegboard in the tiki hut, jerked a flotation vest off a peg, and tossed it to Dylan.

"I know what you're thinking," he said.

"You don't have a fucking clue what I'm thinking, Dylan." She walked on past him, toward flotation tank four, where they would be out of hearing range of anyone in the building and shrouded from sight by the bottlebrush trees that grew along the seawall. "You've never had a clue."

"Look, I'm just doing my job. Learning the lay of the land."

"You left me standing on a goddamn roof as you took off in a chopper and I don't hear anything from you, no explanations, no apologies, nothing. Then you have the gall to show up here and make trouble with my boss's boyfriend."

"She's got lousy taste in men."

"No worse than me."

"That's unfair."

Gail turned her full fury on him, her anger pumping at such extreme levels that she was actually shaking. Her voice trembled with rage. "That's it, Dylan. No more. I'm out of this game. I don't have the energy for this kind of bullshit. I can't make it any clearer than that."

She turned and walked away from him along the seawall, through the shade, and out of his stinking life forever. And for those few moments, she knew the greatest freedom she'd ever experienced, a liberation so total it was as if the weight of gravity itself had fallen away from her. She felt like Peter Pan, like one of the lost boys. If she thought happy thoughts and had a sprinkling of Tinkerbell dust to boot, she would rise from the ground itself and fly on toward morning.

But then he came running up behind her, caught her arm, and spoiled it completely. "It's never finished with us, Gail. That's the whole point. That's how it's always been and how it'll always be. We're like Siamese twins joined at the heart, you and me."

"I'm not joined to anyone's heart, Dylan." She tried to wrench her arm free, but he held on.

"Listen to me," he hissed. "That boat that sank the night you came to my hotel room? It sank because *dolphins attacked it.*"

"I don't give a shit why your stupid boat sank." At the moment, she was more concerned that Lydia or Pintea would see them from the building. She veered into the heavy thickets on the vacant lot beyond the seawall. "And any story you tell me is going to be a lie, so don't bother, Dylan."

She jerked her arm free of his grasp, but he kept pace with her as she crashed through the thick brush. "Somehow, they knew we intended to harm Alpha and they rallied to protect her. Two of my men drowned. Another is still in critical condition. One moment, there were no dolphins in sight and the next moment, Gail, there were dozens, a hundred or more. They arrived *instantaneously and they vanished instantaneously.* That's what they do. Remember how I told you that dolphins were tagged and we thought the electronic devices were flawed? It wasn't our devices. It's the dolphins. Somehow, their sonar interacts with . . . with energy conduits in the planet and it . . . it moves space-time. Or they move through space-time. We still aren't sure which it is."

Gail stopped and stared at him, just stared because she didn't know what to say. He had her full attention now.

"The pod of a thousand dolphins that accompanied Alpha into this center? I'm betting they just *appeared,* Gail. Ask the kids who were in the canoe. Ask them what they saw."

It suddenly dawned on Gail that Dylan didn't want

Alpha dead. He might have at one time, but he didn't now. What he wanted now, she thought, was Alpha alive and under his scrutiny and control. Alpha, the primo navy lab rat, would lead Dylan to the secrets of space-time and he, like the loyal borg that he was, would turn it all over to the military. And given enough time and money, the military would fuck it up.

In the old days, she would leap at the opportunity to be a part of something like this. Dylan, after all, wasn't talking about the usual military cover-ups— agent orange, LSD experiments on U.S. troops, Roswell, the Kennedy assassination. Movement through space-time lay at the very core of true power. Whoever held this secret held the key to planetary control. But in her life, Dylan was the kid who had screamed wolf so many times now that doubts immediately crept in about the veracity of his story. Was any of it true? Were only parts of it true? And if so, which parts? How much did he and his military brothers really know? Or was this just Dylan's private little world?

It suddenly seemed quite likely that Dylan had diverted some of the generous funding for the mammal defense program into his own agenda. He had picked his men and paid them well above the usual military pay. He had his own private troops, for his own private war. A little Caesar, she thought.

"Christ, Gail, would you *say* something?"

"Just leave me alone for a while, Dylan. Please. I need some space." She backed away from him as she spoke. "I need some time." Her hands went up, palms facing him, as if to ward off a blow. "I need to sort stuff out."

Gail saw conflicting emotions in his eyes, a lifetime of conflicting emotions that mirrored her own struggles over the years where their relationship was concerned. It hurt her to see it and she turned and walked quickly through the thicket. He didn't come after her, but he called her name and it echoed through the heat and the brush. She broke into a run and didn't stop running until she reached her car.

(4)

Gone, everyone gone, Natalie mused, glancing around the holding areas. They'd left for lunch, her mother and Arnie and even Gail. The two veterinary students from the university had split a few minutes later and now here she was, the loner in a water world, the kid in charge. She went over to the shaded tiki hut and turned on her boom box. She popped in a Britney Spears tape and bopped back out into the hot noon light, swinging her hips and lip-synching to the music.

It wasn't dolphin music, she thought, but it spoke to a different part of her, the teen part of her who wished that Tom Maynard would slide his arm around her shoulders some night and kiss her. She shut her eyes and threw her arms out at her sides and danced along the edges of the holding tanks, vaguely aware that the dolphin trio splashed and clicked nearby.

She was supposed to hose off the vests and get everything ready for the swims at two this afternoon. But the music had captured her and she sashayed around the tanks, humming to herself. Then suddenly the music went off and a man's voice called, "Excuse me. Hello? Is there an adult I can talk to?"

She turned to see a thin man with curly dark hair going to gray at the sides. His jeans looked uncomfortably tight, the first two buttons on his shirt had come undone, and he clutched a bottle of water in his right hand. She started to say she was the adult in charge, but sensed he wouldn't appreciate the irony. "Who's asking?"

"Lieutenant Nelson." He brought something out of the back pocket of his jeans and flashed it.

Natalie was too far away to see whatever it was, but figured it was his ID. She walked over to him, irritated that he'd turned down her music. "I can't read the fine print at fifty feet."

He grinned, a sort of lopsided grin, then laughed aloud once, and handed her the ID. *Lieutenant Joe Nelson, Blue Mountain Lake, NY, PD.* "Where's Blue Mountain Lake? It sounds like a pretty place."

"It is. I'm looking for Lydia Thomas."

"She isn't here right now. Maybe I can help you."

"What time will she be back?"

"I don't know."

He slipped a piece of paper out of his briefcase and handed it to her. "You seen this guy around here?"

Natalie glanced at the photo. The man looked vaguely familiar, but a lot of people looked vaguely familiar to her, probably because so many people trekked through the center in the course of a year. Under his photo, she read about the reward offer. "Wow. Half a million dollars? What'd he do?"

"He's wanted in connection with the murder of his girlfriend. He probably showed up on the island sometime after June twenty-fifth."

"I haven't seen him around here. At least, not that I remember. But we get a lot of people at the center. You want me to post it on the bulletin board?"

"That'd be great, thanks. My number is on there."

"Okay. I'll make sure everyone sees it."

"Thanks." He raised his eyes and looked out over the tanks and the dolphins. "I, uh, read about what happened here with the dolphins. You one of the kids who was in the canoe?"

"Yeah, but I'm not allowed to talk about it."

"Why not?"

"My mom said so."

He smiled. "Your mother sounds like a wise woman. Make sure she sees that poster, okay?"

"Right."

With that, he headed for the side gate and Natalie walked over to the bulletin board under the tiki hut to pin up the flyer. As soon as she'd put it up, she couldn't stop looking at it. The man's face wasn't merely familiar now; she'd seen him somewhere before, she was sure of it. *But where?*

She unpinned the flyer, pulled a pencil out of her back pocket, and sketched over the man's face, narrowing it. She added glasses, a beard, longer hair, then she pinned it on the bulletin board and stepped back, looking at it. It hit her all at once, hit her so hard that she clutched her arms to her waist and stood there rocking back and forth on her heels, tears welling up in her eyes.

No. Impossible. Not Max.

She tore the flyer off the bulletin board, stuffed it deep down inside her backpack, and hurried outside to her bike. *Not Max. He wouldn't kill anyone. I'm not wrong about him.*

Nineteen

The afternoon light slanted low and bright over the center, nearly blinding Lydia as she moved up and down the catwalks between the tanks, feeding the dolphins. She'd been here twelve hours today, still trying to catch up for the day and a half she'd taken off after she'd gotten her Dear John letter about the grant. All her employees had left for the day; even Natalie had skipped out to spend the night with Corie.

When she finished the feeding, she went upstairs to close the office. She checked the schedule for tomorrow to see how many swims were scheduled. One, she thought, just one afternoon swim and it had been paid in full a month ago. At this rate, the center would close sooner than even she anticipated. She could only stretch the financial reserves so far; she needed a loaves-and-fishes miracle. She shut the schedule book and jotted herself a note to call the bank first thing in the morning about her loan application.

If it didn't come through, then she was out of luck and the center would close in about two weeks and she would have to put the whole place up for sale.

She left with a pall of depression sinking over her and tightness in her chest. Failure: There was no word she hated more than that.

As she got into her golf cart, Max's Explorer pulled

up. "Hey," he called. "I'm glad I caught you. I just wanted to apologize for what happened with Bacall yesterday. I've never seen her act like that."

"Don't worry about it. Gail said he was a nutcase and he didn't even stay for his swim. We get nuts from time to time."

"How about if I fix dinner for you and Nat? It's the least I can do for chasing off a client."

"You a good cook?" she asked, teasing.

"Only with my linguini and shrimp smothered in a white wine sauce."

"It sounds a whole lot more appetizing than yogurt and veggie burgers. You cook, we'll use my kitchen. And Nat's gone for the night."

"I already picked up a few groceries."

"Then follow me."

As he and Bacall followed her, she realized she felt nervous about this dinner in a teenage sort of way. Ian Cameron was the last man she'd invited to her home for dinner and that had been a week before they'd split up. It had also been the last time she'd been to bed with anyone. And for the last nine months, she hadn't missed sex, had hardly thought about it. Nor had she met anyone who remotely interested her physically. But Max interested her and it worried her.

Yes, there were definite drawbacks to no sex life and a lack of emotional intimacy. But for all these months, the advantages had outweighed the drawbacks. Her energy had been more focused and, in some ways, her life had run more smoothly. No distractions about whether the guy would call or when she would see him again or what a prolonged silence really meant. The thought of that entire syndrome, that bullshit game that men and women always seemed to play at some point, exhausted her. By the time she pulled into her driveway, she wished she'd told him she had other plans.

But she found his presence unobtrusive, easygoing, without pretension. The fact that he cooked was a major plus. Ian Cameron had loved to eat, but had never helped her cook. And forget her ex. He had relegated all kitchen duties to "women's work." Halfway through the preparation, Max decided the simmering sauce for their linguini needed a dash of some spice she'd never heard of and he drove over to the market to get what he needed.

In his absence, she set the table on the balcony that overlooked the marsh. She set a lit candle on the table and dropped three hibiscus blooms in a bowl of water as the centerpiece. Bacall seemed hungry, so she dug out her stray animal supplies and found some dry canine food that Bacall inhaled.

Within fifteen minutes, Max was back with everything he needed, plus a loaf of Cuban bread, which she sliced and buttered and popped in the toaster oven. They ate out on the balcony and shared a bottle of wine and personal stories. She already knew from Gracie that he was on sabbatical from some university out West. Now she discovered that he'd requested the sabbatical after his wife had died. This story led to hers about her divorce.

A breeze kicked in off the salt marsh and the gulf. The candle burned down, the wine vanished, and they got up and cleared the table. She rinsed the dishes and he stacked them in the dishwasher and asked about the day Alpha had arrived at the center.

"Was there anything strange that preceded the incident?"

"Strange how? The whole thing was strange."

"Were there lots of birds? Were the dolphins at the center acting unusual in any way?"

"Not that I remember." She rinsed off the frying pan and handed it to him. "But then, I was so focused on Natalie and Corie in that goddamn canoe that I probably wouldn't have noticed anyway." She glanced over at him, seeing him differently now, but unable to pinpoint the difference. "Why do you ask?"

"I don't know." He dried the frying pan and put it away. "I guess because erratic wildlife behavior seems to be a clue to whatever is going on."

"A clue or a symptom?"

"Beats the hell out of me. Where's this go?" He gestured at the glass bowl that had held salad.

"I'll put it away."

When she picked it out of the dish rack, it slipped from her hands and shattered against the top of her foot. Blood rushed out of it and splattered against the floor as she limped over to the nearest chair and collapsed into it. Max grabbed a dish towel and wrapped it around her foot. "Hold it tightly and elevate your foot. You have a first-aid kit?"

"Under the kitchen sink." She propped her foot on the edge of the kitchen table and pressed down to stem the flow of blood, but it began to soak through the towel.

Max hurried over to the table with the first-aid kit, an ice compress, and a stool. He tilted his glasses back onto the top of his head, sat on the stool, and eased her foot onto his thigh. Then he applied the compress to the top of her foot. "Hold it, will you? And keep pressure on it."

He popped open the first-aid kit and proceeded to remove the items he would need. He worked with the smooth assurance of a pro, she noticed, never flinching at the sight of blood, never faltering with uncertainty about what to do next. This guy, she thought, was no college professor on sabbatical.

"Let me guess," she said. "You took an EMT course, right?"

"You got it."

Uh-uh. The expertise with which he treated her foot hinted at something far more than an EMT course, but she didn't say it. Max, she decided, was a man with secrets and those secrets were none of her business.

"I'd better clean up that mess," she said when he was finished, and started to get up.

He touched her shoulders, keeping her in the chair. "I'll get it. You stay put."

Their eyes locked and she knew that hers reflected the same desire that she saw in his. He leaned forward and touched her chin, lifting it ever so slightly, and kissed her. His mouth tasted faintly of wine and undiscovered countries, and the kiss quickly exploded with chemistry. She broke the connection first, pulling back, and ran her hand over his beard. "You're going to make my foot bleed again, Max."

He laughed. "That's easy to take care of." He slid an arm under her legs and picked her up out of the chair and carried her into the bedroom.

It was hardly the most romantic spot in the house, her bed unmade, the desk cluttered with unpaid bills and other financial papers. But Max didn't seem to notice any of it. He set her gently on the bed and stretched out alongside her and kissed her again.

The last of the light slanted through the blinds and fell across the bed in gold bands. He got up at one point and closed the blinds completely and stripped off his clothes. Then he returned to the bed and slowly undressed her, his every caress electric. Sound vanished from the world, her mind emptied, and there was only a sequence of exhilarating sensations, each more exquisite than the last.

He read her with his hands and his mouth and brought her to the edge and held her there, her body twitching, hips rising, fingers knotted in the sheets. She gasped when he finally slipped inside her and the dark tide of her hunger swept her away.

Afterward, they talked quietly in the dark, first about her life on Piper Key, then about his early childhood in upstate New York as the only child of a vet and horse breeder. He didn't mention his marriage or his wife's death, which suited her just fine. None of that belonged in bed with them, something that Cameron, with his string of ex-lovers, had never understood. Now and then, Max lifted up on his elbow to stroke the line of her jaw or brush strands of hair from her forehead and cheek. She liked that, liked the continued contact, and liked it even more when he began to run his hand over her hipbone and between her thighs, stroking her with the sheet between them.

"That makes me crazy," she whispered.

"That's the idea," he whispered back, and reached under the sheet and slipped his fingers inside of her and it started all over again.

She is in the woods, watching the blue light expand and grow. It seems to seep from the ground itself and a soft humming emanates from it. She knows she's supposed to step into it, but fear grips her, she can't move toward it, can't move at all. But she knows she must because the light will lead her to Natalie, her daughter is lost in the light.

Suddenly, Max grabs her hand and together they run toward the light but it moves. It darts through the darkness like a living thing, eluding them, teasing them. They reach the edge of the cliff and can see the light far below them, on the beach, a blue tube that shoots from the sand to the stars. "We have to jump, "Max says.

"It's a hundred feet down," she replies.

"Trust, it's about trust." And then he releases her hand and leaps and vanishes into the light.

She woke abruptly from the dream and lay there, breathing hard, terrified. Max stirred beside her and she turned on her side, toward him, drawing comfort from his presence in the dark. She didn't realize how much she had missed this, the feel of warm skin against her own in the middle of the night.

He reached out and draped his arm over her hip and drew her closer. "You smell good," he murmured.

"I thought you were asleep."

"I was." He ran his hand over her spine, then rolled her onto her back and drew his tongue around her breast. She slid her fingers through his hair, all of it perfectly white, and she wondered if there was a story about it. A father who had been prematurely gray, genes, maybe trauma. She brought his mouth to her own and tasted his sleep, his dreams. It occurred to her that Max kissed well, a subtle art form that her ex had never mastered and that Ian had never gotten, either.

His hands roamed again, intrepid explorers with their own agenda, priming her skin for the slow free fall of his mouth. His tongue left a warm, moist trail across her belly, lingering here, there, as if he were sampling chocolates. Nerves lit up, tissue sprang to life, and her hips raised suddenly from the bed, an instinctive, involuntary motion, as if he were imparting the gift of flight. Then his tongue slipped over her, around her, and her breath exploded from her mouth. Her nails sank into his scalp, his shoulders, but he didn't stop. This languid glide grew progressively more intense, tighter, more powerful. She began to shudder. Her arms dropped to her sides and her fingers clenched the sheets, and just as the waves of intense pleasure began to sweep through her, he slipped inside her.

She cried when she came, cried for all the wrong reasons. It had been so long since she'd felt anything even remotely like this—not just the sex, but the raw power of emotional release, as if she'd been purged of something she hadn't even realized existed.

Piper Key Gazette
Wildlife Column
August 3, 1999

The stirring of a butterfly's wings in Beijing today can cause a storm in New York next month. Sounds preposterous, doesn't it. But the butterfly effect, as it's called, is an intricate part of chaos theory and implies a vital connection among all living things.

Now suppose that the connection is facilitated by electromagnetic energy flows or currents within the planet itself. For centuries, native people have known about these currents. In China, they're known as lung-mei, the paths of the dragon or creation paths. They form the heart of Feng Shui, the Chinese art of placing objects where they are most harmonious with their environment. In Ireland, they are the road of the faeries. The Hopi Indians use these currents for mental communication during rituals. In Australia, the aborigines follow these currents in their walkabouts. In popular culture, these currents are called ley lines and have been used as possible explanations for everything from aircraft that disappear into the Bermuda triangle, UFOs, and even for the alleged disappearance of the USS Eldridge, better known as the ship that vanished in the "Philadelphia experiment."

Is it possible that the electromagnetic surge from these ley lines somehow alters the space-time continuum? Could that be a possible explanation for how the gray wolf and her pup got to Piper Key? Could it explain the sighting of a Florida panther in Kansas City?

If these surges are actually happening, and I be-

lieve they are and that they may even be visible and measurable at certain times, then it's very likely that animals are sensitive to them. Perhaps that's why hundreds of pelicans filled the beaches in Port Orange, Florida. Or why a thousand dolphins converged off the shores of Piper Key. Or why the woman in Houston, Texas, was attacked by owls.

But the more disturbing element is what the surges mean and why the effects seemed to be concentrated primarily at the twenty-ninth parallel. Which brings me back to the butterfly and my own experience with the fluttering of wings.

Many years ago, I was assigned to a high-security military unit at sea. On this ship was a room with a large steel door that was off-limits to everyone. We were told it contained an emergency power generator for the ship, a story that I never bought.

During the days and weeks I was on board the ship, my curiosity about the locked door became so great that I finally decided to break in and see what was really in there. I planned the break-in so carefully that when it came down to the actual event, it went flawlessly.

I stepped into the room at exactly 2:07:00 A.M. I noted the time because I knew I had about five minutes before the security guard's rounds brought him back by the steel door. The moment I stepped into this room, I was drawn to the soft blue glow emitted by a pair of spherical machines that rested against the floor. They weren't large, maybe waist high, and they hummed, a rather pleasant sound that seemed to affect my mood, making me feel quite tranquil, almost cavalier, about where I was.

The machines appeared to vibrate and when I

touched my hand to one of them, I could feel the vibration. They were made out of a material I'd never seen before, something that looked and felt like metal, cool and smooth, and yet I knew the material wasn't really metal. It was camouflage, that's the only way I can describe it.

The machines didn't appear to be connected to anything, except each other, through a long tube made of the same material. I found two switches on the side of each machine. When I flipped one of the switches, the machine's glow instantly dimmed and the glow in its twin instantly brightened. Intrigued, I checked the time just to make sure I wouldn't be caught in there. It was now 2:10 on the nose. I had two minutes to play with before the security guard appeared, so I threw the other switch.

Suddenly, the blue glow enveloped me and filled the room. The hum got louder, then its pitch leaped for the sky. I recall slapping my hands over my ears and squeezing my eyes shut and wishing I was back in my bunk and had never ventured in here. And then, just as suddenly, that's exactly where I was, in my bunk. The time was 2:10:03. In other words, three seconds had passed since I'd thrown the switch.

For a long time afterward, I could still hear the humming. I finally got up and dug out a pair of ear plugs. Once I put them in, I was able to fall asleep. This wasn't a dream or a vision or any kind of hallucination. I had no sense of movement. Over the years, I've reviewed this event thousands of times, seeking some detail I might have missed before. But the specifics and the sequence of events have never changed: the blue glow, the piercing hum, the in-

tense desire to be in my bunk. I've formulated and discarded numerous theories about what happened that night, in those three seconds.

Until now, I've never mentioned this incident to anyone. But I am certain that this flutter of wings, a mere three seconds in the cosmic scheme of things, affected what happened the next night.

We were quite a few miles off the coast, conducting a night experiment with several dolphins that had been caught specifically for training purposes. We had spotlights trained on the dolphins. Suddenly, the ship started vibrating and I heard that same humming that I'd heard in the room the night before. It rapidly increased in pitch and volume and the people around me were frantically trying to cover their ears and get away from the sound. But there was no getting away from it.

I had the earplugs in my pocket and quickly put them in my ears. So while everyone else was running around to get away from the sound, I turned toward the water to see if the dolphins heard it as well. They were swimming in wild, erratic circles very close to the ship, dangerously close. Even though I couldn't hear them because of the plugs, I sensed that they were whistling and shrieking at each other. Suddenly, the older of the two dolphins started to fade and then it just vanished. Moments later, the same thing happened to the second dolphin.

Other people on board saw it, too, and mayhem broke out, utter chaos. By this time, I'd taken out the plugs and I could no longer hear the humming. But I heard shouts and people barking orders, a hundred men and women all moving and talking at

once. Then the first dolphin reappeared. Before anyone had a chance to get into the water to do a
visual check, something slammed into the boat and
we started to sink.

I always wore a flotation vest when I was on
board—call it paranoia, but that vest saved my life.
I inflated it and leaped overboard and that's when
I heard the horrifying shrieks and realized they were
coming from the second dolphin. Its body was embedded in the hull of the ship, as if its skin and
muscles had grown into it. Its head protruded from
one side, its flukes protruded from the other. It
struggled vainly to escape and every time it moved,
the ship rocked violently, taking on more water.

The other dolphin raced back and forth as the
ship sank, banging into the hull, trying to free its
mate, its shrieks filled with excruciating pain. I
started swimming and didn't look back.

I woke up in the base hospital with no memory
of how I got there. But I remembered everything
else in vivid detail. When I was questioned about
the incident, I feigned amnesia. Some months later,
when they were sure I really didn't remember what
had happened, I was transferred. I later discovered
that out of the hundred people on board, only half
of us survived. Of those fifty, another half were discharged for medical reasons. The incident was buried; officially, it never happened.

So what were these machines? In retrospect, I
believe they were able to draw on the earth's electromagnetic energy to generate tremendous amounts
of electrons, which were then harnessed for some
purpose and supplied almost limitless energy.
Maybe these machines actually powered the ship. I

don't know. When I threw the two switches on one machine, I think I altered the output of power, which resulted in an almost instantaneous relocation of energy. In short, these machines were, I believe, capable of pulling space-time from one place to another.

In my case, since I was well within the range of the machines' power, the relocation was to my bunk, the place I most wanted to be at the time. I don't know where the dolphins went where they left. But something went horribly wrong when the second dolphin snapped back.

Years later, I ran into one of the men who had been on that ship. He'd been medically discharged and had had emotional problems ever since. But we talked about that night, he and I, and I believe that we achieved some sort of closure.

There's a certain comfort, after all, in knowing that despite circumstances that were bizarre, extraordinary, and totally impossible according to our current understanding of scientific laws, neither of us was alone. In this way, perhaps, we are like the survivors of any group—from alien abductees to POWs to people who go through near-death experiences. But in this instance, we experienced the same event and agreed on what had happened: the humming, the blue glow to everything, and that a dolphin got stuck in the hull of our ship and that's what sank it.

Unlike my friend, however, I at least have theories about what caused it. I also have quite a bit of guilt because I suspect that my breaking into the locked room and meddling with those switches somehow upset their delicate balance and caused

*them to malfunction the following night. I suspect
I was the butterfly in Beijing who created a storm
elsewhere.*

*Since this column, like all the others, is posted
on our website, available to anyone, let me add this.
The incident I just related won't be found in any
files, classified or unclassified, because, officially,
it never happened. Explanations had to be given to
the families of men who had died, however. So the
dead had died "in the line of duty" and, undoubtedly, a colorful story had been dreamed up.*

*Like the Philadelphia experiment and the truth
about Roswell, this incident has been buried. But
that doesn't mean the research and development of
the technology that led to it has stopped. Perhaps
now the military has bigger and better and more
efficient machines like the pair I saw. Perhaps they
are made of new alloys. Or maybe there's an installation on or near Piper Key that's producing this
kind of energy and the technology now exists to direct it. If so, then we need to be ever vigilant—and
afraid. Very afraid.*

*Witness
Visit our website at
www.piperkeygazette.com*

Twenty

Thorn left without waking Lydia, left with his dog, his guilt, and his confusion, and drove over to a café on the beach for breakfast. He lowered the car windows for Bacall, filled her dish with water, and promised her that he would be back shortly.

He bought a copy of the *Gazette* and sat by himself at an end table on the outside deck, the gulf a smooth blue mirror as far as he could see. There, he struggled with his conscience.

He had betrayed Ellen and the memory of their years together. And for what? A single night of intimacy and human contact? No, more than that. Chemistry, lust, and a deep, inexplicable attraction for Lydia. In his heart, though, he suspected that his anger at Ellen for not marrying him had begun to squeeze out the love he'd felt for her.

In retrospect, he'd come to view her decision not to marry him as the point where his life had diverged, propelling him down a road that had ended here, on Piper Key, hiding from Joe Nelson and old man Bradshaw, and waiting for whatever would happen next.

All this aside, his actions last night may have put him at considerable risk. He had created a colorful fiction of his adult life in Seattle, a fiction so convincing that at times last night he almost had believed it himself. But so many gaps existed in that fiction that Lydia might start asking questions that he couldn't answer. The worst-case scenario was that she would be sufficiently suspicious to lift his prints from her house and have her ex-lover, the cop, run them through the computer. He would end up in jail and Ellen would remain forever lost to him.

The least he could have done was to tell Lydia the truth. *The woman I lived with for seven years faded and disappeared in front of my eyes* . . . Sure. He would sound like a candidate for a padded cell. It was one thing for them to speculate together about what the blue light in the woods had been about. The fact that they hadn't been the only witnesses to it and that Gracie had a theory about it somehow made it easier to swallow. But he'd been the only witness to Ellen's disappearance and was also a man on the lam.

His breakfast arrived and he opened this morning's edition of the *Piper Key Gazette* and turned to the wildlife column. He read it twice, his excitement so palpable that he could barely swallow his food. *This is it, what I've been waiting for. This is the next step. Hell, this may be* it.

He wolfed down his breakfast, grabbed his bill, and went inside to pay. As he stood in line at the register, he happened to glance out at the deck where he'd been sitting and everything around him went still. He couldn't wrench his eyes away from the guy coming up the steps. *Impossible. It can't be him.* He kept staring, trying to get a better look at the guy's face, but he had a baseball cap tugged down low over his eyes.

Then the guy pulled out a chair at one of the tables and sat down, offering Thorn an unimpeded view of his profile. Thorn gaped, his heart slammed into his throat, and he did an about-face and headed for the men's room.

Joe Nelson. Here. Christ. Got to get out today. Immediately.

He locked himself in one of the stalls and almost immediately began to shake. Shudders rocked through him and he backed up to the door, arms clutched against him, certain he would puke. How had Nelson figured out he was here?

Same way you figured out where to go, asshole. Surf the Web, look for the weird shit, follow your hunches. Or through his e-mail?

He waited in the stall, his mind racing, scrambling to slap together a plan. He had to walk out there and pay the bill. That ranked at the top of the plan. He thought he could manage it without Nelson seeing him, but then what? Had Nelson seen his car?

Probably not. He'd parked one street over, where parking spaces were usually easier to come by. Okay, fine. He felt reasonably certain he could get to his car without being seen. This thought calmed him and after a few minutes, he stopped shaking and walked out of the stall.

Get into your car and . . . what? Just what the hell was he going to do? Race back to Gracie's and pack up the camper? And go where? Just how far could he run before someone, somewhere, recognized him or Nelson found him?

He suddenly knew, again, that he wouldn't run, that he couldn't. His best leads lay here, at the source of that blue light and with the man who called himself witness. Find witness, find the source of that light, and he would find Ellen and vindicate himself. *Fuck running.*

He made it to the register, waited in line again, and glanced quickly toward the deck. Nelson had his food now and was reading the *Gazette*.

Take a look at the wildlife column, Joe. Then tell me I'm nuts.

Thorn handed the cashier a ten, pocketed his change, and slipped outside. Then he walked very fast to the next block, where Bacall waited patiently in the passenger seat. She barked when she saw him and licked his hand and arm as he slid behind the wheel. "I know, I know. It's hot out here and you missed me. I missed you, too. But right now, we've got to beat feet, girl."

She cocked her head and gave him one of those looks that made him suspect she understood every word he said.

He drove downtown to the *Gazette* office. Unlike most of the homes on the island, the office didn't stand on stilts. Wedged between a bakery and a real-estate company, it had a WELCOME mat out front and a sign on the door that proudly announced its service to the community since 1875. Thorn pulled into the tiny parking lot, then hesitated.

Maybe Nelson had been here first, stopped by with that same photo the *Times* and other newspapers had run. Just in case, Thorn put on sunglasses and grabbed his baseball cap from the dash. He pulled it down onto his head and looked in the rearview mirror. Did he look like that guy in the photo?

"Not by a long shot," he murmured.

Thorn got out and went into the office, where the elderly woman at the front desk gave him a big smile that dimpled the corners of her mouth. She was on one phone and a second was ringing and in between, he asked if he could speak to the editor.

"You sure can, if we can get him between calls. The response to this morning's column has been absolutely incredible."

A few minutes later he entered a small, cluttered office at the back of the building. Rusty Franklin looked like the Pillsbury doughboy, with a head so bald and polished that it gleamed. "Nice to meet you, Mr. Howard. Have a seat, please. If you can find room," he said with a laugh. "Just set that stuff on the floor."

"I'm a big fan of your wildlife columns."

"You and me both. The phone hasn't stopped ringing since I came in two hours ago. The response to today's column has been incredible."

"I have some information that he might be able to use and was wondering if it might be possible to speak to him in person."

"I wish I could help you, but I don't have the faintest idea who the witness is. I don't even know whether he's a he or a she." He smiled at that. "Or how old he or she is."

"How do you pay him?"

"I don't. He does it for free. Two, maybe three years ago, I got an e-mail from him, with a sample column. He asked if I would run it. I loved it and ran it and the column's been in the paper ever since. I've offered to pay him, but he says he prefers to remain anonymous." Franklin sat forward, his pudgy fingers laced together. "About the only thing you can do, Mr. Howard, is drop him an e-mail and ask him to meet with you. Maybe he will. If you don't have a computer, there's a café just down the block with Internet access."

Franklin's suggestion made Thorn realize it would behoove him if this witness person knew as little as possible about him. The Internet provider the café used would provide that anonymity. Just in case this guy wanted to get in touch with him, Thorn would leave the number of a toll phone somewhere in town and a time for the witness to call that number.

No, that wouldn't work. Suppose this guy didn't pick up his e-mail for a day or two? He didn't want to use his own e-mail address, just in case Joe Nelson was monitoring it. He needed an intermediary, someone who wouldn't ask questions.

Tom Maynard.

Natalie had told Thorn that Maynard was a whiz with computers. Worth a try, he decided. He let Bacall out of the car, snapped a leash on her collar, and walked up the street to the nearest pay phone. Maynard answered on the second ring, his voice gruff and hoarse, as if Thorn had awakened him. "Yo, Ben's Grill."

"I'd like to place an order for delivery," Thorn said with a laugh.

"Hey, Max." He cleared his throat. "Is the sun up yet?"

"It's past nine. Listen, I need a favor."

"Sure thing, man. What's up?"

"I think I'm on to something with that blue light we saw."

"Yeah? You figured out what the hell it was?"

"I'm getting closer. But I need an e-mail address to get a response from someone. Natalie tells me you're the next Bill Gates. Can you set me up something temporary that would be good for, say, two days? I'll pay you whatever your going rate is."

"Forget the pay, man. This is the kinda stuff I love doing. When do you need the e-mail address?"

"The sooner the better."

"Call me back in an hour. I'll have it then."

Thorn hung up and he and his dog walked on toward the café. The morning air already felt oppressive, but he enjoyed the rich, powerful scents of salt water and high summer, of heat simmering against the asphalt road. He liked the dense shadows that the trees cast on the ground, the vividly colored flowers that exploded from such unexpected places, the emerald greens, the pastels of the buildings. Everything on this island existed lushly, excessively, without compromise. Last night with Lydia had held that same quality. For that matter, every experience he'd had since he'd arrived had been of this all-or-nothing variety.

Maybe, he thought, that in itself held a key for him.

Outside the café, he tied Bacall's leash to a tree and she immediately rolled around on the grass. Due to the summer lull in the tourist business, only a few die-hard caffeine addicts occupied the café. Despite the heat, they sat sipping espressos and cappuccinos beneath slow-moving fans that stirred the cool air. The four computer terminals were empty.

Thorn bought an espresso and a croissant and sat at a table, composing his e-mail on a napkin. He kept glancing at his watch and then at the clock on the wall and seventy minutes later, he called Maynard back.

"Okay, for the next forty-eight hours, you're Bogie at yahoo dot com."

Bogie and Bacall. Very cute. "That's it?"

"That's it. It'll come through one of my computers and as soon as I get the response, I'll bring it up to the campground or call you."

"I can't thank you enough, Tom."

"Just let me know what you find out, Max. I need

to know where that stone went that Gracie threw into the light."

And I need to know where Ellen went. "You have my word."

Thorn went over to one of the terminals and went to work. Just from the tone of the wildlife columns, he sensed that the witness, whoever he was, wouldn't question whether Ellen had *really* faded and vanished. This guy wasn't Joe Nelson. He wasn't about consensus reality. He would read the e-mail and he would respond because he would *recognize the event as a part of a pattern.* The big question, however, was whether he would share what he knew with Thorn.

Dear Witness,

    On the morning of June 9th, the woman I'd been living with for seven years went out for her daily run. I watched her for a few minutes and then started to go back inside when she suddenly began to scream. Before I reached her, she started to fade. And then she winked out like a dying star. Vanished completely.

    For moments afterward, I was gripping her legs, holding on to her, holding on to what I couldn't see. And then even that was gone. I didn't live anywhere within the twenty-ninth parallel at that time. The ground within three feet of the vanishing point was utterly barren. Nothing living would come near it. This event was preceded by erratic wildlife behavior among birds.

    Since then, I have observed other similar events in the twenty-ninth parallel. I would like to discuss these events with you. I need answers and feel certain that we each hold pieces of a vast puzzle.

                                        Bogie

When Thorn got back to his camper around noon, Tom Maynard's truck was parked out front. He got out and handed Thorn a sheet of paper. "It's not much, Max."

That was the understatement of the year. The reply consisted of three words: *You have proof?*

"Do you?" Maynard asked.

"Do I what?"

"Have proof."

"I don't know if it's the kind of proof this guy's looking for."

"But you have something?"

"Videotapes. Autopsy results . . ."

"Then you tell him you have proof, right?" Maynard said.

"Right."

"Good. That's what I told him."

Thorn balked. "You already responded?"

"Sure. Tempus fugit and all that shit. He'll be in touch about where and when you should meet."

"You took liberties, Tom."

Maynard leaned against the side of his truck and rubbed his unshaven jaw. He shifted his weight from one foot to the other. He seemed to study the ground right in front of him. Then he raised his large blue eyes and fingered the skinny little ponytail at the back of his head. "Max Thorn, late thirties, veterinarian in the picturesque town of Blue Mountain Lake, wanted for the murder of his lover, Ellen Bradshaw. Her old man is a big shot New York criminal attorney. Lots of family money. Enough family money to put up half a mil for info leading to Thorn's arrest. He assaulted the cop in charge of the investigation when . . ."

"I didn't assault him," Thorn said, hotly. I had to tie him up to get out of there."

They both looked down at the ground. Thorn's heart beat very fast. Neither of them said anything until Thorn finally broke the silence. "How . . ."

"Witness didn't delete your message in his response."

For Thorn, it was the equivalent of a computer programmer way back when forgetting to make the years four digits instead of two. His personal Y2K. And any second now, Joe Nelson would step out from behind the trailer, grinning with glee.

"As soon as I read the part about the birds," Maynard went on, "the rest was pretty easy. The blond hair, beard, and glasses threw me at first, though."

"It apparently wasn't enough."

Maynard jammed his hands in the pockets of his shorts. "Look, man, I got no interest in busting you. Maybe I'd feel different if Nat and I hadn't gone to Gracie's that night. Maybe I'd be talking to the cops right now if I hadn't seen that light or seen it swallow the stone that Gracie threw into it and seen what's been happening with the wildlife around here. Maybe I'd feel a whole lot different if I hadn't gotten zapped. But I did and that changed a lotta shit for me. So I'd like to hear about what happened. I'd like to see your videotape."

"And then what?"

Maynard, eighteen years old and wise beyond Thorn's comprehension, merely shrugged. "Either way, I'm not the guy who turns you into the cops."

Thorn hesitated. His new life, his new world, had been insulated so well that he didn't know what the hell to make of this kid. But Christ, he needed input, another opinion, another brain. He needed knowledge and insight that Maynard might just have. He needed an ally.

"Come on in," Thorn said.

Twenty-one

(1)

The ringing seemed distant at first, the way sounds often had whenever she was diving in the Pacific waters off Australia. And Gail, groggy from only two hours of sleep, thought it was the doorbell.

"Go away," she murmured, and pressed her face deeper into the pillow, trying to slide back into the dream she'd been having. Something about Dylan in happier, better times.

On the second ring, she realized it was her fax line and sat straight up in bed, blinking hard to clear her eyes of sleep. She looked over at the clock, saw that it was only 6 A.M., and knew the fax was from Dylan. What lie would it be this time? Or, more to the point, what did he want from her? She hadn't returned his calls since the day he'd shown up at the center, so this was right in keeping with his usual behavior. She supposed that if she didn't respond to his fax, he would show up here with flowers or gifts, all those sweet nothings.

But this time, she thought, she wouldn't be here.

She'd stayed up until four this morning, weeding through her belongings, selecting what she would store and what she would take with her. She didn't have any idea where she would go, but the where didn't much matter. Distance mattered. Australia. Chile. Greece. Some place where his vast resources didn't amount to anything.

She shuffled into her den. Two pages of the fax had already slid into the tray and a third was on the way. She picked up the first two sheets. The top one, the cover sheet, had three words scrawled on it: *butterflies in bejing,* as if she were supposed to know what the hell that meant. Gail glanced at the second sheet, expecting a serious letter from Dylan. Instead, it was the most recent wildlife column from the *Piper Key Gazette,* a paper she'd never read and had used, in fact, for wrapping fish.

The article astonished her—not that the described incidents had happened, but that the information brought together the numerous loose ends in her knowledge and did it simply, which was something Dylan, with all his lies and machinations, had never managed to do. The fact that he'd faxed it to her, that he'd brought it to her attention at six in the morning, meant that he'd known about it and that it was true.

And it means he sees it as a threat to whatever is really going on now.

The last page confirmed it. Dylan had written: *Gail, if you have any idea who this witness person is, please call my cell phone # ASAP. As always, D*

She couldn't find a fax number anywhere on the sheets and her caller ID showed the number as unavailable. It annoyed her, all this secrecy. She argued with herself, mentally listing the numerous reasons why his location didn't matter. In the end, though, her curiosity won. She opened the bottom drawer of her desk and brought out a minicassette recorder and a gadget Dylan had given her several years ago, when she'd gotten a string of hang-up calls.

She connected the gadget to the recorder, turned it on, and hit *Redial*. As the recorder picked up the digital sounds of the numbers as they were redialed, they appeared one by one in the gadget's window. The area code was the same as hers, but she didn't recognize the number. *Okay, Gail. Do you really want to open this envelope?*

"Absolutely," she murmured, and called her contact at Alachua Bell.

Twenty minutes later, she had an address outside of Roberta and a name, a female name: Liv Ingston. Dylan's honey, a European babe along the same lines as Liv Ulman, but probably younger, much younger, Gail mused. She imagined a svelte young thing whom Dylan had set up in a house, a job, a life. Or maybe the woman was closer to his own age, a divorcee or a widow, someone with kids. Maybe she'd had kids with Dylan.

Oddly, she didn't feel enraged or depressed or even sad about this new information. She felt nothing at all. She'd spent so many years expecting something like this, preparing herself emotionally for this discovery, that it seemed she'd bottomed out in the feeling department.

She made copies of the fax and the column, then went over to the closet and brought down a thick photo album. She ran her hand slowly over the cover and touched her fingertips to the meticulous lettering on the front: *Dylan*.

She slipped the original fax and a copy of the column between the transparent pages toward the back of the album, right after the note that had accompanied the bouquet of flowers that Dylan had left on her coffee table earlier this summer. She now had an even dozen of these albums, crammed with photos and memorabilia from the best and worst of times with Dylan. The earliest photo in the albums dated from the days in Cuba, when she and Dylan were toddlers in diapers. This album had nearly reached the end, but she doubted she would be buying a thirteenth to continue the tradition.

She returned the album to the shelf and opened a drawer of her file cabinet. It held about fifty files, each one neatly dated and categorized according to type. Letters. Faxes. Notes. Miscellaneous. She selected certain pieces, only the passionate and the profane, the extremes, and made sure they covered at least twenty years. She put these in a separate file folder and printed *Liv Ingston* on the label.

Her cool detachment surprised her. It seemed that on some level her preparation for this moment had been more thorough than she consciously had realized. She knew how this would go, what she would do. She would knock on this woman's door. She would introduce herself. She would hand her the file and say, *When he starts calling you Livvy, run for the hills.*

Liv, naturally curious about who the hell Gail was, would open the file and read it. And when Liv saw Dylan, who undoubtedly had told her nothing about Gail or their long and convoluted history, she would thrust the file at him and demand to know the truth. The shit would hit the proverbial fan.

Gail smiled as this sequence of events unrolled in her head. She couldn't change Dylan. She couldn't fight him anymore. She understood that clearly now. She couldn't hate him or love him without driving herself crazy. But she could definitely get even with him.

* * *

(2)

Lydia eased her body over the edge of the catwalk, into the warm gulf waters. On the other side of the tank, Alpha swam languidly, eyeing her. Rainbow and Kit hovered nearby, alert but trusting.

She let a little air out of her flotation vest and treaded water in the middle of the tank, waiting for one of the dolphins to approach her. *I need to talk to you,* she thought. *I need to explain what's going to be happening.* Alpha approached her first, moving neither slowly nor fast, as if to say she merely felt curious. Lydia placed her palms flat against the water and the dolphin came up under them, inviting her to grab on to her dorsal for a playful swim. Lydia gripped the dorsal and Alpha sped across the tank toward her two buddies, and passed her off to Kit, who then passed her off to Rainbow. It was like a relay race, Lydia thought, exhilarating but beside the point. She finally let go of Kit's dorsal and treaded water in the middle of the tank.

"Here's the deal. The bank turned me down." Her voice dropped at the end of the last sentence; emotion bubbled up in the back of her throat. "Greenpeace is fascinated with our work here, but they're strapped for funds right now. The vet school in Gainesville is pleased with our little exchange program, but they don't have the kind of funds I need. So I've got to sell." Her voice broke. Tears rolled down her cheeks. Alpha circled Lydia as she talked. "By tomorrow, the facility will be listed for sale on the net and for-sale signs are going up. I can keep you guys another week, then I have to release you."

Alpha clicked, scanning Lydia from every angle, then

came right up to her and opened her mouth. Lydia, sobbing almost uncontrollably now, reached out and stroked the dolphin's tongue. She kept clicking and the other two dolphins now approached, clicking and whistling. Several yards from Lydia, they separated and Rainbow swam up on Lydia's left and Kit, on her right. They surrounded her, their clicks and whistles creating sounds she'd never heard before, sounds that swirled around her until she heard the music in those swirls, the subtleties of composition.

Then, from somewhere behind her, she heard flute music, and she turned in the water and saw her daughter moving quickly down the catwalk, a silhouette against the light, her head held high, the flute to her mouth. She looked like a mythical piped piper, a little Kokopelli, a being so magical that Lydia suddenly wondered how they could possibly be related. The exquisite notes drifted through the heat, out over the water, and the three dolphins responded with music that was equally exquisite and mysterious.

This is what Natalie heard the day she fell into the tank and Kit rescued her. This is why she plays the flute.

Natalie, still playing, stepped down onto the floating catwalk. Rainbow and Kit moved toward her and Alpha sank and came up under Lydia, lifting her out of the water on her massive back. Then she sped across the tank. The hot wind burned Lydia's eyes and she threw herself forward, arms embracing Alpha's sides so she wouldn't fall off. She pressed her cheek to the scarred, rubbery skin along the dolphin's back and shut her eyes. The music followed her, surrounded her, suffused her tissues, her very blood. Then Alpha dived, water closed over Lydia, and there was only the vast, eerie silence of a world that would never be her world.

Moments later, the dolphin surfaced again and turned so abruptly that Lydia slid off. Her vest had lost its air and hung limply against her chest, but it didn't matter. Alpha had left her at the edge of the catwalk and Natalie reached out her hand and pulled Lydia out of the water.

She sat there, her limbs tingling, her chest rising and falling, and watched the trio swim away. Natalie touched her shoulder. "You okay, Mom?"

Lydia nodded. "They understood, Nat. They understood that I've got to sell the center."

The horror in her daughter's expression reflected everything that Lydia had felt before she'd gotten into the water. "But not all the dolphins are ready. . . ."

"I'll find places for the ones that aren't ready. I have contacts all over the state. I don't have any choice, honey."

Natalie unzipped her pack and pulled out a page from the *Gazette*. "Did you see this? It was in yesterday's paper. This is what's happening here on the island, Mom. *This* is why you saw hourglass dolphins and why the stone disappeared into that blue light, and why there are wolves on Piper Key. The day that Corie and I brought in Alpha, it was just her, Rainbow and Kit at first. Then suddenly there were hundreds of dolphins, then a thousand of them. *And this is why.*"

Natalie's cheeks burned with color and she waved the page in Lydia's face. Lydia snatched it out of her hand. "Okay, calm down. Let me see it."

She read the article once, then again and again, trying to connect this information with the various incidents she'd experienced. If what witness said was true and if his speculation that an installation might exist somewhere on or near Piper Key, then *where* was it? She'd lived here fifteen years and couldn't think of any place where such an installation might exist without someone knowing about it.

Except in the hills or the wilderness preserve.

"See what I mean?" Natalie said.

"Who is this witness person? Any ideas?"

Natalie shook her head. She started to say something, but Lydia's cell phone, resting on a mound of clothes and towels next to Natalie, started to ring. Natalie grabbed it, tossed it to Lydia. "Dolphins on the Gulf."

"Hey, it's Ian. I need some advice, Lydia. You have some free time?"

In about a week, I'll be unemployed and have plenty of free time. "What's up?"

"I'm at old man Livingston's place. You know where it is?"

Everyone on the island who had a pet knew about old man Livingston. Whenever a cat or dog got lost, Livingston's was the first place they went to look for it. He collected strays the way the homeless collected grocery store carts and cardboard boxes and reputedly sold the animals to labs that tested on animals, something that Cameron had never been able to prove.

"Can you tell me over the phone what it is, Ian?"

"You have to see it. Something's happened up here and I'm not sure what it is."

"Okay. Give me half an hour."

"Don't bring Nat."

Then it had to be bad. "Okay."

"And bring or wear boots. High boots."

"Meet him where?" Natalie asked as Lydia hung up.

"Livingston's."

Natalie made a face. "I'm not going up to *that* place."

"You're going to Gracie's."

As they headed into the hills toward Gracie's, sunlight exploded above the trees and spilled down between the branches, turning everything a soft gold. A flock of wild green parrots flew past overhead, squawking noisily in the morning air.

"Are you still going to put the center up for sale?" Natalie asked.

"Unless a miracle happens, yeah. But I'm going to hold off for a couple of days and try to find out who witness is. Maybe he knows what Alpha is really about. I mean, all this strange phenomena started happening about the same time that Alpha showed up, which makes me think she might be integral to whatever is going on."

"She is."

The conviction with which Natalie said this caused Lydia to look over at her. "You sound pretty sure about that."

"I talk to her, Mom. I know you don't believe it, but it's true. It's been true ever since I fell in the tank."

"If you can talk to her, then how come you don't know where she came from or how she's involved?"

"It's not like talking to a person, Mom." Exasperation had crept into her voice. "It's a feeling. It's . . . *routes*. I see routes."

"Roots? What's that mean? Roots grow in the ground."

"R-o-u-t-e-s. Like highways. The day I first touched

Alpha, I saw a lot of *routes,* but it didn't make much sense then. Now I think I understand it a little better."

"Great. Illuminate me."

"The *routes* are, well, like possibilities, I guess. The clear, bright *routes* are the ones that are most likely to happen." She related what she'd seen when Corie had asked if her parents were ever going to buy their own place. "With Alpha, every *route* I saw looked bright and clear, all of them equally possible."

"Give me some specifics, Nat. Where'd she come from?"

"North of us."

"North. Okay. That's a start. Was she in an aquarium?"

"I don't think so. I saw her with this thing attached to her beak. I think she was supposed to put it somewhere, but instead, she put it somewhere else and it exploded."

Mammal defense program? "Why didn't you tell me this stuff before?"

"It's taken me a while to sort it out." She shrugged. "And I didn't think you'd believe me."

Yes, there was that. "The light in the woods changed my concepts of what's possible, honey. And I'm sorry that you've felt you had to keep things from me because I wouldn't believe you."

"Then believe me when I tell you that Alpha knows Gail from somewhere. Remember when I asked you about the Frisbee?"

Here it comes. "Yeah. So?"

And the story came spilling out, how she'd gotten up early to swim with the trio and had hidden under the dock when Gail had appeared and the details of what she'd witnessed. "Then she called some guy named Dylan, Colonel Steve Dylan. . . ."

"You're sure that's what you heard?"

"Yes. That was it."

Shit. Eight years ago when she'd gotten a research grant from the government, a Steve Dylan had been her liaison. Part of the grant had included hiring Gail Campbell, whose salary for that first year was included in the grant. She'd never met the man, only talked to him over the phone, and he hadn't said anything about being a *colonel.* But he had to be the same guy.

But what's it mean?

As Lydia turned onto the road that led through the campground, Bacall darted out of the trees, carrying a Frisbee in her mouth. Lydia braked and, moments later, Max loped out of the trees, shouting at Bacall. He saw her car, grinned, and stuck out his thumb.

Laughing, Lydia pulled alongside him. "You're up early."

"I was just about to say the same thing about you two." He crouched and winked at Natalie. "Hey, kiddo."

"Hey, yourself. Max, can you go with Mom up to Livingston's? I don't think she should go alone."

Lydia gave her a sharp look. "What're you talking about?"

"I have a bad feeling about it."

"What's Livingston's?" Max asked.

Lydia quickly explained. "You'd have to bring boots."

"If Nat can watch Bacall, I'll ride up with you."

Natalie's eyes lit up. "You bet."

Ten minutes later, Lydia drove into the emerald hills, Max in the passenger seat and their night of intimacy jammed between them. She hadn't thought much of the way he'd left the morning after, just splitting the way he did without saying good-bye, without even leaving a note. He hadn't called yesterday and probably wouldn't have called today, either. In fact, if they hadn't run into each other, she wondered if she would have seen him again.

Yet, here he was and she didn't know what to say.

"I apologize for leaving like I did the other morning," he said suddenly.

As if he'd read her mind. "I thought maybe I'd forgotten to brush my teeth."

He laughed. "You looked so peaceful, I didn't want to wake you."

Flattery. He knew what to say, all right, and yes, she liked hearing it. A part of her knew it wouldn't take much for her to fall in love with this man and that same part of her suspected that she loved him already. "That's it? No wife or girlfriend stashed away somewhere, Max? No deep dark secrets?" She grinned as she said it, but was only half joking. She hadn't forgotten the deftness and certainty he'd shown when he'd tended to her foot, the skill that hinted at medicine as a profession, and not just because his old man had been a vet, as Gracie had told her.

"Just the usual," he said. "I'm wanted for allegedly murdering my girlfriend, the cop in charge of the case is already here on Piper Key, and of course I'm innocent. You know, ordinary stuff."

She looked over at him and they both laughed.

Part Three

The Void

August 5–7, 1999

"If we can become architects of space-time . . . then it may be that we can also create entirely new, viable universes."

—David Darling
equations of eternity

Twenty-two

As the crow flies, Roberta lay only a few miles in-
land from Piper Key. But the winding road added mile-
age and time. Thorn had driven this route many times,
but had never explored off the beaten path because
everyone he'd seen looked like they'd just stepped off
the set of *Deliverance*.

Thanks to the speed at which Lydia drove, they
reached the outskirts of town in about twenty minutes.
She slowed, but not by much, as they passed through
the downtown. Magnificent live oaks lined the road on
both sides, Spanish moss spilling from the branches
like bluish green lace shawls. He spotted parks, an elementary school, a restaurant, a bookshop. So far, so
good. The town looked inviting, tranquil in the southern
sense, as if in the next pool of shade he would glimpse
darkies in white uniforms serving mint julep tea to the
southern belles.

He reached across the seat and touched his fingertip
to Lydia's cheek. It startled her and she flinched, then
glanced at him and smiled. "Thanks for coming with
me, Max."

And suddenly it dawned on him that Ian Cameron
was a cop. This information had been imparted at some
point during that long night of great sex and immense

guilt and even though Cameron investigated only animal abuse cases, he was still a cop. That meant computers, FBI files, privileged info. And the way his life had been running lately, it wouldn't surprise him if he discovered that Ian Cameron was Joe Nelson's cousin four times removed. It disturbed him. It scared him shitless. He suddenly felt like a gladiator entering the lion's den.

"Is something still going on between you and Cameron?" he asked.

"Nope. Not for me."

"But there is for him."

"I doubt it. We split up because he couldn't talk about what he felt."

He wondered if she thought the same thing of him and felt briefly tempted to come clean, to confess, to tell her about the copies of the videotapes he'd mailed to witness, courtesy of a post office box on Piper Key. But now wasn't the time.

The trees ended. Squalor now dotted the landscape in every conceivable shape and form. Abandoned vehicles rusted in overgrown front yards—trailers, trucks, boats, bikes. Shacks cropped up, half-hidden in the trees. Barbed wire encircled tiny cement block homes.

Lydia turned off on a dirt road and followed signs for Livingston Farms that brought them to a compound of squalor surrounded by a wire mesh fence. Beyond the fence lay abandoned cages resting on rickety wooden benches, abandoned pens, and rusted heaps of refuse—a fridge, a car without wheels, two bikes, a floor freezer. Nightmare country, Thorn thought.

She drove through the open gates and pulled up alongside a black pickup truck. In front of them stood a single-wide trailer that looked as if it had sat in this same spot for so long it had merged with the landscape. Branches and leaves covered its roof, dirt and mud streaked its windows, and the aluminum porch roof sagged at one end, as if beneath the weight of its own decay.

"Pretty creepy," Thorn remarked.

"Livingston should've been shut down years ago."

They pulled on their boots and got out of the van. Just then, a guy in jeans, boots, and a blue work shirt came around the side of the trailer. With his sunburned face and pale, rather long hair, he looked like a throwback to frontier times, handsome and macho. He extended his hand when Lydia introduced them and Thorn didn't discern any jealousy.

"I'm surprised the health department didn't shut this place down," Lydia remarked.

"They tried a number of times, but never got anywhere. I've always suspected someone was paid off, but could never prove it," Cameron replied. "What I want to show you is inside the trailer."

"Where's Livingston?" Thorn asked.

"Not here. No one's seen him for three or four days. That's why I drove out here to begin with."

Cameron opened the door to the trailer and they filed inside. The interior looked worse than the exterior. Filth everywhere, the carpet either worn away or covered in grime, dirty dishes piled high in the sink. The windows weren't open and the air wasn't on. The temperature in here, Thorn thought, probably hovered around ninety-five. And the stench was bad, of eggs left to rot in the sun. Beneath that stench lay something else, something worse, but he couldn't define it immediately.

A long line of ants emerged from under a pile of dirty laundry on the floor and proceeded down the hall, in the same direction Thorn's group was going. They looked too large to be fire ants, but Thorn was careful to avoid them nonetheless. At the end of the hall, Cameron kicked the door open with the toe of his boot and, still using his foot, pushed a brick in front of the door to hold it open. The ants scurried in and out of the room, maintaining their orderly, efficient line.

They stepped into the pigsty of old man Livingston's bedroom—laundry everywhere, dirty dishes on the floor and the dresser and under the bed, torn curtains, bare mattress, a broken window. A chair lay on its side, a telephone sat in the middle of the mattress, a videotape balanced like a seesaw on the sill of the busted window. Beads of moisture had gathered on the walls.

"Now keep in mind that when I got here," Cameron said, "the bathroom was locked from the inside and there's no window in there."

"Meaning what? There's a dead body in there?" Lydia pointed at the line of ants that marched past them and vanished under the door. "They found it first."

"No dead people. No dead Livingston." Cameron pointed at the splintered wood of the doorjamb. "I had to bust the damn dead bolt open to get in." He pushed the door all the way open with his foot and they crowded into the room.

Thorn nearly gagged on the stench and pressed his hand over his mouth and nose. Without a window or lights in here, the room was too shadowed to see much of anything except the ants, which marched over to the bathtub and under the shower curtain. Cameron turned on a lantern flashlight, hooked it over the shower curtain rod, then jerked the curtain open.

When Thorn looked down into the tub, the florid light exposed the utter horror of what lay there and that horror catapulted Thorn back into the field on the morning that Ellen had faded and vanished. He groped for something to hold on to, to steady himself, and as soon as his hand came away from his mouth and nose, the stench rushed into his nostrils again. *The same smell, the same hideous reality.*

Dead birds filled the tub from one end to the other, from top to bottom, as if someone had dumped them there. They came in different colors, sizes, shapes, and species, and the ones on top appeared to have died quickly, with their wings still spread, perhaps as they'd tried to flee. Hummingbirds. Pelicans. Amazonian blue parrots, finches, sparrows, robins, woodpeckers, owls, wood thrushes, a scarlet macaw, a yellow-headed parrot, a hooded warbler. And that was just the top layer, the birds that were immediately visible and identifiable.

Thorn jerked a dirty towel off the nearest rack, wrapped it around his hand, and leaned forward to turn a bird over. The gaping hole in its chest told him everything he needed to know. *It happened here.* And suddenly, he knew that old man Livingston had gone the same place that Ellen had, into the twilight zone.

"Max?"

Max Max Max: Lydia's voice echoed in his skull. He dropped the towel and straightened up. When he glanced at her, he knew that his horror showed because she frowned and murmured, "You okay?"

"The smell . . . Jesus, it's bad."

Cameron handed him a kerchief. "Tie it around your nose and mouth. I slathered it with Vick's Vaporub. That'll help." He snapped on a pair of latex gloves, handed a pair to each of them, then turned on the shower, washing away the ants that swarmed over the corpses. "A lot of these birds aren't even native to Florida."

"They aren't native to the *Southeast*," Thorn said, working the gloves over his fingers. The smell of the Vick's cleared his head.

"We need experts here," Lydia said. "Ornithologists from the university, state cops . . ."

"No way." Cameron shook his head. "Within thirty minutes, we'd have a media circus that would surpass anything you experienced with the dolphin incident, Lydia. You've got to perform autopsies on some of these birds. That'll tell us what killed them and why they've got these huge holes in their chests."

"I'm a marine biologist, Ian. I wouldn't know what the hell to look for."

"I need answers."

"Then you'll have to find a vet who'll do the necropsies."

Thorn removed the shower curtain from the rod and spread it open on the floor. "Let's put the birds in here and then bury them."

Cameron nodded. "Good idea. But I want several on ice so Lydia can cut them open."

"You apparently didn't hear me the first time, Ian. I'm not qualified to do a necropsy."

"We don't need necropsies," Thorn said. "Their hearts imploded. That's what killed them."

"You a vet?" Cameron shot back.

He remembered the fiction he'd told Lydia. "My father was a vet and I worked for him for years."

"And that qualifies you to make that sort of snap judgment?"

"Look, Mr. Cameron. I'm not trying to challenge your authority here, okay?" He picked up one of the larger birds and held it up close to Cameron's face. "But this is precisely where the bird's heart was." He stuck his gloved finger into the hole and scooped out the remainder of the heart muscle. "And here's what's left of it."

Cameron shoved his arm away. "Okay, man, you made your goddamn point. But even if you're right, what would cause it?"

Thorn set the bird on the shower curtain and picked up another. "An aneurysm in the ventricle wall." He scooped out another bird, a Canadian goose that had no hole in its chest. "The real questions are what caused the aneurysms and what created the fear that made them blow."

"The light?" Lydia asked.

"Not the light," Thorn said. "The electromagnetic surge that creates the light."

Cameron looked from one to the other. "What light? What the hell are you talking about?"

"Did you read yesterday's wildlife column?" Lydia asked.

Cameron's eyes narrowed. "What about it?"

"Witness described a soft blue glow that emanated from those machines that he saw. We saw something similar in the woods behind Gracie's place."

"You saw it, too?" His eyes slid to Thorn.

"Yeah. And there was a hum and we got zapped."

"Let's get these birds outside, then I'd like to hear more about it."

They worked silently after that, cleaning every last bird out of the tub. Cameron pulled the bundle out through the trailer, with Lydia and Thorn hurrying along ahead of him. As soon as Thorn got outside, he tore the Vick's-scented kerchief off his face and gulped at the fresh air. "I'm going to find a couple of shovels."

Lydia moved quickly to his side. "I'll come with you. Ian, we're going to find shovels," she called.

"Out back," Cameron said. "In the shed."

As soon as they were out of Cameron's hearing range, Lydia whispered, "Christ, maybe I shouldn't have blurted all that."

"Do you trust him enough to describe the rest of it?"

"Yes, but . . . What's the big deal, right? We saw a blue light that appeared suddenly in the woods and when we got too close to it, we got zapped." She started to laugh, a nervous staccato laugh. "It sounds wacko."

"If you told this to someone who wasn't here, it'd sound wacko, too." *And you heard how Ellen faded . . .* "You know him, you decide how much to tell him."

The shed door had a padlock on it, but the damn thing had rusted so badly that when Thorn threw his weight against the door, it popped loose. He pulled out three shovels, a wheelbarrow, a 30-06 rifle and a box of shells. And just in case they couldn't find a place to bury the fifty-seven birds without polluting the water table, he brought out a pair of ten-gallon cans of kerosene. They loaded everything into the wheelbarrow and headed around to the front of the trailer again.

"You know how to use that rifle?" she asked.

"Nope. But the place is creepy and I feel better having it."

Lydia picked it up, found the box of shells, and loaded it with the ease of a pro. "They teach you that in marine biology school?" he asked, dryly.

"My grandfather was a hunter."

Thorn sensed she mentioned it in an attempt to impose some semblance of normalcy on their circumstances. "How'd you feel about that?"

"I hated him for it. But right now, I'm grateful he taught me how to shoot a gun."

They joined up with Cameron, who hoisted the bundle of birds into the wheelbarrow. Thorn noticed that he, too, was now armed. "Let's get this over with as quickly as possible. I put two birds in a cooler." He looked around uneasily. "Hear how silent it is? No birds are singing."

No birds, no bees, no butterflies, no reptiles, not even a live fire ant anywhere in sight, Thorn noticed. The parallels to his own experience in the aftermath of Ellen's disappearance, out in the field, disturbed him, but didn't surprise him. Were there barren, frigid areas on the property? Would they stumble across the corpses of other animals? And what had happened to the animals that had lived in all those empty cages and pens? Had they gone to the same place that Livingston had?

A quarter of a mile into the woods, they found what looked like an ideal spot to dig a hole for the burial of the birds. Without speaking, they each took a shovel and started digging. The humid stillness didn't just surround them, it pressed in around them, permeating the air they breathed, sucking the moisture from their bodies. And within that stillness, Thorn became aware of noises, soft, strange noises. Cameron and Lydia apparently heard them also because they all stopped digging and leaned against their shovels, listening.

"You hear it?" Lydia whispered.

Cameron pointed off to his left. "Over there."

"Let's go," Thorn said, and dropped his shovel.

Lydia grabbed the rifle and they moved toward the sound, fanning out through the trees, their boots crushing the dry, overgrown grass. The noises got louder, stranger, and assumed a frantic, wounded quality. Gooseflesh broke out on Thorn's arms. He broke into a run.

The sound stopped and so did they, breathing hard, their faces now bright with sweat. And then Thorn saw it, saw it in a place he'd looked at before but hadn't really seen because his eyes weren't attuned to this kind of seeing, to the seeing of the impossible, the grotesque, the incomprehensible.

Embedded in the trunk of a live oak tree in front of him, embedded so perfectly that it seemed to be growing out of the tree, were the head and front paws of a rottweiler. The rest of its body was trapped in the trunk, encased within the wood, *vanished* inside of it.

Bile surged in Thorn's throat and he stumbled back. Cameron's shovel dropped with a noisy clatter against the rocks. But Lydia, Christ, Lydia sounded as though she was choking, gasping for breath. Then the dog's eyes opened, liquid with agony, with unimaginable pain, and it emitted the noise that had drawn them here. Lydia screamed something unintelligible and ran toward it, tears streaming down her face. She stopped a yard short, staring at the creature for a fraction of a second, then raised the rifle and fired twice, ending its misery.

The explosions blew apart the silence in the woods and echoed for moments afterward. In that brief pocket of time, Thorn just stood there, shocked into paralysis, a part of him terrified that if he moved, if he acted, if he tried to deal with what he saw, he would end up as he had when Ellen had vanished. He would end up roaming the woods like a madman, wake up in a psych unit, and a different version of the nightmare would unfold.

Then something broke inside of him. With the echo of gunfire still ringing in his ears, he ran over to the wheelbarrow and grabbed the cans of kerosene. Burn it, he thought. Burn all of it. Burn the whole fucking, fetid mess. Purge it. He thrust one of the cans into Cameron's arms, then proceeded to splash kerosene over the bird corpses and the shower curtain, the dry grass, and around the base of the live oak. He splashed kerosene until the can was empty. He tossed the spent can into the wheelbarrow.

Cameron moved backward from the tree, pouring a neat line of kerosene across the ground, leading away from the area Thorn had just saturated.

"Get back," Lydia shouted from behind them. "You're still too close."

Thorn glanced back and saw her raise the rifle, aim. He and Cameron beat a hasty retreat and were well behind Lydia when she fired the first shot.

The shot ignited the neat line of kerosene that Cameron had put down. Lydia fired again and a ring of flames sped around the base of the tree. Fed by the dry leaves and grass, the fire quickly gained momentum and height and strength. Black plumes of smoke billowed upward.

The three of them raced away. Thorn didn't know how long they ran or how far, but they outraced the fire and exploded out of the woods and into the clearing where the trailer stood. The stench of smoke and fire had thickened. Ash and embers floated down through the air. Thorn knew they didn't have much time before the fire reached the trailer. But he didn't want to leave anything for investigators to find, no evidence that would help them piece together a picture of arson.

He shouted at Cameron to put the empty cans in his

truck and ran over to the propane tank at the side of the trailer. He disconnected it and carried it over to the sagging porch. He spun the valve and yelled, "As soon as we get the cars, set it off, Lydia."

Cameron raced for his truck and Thorn made a bee-line for the van and scrambled inside. Lydia had left the key in the ignition, so he gunned the engine, backed up, and swerved until the van was parallel with the trailer. He threw open the passenger door and Lydia leaped inside, aimed the rifle through the open window, and fired three shots.

Thorn slammed his foot to the accelerator and sped away, following the dust from Cameron's truck. A heartbeat later, the trailer went up, an explosion that sent a fireball fifty feet into the air and blew apart the whole stinking mess. Pieces of the trailer rained down, scorched wall panels and shards of glass, lengths of pipe and parts of a chair. Pines caught fire and exploded, spewing bark and burning branches. A skin of ash coated the windshield.

He fishtailed through the gate and raced toward the highway.

Twenty-three

(1)

"Dolphins on the Gulf. Natalie speaking."

"Oh. Natalie," said Gail. "I didn't think anyone would be there."

"I came in early to do the feeding so Mom could sleep."

"Let your mom know I won't be coming in today. I've got a fever and feel like I'm coming down with the flu."

To Natalie, it sounded as if Gail was pinching her nostrils. "I'll tell her. Did you have any swims today? Anything special I should take care of?" She tried to keep Gail on the line while she punched out Tom Maynard's number on the fax phone.

When he answered, she asked Gail to hold while she took another call and quickly told Tom what she needed. Gail was still waiting when she went back on the line. Natalie managed to keep her talking long enough for Tom to haul himself out of bed and down to his car. As soon as she hung up from the call with Gail, she scribbled a note to her mother. *Emergency at Tom's, I'll call on cell phone. Love, N.*

She grabbed her pack and ran outside. Already, she regretted the lie to her mother, but she couldn't call her and wake her up and tell her the truth. *Gail's up to something, Mom, and I'm going to find out what it is.* It wasn't as though she would be in any danger. She and Tom would follow Gail, that was all. But her mother would worry and fret.

She raced parallel to the runway, then halfway down the road that connected with the main route to town. Tom's truck came barreling toward her and screeched to a halt. He threw open the passenger door. "This better be good, Nat. I've hardly got my eyes open and I'm hungry as hell."

Natalie grinned and slid into the passenger seat. "It's good." And she told him.

All along, she had confided in Maynard about her small discoveries, her little epiphanies. She was the figure in the Sunday cartoon with a lightbulb lighting up over her head. *Hello, Natalie. Do you get it?* Well, she got it now, all right. Gail Campbell would lead her to this Dylan person, who would lead her deeper into the mystery, whatever it was. And somewhere in the heart of that mystery, she would uncover the truth about Alpha and save her mother's center.

"Okay, it's good," he agreed. "But I need something to eat." He stabbed his thumb over his shoulder. "There's a cooler in the back with some fruit and stuff in it. Could you take a look?"

Four minutes later, they pulled into a field at the end of Gail's street. A very bare field. Yeah, the grass grew high, but they were in full view of anyone who drove by. They both slid down in their seats and waited. Gail wouldn't be expecting to see Tom's truck out here; therefore, she probably wouldn't notice it. Expectations, Natalie thought, molded reality. You saw only what you expected to see, which was why Gail wouldn't see them and why she hadn't recognized Max as soon as that cop had shown her the photo.

At 7:17 on the nose, Gail Campbell drove past in her Cherokee, her head tilted back slightly, so that in profile she looked as though she had her nose in the air. Natalie and Tom exchanged a look and he remarked, dryly, "She looks pretty healthy to me."

As Gail's Cherokee turned another corner, Tom fired up his truck. "You committed?"

"Absolutely."

"In for the long haul, regardless of where it takes us?"

"Yup."

He stepped on the accelerator and the truck shot forward, burning rubber.

(2)

Just in case Liv Ingston had to be to work early, Gail timed her visit so she would be sure to catch her before she left her house in Roberta. She had rehearsed her little speech so many times she could now recite it in her sleep. But just in case, she rehearsed it again as she drove up into the hills, following the map to the address the Alachua Bell operator had given her.

According to the map, the address would bring her close to Livingston's place, not a location she had any desire to revisit. Sometimes at night, she could still smell that goat's blood on her hands and imagined that she could hear the rabbit's frightened squeals. She'd kept the rabbit about a week, a part of her hoping that it eventually would lose its fear of her. But it didn't and she finally released it down near the salt marsh, where she occasionally spotted it in the evening, munching contentedly on grass. Releasing the rabbit was probably one of her more humane deeds, but it didn't compensate for what she'd done to the goat.

She came down out of the hills and passed numerous dirt roads that meandered into the woods on either side of her. The road where Liv lived missed old man Livingston's place by maybe half a mile. Gail turned onto it and just after the first curve, ran into a blockade of military vehicles. "What the hell." She pulled up short of the blockade and stuck her head out the window.

An armed soldier came over to the car. A tall guy, young and cute and polite. "Morning, ma'am. I'm afraid you're going to have to turn around and go back the way you came. This area is off limits."

"This is a public road and I've got an appointment with someone who lives along here."

"This is actually a private road, ma'am. And it's under the jurisdiction of the CDC right now."

"Since when does the CDC have soldiers working for them?" *Or are you part of Dylan's private little army?* "Oh, forget it. Tell Colonel Dylan that Dr. Campbell is here to see him."

The sudden change in his expression said that he knew Dylan. "I'll need to see some ID, ma'am."

Gail gave him her driver's license. He looked at the photo, then at her, but didn't return the license. "Please wait here and don't get out of your car, ma'am."

She turned off the engine, resigned to what might be a lengthy wait. The heat that poured through her open window smelled faintly of smoke and she noticed a scattering of ash across the ground. Something more than a fire had happened in there for this sort of turn-out of military vehicles. Dylan's involvement in whatever it was meant that she probably wasn't going to like it very much.

Ten minutes later, the soldier hurried back over to her car. "I'll drive you to Colonel Dylan, ma'am." He opened her door to get in and she slid over into the passenger seat.

"So what happened in here?" she asked once they were under way.

"I'm not at liberty to say, ma'am."

No surprise. "What division of the military are you with?"

"Naval Intelligence, ma'am."

DNI. Dylan's boys, for sure, she thought, and sat back, resigned to the silence.

The soldier drove her car through the blockade and along the dusty road to the next blockade, where they left her car and got into a Power Ranger, an all-terrain vehicle that took them straight through the woods. The stink of smoke got stronger. Ash and soot appeared on the ground, the branches, even on the leaves.

They emerged in a charred clearing where several containment tents had been erected over a large area. They looked like giant white mushrooms growing together in a tight cluster. Beyond them stood scorched tree trunks, their branches and leaves gone, and the remains of glorious pines that looked as if they had imploded. Way off to her left rose mounds of debris. The area had changed so drastically that it took her several moments to realize the soldier had brought her to the Livingston farm.

The Power Ranger stopped alongside one of three mobile units. "Stay in the car, ma'am. I'll tell Colonel Dylan you're here."

The soldier swung gracefully out of the vehicle and

Gail sat there, a knot of dread aching in the center of her chest.

(3)

One moment they were doing fifty down a dirt road and the next moment, Tom's truck swerved so suddenly and violently that Natalie was thrown forward. In the next moment, he slammed on the brakes and her body snapped back and the truck screeched to a halt, a cloud of dust flying around them.

The engine ticked in the silence, dust drifted through the open windows. She had no idea what had happened, but Tom shouted at her to get out now, fast, and she threw open her door and scrambled out. She ran to the front of the truck, where Tom was, and stood there beside him, struggling to make sense of what she saw.

A wave of air, quivering like heat above a pavement on a hot day, seemed to be moving across the road in front of them, its shape changing constantly, from an oblong to a sphere to a tall cone to a rectangle the shape of a door. It was pitch-black, like onyx, and didn't move fast. In fact, its movement was wavelike, and its direction never varied.

The waves around the shape were transparent and distorted everything that lay on the other side—the road, trees, rocks. It was like looking at a fun house mirror that distorted the shape of your body. But the center of the shape was dense and dark, like a black door, and it seemed to emit a faint hum.

Wherever the black door touched the road, the road vanished. Or became something else. She didn't know which. The road just wasn't there anymore and in its place was a long, wide strip of blackness, as if some-one had poured paint over the road, the dirt and rocks and brush, covering all of it in a ribbon of black.

Before it reached the trees on the other side of the road, it began to shrink, to contract like the pupil of an eye until it just wasn't there anymore. Neither of them spoke. They simply looked at each other, then Tom took her hand and moved closer to the strip of blackness that had cut the road in half.

On the other side of it, Natalie could see the road, trees, everything as it should be. But between them stood a chasm about four feet wide and endlessly deep. She didn't see rocks or dirt or anything else inside the chasm. Just the bottomless blackness.

Tom picked up several stones. He tossed one into the chasm and it vanished. He threw the other about four feet above the chasm. It landed on the other side. By throwing the stones at various levels, they deter-mined that the effects of the chasm, whatever it was, extended upward about three and a half feet.

"We need to find another way across the road," he said. "Through the woods."

They got back into the truck and he drove through the trees, parallel to the chasm for a quarter of a mile or so. Then the chasm ended and they got out again. "This must be where it started."

"Started out of what?"

"Shit, I don't know. We need new language to de-scribe this. But this must be where it popped into be-ing, where its reality coincided with ours."

"But what's that *mean?*"

"I don't know. C'mon, let's get outta here."

He drove through the woods, the truck bumping along a footpath for several miles, the road occasionally visible through the trees on their left. He could have taken the road, of course, but she understood that Tom, like herself, felt an intense need to remain hidden, camouflaged.

"We've lost Gail," Natalie said.

"She took one of these roads. I'm sure of it. The . . ." He stopped suddenly and pointed through the trees. "There. See it?"

Three military jeeps sped by on the road. Tom slowed and nosed the truck between a pair of thickets, where it wouldn't be visible from the road. "Let's take the mountain bikes. It'll be safer."

They crossed the road on their bikes and went into the trees on the other side. The terrain was rough and hilly, thick with pines and live oaks. But before long, Natalie smelled the residue of smoke and heard music, faint but unmistakable. They stopped, laid their bikes on the ground, and covered them with dead leaves and branches. Then they moved forward on foot, closer to the source of the music, neither of them daring to speak. The heat became almost unbearable. Her shirt stuck to her body and her jeans felt heavy and weighted against her legs. They passed a water bottle back and forth and shared one of the apples in her fanny pack.

As the music grew louder, they hunkered down and crept from tree to tree. Live oaks now gave way to pines. The stink of smoke got stronger. Ash covered parts of the ground. Tom suddenly stopped, dropped to his knees, and pointed.

Six or seven yards away was a lone soldier, seated on a large rock, smoking a cigarette and listening to a portable CD player. They watched him for several minutes, then Tom gestured to the right, indicating that they would circle around him. Three hundred yards later, an-

other soldier stood watch, and he wasn't distracted by
a cigarette or music. He kept turning slowly in place,
alert, his weapon ready.

Tom waited until the man's back was to them again,
then hurled the apple core through the trees, somewhere
beyond him. The soldier heard the core when it came
down and immediately hurried off to investigate. Tom
and Natalie quickly moved forward.

They saw other soldiers here and there through the
trees, but managed to stay clear of them until they approached what looked like the remains of a fire. Trees
burned to stumps, brush scorched to the ground, ash
covering rocks. Beyond this, in a clearing, Natalie saw
dozens of military vehicles—jeeps, covered trucks, even
small tractors that appeared to be clearing debris.

"We need to get closer," Tom whispered.

"We need to get outta here," she whispered back.

"Just a little farther."

To the west of ground zero, the trees brought them
a little closer to what appeared to be some sort of mobile medical unit, like the bloodmobile that made the
rounds every month on the island. But this vehicle was
much longer, with darkened windows. White tents rose
on the other side of it, containment units that reminded
her of scenes from *E.T.*

"Take a look," Tom whispered, and passed her a pair
of binoculars.

When she focused the binoculars, everything sprang
clearly into view—shadows moving against the inside
of the containment unit closest to them, some sort of
large hose or tube that connected it to the mobile unit,
and Gail Campbell and a man walking quickly toward
it.

Natalie zoomed in on the man's face, then on the ID badge that hung around his neck. *Col. Steve Dylan.*

He and Gail seemed to be arguing. Her hands sliced the air as she talked, her face looked flushed, and at one point she stopped and threw out her arms, a gesture that took in not just Livingston Farms, but all the military vehicles. Then they went inside the mobile unit and emerged about ten minutes later, wearing white astronaut suits with helmets, oxygen tanks, the whole nine yards, and vanished into the containment unit.

Tom touched Natalie's elbow and tilted his head toward the woods. They ran back the way they'd come, but as they neared the place where they'd left their bikes, Natalie heard voices. Tom heard them, too, took one glance around, and pointed at the live oak that was closest to them.

Climb, he mouthed. *Climb fast,* and offered her a foothold so she could reach one of the lower branches. She grabbed on to it, swung her body in toward the trunk, found a place for her foot, and climbed high into the branches, Tom right behind her.

Moments later, two men in fatigues walked into view. They lit cigarettes and stood in the shade, puffing away. "You think they'll have the area secured by dusk?" asked one.

"They can secure an area in an hour if that's what they decide to do. You get a look in that tent?"

"Nope. You?"

"Naw. It was set up before I got called in."

"What do you think's in there?"

"Dunno. Don't want to know."

"Kramer was here last night, when they set up the tent. He said he heard screaming. Human screams."

Natalie tightened her grip on the branch. Her feet,

squashed into a fork between two branches, ached. Every time she looked down, she got dizzy and had to shut her eyes.

"Let me give you a piece of advice," said the second man. "Don't get too curious about anything. I've worked with Dylan before. If he thinks you're the curious type, you'll find yourself on a sub in the Arctic."

"You mean you're not even curious about what's in that tent?"

"Sure, I'm curious. But our job is to secure and quarantine the area and enforce the curfew. We get double time with a hazard bonus. After that, we go home and my wife and I head to the Caribbean just on what I'm earning here. So why be curious?"

"Good point."

"Hell, it's not just a point, man. It's the bottom line. C'mon, we'd better get back."

Natalie opened her eyes and peered below, down through the branches and the layers of green, watching as the two men moved away. She shifted her upper body and lifted her right foot off her left, then brought it down to a lower branch. She tried to move her left foot, but her shoe had gotten wedged in the forked branch. She had to untie her sneaker and slide her foot out. She pulled on the sneaker, trying to work it free, and when it finally popped loose, she wasn't ready for it and nearly lost her balance. The sneaker slipped out of her hand and tumbled down through the branches, breaking off dry twigs, shaking loose dead branches, and hit the ground.

"Shit," she whispered.

"They're too far away to hear it," Tom whispered back. "Just climb down. Fast. Let's get outta here."

Natalie took off her other sneaker, tied it to the strap

of her backpack, and started down the tree, barefoot, her hands sweating from the heat, the inside of her mouth dry and sour with fear. She dropped to the ground, scooped up her other shoe, and tore into the woods. Her bare feet pounded over stickers and twigs, but she didn't dare stop to put on her shoes.

They reached their bikes and pedaled madly through the trees. Everything around her seemed to blur, greens melting like wax into deeper greens, shadows merging with deeper shadows. Branches slapped her in the face and clawed at her clothes. The bike pounded over rocks and thick roots that protruded from the ground. The wind whistled past her ears.

By the time they reached the truck, Natalie could barely breathe. Her heart hammered. Fear coursed through her, a powerful current that short-circuited everything except her need to get out of here, to get home, to the center, to safety.

They tossed the bikes into the rear of the truck and scrambled into the front seat. Tom sped recklessly through the trees, toward the road, and Natalie kept turning in her seat to look back. But they weren't being followed, no one had seen them. And just when she allowed herself to believe they would make it back to Piper Key in one piece, she saw a military Humvee just in front of them, on the road where they would be in seconds. She screamed and Tom swerved and his truck slammed through a ditch and onto the pavement and skidded. The engine stalled.

Natalie whipped around in her seat to see the Humvee barreling toward them. "It's coming!" she shrieked.

Then from the right, a jeep shot toward them.

"Get out and run!" Tom shouted.

Natalie threw herself out of the truck and stumbled

into the trees, her chest burning, sweat pouring into her eyes. She didn't look back, she didn't have to. She heard the jeep roaring behind her and knew she couldn't outrun it. Her arms pumped at her sides, the ground blurred beneath her, and she jagged right, left, right again. The jeep raced alongside her, two men inside, one in the back.

Natalie turned sharply and crashed through undergrowth. The jeep's engine strained as it swung into a U-turn. Just head, she saw more trees, very dense trees. *Not much farther, you can make it. . . .*

Then she tripped and felt herself flying forward and her arms shot out to break her fall. She landed hard on her side and seconds later, hands jerked her to her feet, a soldier snapped handcuffs on her, then lifted her and carried her to the jeep and dropped her in the back with the other soldier.

He pointed his rifle at her. "Don't even think about moving, kid."

Natalie lay there, her upper body propped up against a cooler, too terrified to speak, to move, to do anything at all. What had happened to Tom? Had he gotten away?

The jeep roared back through the woods, slammed down hard as it hit the paved road, and raced in the same direction the Humvee had gone.

The road dipped steeply downward and curved sharply to the left. The jeep whipped into the curve on two wheels and Natalie's body slid left, giving her a better view of the road. As the curve straightened out, she saw the Humvee clearly just ahead of them and—beyond it, in front of it—the black void, that looming chasm, that *impossible thing.*

"Watch out!" she shrieked. "Don't get near it!"

The Humvee hit the chasm—and vanished.

The jeep spun left, swerved onto the shoulder, crashed down over rocks, branches, ruts. Then it slammed into a tree, hurling her into the soldier. Her head hit something and the world went instantly black.

Twenty-four

(1)

Gail didn't want to go into the containment area. Dylan still hadn't told her what was being contained. But already, she had visions of little *E.T.* bodies hooked up to life-support machines or floating in some sort of preservative liquid. Already, her stomach felt tight and fluttery, as if she might puke, and she wished to hell she'd never come up here.

She realized now that there was no *Liv Ingston,* no little honey stashed away somewhere. There was only old man *Livingston,* who apparently had a business arrangement with Dylan concerning his land. She had the distinctly uneasy feeling that she was about to discover the exact nature of that business deal.

Dylan led her into the tent, where other figures in containment suits moved around, carrying metal trays, vials, and syringes. At least five computers were up and running, monitoring various machines and medical systems. She followed Dylan to the other side of the tent, where maybe half a dozen people dressed just like her hovered around whatever Dylan had brought her in here to see.

"BP holding steady at one-ten over sixty," said one.

"Heartbeat still fast at ninety-two," said another.

"Let's speed up that morphine drip a little," said a third.

"In twelve minutes, we need another blood sample," said a fourth.

"How're we doing?" asked Dylan, and the huddle parted to accommodate him and Gail.

From the moment she stepped into the huddle, everything around her stopped. She no longer heard voices or the hum of machines or the sound of her own breathing. Her peripheral vision shrank and she felt as if she were peering down a very dark and narrow tunnel to a light at the end. But the light was only the faint glow of the machines washing over a steel table that held a metal, four-drawer filing cabinet that lay on its back.

Embedded in the cabinet, like mosaic inlaid in stone, was old man Livingston. Most of his skull appeared to have grown into the first drawer, with just his face, right temple, and right ear showing. His right hand and forearm were free; his left hand and arm vanished into the filing cabinet. His legs protruded from the end, but his body from the groin to the solar plexus lay within the cabinet. Tubes and catheters snaked from his right arm, his feet, and his chest. His chest moved up and down, but very slowly and then his eyes opened and sound suddenly rushed back into Gail's world, a high-pitched keening filled with such abysmal horror that it sundered her soul.

She realized it was coming from her.

She spun and ran out of the tent and tore off her helmet and hurled it away from her. She kept running until she tripped and fell to her knees. Her stomach heaved and she vomited and that was how Dylan found her, puking in the hot light at the edge of the trees.

"You need to get inside where it's cool," he said, trying to help her to her feet.

Gail wrenched free of his grasp and ran the back of her hand across her mouth. The bitter taste of vomit filled her mouth. "Don't touch me, Dylan," she snapped. "Just don't touch me."

His arms swung to his sides and he crouched beside her in the burned grass, his helmet off now. Distantly, way out in the woods, she heard the warble of birds. But here, right here where she and Dylan were, she heard no wildlife at all—no birds, no insects, not even a goddamn lizard was in sight.

"Why?" she finally whispered. "Why keep him alive? And if you're going to keep him alive, at least cut him out of the . . . the cabinet, for Christ's sake."

"He'd die for sure if we tried to cut him out. And we have to keep him alive because he may be our only hope in stopping this thing."

"What *thing*, Dylan? A repeat of the Philadelphia experiment? Teleportation? Just what the hell are we talking about here?"

"It's complicated. It isn't just *one* thing, Gail. Something went wrong and we're trying to correct it, but we don't know if we can. Right now, it seems to be concentrated from here to Piper Key, so we may be able to contain it. But I don't know if we can rectify it."

"Help me get this goddamn suit off," she said.

He did and then she helped him and one of the soldiers came over and picked up the suits and carried them into the mobile unit. Dylan touched her arm and they walked a ways through the woods, neither of them speaking. It was somewhat cooler here and pine scented the air. Her nausea ebbed.

When they finally settled on the ground, backs

against a live oak tree, she felt as she had when they were kids, sneaking out in the middle of the night to do some forbidden thing. But in the realm of forbidden things, this was totally *out there* and leagues beyond even *her* idea of travesty.

"You don't have the authority to seal off this area, Dylan."

"It's gone way beyond my authority, Gail. The column witness wrote is essentially correct. Except that he wrote about something that happened fifteen years ago. And in fifteen years, the technology has surpassed anything any of us could imagine."

"A machine like he describes actually *exists?*"

"Several prototypes exist, none of them perfect. But Livingston and our other mistakes are helping us understand how to correct the flaws."

A man embedded in a filing cabinet is helping them understand flaws. Jesus, I can't believe I'm hearing this. "And they're powered by these . . . these currents in the earth?"

"The currents seem to boost the power, especially when a machine is located in an area where several currents merge. One of the peculiarities of these machines is that although they exist in our reality, they don't seem to be subject to the same physical laws that we are. They're anomalies, no less strange or mysterious than UFOs. Witness said the machine he saw was built of a material he'd never seen before. He was right. Fifteen years ago, the original prototype was built from samples that we brought back from the moon. Now, the machines are built of a new alloy created from crystals grown in space."

He paused and ran his hands over his face and, suddenly, he looked old to her. Old and tired and used up.

But for the first time in their adult lives, Gail knew that he was telling her the truth, the whole unvarnished truth, the very thing she had wanted desperately to know for so many years. "That mobile unit back there?" Dylan stabbed a thumb over his shoulder. "It's powered by a much smaller portable unit. And our installation here . . . The machine supplies us with unlimited power."

The installation where he'd faxed her from yesterday morning. "Where's the installation?"

"A couple miles into the woods."

"On Livingston's property?"

"Yes. There's an old mine two miles back into the woods. We were paying old man Livingston for the use of it. That's why he was never permanently shut down when he was cited by the health department and the animal abuse department and anyone else who was after him. He never had any idea what we were doing, but he was eager to take our money."

"So this is why you want Alpha—alive."

He nodded. "She's the first dolphin who was observed vanishing and then reappearing. Until then, it had only been observed on radar."

Gail felt like asking what else he'd kept from her all these years. In the end, she realized, Dylan's worst lies had been those of omission. "Then the incident witness wrote about actually happened? And that was Alpha?"

"Yes. It was an accident. We'd installed a pair of prototypes on a research vessel. We intended to run tests at some point to see how they performed, but we never had the chance because the machines malfunctioned. At least, that's what we thought at the time. Until I read that column, I was never quite sure of the specifics involved. Now I'm sure the machines malfunctioned because this guy messed around with them. Whatever he did created a field that extended out into the water and it caused the two dolphins in the area to teleport." He paused and rubbed his hands over his eyes again. "The dolphin that ended up embedded in the hull of the ship had been in our training program for about five years. He was Alpha's mate."

Gail rubbed her hands over her face, trying to absorb all this.

"I know what you're thinking," he added quickly. "That it's just one more thing I kept from you and why should you ever trust me again. You don't know how many times I wanted to tell you over the years, but I couldn't. Just by taking you into that tent, I violated every security code this project has had. But if you and I are going to continue, Gail, I can't go into it with so many secrets. I want you to be fully involved in this."

Even though she'd spent most of her adult life waiting to hear Dylan commit to her in exactly this way, the only thing she felt just then was numbness. "I wish you'd told me all this eight years ago, Dylan, before I ever started working with Alpha."

"I doubt if you were prepared to hear all this eight years ago."

She wasn't so sure she was prepared to hear all this now, either.

"Even though we believe dolphins have been teleporting along ley lines for centuries, no one ever actually saw it happen, except on radar, until the night that witness wrote about in the column. The fact that Alpha was teleported as the result of a malfunction and then watched her mate suffer such an excruciating death changed her at some fundamental level. Afterward, she began to exhibit behaviors like she did the day she fled from us—vast and complex intelligence, the ability to strategize, and to carry out plans."

In other words, Alpha was one of a kind, Gail thought. "Where did you find Livingston?"

"In the woods."

"And he's part of what has gone wrong?"

"He's a product of what has gone wrong. It seems the old saying about messing around with Mother Nature is true. By tampering with the currents that run through the ley lines, we seem to have created tremendous surges of power at points where the lines converge. Several points converge here on Livingston's property. And that's why he's where he is. Most of these surges have happened along the twenty-ninth parallel, which runs right through this area. The surges seem to drastically alter the fabric of space-time."

The fabric of space-time: He said this almost casually, in the same way that a seamstress might refer to fabric. She had sudden visions of other space-time snafus, none of them pretty. People with their hands sinking into the desktops. Cars embedded in roofs. Legs sinking into sidewalks. Trees growing in the middle of kitchens. Multiply these scenarios by the number of people who lived in this area—*including Piper Key, he mentioned the island*—and the nightmare would escalate quickly into a fullblown cataclysm. Was this the kind of shit Dylan was talking about?

"So turn the damn machines off."

"We can't."

"Can't or won't?"

"Can't. They aren't like our machines. They don't plug into walls. They aren't powered that way. Jesus, haven't you been listening to anything I've been saying?"

"What you've been saying, pal, is that technology at the end of the twentieth century and the beginning of the new millennium is going to bring down western civilization. What you're saying is that you fucked around with stuff you had no right to fuck with and now the rest of us are going to pay for it."

Very softly, he replied: "Unless we find a way to mitigate or remedy the problem."

"Blow up the machines."

"We don't know what would happen if we blew them up. We don't even know if they *can* be destroyed. We can't risk trying, because then we would lose the technology. The people who built those machines are dead."

"And they didn't leave notes? Directions? Diagrams? Blueprints?"

"No. Nothing."

"Then what're your options?"

"It begins with a quarantine on Roberta and everything west of it."

Quarantine. Then FEMA—the Federal Emergency Management Administration—would step in and declare martial law. Under FEMA regs, the government basically could do anything it wanted to do. FEMA spelled police state. They could take your kids, your property, your home, and toss you in jail on top of it and there would be nothing you could do about it. FEMA swallowed your civil rights.

"You can't quarantine the entire twenty-ninth parallel."

"It doesn't matter. The bulk of the disturbance centers here. Even in a best-case scenario, there are still going to be anomalies."

"What follows the quarantine?"

"An explosion that generates so much energy in a

particular place that it essentially overwhelms the energy pouring through in these surges and cancels it out."

"Nuke 'em, Dylan? Is that it?"

"Too dangerous to everyone else."

Hardly a comforting thought, considering what lay in that tent. "It's going to take you some time to evacuate the area, Dylan."

He didn't reply.

"You *are* going to evacuate the island, aren't you?"

He shook his head.

Sweet Christ.

"We can't risk it. Suppose this witness person came forward and was interviewed by *Oprah?* Or *Nightline?* Or Brokaw or Rather?" He shook his head again. "It would blow everything."

"Nearly three thousand people gone in the blink of an eye?" She struggled to keep her voice calm, low, but failed. And as soon as her voice reached a crescendo and echoed through the woods, Dylan flinched and shot to his feet, his face the color of radishes.

"This isn't my decision, Campbell. I can't stop what's been set in motion, okay? I may not like it, but *I can't stop it."*

Of course he couldn't stop it. Dylan was what he was, the offspring of military parents who had never been able to get beyond that. The military wasn't just his job or his career; it had been and always would be his mistress, his religion, his god. Forty-four years rushed between them, around them, through them. Gail got to her feet, her eyes never straying from his; then they stood there in the warm shadows of the fragrant woods, looking at each other and saying nothing because there was nothing more to say.

In the end, she and Dylan were silent travelers, apparently fated to take their personal foibles and weaknesses into a much larger arena that affected people other than themselves. In the immediate future, that added up to thousands of lives. In the near future, more thousands or millions of lives. And for what? Getting from point A to point Z without having to take a single goddamn step? Presto and you're there?

She turned and began walking away from him, back toward her car. He called out, "The curfew goes into effect at dusk tonight, Gail. You've got till then to get the hell off Piper Key. After that, I can't do anything to help you."

Gail kept walking and Dylan didn't follow her. When she reached the containment area, she asked one of the soldiers to please drive her back to her car. As they started off in the Power Ranger, a jeep came up the road, towing a second jeep with its front end crumpled. The driver of the first jeep leaped out and shouted, "Get the medics over here. We've got three people with injuries.

Gail turned in her seat, watching the commotion, and saw a girl as limp as a wet towel being lifted out of the back of the jeep. Natalie. It was Natalie. She started to interfere, to tell the soldier to stop, but knew that she wouldn't stand a chance. If she intervened now, Dylan would put a gun to her head and pull the trigger. She had become as expendable as everyone else on Piper Key.

(2)

Thorn put the videotapes and autopsy report into a black canvas bag, just as witness had stipulated in his last e-mail. They were to meet at four, at the café on the pier where he'd seen Joe Nelson the other day. Besides the trip to Livingston Farms last night with Lydia, he hadn't ventured very far from the campground and the thought of returning to the café troubled him.

Tom was supposed to go with him, but he was late. Thorn would give him another five minutes, then would leave without him. He slung the bag over his shoulder and glanced around to make sure he hadn't forgotten anything. Outside, Bacall barked, a friendly bark, a greeting for someone she knew. Probably Gracie. Thorn had told her he had to go into town and she'd invited the dog to stay at the house, where it was cooler, until he got back. He grabbed the leash off the wall hook and stepped outside, whistling for Bacall. She bounded around the corner of the camper, tail wagging.

"Hey, who were you talking to, Bacall?" She sat down at his feet and barked. He snapped on her leash. "We're going to walk up to Gracie's and you can play with the skunk for a while."

"Sounds like a shitload of fun, Max. Now turn nice and slow, hands locked on top of your head. I've got a nine millimeter aimed right at your back."

Fuck. Thorn dropped the leash, locked his hands on top of his head, and turned to face Nelson. Bacall trotted over to him, barking with friendly zeal. She apparently didn't remember what was going on the last time she'd seen him; she only recalled that he'd helped her when she needed help and had been responsible for bringing Thorn back to her.

"Hi, Joe."

"Hi Joe?" Nelson scoffed. "That's all you've got to say?"

"Nice piece of detective work."

"Bet your ass. It's amazing what lengths a man will go to for half a mil, Max." He gestured with the gun toward the picnic table. "Sit down there nice and slow."

Thorn sidestepped toward the picnic table, his thoughts darting about, seeking a way out. *Keep him talking*. "So how'd you find me, Joe?"

"I figured I had to think like you think." Nelson cuffed him to the picnic table. "So that's what I did. Found the weird shit on the Web, narrowed the possible cities to the largest and the smallest, and came to the smallest first. I checked every hotel on the island and got nowhere. So then I started with campgrounds and what d'you know? Spotted Bacall and the rest is history.

"And her old man is footing your bill?"

"Department's doing that. Bradshaw offered me half a mil to bring you in."

"I bet he'd pay you twice that if you brought his daughter back."

Nelson rolled his eyes and picked up the end of Bacall's leash. He coaxed her inside the camper and kicked the door shut. "Ellen's dead, Max. You killed her. That's a fact. So there won't be any bringing Ellen back."

"Wrong," Thorn said. "I have every reason to believe we'll find her up at a place called Livingston Farms. . . ."

Something changed in Nelson's expression. "Yeah? Why's that?"

"You want the thirty-second version or the blow-by-blow?"

"Thirty seconds."

Inside the camper, Bacall kept barking and whining and scratching at the door. As Thorn started his thirty-second version of life in the twilight zone, a shadow fell across the concrete slab behind Nelson. Thorn didn't intend to tip off Nelson, so he kept his eyes on Nelson's face and extended the thirty-second version.

The shadow withdrew. Moments later, a white Ford rolled slowly past the camper. "You driving a white Ford, Joe?"

"Yeah. What about it?"

"It's rolling down the driveway."

Nelson grinned. "Sure, it is, Max."

Thorn shrugged. "Suit yourself."

But Nelson edged to the side and glanced toward the driveway, where the white Ford now gathered speed. "Hey!" he shouted and ran after it until it came to rest in a thicket of gardenias. He reached to open the passenger door, but it suddenly flew open, slamming into him, and knocked him flat off his feet and out like a light.

Ian Cameron scrambled out of the car, handcuffed Nelson, went through his pockets, and loped over to Thorn with the key to the cuffs. "Who the hell is that guy?"

"It's a long story."

The cuffs fell away and Thorn rubbed his wrists, wondering how he would get out of this one. Cameron was just another cop. "Help me get him into the back of the car," Cameron said.

"He's a cop."

"Not a local." He picked up Nelson by the feet, Thorn seized his shoulders, and they carried him toward the Ford. "And if he's not a local or a fed, he's got no jurisdiction on the island."

At the car, Cameron dropped Nelson's feet to open the door, then they slid him onto the backseat. Cameron gagged him, slammed the door, and looked at Thorn. "Let's drive up to your camper and take a look at what you've got in that black canvas bag, Bogie."

"*You?*" Thorn nearly choked on the word. This guy was *witness?*

"I had to be as careful as you. I've been carrying my secret a lot longer. I stopped by Gracie's to pick up some herbs and she happened to mention your dog. Bacall. As soon as I heard it, I knew."

"So Gracie knows, too?"

"She does now."

"What about Nelson? He's after the half million reward."

"It's up to you. I can toss him in the can in Roberta or we can leave him in Gracie's cellar until we find Ellen. That's her name, right?"

"Yes." Ellen Bradshaw, whose refusal to marry him had been to placate her old man. This thought bumped around in his skull, as if to remind him why he was now sitting in a car with a man he barely knew, but with whom he felt a camaraderie.

Cameron backed the Ford out of the gardenia bushes and drove in reverse up the driveway. Nelson was beginning to come around. "He's making noises. We'd better decide what to do with him," Cameron said.

"The cellar until we find Ellen."

"No problem. I'd like to see your evidence first. There might be something in it that'll give us an edge."

"The source of it is somewhere on Livingston's property," Thorn said. "It has to be, given what we . . . we saw yesterday."

"I'm sure of it. I went up there earlier today to sift through everything and I couldn't get in. There are soldiers, military vehicles. . . . The place is under quarantine."

"Quarantine for what?"

"The story they gave me—and the mayor of Roberta, incidentally—is that old man Livingston's body was found somewhere in the woods and that he died of some highly contagious bacterial infection. They say they set the fire to burn his clothes and so on."

"Don't they have to alert local authorities to do something like that?"

Cameron stopped the car in front of the camper. "Under martial law, the military doesn't have to explain themselves to anyone."

"We're not under martial law."

"Not yet," Cameron said, and got out of the car.

Twenty-five

(1)

Lydia closed up the center, irritated that Gail had never shown up today, that Natalie had taken off with Tom, that no one answered at Tom's, that she had a million questions and no answers. But the bottom line, she thought, lay in her anxiety about her daughter.

Yes, Natalie had stayed away from the center for a full day before and yes, they'd had their share of disagreements and arguments about it. But this felt different. This felt like the moment years ago when her eighteen-month-old daughter had fallen into the dolphin tank and not come up. A lapse in attention, a brief distraction: That was all it had taken back then. Multiply those lapses and distractions a thousand times, she thought, and it brought her here, now, to this moment in time.

Lydia walked a little faster down the ramp toward the parking area where her electric cart had been since nine this morning. The heat bore down, the hot light quivered against the black asphalt of the runway just beyond her. Could she redeem herself as a mother? She didn't know. For her entire adult life, she had loved dolphins nearly as much as she had loved her daughter. But both had tugged at her from different directions.

Yeah, and so what? Plenty of obsessed people managed to succeed in more than one area of their lives. But she hadn't succeeded in any area of her life. Her marriage had gone down the tubes, she'd neglected her daughter in favor of her work, and now the closing of the center loomed like some huge exclamation point to her failure on the professional level. In other words, it all amounted to a big, fat zero.

She didn't know where Max fit into any of it, didn't understand a damn thing about what had happened between them, how any of what she'd seen at Livingston's could even be possible, and she didn't have a clue about what she should do next. Christ, she didn't even know who else she should call next to try to get a lead on where Natalie was.

She started across the runway, as she did every morning and evening, and saw a car flying toward her.

Gail Campbell's car.

It screeched to a stop just short of her front end and Gail leaped out and ran over to the electric cart. Her hair sprang wildly from her head, her cheeks had flushed bright pink, either with anger or sunburn, Lydia couldn't tell which, and her eyes looked strangely dark. "They have Natalie." This came out in a breathless rush, *theyhavenatalie,* the words and syllables all pushed together, everything truncated, a kind of shorthand that Lydia knew that Gail knew she would understand. And she did.

They have Natalie.

Thanks to what had happened at Livingston's, she understood "they," even though she didn't have names, and she understood "have," but she didn't understand anything else. And when she didn't understand, she got mad. She lunged toward Gail and grabbed her by the front of her shirt and jerked her forward. "Who the fuck are *they?*"

She screamed the words, screamed them right into Gail's face and Gail wrenched back and threw off Lydia's hands and pedaled back away from the cart. "I'm only going to say this once," and she let loose with her story.

Dylan. Livingston. Dylan and the machine. Dylan and Alpha. Dylan and Natalie. *Dylan.* As though he were a god.

Fuck Dylan.

"You know where this installation is?" Lydia snapped.

"A mine," Gail replied. "A mine somewhere on Livingston's property. I snuck around up there, trying to work my way in on foot, but it's impossible in the daylight. There're too many soldiers, too many jeeps. And we have to hurry. By dusk, the island will be under quarantine."

Quarantine? Lydia rocked back on her heels and leaned against the electric cart. "Why should I trust you, Gail? Give me one good reason. All along you've been trying to sabotage my center and suddenly you're concerned about my daughter?" She laughed, a sharp, ugly sound. "I don't buy it."

"You'd better buy it, Lydia. Not only do they have Nat, but they're going to blow up the island once everyone is quarantined. It's supposedly the only way they can fix the problems that witness wrote about. And the source of the problem is in that mine."

"If that's true, Gail, then why don't you go to the press?"

"Sure. And just what the hell am I going to tell them? That Armageddon is on the way and ground zero is going to be Piper Key and Roberta? Who's going to believe that? Dylan has gone off the deep end and, unfortunately for the rest of us, he has the clout to do what he says he's going to do."

A trick, it's a trick. Don't listen to her. "Just what are you proposing?"

"We need people and weapons and we need to get into the mine. We destroy the machine or the technology of whatever it is that's messing everything up."

"Are you willing to tell other people what you just told me?"

"Absolutely."

"Why? Why not just get into your car and drive away, Gail? Why should you give a shit what happens here?"

A dark, crippling pain came into her eyes, the strangest and most powerful emotional response that Lydia had ever seen in her. "Because that's what I've been doing most of my life," she said softly. "And I just can't do it anymore."

Can I trust her? She had to trust her. Right now, Gail Campbell was the only person who could lead Lydia to her daughter. "Follow me to my place. We'll take my car."

(2)

Joe Nelson heard every word they said. He saw the videotape. He watched and listened from the chair to which he'd been tied inside Thorn's camper and decided there were only two choices. Thorn and Cameron were both wacko or what they said was true.

What frightened him most of all was that what they

said seemed plausible, particularly in light of what he'd seen when he'd taken a leak in the woods on old man Livingston's land. Those spiders, so goddamn many of them, suddenly *there,* surrounding him with their fine silvery threads, acting with such *intent,* then *not there.*

But maybe he imagined the intent. Maybe the spiders had been there all along, in the trees, and his presence had spooked them. Maybe they were trying to get away from *him.* He wanted to tell Thorn and Cameron about the spiders, but he was still gagged and when he made noises, they ignored him.

Suddenly, the door to the camper exploded open and a tall kid with torn clothes and dried blood on his face stumbled inside. Thorn shot to his feet so fast his chair toppled over. "Jesus, Tom." He helped him to a chair, Cameron handed him a glass of ice water, and the kid gulped, coughed, gulped again.

"The Humvee," the kid murmured. "The Humvee . . . It hit this . . . this black strip across the road and . . . and vanished. And they got . . . Natalie. I . . ." And the entire story spilled out—following Gail, the quivering air, the black sphere, the bottomless chasm, the containment tents, the quarantine, the vanished Humvee, the jeeps, Natalie, and how he'd run and hidden in the woods until he could get back to his bicycle.

He started coughing again and Cameron picked up the phone. "I'm calling Gracie to take a look at him." He put the phone to his ear, frowned, hung up the receiver, picked it up again. "Phone's dead. I'm going to run up to the house."

Nelson kicked his bound legs and screamed into the gag. The kid now glanced over at him, then looked back at Thorn. "Who's he?"

"The cop I assaulted."

"What? How . . ." Then, in a softer voice: "Ian knows?"

Thorn nodded and Nelson screamed into the gag again and threw himself from side to side until his chair fell over. Thorn came over, pushed the chair upright, and leaned into Nelson's face. "I'm going to take the gag off, Joe. I don't give a shit how loud you scream, but you're going to be doing it from Gracie's cellar. Understood?"

Nelson grunted and Thorn removed the gag. "I won't scream," he said quickly. "I . . . I saw the military people the day I got here. I took a leak on Livingston's land. You can't leave me here, Max. We . . . we have to get off the island, we . . ."

"Shut up, Joe," Thorn snapped.

"He's right," Tom said. "We need to get out of here before dark. We need weapons, vehicles that'll go through the woods without losing an axle, food and water, cell phones . . . They won't be able to disable every cell phone tower. . . ."

"Slow down." Thorn patted the air with his hands. "Just slow down."

"He's right," Nelson said breathlessly. "The kid's right. I've got radios, Max, and a handgun and . . ."

"Uh, excuse me if I misunderstood the situation, Joe, but an hour ago you were ready to shoot my fucking kneecaps off."

"Everything's changed. All bets are off. I can help. And if you don't want my help, fine. At least let me drive out of here and you'll never see me again."

"We need as many people as we can get, Max," the kid said.

"No. We need as many people as we can trust,"

Thorn corrected him. "And I don't have one goddamn reason to trust Joe."

Nelson sat forward. "Hello, I'm right here. You don't have to refer to me in the third person. You trusted me for years, Max. Both you and Ellen did. But put yourself in my shoes. Suppose you found me in the woods, out of my mind, babbling about birds falling out of the sky and my lady friend vanishing in front of my eyes. How would that sound to you?"

The kid said, "He's got a point, Max."

"Damn right I do. I was just doing my job."

"Bullshit," Thorn replied. "Bradshaw wagged a half mil in front of your face, Joe."

"Not until later. Not until days after you'd punched me out and tied me up."

"Okay, here's the deal. I'll untie you. But you don't get a weapon until I say you do."

"That's fair."

"You're either with us or against us."

"Absolutely."

"You agree, Tom?"

"Sure, man. Let's just get moving."

Just then, the door opened again and Cameron came in, followed by three women. Thorn took one look at the middle woman and snapped, "What the hell is *Gail* doing here?"

(3)

In the end, they numbered seven, four men and three women crowded into Thorn's camper, and none of them had secrets anymore, not even Thorn. He noticed that

Lydia would no longer look at him and he couldn't blame her. In her shoes, he wouldn't look, either.

Gail Campbell—the last person Thorn had ever expected to see as part of their group—told her part of the story, supplying information and pieces of puzzle that no one else had. Thorn didn't trust her any more than he trusted Nelson. But in extreme times, with a larger and more profound threat confronting them, loyalties were redefined, personal boundaries shifted, the utterly impossible became not only possible, but a reality.

According to Gail, after all, old man Livingston had met the same fate as the rottweiler, but he was embedded in a metal filing cabinet rather than a tree and was being kept alive. Would he find Ellen in the same condition? Was that what awaited him at the end of his nightmare journey into the twilight zone? He couldn't allow himself to think along these lines too long or he would lose his nerve and run until there was no place else to run.

As a group, their main priority was to get off the island and deep into the hills before dusk. Thorn figured they would have several hours beyond that to find the mine, the machine, and Natalie, before the military blew the island to smithereens. They'd talked about warning the island's twenty-five hundred other residents to get out while they still could, but decided against it. Widespread panic might prompt Dylan and his people to act sooner.

He finished packing up the camper, which would serve as their base for supplies, Bacall, and Gracie's pets. They would take two cars—his Explorer, which would pull the camper, and Gracie's Explorer. They had seven mountain bikes, at least one weapon for each of them, half a dozen explosives, and two guns that shot tranquilizer darts. They had radios, cell phones, and copies of the map that Gracie had provided, as well as medical supplies. They would be as well prepared as they could be, given what they knew. The problem, as Thorn saw it, was everything they didn't know. What was the exact location of the machine? Where was Natalie being held? Would they even be able to get close to the mine, much less into it, without getting themselves killed?

As he whistled for Bacall, Lydia trotted toward him. "Max, hold on."

She stopped and for moments, they simply looked at each other. She opened her mouth to say something, then just shook her head and shrugged, palms upward. "I wish you'd trusted me enough to tell me the truth," she said finally.

"Would you have believed me?"

She jammed her hands in the pockets of her jeans. "Probably not. I wasn't sure what I believed about any of this weirdness until we . . . we went to Livingston's."

"It was never a matter of trust, Lydia. If I was going to confess anything to anyone, it would have been to you."

She smiled at that, a quick, enigmatic smile. "I guess I should take that as a compliment. You want to follow me out of here?"

He nodded and she turned away without another word. He hesitated, then hurried after her, caught up to her, and caught her hand. "Wait," he said softly, and put his arms around her. Holding her, inhaling the sweet scent of her hair, her skin. "If we all get through this in one piece, you need a vet at your center?"

She pulled back slightly, eyes bright with emotion. "Definitely. But can I afford you?"

Thorn ran his hands under her hair, lifting it from the nape of her neck. "I think we can work out something." He kissed her gently on the mouth and suddenly knew that if they got through this, Lydia would be a major part of his future.

"Hey," Gracie shouted. "Let's get moving."

Lydia broke the embrace and he squeezed her hand. "Love you," he said softly, and realized that he meant it.

She kissed him once, quickly, and hurried on up the driveway to her car.

Thorn whistled again for Bacall and opened the car door for her. She leaped up into the front seat and Thorn slid behind the wheel. For the first time since his arrival, he pulled his camper out of the site he'd called home and headed up toward Gracie's to meet the others and embrace the unknown.

Twenty-six

(1)

From the moment she'd heard the words *They've got Natalie,* it was apparent to Lydia that she couldn't find her daughter alone. She had no guarantee that she would find her now, either, but the odds had improved.

The irony didn't escape her. For the last fifteen years, she had always tried to do everything herself and now, faced with the loss of her daughter, she had to depend on others. One of those others had been working with the enemy and another had lied to her from the very moment she'd met him. But she had to look beyond the personal because her daughter's life depended on exactly that.

"I've got to release the dolphins," she said. "Gracie, could you radio Max and let him know?"

Cameron leaned forward. "We're already pushing our luck, Lydia. They can get out of the tanks and the cove if they need to."

"Five minutes, Ian. I have to do it."

"Less," Gail said. "One of us can open the gates and the other can release the net. They may have the airport blocked," she added, "so we should be ready."

Gracie set the radio on the dash. "Max is sticking with us. I told him to be ready for trouble."

They passed no other cars and she sped down the deserted road toward the runway. The whole area looked abandoned—no cars, no planes, and no military jeeps. No people were out and about, either, which seemed strange to Lydia, but no stranger than anything else that had happened. It struck her that in the last forty-eight hours, everything that had previously defined her sense of the ordinary, her consensus reality, had shifted. She no longer knew what was *normal*.

She screeched to a stop near the side entrance and she and Gail scrambled out. Lydia unlocked the gate and they raced inside the tank area, already raucous with shrieks and clicks and whistles.

They sensed it, she thought. They sensed what was coming and they wanted out.

She and Gail ran across the deck and up two flights to the control room. It occurred to her that now she was consorting with the enemy. This was the woman, after all, who had been intimately involved with training dolphins as weapons and had come to the center as Dylan's spy. Because of her, because of what she'd reported to Dylan, Lydia hadn't gotten her grant and, ultimately, would have to close the center.

But by tomorrow, there might not even *be* a center. There might not be a Piper Key or a town called Roberta and she might not have a daughter anymore. None of that was Gail's fault. For the first time in her adult life, Lydia realized that people really could change and that the change was accelerated when they united with others against a common enemy.

Lydia hit two switches on the control panel. "We're on manual. There's no time to boot up the computers."

"Got it."

While Gail hurried over to the control panel for the

net, Lydia pressed down on the lever that controlled the gate for holding tank one. The glowing red light changed to green. Then, in rapid succession, she pressed down on levers two, three, and four, and glanced out the window that overlooked the tanks.

"Go," she whispered. "Go now. *Fast*"

Even in here she heard their whistles and shrieks as they shot out of the tanks, Rainbow in the lead, followed by Alpha and Kit. The other dolphins followed quickly, a moving line of dorsal fins and flukes, headed for the open sea and freedom.

"My God, Lydia. Look." Gail touched Lydia's arm and pointed out the other window, which overlooked the cove and the gulf beyond it.

There, in the waning light, thousands of dolphins waited, a surging dark wave that extended nearly to the horizon. And as they watched, the wave expanded simultaneously to the left and right. Lydia and Gail ran for the door and tore up another flight of stairs to the deck.

From here, Lydia saw Rainbow, Alpha, and Kit racing into the cove, their bodies rising, shimmering, diving again. The dolphins in the open waters—ten or twenty thousand, maybe more—instantly parted to accommodate them and the air burst with the most exquisite music Lydia had ever heard. This was the dolphin equivalent of Mozart and The Beatles, Beethoven and Jerry Garcia jamming at the same concert, beneath the same glorious light, an instant of magic. This, she knew, was what her daughter had heard the day she'd fallen into the holding tank and Kit had saved her.

They stood still, neither of them speaking, until the dark wave of dolphins closed around Rainbow, Kit, and

Alpha. Lydia's hands clenched against the railing, a part of her trying to hold on to the moment, to seize it and never let it go. Then the wave just disappeared, as if it had never been there.

Gail made a sound, a sharp intake of breath or a sob, Lydia didn't know which until Gail turned toward her, tears glistening on her cheeks. "We need to get outta here. Now."

She cries.

"*C'mon,* Lydia." Gail grabbed her arm and they ran.

When the gate in the fence banged open sixty seconds later, three military jeeps had boxed in the Explorers and several soldiers advanced on Max, who was getting out of the car. "Let me handle this," Gail said, and moved briskly toward the soldiers, pulling out ahead of Lydia.

(2)

Dylan's boys. She knew their language, had spoken it in one form or another all her life. She pulled out her Pensacola ID, the stupid piece of laminated plastic that held her photo, the words *Mammal Defense,* with Dylan's name beneath it. "Hey, soldier," she snapped. "Is there a problem here?"

He took a quick look at her ID and lowered his weapon. "No, ma'am. We're just checking the airport. Are both cars in your party?"

"Yes."

"All personnel were supposed to be off the island an hour ago," he said. "I'll have a jeep escort you to the bridge, ma'am."

"Thanks."

Gail turned on her heel and made a beeline toward the Explorers. She went right over to Max and said, "A jeep is going to escort us to the bridge. If we get stopped again, refer them to me." Then she hurried on toward the other car and, moments later, the jeep led them up the runway and away from the center.

(3)

Lydia didn't have any idea what Gail had shown the soldiers or what she'd said to them, but she now understood that in the military scheme of things, she was a valuable asset.

As they turned onto the main road through town, she saw checkpoints and soldiers, jeeps, and barricades all the way to the bridge. Other cars were on the road, a few commuters, oblivious locals on their way to dinner off island, a few islanders who knew the scoop and were trying to get out. Most of them were turned away.

The jeep got them through two major checkpoints, but at the third, their luck ran out. "You'll have to turn back, ma'am," said the soldier who leaned into her window.

Gail, now seated in the passenger seat, held out her ID. "This car and the one behind us are personnel, soldier."

He leaned farther into her window, checking out everyone. "I need to run your ID, ma'am."

"Sure."

Gail passed it to him and he walked off with it. Lydia adjusted the rearview mirror, watching him. "Gracie, alert Max that we may have a problem." She spoke softly. Her voice cracked. She had never been so afraid.

Gail adjusted the side mirror, watching the soldier.

In the backseat, Gracie and Cameron turned, also watching.

"Shit," Gracie said, the radio still close to her mouth. "I don't like this, Lydia. I don't like it one god—the bridge! The bridge is going up!"

For a single, paralyzing instant, Lydia simply stared at it, at the old, creaking bridge, and thought: *If we hadn't gone to the center, if we hadn't lingered there . . .*

No. No more of that. No more choices between dolphins and her daughter. No. *Fuck all of you,* she thought, and swerved around the jeep, out of the line, out of the line of cars, out, away, gone. The Explorer shot along the shoulder of the road, gravel flying up, pinging against the underside, the fender, the sides. Sirens sounded, bells rang, and if there had been any boats down there on the water, they would be revving their engines, preparing to move forward. But there wasn't a boat in sight, only three dolphins surfacing, diving, surfacing again.

She guessed she hit the bridge when it stood at about a fifteen-degree angle to the setting sun. She hit it hard and someone screamed and then they were airborne, the Explorer riding nothing but air and empty dreams. Seconds, only seconds, that was all it took until the tires struck the other side. The impact jarred her to the bone, her tires spun, the engine shrieked, then the tires found purchase and the Explorer shot forward, past several military vehicles and more soldiers.

Gunfire exploded around them and Lydia screamed, "Get down, everyone get down!"

Her side mirror shattered and the glass would have struck her if the window hadn't been up.

Her eyes darted to the rearview mirror and she saw

the other Explorer right behind her and jeeps behind it, racing to close the gap. Lydia jammed the accelerator to the floor and sped into the darkening hills.

(4)

No one spoke in Thorn's car. There was nothing to say. They all understood that if the soldiers had been better organized, the story might have turned out much differently, he thought.

Now and then, Bacall howled, making it clear that she wasn't happy, a perfect expression of how they all felt.

When Lydia left the road, he did, too. When she went deeper into the woods, he followed, the Explorer pounding over rocks, fallen branches, deep gullies. Darkness closed around them. They kept in touch by radio, avoiding the area where Tom and Natalie had seen the chasm of nothingness.

Sometime later, Lydia stopped and Thorn pulled in alongside her. They had gone so deep into the woods that Thorn wondered how the hell they would find their way out. He killed the headlights, lowered the window, and shone the flashlight around, checking the surrounding area for anomalies.

"It looks okay on this side," Thorn said.

"Okay over here," Tom added.

"Same here," Lydia called.

All seven of them got out and stood there in the eerie silence. Bacall, her head poking out the window, started whining and Thorn patted her and snapped on her leash. When he opened the door for her, though, she refused to get out.

"Okay, let's get started," Thorn said, and turned on one of the hurricane lanterns and hung it from a low branch. "Watch where you step. Tom, grab the trank rifle and take the first watch. We'll change watch every fifteen minutes."

He nodded, Cameron handed him the trank rifle, and he moved around to the front of the vehicles.

"Maybe we shouldn't have this much light," Nelson remarked, wiping his arm across his sweaty face.

"We don't have any choice," Gail replied. "We need light to set up the camper. The trees are densely packed in here. I think it's okay."

For the next fifteen minutes, they worked in silence, setting up the camper. Nelson took the second watch. Other than the strange, unnatural silence, nothing happened. Thirty-five minutes later, they all piled into the camper with the animals and sorted out their supplies. They dressed in dark clothes and high boots and each of them selected a weapon. Thorn seemed to be the only one among them who had almost no experience with weapons.

While Gracie smoothed the map open, Thorn put out food and water for Bacall, the skunk, and the cat. Bacall wolfed down the food, then eyed him warily, as if she understood she was going to be left behind. Thorn had mixed feelings about leaving her. Even though she didn't know this area any more than he did, she had a keen sense of smell, acute instincts, and might sense any anomalies before the rest of them. He decided to bring her along and put extra water and dog food in his pack.

Gracie marked their approximate location on the map. "I figure we're about five miles north of the mine. There's a creek four miles from here that's the official border for the town of Roberta. This is *not* going to be easy on mountain bikes and I think the sooner we appropriate a jeep and uniforms, the better off we'll be."

Cameron spoke up. "Since Joe and I are both experienced cops, one of us should be in the lead, then the rest of us should pair off. That way, no one is left alone at the back of the line."

"I'm taking Bacall," Thorn said. "Anyone have a problem with that?"

Lydia nodded. "Of course she's going. She's going to find Natalie and the mine for us. She should be in the lead."

Ten minutes later, as the others mounted up, Thorn crouched in front of his dog and ran his hands over her fur. "Find Natalie," he said. "Find the safest path to Natalie." She whined and pawed the ground, then Thorn told her to go to the front of the line and she took off.

With Bacall and Cameron in the lead, they started out of the dense trees. He and Lydia brought up the rear, with Gracie and Tom in front of them, and Gail and Nelson directly behind Cameron. Bacall stayed five or six yards ahead of the line, nose to the ground one moment, then sniffing at the air the next moment.

Stars now glinted through the trees, providing enough light to see by. Now and then, Thorn thought he glimpsed movement in his peripheral vision, but whenever he looked, he didn't see anything except trees and the darkness between them. The back of his neck turned prickly, though, a sure sign that something wasn't right.

"You feel it?" Lydia whispered suddenly.

"Yeah, but what the hell is it?"

"I don't know."

Thorn smelled a deeper lushness to the woods now, a lushness he associated with water, and figured they were coming up on the creek. He pulled out to the side of the line, sighted Bacall, and saw that she'd suddenly stopped and flattened out against the ground. Cameron now halted and motioned for them to dismount, lay their bikes on the ground, and follow him.

They advanced toward Bacall slowly, soundlessly, and dropped to their knees around her, peering through the tall, thick brush at the creek—and at the pair of jeeps parked on the other side of it. The first line of defense, Thorn thought.

"Two guys," Cameron whispered.

"Three," Gail corrected. "The other guy is down by the water, under that thick overhang of branches. That'd be a good place to cross if he weren't there."

"I'll trank him first," Tom said. "Then the rest of you cross and I'll pull him into the brush."

"Then we split into two groups and take the other guys," Cameron finished.

Thorn motioned for Bacall to move forward and they followed her. She skulked along the line of bushes, between starlight and shadows, her body close to the ground. The inside of Thorn's mouth had gone dry with fear. How many times would they have to repeat this? They were only seven and no telling how many men Dylan had. Their best hope, he realized, was that most of Dylan's troops were on Piper Key and in Roberta, involved in imposing the phony quarantine.

They stopped just short of where the brush thinned. Thorn took hold of Bacall's collar, whispered, "Heel," and she flattened against the ground.

Tom raised the trank rifle, sighted, and a breath later,

the soldier toppled sideways, one hand to his neck, where the dart had gone in. They crept out one by one and moved down a sloping bank, through the huge banyan trees, toward the creek. Bacall hugged Thorn's side until they neared the water, then she darted ahead and found a shallow place to cross.

Just as Thorn came out from under the protective overhang of banyan branches, one of the guys in the jeep shouted, "Hey, Luke, let's get moving."

Thorn dived for the ground on the other side and crawled forward on his hands and knees, through the dry, overgrown grass, Lydia on one side of him, Gail on the other, Nelson and Cameron behind them. He couldn't see Bacall anymore and worried that she might dart out of the grass toward the jeeps and get herself killed.

"What the hell," said one of the men, his voice booming in the silence. "Jim, there's a dog over here. I think it's hurt."

Shit. Thorn rocked on his heels and gazed over the top of the grass. Bacall lay in a pool of starlight near the jeep, whimpering in a way that would break even the coldest heart. Now the two men stood side by side, staring at her, discussing her.

"Don't touch it," said one. "The colonel said we'd be seeing weird shit that suddenly appeared and vanished."

"Oh, for Christ's sake. She's real."

"Then where'd she come from? She wasn't here sixty seconds ago."

Gail suddenly rocked onto her knees, aimed the trank rifle, and shot the man closest to them. She reloaded before the guy hit the ground and just as his companion spun around, she shot him in the chest. He fell backward and Bacall scrambled up and ran over to him, growling softly.

By the time Thorn and the others reached the two men, the second soldier was as far gone as his companion. The tranquilizer would last four to six hours and, with any luck, they would be long gone by then. Thorn and Cameron quickly removed the men's uniforms, then pulled them across the ground to where Tom had left the other guy.

They took inventory of the jeeps. Besides the three uniforms they removed from the soldiers, they found a chest filled with weapons and ammo, two canvas tarps, a cooler of cold bottled water, another uniform, several pairs of boots, and a tin box filled with earplugs.

For the high-pitched humming, Thorn thought, and passed out pairs to everyone.

They debated briefly about who should drive the jeeps and who should get a uniform. It came down in the men's favor, until Gail pointed out that there were probably women in Dylan's band and she, a military brat, knew how to talk to "these people." She agreed to ride shotgun with Cameron in one jeep, with Nelson and Gracie in back, hidden under the tarp. Thorn got the other jeep, with Lydia and Tom and Bacall hidden in the back.

They changed into uniforms, packed a mountain bike in each jeep, oriented themselves according to Gracie's map. Then they started out, Cameron's jeep in the lead, headed through a corridor of starlight between the tall, graceful pines in the distance.

They went about two miles, headlights off, through the corridor of starlight; then the trees thickened again and the terrain turned rough and hilly. A mile later, the trees ended and Cameron suddenly slammed on his brakes. Thorn swerved to the left to avoid hitting him and saw why Cameron had stopped.

Language abandoned him, all he could do was gape. Three, maybe four hundred yards away, the landscape simply ended. *Ended.* Even the stars were gone. Blackness stretched as far in every direction as he could see.

Twenty-seven

Lydia

She knew she was on her knees, peering over the edge of the passenger seat, that Bacall was barking and trying to scramble into the front with Thorn, that Tom was shouting. Sensory impressions hadn't left her; but everything else had. She felt as if she'd been unplugged from the familiar and hurled into a bubbling, primal sea.

The blackness seemed to be spreading—not fast, not in any discernible direction, but like india ink spilling across a starlit canvas or like a slow-moving river that had risen above its banks. Even those analogies didn't really fit, though. Nothing familiar fit into this.

Cameron's jeep moved forward first, turning left; Thorn followed. For a while, they paralleled the blackness, driving very slowly, barely five miles an hour. They remained a safe distance away, close enough to see that there was nothing in the blackness, but far enough away so that the blackness couldn't touch them. Then the jeeps stopped and everyone got out, except for Bacall, who wanted nothing to do with any of it.

They walked in a single file along the edge of the blackness, about thirty yards away from it. To Lydia, it looked like some vast undiscovered continent or an ocean that covered the face of the rest of the world. She thought she heard a faint humming similar to what she'd heard in the woods that night behind Gracie's. She craned her neck back and looked up into the belly of the sky just above them and oriented herself.

Stars. Orion, the gibbous moon, and farther away, Jupiter. Then she gazed out into the blackness again, into the face of nothingness, and when her eyes skipped upward, only blackness remained. The humming got louder, but so far, she hadn't run into any cold spots and no blue light had appeared. She jammed her hands into the pockets of her jeans—and found a shell that had probably been in the pocket since last winter. She slipped it out and hurled it into the blackness.

It never made a sound; the blackness swallowed it.

Tom finally broke the silence. "It's like the chasm that Natalie and I saw, the black hole that swallowed the Humvee. Only it's bigger. Much, much bigger."

"Let's go back," Nelson suggested. He had stepped out of the line and paced restlessly about forty feet from the edge. "There're other ways to get to the mine."

"Yeah? And where's that, Joe?" asked Gail. "You see anything out there that looks the least bit familiar?"

Nelson spun around. "We've got two choices," he hissed. "Go back or go forward. That's it, the bottom line."

"Go back to what?" Gail snapped. "And go forward into what?"

Noise erupted behind them and Lydia turned to see what it was. She didn't know what she expected to see, but knew that it wasn't this, a dense bright glow of headlights aimed straight at them. A village of headlights. Troops.

"Back in the jeeps!" Thorn shouted, and they all scattered like fleas.

Lydia and Tom clambered into the back of the jeep Thorn was driving, crawled over the mountain bike and other supplies, and began firing on the advancing vehicles. Bacall howled, a sound so wild, so primal, that gooseflesh broke out on her arms.

A Humvee pulled out in front of the other vehicles, its low, squat body glinting in the starlight like some silvery and giant spider scrambling after its prey. Lydia grabbed a hand grenade, pulled out the pin, and hurled it at the Humvee. It exploded too wide and she thought, *We aren't going to make it.* They had nowhere to run.

The Humvee opened fire on them and Thorn swerved left and right and left again in a crazy zigzag to make them a more difficult target. With each swerve to the right, he got closer and closer to the blackness and Bacall's howls got louder and wilder.

Bullets whistled around them, Lydia ducked to reload, and when she raised up again, Thorn looped erratically to the right, dangerously close to the blackness. Bullets struck the ground inches from the back tires. He veered into another zigzag and the left rear tire blew.

"We're fucked!" Tom shouted.

"Hold on!" Thorn yelled back, and the jeep shot forward, the blown back tire flapping against the ground. For seconds, they raced neck and neck with the other jeep, then both swerved sharply to the right, as if Thorn and Cameron had the same idea at the same time. Together, they sped toward the blackness, the ubiquitous void.

* * *

Gail

She ran up the rocky beach behind her house, excited about seeing Dylan and telling him about the hermit crabs she'd discovered under the bridge. The water, a liquid sapphire, was so clear she could see shells sticking up out of the sand.

She picked several shells out of the sand, pocketed them, and trotted on until she saw Dylan at the water's edge. His jeans were rolled up to his knees, he wore his father's fishing cap, and he held a fishing pole. He waved when he saw her. "Gail, you gotta see this."

She stopped beside him. "What?"

He pointed at the shallows. "There, see it? A sand shark."

She looked where he pointed and saw only shadows. "That's no sand shark."

He burst out laughing. "Fooled you."

"You did not."

"Did, too."

"Did not."

Then they both laughed and he dropped his fishing pole and grabbed her around the waist and pulled her down onto the sand and kissed her. Maybe it was the kiss that tipped her off, a passionate adult kiss, not the kiss of a teenage kid. She pulled back and whispered, "Something's wrong about this."

Wrong wrong wrong . . .

The beach and Dylan faded into the bridge between Berkeley and Frisco. She knew immediately this was the day her divorce had become final. It wasn't just a memory. It was real in the same sense that the keys had been real, with the pleasant wind blowing off the bay and the city visible in the distance, all those buildings on all those hills. The only difference was that she felt she had lived these moments before.

She stopped and got off her bike just to feel the concrete under her feet. She walked over to the railing and looked down and saw three dolphins surfacing, diving, surfacing again, making their way out to sea. She knew she would return to an empty apartment and smoke a joint and open a bottle of wine. She knew that at exactly one minute after eleven, as soon as the rates went down, her phone would ring and it would be Dylan.

I'm getting married, he would say.

She would start to cry and tell him her divorce was final today and why the fuck did he have to go and get married to someone else when he should be marrying her? It occurred to her that since she had already lived that experience, she would change it now. She would get on her bike again and pedal back to Berkeley and stay with friends so that she wouldn't be home when Dylan called.

So she lifted her bike up, aimed it toward Berkeley, and pedaled madly away from that past and onto the floating platform off the coast of Pensacola. Alpha swam nearby and Gail tossed her a handful of herring. She played to Dylan's camera, doing aquarium tricks, swimming backward through the water. Gail blew her whistle, a signal for Alpha to return. Instead, she dived.

Right then, Gail recognized this for what it was—*been here, done that*—and instantly she was in the jeep again, gripping the edges of the seat as Cameron drove it like a madman toward the void. She screamed, *"Don't do it, don't . . ."*

. . . and she was inside the white containment tent, staring at a steel table that held a metal, four-drawer filing cabinet that lay on its back. Embedded in it was old man Livingston. His chest moved and his eyes opened very slowly, like eyes in a dream. . . .

Lydia

Lydia stood by the holding tanks, the hot summer sun beating against her head, the heat so oppressive that her chest felt as if it were filled with cotton. She and her husband were arguing about the center, about how much money it took to maintain the place. Her head pounded, the muscles in her neck hurt, all of it connected to the argument, this same endless loop of bullshit.

Her attention lapsed. She forgot that Natalie was waddling across the deck, forgot her eighteen-month-old baby was even there until she heard the splash. When she spun around, Natalie was already sinking like a stone, down through the crystal waters.

For a horrifying moment, she simply stood there, paralyzed, waiting for Natalie to bob to the surface as she was supposed to do. Her husband kept shouting, *"Do something, do something,"* as if this, like everything else, were solely her responsibility. She couldn't move, couldn't think, couldn't do anything at all. Suddenly, her husband dived into the tank and water splashed against her legs, shocking her into action. Lydia leaped into the tank and swam down, down, the salt water stinging her eyes, her heart pounding so hard she could hear it, her lungs nearly bursting.

Her husband shot to the surface, up through the bubbles and the fractured sunlight, Natalie in his arms. Lydia swam frantically after him and surfaced seconds later. Her daughter, her sweet little baby, lay on the deck and her husband was leaning over her, mouth mashed to hers, blowing air into her lungs.

Nonono. It didn't happen like this.

Now she sat in her bedroom, her mouth puckered around the end of a pistol . . .

No, this is wrong . . .

. . . and she leaped into the holding tank. As her feet struck the water, a dolphin shot past her, pushing her baby to the surface, then flicking her out onto the deck. Natalie coughed and wailed and spat up water and Lydia swept her up—*she's alive, alive, dear God, she's alive*—and ran with her into the shade.

The air shimmered and shifted, as it does in intense heat, and everything around her blurred. It seemed that she moved at luminous speeds—or that the world sped toward her, she couldn't tell which—and suddenly she was running through a cool, twilit tunnel, her boots slapping the hard ground. She saw Thorn and Bacall just ahead of her and ran faster, arms pumping at her sides.

"Max!" she shouted, and the tunnel became a rocky slope that burned against her bare feet. Out there in the distance she saw the dolphins, hundreds of them, and the canoe with Natalie and Corie inside.

She blinked against the glare of the light, a sense of déjà vu sweeping over her. *I've lived this moment.* With this thought, her consciousness split like an atom and awareness flooded through her. She had been in the jeep, they had driven into the blackness, into the void, into no time or all time. And now she was here again, in this moment where it had all begun. Or maybe it hadn't begun here. She no longer knew, could no longer be certain.

Lydia dived off the rocky jetty, hoping that if she was right, Corie wouldn't be in the canoe in this version of events. She swam fast and hard, grabbed on to the sides.

No Corie.

Natalie, her face white, said, "I'm okay, Mom."

She started to say what she had said the first time she'd lived through this, but caught herself. *"Play your flute. Fast. Now."*

Natalie

She hid in the woods with Tom, watching as Gail and the man named Dylan came out of the mobile unit wearing white astronaut suits with helmets, oxygen masks, the whole nine yards, and vanished into the containment tent.

Tom touched her elbow and tilted his head toward the woods. The instant seemed familiar to her somehow, as if she'd lived it before. As soon as she thought this, *routes* lit up in her head. The Humvee. Tom's truck not starting. Both of them running. Jeeps chasing her, running her down. Along that route, she would be put into the containment tent with—what?

Then it flooded through her, the tent and old man Livingston, and the mobile unit that held the machine witness had written about.

"We can't leave," she whispered to Tom. "This time we have to do it differently."

"What? What're you talking about?"

"We have to go into the tent. Now."

Before he could stop her, she pulled her flute out of her backpack, put it to her mouth, and started to play it. Then she walked out of the trees.

Thorn

One moment Thorn tore down a concrete corridor with Lydia and Bacall, and the next instant he was staring up at the birds.

A hundred or more of them now fluttered and twittered in the branches of a pair of maples that stood just outside his kitchen window. More arrived by the minute and the longer Thorn watched, the more familiar it all seemed to him, although he couldn't say why.

After a while, Ellen came out, dressed for her morning run. This, too, seemed eerily familiar to him, but then, why shouldn't it? She ran most mornings. She remarked about the birds and Thorn felt spooked now and raced toward them, waving his arms and shouting. They flew away, lifting up toward the sky in a huge black cloud.

"We've got two horses reserved at the stable for nine," she said, and bussed him on the cheek.

Maybe it was that kiss, the cool brush of her lips that did it, maybe it something else, but Thorn suddenly knew that she could NOT go running, that if she ran out into the field she would never come back.

"Don't go." He tightened his arms around her waist. "Let's go into town for breakfast or something. Just don't go running."

She laughed and kissed him lightly at the tip of his nose. "I'll be back in twenty minutes. Set your timer."

She wiggled free of his embrace, but Thorn caught her hand. "Ellen, marry me. We can go down to the justice of the peace this afternoon and do the paper-work, get our blood tests tomorrow, and be married in two days."

Ellen's frown brought her lovely eyes too close to-gether, so that she almost seemed to be scowling. "What brought all this on, Max? I thought we'd re-solved that issue."

"I just resigned myself to it." He would keep her talking, keep her here, and then everything would be okay, she wouldn't—what? What the hell was he so afraid of?

Then she won't disappear.

The notion bumped around inside him, almost like an afterthought, a postscript. But as Thorn seized it, he *remembered* . . .

. . . and stood over Joe Nelson, tied up like a pret-zel on the office floor, and tried to explain what had really happened. "And then she began to *fade*. . . ."

Memory shuddered through him and Thorn started to shake. His teeth literally chattered. He dropped to his knees and leaned into Nelson's face, whispering. "Joe, listen to me. Joe . . . we've done this. You and I. *We've lived this moment before."*

Nelson burst out laughing, spittle flying from his mouth. "Yeah, deja shit vu and . . ." The contempt in his face abruptly collapsed and his eyes widened until they were as round as paper plates. "The void," he whispered.

With those two words, everything rushed into Thorn.

Lydia

Lydia turned to look for Thorn and Bacall, but they were gone and the concrete corridor stretched forever behind her. Confused and scared, she stopped and rubbed her eyes, desperately trying to remember something. *Natalie, where's Natalie? What am I doing?*

The void, she remembered the void and . . .

Panic surged in her chest and her arms dropped to her sides and suddenly she and Natalie were with Tom in the woods. Crouching in the woods. Watching.

"I . . ."

"Sshh," Tom whispered. "They'll hear us."

And she raised up enough to see her daughter moving toward an encampment of some kind with a white tent in the center of it and a mobile unit of some kind to the right of the tent. "No, Christ, no, she can't . . ."

Tom grabbed the back of her shirt, jerking her back. "She knows what she's doing. Go fast, Lydia. Into the woods. I'll meet you there."

"It's all messed up. This never happened, Tom." The words rushed out of her, a hissing, whispered stream of words, and Tom's eyes widened with astonishment.

"I remember," he whispered back. "The jeep, the . . ."

Pandemonium erupted from the containment area and Lydia shot to her feet and shouted her daughter's name.

Gail

Old man Livingston's eyes opened all the way and the corner of his mouth, the only visible part of it, twitched, trying to form words. He finally succeeded, two words, that was all, two words uttered like a prayer.

Help me.

Gail wrenched back, sucking at the air in her helmet, her stomach heaving. She tore the helmet off and stumbled into one of the machines behind her and things struck the floor.

Dylan snapped, "Watch it, damn it," and one of the other white-suited sadists demanded that he get her out of there.

He grabbed her arm and she tore it out of his grasp and swung her helmet at him. It slammed into the glass face of his helmet and fissures spread across it, tiny fault lines that burst from a center. Dylan stumbled back, Gail whipped around, a gun in her hand, the gun she'd stuck in the suit when they'd changed. She raised it, her arm shaking, the sadists leaping out of the way. The old man's eyes locked on hers and the visible corner of his mouth seemed to curve upward in a grateful smile. Then he shut his eyes and whispered, *Yes, please, yes.*

Like the goat, she thought, *those same pitiful eyes.* And she fired. She emptied the gun in his face and the machines went berserk, buzzing, ringing, clattering. Then someone slammed into her from behind, knocking her to the floor of the tent.

Natalie

Gunshots, screams, shouts, pandemonium, all of it came at her so fast that she barely resisted the urge to race back into the woods where she'd left Tom and her mother. There seemed to be something wrong with that, with her mother being here, but she couldn't think about it now. She had to keep playing.

She shut her eyes and kept walking and playing, knowing that if she didn't focus on the music, just the music, it would all come undone.

When she opened her eyes again, the trees were behind her and the containment tent seemed to be collapsing. Soldiers shouted and ran in a dozen directions. She smelled smoke. Tongues of fire curled up around the bottom edge of the tent and people poured out of it, men in space suits stumbling over each other, trampling each other.

Among them was the man named Dylan. He shot toward her, panicked and enraged, and slammed into her. The flute flew out of her hands and she crashed to the ground and he straddled her like a horse, nearly crushing the air from her chest. He grabbed her by the hair, jerked her head upward.

"You," he spat. "They come to you and your music. . . .

. . . And she cowered now in a corner of the mobile unit, cold air blowing in her face, a flute frozen in her hand. *"Play,"* Dylan whispered in her face. *"Play the fucking flute. Bring them here. They have the secret."*

But she refused to play and he struck her across the face with the back of his hand, struck her again and again. Her lip split open, blood oozed from it, and Natalie knew that he would hit her until she died unless she bargained with him.

"Show me the machine. Then I'll play. . . ."

. . . And they were outside again, on the ground, Dylan's fetid breath a wave of filth in her face. Gail burst out of the tent, flames leaping up from her space suit, and screamed, *"No!"* Then she crashed into him, shoving him away from Natalie, off her chest.

Natalie sprang to her feet and backed away from Gail and the man named Dylan, her flute clutched in her hand. Her head ached, her eyes burned, she didn't know what was going on. One moment she'd been in the woods with her mother and Tom, then she was in the canoe with her mother hanging on to the side and demanding that she play the flute, now she was here. . . .

The flute. Play, play, fast. . . . The music is forever. The music is the bridge that connects everything.

She squeezed her eyes shut and started to play, played as she had never played before, the music drawing the world around her. . . .

Thorn

He understood now. He realized he'd lived so much of this before. Or was living it now. Or would live it in the future. These types of distinctions no longer served him as reference points.

He was a soul at the banks of the river Styx. If he plunged into the river and swallowed any of the water, he would forget where he'd been. He would forget everything. He would live out some version of his life in blissful ignorance, only puzzled, perhaps, by certain feelings and blurred, very hazy memories that occasionally rose up inside him.

If he didn't drink the water, he wouldn't go anywhere. His life would continue in an endless loop, repeating the same old versions of the same old events. That wasn't necessarily bad, but he knew now that it wasn't what he wanted.

So he plunged into the river, plunged with the understanding that the act itself would create a new version of events and that he probably wouldn't remember what had gone before. He plunged with the realization that, in the final analysis, the creator had endowed them all with *the will to choose* . . .

. . . and he exploded through the door of the mobile unit, Nelson tight at his heels, and there she was. Ellen. Ellen. She still wore her white jogging outfit, that flat, slightly tanned midriff showing, but nothing else remained the same. From the waist down, she had grown into the walls of the mobile unit and Thorn suddenly understood that the mobile unit was the machine or some version of it that witness had described.

The walls now began to move, to quiver as if with life, and Thorn realized they were made of some sort of organic substance that was pliable, like soft contact lenses. He couldn't see her arms; they were buried in the unit's walls, but he clearly saw her face.

Her eyes glowed a bright, sapphire blue. When she opened her mouth, the humming got louder and he wanted to go over to her, to touch her, to be with her. He remembered the earplugs and quickly retrieved them from his pocket and shoved them in his ears. But her eyes beckoned and he moved closer to her.

Her hands folded out of the organic walls, soft, beautiful hands that had grown so pale he could see the network of veins and tendons on the backs of them. Her hands turned over, palms up, and motioned for him to come closer, closer.

Her mouth moved again and he read her lips. *I wasn't the first. But make me the last.*

The door exploded inward and Nelson stumbled in.

Gail

She and Dylan, locked together in a ridiculous embrace, rolled across the ground, through the stink of smoke and fire, and she tried desperately to get her hands around his throat, to squeeze and squeeze and never let go. . . .

. . . And she pedaled fast along the Golden Gate bridge. She was crying so hard she could barely see where she was going. Dylan had called her at a friend's place to tell her he was getting married. Gail had begged and pleaded with him not to do it. She had groveled without shame. How could he do this, especially on the very day her own divorce had become final?

Because she's pregnant, he said.

Pregnant, the bimbo was pregnant.

Gail reached the middle of the bridge and dismounted from her bike. No traffic at this hour, no pedestrians around. No one to stop her. She went over to the railing and gazed down at the velvet-black waters. The air smelled good here, the breeze held a tinge of autumn. Fog was rolling in, surrounding Alcatraz and moving closer to the city.

You won't feel a thing.

She climbed up onto the railing, one arm wrapped around a post, and thought of all that might have been. For just a moment, it seemed that she remembered things that seemed to have happened—an island somewhere, dolphins, and Dylan's elaborate web of lies. She sensed that her decision would make a vital difference for the people on that island, but had no idea what any of that meant, since the island hadn't happened, had it?

She started to let go of the post, but anger overpowered her, a rage at Dylan, at herself, and she quickly grabbed on to the post again, her heart racing, the water below her blurring.

No. . . .

Gail leaped down from the railing, onto the bridge, and stumbled back, shocked at what had nearly happened, what she had nearly done. She kept moving backward until she stumbled over her bike, then whipped around and pedaled madly off the bridge, away from the bridge, away from *that version of events.* . . . Why should she be the one to die? Dylan was at fault, Dylan was to blame.

If Dylan dies, everything will happen differently. A new version of events will come into being. . . .

The instant she thought this, she and Dylan were on the ground again, struggling for the gun, the machines ringing and clattering, alarms shrieking. He gripped her hair and slammed her head repeatedly against the ground. *He means to kill me.* The realization opened whatever meager reserves of adrenaline that she had left and she wrenched her leg free and jerked her knee upward, into Dylan's groin.

He blanched, maybe he screamed, she didn't know, didn't care. Her arms popped free and snapped upward and she aimed the gun and fired. . . .

. . . And now she stood in an office in the dolphin center on Piper Key, where a pretty young woman handed her a set of keys. "Welcome to Dolphins on the Gulf, Gail. We're delighted to have you on board. My daughter will show you around and introduce you to the dolphins."

A girl of eleven or twelve took her on the grand tour and kept looking at her and frowning and finally blurted, "Have we met before?"

And with that simple question, all the memories rushed back into her and . . .

* * *

Thorn

"Wha the fu . . ." Nelson murmured, breathing hard. His eyes widened as he stared at the wall, at Ellen. "Jesus, it's . . ."

"Let me have the gun, Joe," Thorn said quietly, moving toward him.

"It's . . . grotesque," Nelson whispered. "It's . . . it's not *her,* Max. It's an abomination, a . . . Jesus God. . . ." And his hand jerked up and Thorn hurled himself at Nelson.

It was already too late.

Nelson squeezed the trigger.

Gail

Gail fired at point-blank range, fired into Dylan's face, and his forehead exploded in a spray of blood and bone. Then he collapsed against her. The lights blinked, the alarms kept shrieking, the cacophony now deafening. She shoved Dylan away from her, her clothes stained with his blood, the stink of his death in her skin, her very cells. She leaped up, her head snapping wildly from left to right. Woods, darkness, the tent, people running everywhere, and a voice booming over a PA system. *Evacuate the area. Evacuate the area.*

What now? She remembered shoving Dylan off of Natalie, but where was she? *Where am I?* Even more to the point, how the fuck did she get out of wherever she was? *Think, calm down.* She slammed another clip into the gun and whirled around just as the tent erupted into flames.

Thorn stumbled out, coughing and wheezing, and Gail ran over to him and helped him away from the smoke. "Find the others," he gasped. "Got to find the others . . . get out of here. . . ."

"How?" she shouted over the endless noise. "Where's the exit?"

Thorn shook his head, he didn't know. Gail pulled him toward the woods, pulled him as he continued to cough and wheeze, and refused to look down when she stumbled over Dylan's body.

Suddenly, one of the jeeps tore out of the woods, Cameron at the wheel, gesturing madly for them to get in, and Bacall howling. Gail jerked Thorn forward, her urgency like a disease. Hot, orange light from the burning tent spilled everywhere, illuminating the trees just beyond them—and Tom, then Lydia tearing out of the woods.

"*There, Lydia and Tom!*" Gail shouted, pointing.

"The whole place is gonna blow!" Cameron screamed, and pulled Thorn into the jeep as Gail scrambled into the back. Then he swung the jeep into a tight turn and aimed it straight at them.

Lydia

The music seemed to come from everywhere and nowhere, a sound so pure and powerful that it obliterated every other sound. Lydia shot to her feet, and gripped the back of Cameron's seat. "Follow it, follow the music!" she screamed.

"Where's it coming from?" he yelled back.

From the canoe. From Natalie in the canoe. But where was the canoe? Where was the cove? Forget the canoe, she decided. The music was the point. The music was all that mattered. The jeep plunged into the woods, pounded over holes, fallen branches, rocks.

"Go right," Gail shouted. "The road where the Humvee vanished is to the right."

Cameron made an abrupt right turn and the music suddenly got louder, more powerful. Bacall tried to scramble out of the jeep, but Thorn grabbed her collar, holding her back. Then they hit the road, hit so hard that Lydia was knocked back and fell into Gail.

Before she could react, an explosion behind them sundered the air and lit up the darkness like the Fourth of July. The only thing she saw was the greater darkness in front of them, the ocean of blackness, the goddamn void they'd driven into lifetimes ago.

"Hold on!" Cameron screamed.

The jeep gathered speed, pounding over the rutted road, the engine racing. Another explosion ripped apart her eardrums, and a fireball rose up behind them. Then they plunged into the void.

Twenty-eight

Two canoes, alone in the cove, but Natalie sensed that the dolphins were nearby. "You guys ready?" she asked.

Gail gave an exaggerated yawn. "I've been ready for the last thirty minutes. You get me out of bed in the middle of the night, so this better be good. Hey, Tom, give me some steering closer to Natalie's canoe."

"Gotcha," he murmured.

"So what're we going to see?" Thorn asked. He and Bacall were behind Natalie and her mother was in the front.

"Something no one has seen before," she promised.

"I brought the videocamera," her mother said. "So let's not get tipped over."

"Not a chance that'll happen," Natalie said, and raised the flute to her mouth.

She started to play, each note a world unto itself, as perfect as anything she had played since the day Kit had given her the music so many years ago. The haunted melody floated out over the dark waters, into the moonlight, and suddenly dolphins began to appear. A dozen, then two dozen, then more and more. Their calls and whistles echoed through the moonlight, sounds as pure and lovely as the music that had called them.

"Where the hell are they coming from?" Thorn breathed.

"They weren't here seconds ago," Lydia said, and brought the videocamera to her eye.

Natalie turned slightly in her seat, glancing over at Tom and Gail. Moonlight spilled across their startled faces, and for seconds, Gail Campbell looked at her, at Natalie, as if trying to remember something. Tom grinned and flashed her a thumbs-up.

Dozens of dolphins became hundreds, became thousands, and the lead dolphins—Kit, Rainbow, and Alpha—pressed up against the sides of the canoes and lifted them completely out of the water.

Tom laughed with delight and Natalie played, her fingers sliding along the flute as if with a will of their own. When she looked at Gail again, the truth passed between them. She saw it on Gail's face, confusion, then astonishment, then complete surrender as the memories of what had happened in the void washed through her. Gail glanced off in the distance, toward Roberta, and Natalie knew she was looking for some sign of the explosion. But the sky was clear, the moonlight brilliant. This was a new present.

In time, the others might remember, too, Natalie thought. But for now, only the music mattered.